COLD PRESSED MURDER

"If you enjoy Southern cozies, family driven mysteries, [and] well-written characters and story lines, this is the book for you."   —Open Book Society

"Interesting plot twists that will have readers guessing and second-guessing who they think the murderer is. The shocking truth will surprise readers."   —*RT Book Reviews*

"[A] whole passel of sisterly secrets and gossipy townsfolk."   —Criminal Element

ONE FOOT IN THE GROVE

"This story flows as smoothly as the heroine's olive oil, with fresh characters, an intriguing mystery, and plenty of Southern atmosphere."

—Peg Cochran, national bestselling
author of the Gourmet De-Lite Mysteries

"Charming characters and an atmospheric Southern setting make this a tasty debut for food cozy aficionados."

—*Library Journal* (starred review)

"[A] great new series about a town full of Southern charm and more than its share of locals who love to gossip."

—*RT Book Reviews*

Berkley Prime Crime titles by Kelly Lane

ONE FOOT IN THE GROVE
COLD PRESSED MURDER
DIPPED TO DEATH

DIPPED TO DEATH

KELLY LANE

BERKLEY PRIME CRIME
New York

BERKLEY PRIME CRIME
Published by Berkley
An imprint of Penguin Random House LLC
375 Hudson Street, New York, New York 10014

Copyright © 2018 by Claire Talbot Eddins
Penguin Random House supports copyright. Copyright fuels creativity, encourages
diverse voices, promotes free speech, and creates a vibrant culture. Thank you for buying
an authorized edition of this book and for complying with copyright laws by not
reproducing, scanning, or distributing any part of it in any form without permission.
You are supporting writers and allowing Penguin Random House to continue to
publish books for every reader.

BERKLEY is a registered trademark and BERKLEY PRIME CRIME and the B colophon
are trademarks of Penguin Random House LLC.

ISBN: 9780425277249

First Edition: March 2018

Printed in the United States of America
1 3 5 7 9 10 8 6 4 2

Cover illustration by Anne Wertheim
Cover design by Sarah Oberrender
Book design by Laura K. Corless

For Wyatt and David, in loving memory of Dolly

ACKNOWLEDGMENTS

As always, I'm indebted to literary agent John Talbot—my partner in crime developing and championing the Olive Grove Mysteries. John, your intuition, patience, and tutelage brought this slippery-fun cozy series to life. Thank you.

Lily Choi, my wonderful editor for *Dipped to Death*, thank you for your dedication to the Olive Grove Mysteries, as well as your patience and accessibility, insight, amenability, and unflappable good humor. While unforeseen events rock the boat on my home front, you're always a calm port in the storm—it's an absolute joy to work with you!

During a time of unprecedented change within the publishing industry, I've collaborated with a different Berkley Prime Crime editorial/production team for each of the three Olive Grove Mystery books—with the notable exception of cover designer Sarah Oberrender and cover illustrator Anne Wertheim, who've been on the ride from the very beginning. Thank you both, so very much, for your vision and skill bringing to life three *darling* concepts! I'm totally smitten with each whimsical cover . . . they're without a doubt some of the most appealing and endearing book covers in the genre today. Also, Laura K. Corless, thank you for your original interior text design for the series—you've added the perfect touch!

Michelle Vega, I'm most appreciative that you took on a new series submitted by an unpublished author of fiction after reading just a proposal and fifty pages of *One Foot in the Grove*. Thank you so very much for believing in me as well as the series.

Likewise, Bethany Blair, I'm grateful for your astute editorial guidance for *Cold Pressed Murder*. Your input is invaluable to the series.

With respect to *Dipped to Death*, special thanks to these superb professionals at Berkley Prime Crime: Stacy Edwards, senior production editor; Kelly Lipovich, interior text designer; Marianne Aguiar, copyeditor; Elisha Katz, marketing; and Tara O'Connor, publicity. I appreciate the time, effort, and unique talent you've each shared to help make this series a success.

Bibiana Heymann, your wholehearted, nonstop verve and devotion to our friendship and to the Olive Grove Mysteries leaves me excitedly breathless, buoyed up, and inspired each time we connect. If only I had a smidgen of your brilliance and energy! Martha Austin, the years and years you've shared your steadfast friendship, wisdom, and support are second to none. Having you in my corner humbles, grounds, and invigorates me. Thank you both, Bibiana and Martha, for your constant warmth as well as your help nurturing my dreams and aspirations.

Paul McCubbin, thank you for enthusiastically sharing news about Kelly Lane books with the folks from Ridgewood, New Jersey. I'm most appreciative of your kind efforts on my behalf. Margaret Ann Curran, you've got my heartfelt thanks for taking time to ensure that the Greene County Library in Stanardsville, Virginia, is onto the Olive Grove Mysteries. Caitlin Tirri, I appreciate the encouragement and backing you provided, giving me the "headspace" I needed to wrap up the *Dipped to Death* manuscript.

And to the folks at Georgia Olive Farms in Lakeland, Georgia, you're the inspiration for the series. Recently, I was thrilled to discover a bottle of your Chef's Blend Extra Virgin Olive Oil at the local Target store, here in Virginia. When I first read about Georgia Olive Farms' fledgling business a few years ago, folks were wondering if big-scale production of such an oil in South Georgia was even possible . . .

Also, here's a shout-out to friends and associates from Sisters in Crime, a group that is always welcoming, supportive, and an invaluable resource for mystery authors. And I must mention my

Alma Mater, Mount Holyoke College—I can't imagine Eva Knox attending any other school!

David Eddins and Wyatt Morin, you're my rock and inspiration as I teeter and totter from one massive undertaking to another. I'm forever grateful for your unparalleled patience, love, support, and understanding as I ensconce myself in words and stories. I love you both.

Lastly, this series would not be complete without sweet Dolly, whose big heart, boundless enthusiasm, and exquisite joy for life inspires so much of the stories. Our recent and heartbreakingly unexpected loss of Dolly is only countered by the knowledge that our beloved pup forever lives on in this world, happily romping through the pages of the Olive Grove Mysteries.

CHAPTER 1

Given the bizarreness of the night before, all in all, it'd been a pretty ho-hum September day in Abundance, Georgia. Right up until the moment Dolly and I spied that odd mop of brown stuff bobbing in the pond.

Of course, the last thing I expected to find was *another* dead body.

But, there he was.

Even though we had a full house of guests at Knox Plantation, earlier that day my boss—who happened to be my oldest sister, social butterfly, and self-proclaimed Southern belle, par excellence, Daphne Knox Bouvier—had offered me the Saturday afternoon off. As head of PR and guest relations for our plantation and guest inn, I'd worked nonstop for weeks at my family's old farmhouse—we called it the "big house"—tackling a full load of service and housekeeping, in addition to my usual PR duties.

That's because the duo my sister'd hired to handle housework and guest service—twenty-something twins Charlene and Darlene Greene—had rarely shown up for work that summer. They'd gotten away with their schlocky schedule because they were Daphne's best friend Earlene Azalea Greene's kids. Firing them had not been an option.

Anyway, by midday, I was hot, overtired, and decidedly cranky as I'd labored for hours in the sweltering summer heat, slogging away in place of the MIA twins. Then in the laundry room, I'd stubbed my toe—hard—and dropped a huge armload of just-cleaned, just-folded bath towels that I'd *just* been about to carry up to the guest rooms. As I'd hopped around on one foot, Daphne'd overheard me cursing and grumbling, complaining like a wet hen about Daphne's ever-in-absentia employees.

"Eva!"

Daphne's fancy Italian slingbacks click-clacked across the floor as she entered the laundry room.

"Y'all need to stop that hissy fit you're havin' 'cause everyone in the house will *hear* you," she scolded in a loud whisper. "We have *guests*!"

Even in her hushed voice my sister spoke with a thick-as-molasses Southern drawl. Daphne's accent was far more pronounced than anyone else's in my family . . . more than anyone else's in the entire county of Abundance, really. No doubt, the affectation made my sister feel more Southern than everyone around her. And I imagine that being *more* of something—anything—assured Daphne that she was the *best* . . . as in: good, better, *best*.

A stickler for perfection, Daphne always had to be the best.

She threaded a lily-white finger under a wayward wisp of my hair, securing the strawberry-blonde tendril behind my ear. With mingled scents of sparkly aldehydes, potent florals and powders, along with oakmoss, amber, and musk, my sister's iconic Chanel perfume suffused the cramped laundry room.

"Eva, *dahhwr-lin*, you've got a thumpin' gizzard for a heart sometimes," Daphne cooed as she patted me on the head. Her signature gold charm bracelet jangled as the Southern diva turned her attention to a pile of freshly folded bed linens on the counter. "We're plum lucky to have the twins helpin' us at all. Lord knows, I couldn't manage the business without them. Y'all really should be more appreciative."

She straightened the pile of linens.

Like many folks in our backwater Southern hamlet, whenever Daphne addressed me with the plural contraction "y'all"—a term usually intended to address more than one person—it was a signal that I was on the receiving end of a polite dress-down or diss. Or, it was used to soften an order. Somehow, it sounded less bossy to say "y'all" do this or that, rather than to demand "you" do this or that. It was all part of the subtle art of being an Abundance woman of stature. Or at least that was Daphne's take on it.

And, of course, Daphne was always right.

Sigh.

Primped and polished to the nines as usual, wearing a conservative, fitted linen dress accented with gold Van Cleef and Arpels ear clips—gifts from Daphne's pro-ball-playing ex-husband before he went splitsville—not one glossy, strawberry-blonde hair fell out of place from her flawless chignon as my exquisite sister curtsied over and picked up each towel with her fingertips, one by one, from the floor. Then, one by one, she tossed each towel into the dirty laundry hamper.

I'd have to wash, dry, and fold the *entire* load all over again.

"Argh!"

I pretended to pull my hair out.

"Please, Eva. Man-up," chided Daphne. Treating me like an unruly child was a holdover from the time she helped Daddy raise me and my middle sister, Pep, after Mother abandoned us as children.

Smiling ever so sweetly, Daphne pointed me toward an enormous wad of soiled bed linens in another hamper.

"I need y'all to clean, dry, and fold those ASAP. And, of course, the towels. Don't forget softener."

She turned on her heels and click-clacked back to the kitchen.

"Yes, ma'am," I mumbled, rolling my eyes.

Miffed, I yanked open the door to the oversize washing machine and started jamming in the soiled bedsheets and pillowcases.

I heard more click-clacking, then Daphne peeked back around the doorframe.

"And really, Eva," she said with a sniff, "I do wish y'all wouldn't come to work looking so . . . *pedestrian*."

I slammed the washer door.

Daphne frowned as I reached for the container of liquid laundry detergent. She couldn't mask her obvious disdain for my torn jeans and dime-store sneakers. Of course it was a no-brainer that she'd not "approve" of the promotional tee shirt I'd had made downtown at Hot Pressed Tees. It was printed with the slogan, O-LIVE OR DIE. Underneath, in smaller print, it read, KNOX PLANTATION.

I thought the slogan was pretty clever, actually. I mean, if Daddy hadn't started growing olive trees a few years back, we really *would've* died . . . or at least the plantation would've died. Growing olive trees and producing olive oil saved our homestead during a time when sales of more traditional crops had dwindled to nearly nothing.

Finished with the detergent, I turned on the machine and tromped from the laundry room.

"I don't know why y'all won't wear a uniform," my sister huffed in the kitchen.

Her bracelet jingled as she picked some lint off my shirt while I reached up and took a tall drinking glass from the upper cabinet. I set the glass on the red laminate countertop. Same counter we'd had growing up.

"Stop, Daph," I said.

"Why don't y'all just know it," she yammered, "our guests just *ahh-dowr* the twins in their little Knox Plantation uniforms. They look cuter than a sack full of puppies!"

Ignoring her, I opened the big Sub-Zero freezer and filled my glass with ice cubes.

I had to agree about one thing. Our guests—the men, anyway—did seem to enjoy taking in an eyeful of the twins as they bent over and served meals in their ridiculous, skimpy uniforms. To me, the ruffled, off-the-shoulder, too-short, poofy-skirted getups that Daphne'd designed to look like "charming Southern belle dresses" looked more like cheesy French maid frocks. Naturally, despite Daphne's protestations, I refused to wear one. Service and housekeeping weren't my official duties, anyway.

"I don't see *you* wearing one, Daph," I shot back hotly, slamming the freezer door.

With her svelte figure—she was taller and less curvy than I was—Daphne probably could've gotten away with wearing one of her stupid uniforms, scanty as they were, despite the fact that she was well into her forties.

"Don't y'all be silly, Eva. Of course I'm not wearing a *uniform*."

Daphne sniffed with indignation. Still trying to smile and keep her composure, she ended up looking like she'd just taken a whiff of some stinky cheese. Daphne hated cheese.

She continued. "I'm ten years older than you are, Eva. It wouldn't be age appropriate. Besides, I'm the *lady* of the house."

What Daphne really meant to say was that wearing a skimpy worker's costume wasn't her *station*. And in the same light, heaven forbid should la-di-da Daphne strip a soiled bed, or place *her* delicate hands around the handle of a scrub brush and stare down a dirty toilet bowl . . . *oh no*. That type of job was for the plebeians in life.

And younger sisters.

Still, when you cut to the chase, it was all for our *family* business. That's why I'd stepped in for the twins, time and time again that summer. I'd done way more than my fair share of vacuuming, dusting, changing bed linens, washing laundry, scouring pots and pans, and scrubbing toilets in the big house. And all through the summer, I'd endured Daphne's holier-than-thou attitude.

Like everyone *always* did.

So, on that stifling September morning—overtired, nursing a sore stubbed toe, aggravated with my nagging boss, and seeing nothing but mountains of dirty laundry ahead of

me—I'd nearly reached the end of my string. Plus, on top of
it all, there'd been the unexpected stress of the day before.
Dex Codman and his Boston cronies had just *shown up* at
Knox Plantation, completely out of the blue.

After all those years.

And right after serving them their first dinner at the plantation, I'd had a big blowout with Dex in front of *everyone*
during the after-dinner olive oil tasting party. Later that night
in my one-room cottage behind the big house, I'd actually
been so upset about the scene I'd made with Dex that I'd
downed a couple of glasses of wine before bed, to help me
sleep. A chronic insomniac, I rarely slept, anyway. Especially
that summer. And I rarely drank alcohol . . . certainly not
alone. However, with the shock and stress of Dex and the
others staying on at the plantation, I'd recognized that it would
take something extra to get me to sleep. That's where the wine
had come in.

And for once, it'd worked.

The wine, combined with the allergy pill I'd taken earlier,
had done the trick. I'd slept like a baby, only awakening one
time in the middle of the night, after a weird dream—but
then, I *always* had weird dreams.

In the dream, somewhere in the dark of night, a half-naked
man with two heads was singing and dancing, mocking and
chanting obscenities at me, while trying to pull off my clothes.
He laughed raucously. Then suddenly, I found myself underwater. The same man was tightly holding my wrist, and he
was pulling me down . . . down, deeper into the dark water
as I struggled and gasped for air. Then again, the dream
switched gears. It was still night, and a growling black bear
was chasing me through the woods, gnashing his teeth and
clawing at me. The man was still calling my name. I couldn't
see him. And I couldn't find my way out of the dark and scary
woods. Terrified, I felt a bear claw tearing though my clothes.
There was wet slobber on my shoulder as I still tried to get
away. But I was paralyzed and couldn't seem to move, let
alone run. I heard the man laughing. Then I felt the beast

breathing and slobbering on my cheek, growling in my ear. I was sure that I was about to die . . .

That's when I'd jumped up, awakening with a start, only to realize the attacking bear had actually been my little black dog, Dolly, licking me on the face. She'd been in my cottage with me, up on my grandma Knox's antique four-poster bed.

After that, Dolly'd jumped down to the floor before skittering to the screen door, whimpering.

Probably some critter outside, I'd thought, still groggy with sleep.

Dolly hadn't even bothered to wait for me to get out of bed. Pulling the screen door open with her paw, she'd let herself out of my cottage and onto the stoop outside. Exhausted and barely conscious, I'd put my head back down on the pillow, meaning to get up and let Dolly back in after a moment or two, after my heart stopped pounding and I'd sorted through my dream. Instead, I'd fallen right back to sleep, dead to the world.

Miracles *do* happen . . .

Several hours later that Saturday morning, as I sipped my cool glass of water in the big house kitchen while the blasted bed linens tumbled in the washing machine, Daphne stopped mid-sentence and sighed. She crossed her arms.

"Eva, are you even *listening* to me? I do declare, y'all look like ten miles of bad road today."

Above the farmhouse sink, the curtains at the kitchen window puffed in the warm breeze. I peeped outside, taking in Daphne's riot of flowers blooming in the garden. I caught a heady whiff of sweet-scented Gertrude Jekyll roses, tall, purple bearded irises, and gargantuan, snow-white Casa Blanca lilies as they bobbed in the breeze. Across the green lawn, birds chattered in a live oak tree laden with Spanish moss. I'd managed to avoid Dex and the others that morning while they were out on some sort of nature walk. Still, I thought, it was only a matter of time before I'd run into them. Or worse, if the twins didn't show up, I'd have to *serve* Dex and his Boston buddies. Again.

I need to get away.

I set the glass of water down in the sink.

"Eva? Hello? Are y'all paying me *any* mind?" Daphne tapped her foot as I turned to face her. Her bracelet jingled as she crossed her arms. "Gracious to goodness, y'all are about as useless as tits on a boar today, Eva." She let out an exasperated sigh. "Y'all are no help to me at all like this. I'm sure the twins will be here soon, so, I'm *ordering* you to take the afternoon off."

I laughed. Only Daphne could imagine she'd need to "order" me to take a summer afternoon off.

"Hooray! Thanks, Daph," I said. "Except now, I kinda feel bad about all the despicable things I've thought about you this summer." I grinned.

Daphne threw her hands up, looking positively scandalized. The door from the dining room swung open.

"*Woo-wee!* It's hotter than the Devil's armpit in here!"

Precious Darling, who worked as our "temporary" chef at Knox Plantation—when she wasn't working as estate manager for the Gatsby-esque Greatwoods Plantation next door— clomped into the kitchen. Well over six feet tall, Precious was built like an Amazon warrior maiden. She had beautiful coppery skin, with matching short-cropped hair, and always wore Louboutin shoes and designer duds, even when she worked in the kitchen. Best of all, Precious was a spectacular cook.

"Miss Daphne, you got somethin' you need me to do before I head back to Greatwoods?"

Per Daphne's orders, Precious proceeded to pack me a picnic lunch in an old willow basket.

"I'm tryin' out new recipes for the guests," Precious said later, handing me the stuffed picnic basket. "You're my guinea pig."

"Great!" I cried, eagerly snagging the load. "Thanks, Precious."

"My pleasure, Sunshine."

I hauled the big basket out the kitchen door, down the back porch steps, through Daphne's cutting garden, and across several acres of lawn behind the big house, heading toward my cottage. High above me, big cottony clouds floated in a sultry late-summer breeze, blocking and releasing a blazing hot sun.

It's a perfect day to spend down at the pond, I thought.

More importantly, the free afternoon was an opportune time for me to figure out what the heck I was going to do about Dex.

Why, oh why, after all these years, has Dex suddenly shown up in Abundance?

I agonized about having to come clean about what had happened between us all those years ago.

Crap.

Dolly greeted me with licks and wags as I yanked open the flimsy screen door to my cottage—a pre–Civil War cook's quarters that Daphne'd renovated and furnished with old family pieces right before I'd moved back home earlier that summer. Without air-conditioning, the place was too hot and stuffy inside to keep it closed up during summertime. I always left the main door open, and used just the screen door.

"Hi, Dolly!"

I reached down and patted my pup as she shot past me, leaping over the stoop into the yard.

Quickly, I changed clothes, throwing my soiled stuff on the four-poster bed and pulling on my one-piece swimsuit and a pair of cutoffs. I tied my strawberry-blonde hair in a ponytail, shoved my feet into a pair of flip-flops, and plopped a big, floppy straw hat on my head before throwing into the basket a tube of sunscreen, a mystery paperback, and my vintage Jackie O–style sunglasses—a gift from Daphne; her style, not mine. As an afterthought, I grabbed the local paper, the *Abundance Record*, sitting on my grandmother's old Sheridan dresser near the door.

Then, Dolly and I headed out back, passing another one of Daphne's perennial gardens behind the cottage. We moseyed down the grassy green knoll toward the pond where we made our way around the watering hole.

Conk-la-ree! A red-winged blackbird trilled.

Skittering ahead of me, Dolly chased a squirrel through

the tall grasses around the edge of the pond. Then about halfway around the pond, she came to an ancient olive tree. The squirrel scooted up the great, grizzled, twisted olive tree trunk and was soon hidden from view by ribbons of slender sage green leaves cascading from gnarled branches. Barking wildly, Dolly started scrambling up the tree.

"Dolly! No!"

I hurried over, giggling at the sight of my little pup actually hoisting herself up the tree.

"Stop, Dolly!"

By the time I'd finally managed to pull her down, Dolly'd already made it nearly three feet up the tree trunk.

"No squirrels," I said, holding back giggles as I scolded my naughty pup.

Still eagerly waiting for the squirrel to make an appearance, Dolly sat at my feet, whimpering as she looked up at the old olive tree.

Daddy'd told me once that the tree must've been at least three or four hundred years old—most likely planted by Spanish missionaries who'd long ago inhabited what's now the southeastern United States. Still, the single olive tree at our place had always been a bit of a mystery. As far as anyone knew, there were no other signs in Abundance that missions ever existed in our little corner of Georgia's wire grass country, a place where—unless you farmed or worked at the local chemical plant or the prison on the far side of town—up until recent times there'd never been much reason to stick around.

Except for a few awe-inspiring mansions and estates built during the Gilded Age by wealthy Northerners who wanted lush winter getaways and hunting retreats, Abundance was mostly known for its run-down farms, big, nasty swamps, and untamed forests.

Of course, along with those untamed forests came trees. And with those trees came loggers and logging. The area was chock-full of longleaf pines—those tall, straight trees that grow for hundreds of years and make perfect telephone poles. Loggers loved them, while tree huggers harped about saving the ancient pines, which sounded nice until it came to putting food on the table . . . For most folks in the area, that hadn't always been easy.

Since the railroad went bust after the boom times of the Gilded Age, except for hunters and a few crooks hiding from the law, almost no one came to Abundance, at least during all the years I'd been raised there. For most of my life, Abundance County had pretty much been at death's door.

Then the Internet happened.

Sometime during the eighteen years I'd lived up in New England, a few local folks had fixed up some ramshackle Victorian shops and buildings downtown. Then they'd advertised on the Internet. Some adventurous tourists had shown up, and word had spread about Abundance's "cute," "unspoiled" little village. More new businesses had opened. And instead of driving forty-five minutes to the nearest big-box store in the next county, even local folks in Abundance had begun to shop locally. Garden club members had volunteered to maintain plantings on the tree-lined village boulevard. More locals had renovated more downtown Victorians. And more village shops, guest inns, and local businesses had opened, followed by more shoppers and more tourists. Before everyone knew it, the village had become chock-full of new businesses. Shops. Restaurants. Professional services. There were handmade signs. Striped awnings. Cute window displays. New brick sidewalks. Flower boxes. And outside the village, wildlife tours and a host of agritourist destinations had sprouted up throughout the county.

Abundance had made a comeback, of sorts. Or, perhaps more accurately, a start-up.

In fact, the old olive tree near our pond had been the inspiration for Daddy's new olive oil business. After being hard-hit by the recession, Daddy's traditional peach and blueberry crops hadn't been selling; he needed to save the farm that'd been in our family for six generations. Daddy knew there was a huge international market for olive oil, and the United States had tapped into no more than two percent of that worldwide market. So he took out one big, last loan and gave growing olive trees a try. With the help of his right-hand gal, my middle sister, Pep—a mechanical genius—Daddy's new olive oils quickly became a hit. They'd even won some awards.

More recently, Daddy moved into a small, private retreat nestled in some woods on the plantation. Then after her messy divorce in Atlanta, my oldest sister, Daphne, and her five kids moved back home into the big house. She fixed up the place with money she'd wrangled from her cheating ex-husband. Daphne and the kids moved up to the third floor so paying guests could stay in the second-floor bedrooms. After some well-placed ads and a couple of articles I wrote about Daphne's new hospitality business hit the public—I'd had a little PR business up in Boston—suddenly, Knox Plantation became a hot spot for foodies, nature-lovers, history buffs, and agritourists.

That is, until I moved back home and the dead bodies started piling up.

After two murders and another man found dead from natural causes at our place, just since I'd returned home that summer, the Knox family was getting plenty of publicity . . . more than our share, I'd say. And I'd been the one tripping over and falling into each and every dead person . . . quite literally. Sheriff Buck Tanner had even called me a "magnet for disaster."

So, just when things were finally quieting down and I'd been feeling that all the dead bodies and badness from earlier that summer were finally behind us, suddenly, I had to deal with *him*.

Dex.

"At least Dex isn't dead, Dolly," I said, like a smart aleck. *Conk-la-ree!*

I reached up and plucked an olive from the ancient tree. Not much bigger than a marble, apple green in color with dashes of bruised purple, the oval-shaped stone fruit felt firm when I squeezed it between my fingers. It'd be another few weeks before this fruit, like the olives growing on Daddy's young Arbequina, Arbosana, and Koroneiki trees planted on the one-hundred-acre orchard on the other side of the farm, would be ready for harvest. I tossed the olive into the tall weeds. Pretty to look at, it was too bitter to eat without pickling it first or making it into an oil or paste. Even birds wouldn't eat the tart fruit.

Cheer-up, cheer-up cheer-ree!

A robin sang from somewhere up in the yard, its melodious call distinct from the twitters and warbles of the finches and sparrows around me.

I turned and headed toward the low pier jutting over the pond, slogging through knee-high grasses, sedges, and weeds. Frogs *ker-plunked* from the muddy bank into the water. About ten feet ahead of me, Dolly stopped, barely visible in the grasses. She looked back over her shoulder and yipped. Then with her tail wagging over her back, she jumped up and onto the rickety wooden pier, galloping down to the end of the planks where a small wooden dinghy bobbed in the water.

I smiled.

As a kid, I'd spent countless afternoons in that little boat, painted white on the inside and fire-engine red on the outside, rowing around the pond, fishing, sunning, and swimming.

Good memories.

Dolly looked down at the water, ready to jump.

"No! No! Dolly! Don't jump!"

Dolly scratched and whimpered at the end of the pier.

"No!"

I rushed through the weeds toward the pier as the big basket banged against my legs.

She whimpered again, this time digging and scratching at the wooden planks.

"Dolly! I said, *no*!"

She sat and waited.

Hoisting the basket, I hopped up from the grass onto the wooden planks of the pier and followed Dolly to the end. I set the basket down and rubbed my pup.

"Good girl, Dolly." I planted a kiss atop her head. Her wavy fur felt smooth as satin.

Reaching inside the basket, I pulled out the ginormous ham hock that Precious had packed, just for Dolly. Before I could give it to her, Dolly jumped up and stole the big bone from my hand. Racing back down the pier, she tossed the bone into the air then pounced on it as it clattered on the wooden planks.

"Don't go far, Dolly!"

I unfolded a red-checkered tablecloth and set out the contents of the basket. Precious had prepared a cold plate of bourbon and ginger barbecued chicken sliced atop her limey summer pasta salad—a concoction of bow tie pasta, apples, celery, grapes, parsley, and her roasted sweet, salty, 'n spicy pecans, all drenched in a ridiculously delicious lime vinaigrette. As a side, Precious had prepared corn pudding, and for dessert, she'd added a huge wedge of chocolate olive oil cake with scrumptious mascarpone frosting. Of course, every dish was prepared with our Knox Liquid Gold Extra Virgin Olive Oil. Also, there were some strawberries and a cooler of iced lemonade to wash it all down. It was a feast fit for a queen. More than enough to quell a jag of nervous eating while I figured out what the heck I was going to do about my problem guests.

First, I'm going to relax and enjoy my feast, I thought. *I've earned it.*

Settling in at the end of the pier, under the protective shade of my floppy hat, I listened to the birds in the yard and the smack of the little red dinghy as it bobbed in the water and bumped the pier while Dolly gnashed at her bone on the wooden planks behind me. I savored each and every morsel of my mouthwatering meal.

Thirty or more minutes later, there wasn't a bite left to eat. I sighed happily as I packed up the spoils of my picnic and covered the basket. Then, reality sank back in . . .

My little voice inside was screaming. I needed to deal with Dex.

Not yet.

I grabbed the newspaper and scanned the headlines: "Twiggs Shoots Self, Dies While Cleaning Firearm"; "Naturalists Celebrate Abundance Peeps Week with Parade"; "Teen Flips Auto at Benderman's Curve"; "Real Estate Board

Reports Surge in Local Property Sales"; "Nursing Home Volunteers Make Kindness a Priority"; "Clatterbuck Benefit Raises Thousands"; "Anonymous Benefactor Donates Rescue Boat to Fire Department"; "High School Cross-Country Team Stomps Competitors"; "Library Posts New Hours" . . . the usual stuff.

I was just happy not to read anything about me, for once. Local reporter Pat Butts and her sidekick, photographer Tam See, were always popping up at the most inopportune times to record my misfortunes, mostly with dead men.

I tossed the rag aside and grabbed my mystery book. Behind me, Dolly continued happily gnawing away at her ham bone. A little breeze kissed my cheek as I opened the paperback and began reading, trying to distract my mind with the details of a whodunit. With my bare feet dangling over the pier, splashing in the cool water, I concentrated on the mystery, barely noticing as birds sang and long strands of leaves waved and hissed from the ancient olive tree and the willow trees on the far side of the pond. It was a perfect afternoon.

At least for a few minutes . . .

Conk-la-ree!

A stiff breeze blew. Slender leaves in the olive tree chittered in the wind and the boat bumped against the pier. I reached up to grab my hat before it sailed away. Something *kur-thunked* from the side of the pond with a splash. Dolly's bone clattered on the boards as she dropped it to listen. Looking up from my book, I shielded my eyes with my hand, squinting through my Jackie O glasses to see.

Was it a frog? Trout?

Over on the marshy side of the pond, I heard a chorus of bullfrogs burping and grunting, reminding me of sounds my two sisters and I used to make when we'd plucked rubber bands wrapped around old tissue boxes, our homemade "instruments."

There was another *kur-thunk*. Dolly looked up again.

"It was a frog, Dolly."

She went back to her bone.

Even under my hat, the afternoon sun was bright and felt

blistering hot on my skin. Returning home earlier that summer after eighteen years up in New England, I still wasn't acclimated to my hometown's sultry climate. The preposterous heat, coupled with the unexpected problems that came with *Dex's* arrival, plagued me . . .

I dropped the book. Reaching into the picnic basket, I pulled out the tube of sunscreen. Opening the tube, I slathered the goo on my face, chest, shoulders, and arms, careful not to get it on my baby blue swimsuit. I was tanned, but with my fair skin and my love for the outdoors, I worked hard not to burn. I had my share of freckles; I didn't need any more.

I secured my hat with a tug and went back to my book, flipping to a new page as a puffy white cloud crossed overhead, blocking the bright sun. From the yard up the hill, I could hear noisy blue jays squabbling from moss-covered limbs in the live oak trees. The long, pointed leaves of palmetto trees in the yard twisted in the wind as I got a whiff of Daphne's flowers. The cloud moved on, releasing the glaring sun again. Then a smaller shadow crossed my legs. I looked up to see a buzzard circling slowly overhead.

Looking for field mice.

The breeze blew ripples across the pond. Next to me, the red dinghy bobbed in little waves, nudging the pier.

Thunk. Thunk.

The buzzard flew off just before a brown pelican dropped like an arrow from the sky, splashing straight down into the black pond water where it disappeared. A moment later, the big bird emerged from the pond, flying up and then soaring off with a small trout in its bill. Dolly woofed and wagged her tail as she watched the pelican.

"C'mon, Dolly. That bird's got the right idea. It's too hot to just sit here. Let's go for a row."

I dog-eared a page and tossed my mystery book inside the basket. Dolly released her bone with a clatter and galloped down the pier. I reached down and scooped her up in my arms.

"Omigosh! Dolly! You weigh a *ton.*"

Cradling Dolly felt more like I was cradling a cinder block. Squirming in my arms—with brown button eyes, floppy ears, a long tail curled over wavy black fur on her back—she whimpered excitedly as she licked my face.

"Dolly, your breath is *terrible!*" *Ix-nay on the ham bones*, I thought. *Sheesh.* "How can you be so fat, Dolly? I hate to put you on a diet. I barely feed you as it is!"

With porky Dolly pressed tight against my chest, I carefully slithered down from the wooden pier into the tiny boat bobbing in the wavelets below. No more than five or six feet long, the dinghy rocked furiously back and forth as I stepped down inside, trying to balance with Dolly in my arms.

Dolly wriggled free and jumped down—landing with the athletic prowess of a log—to stand panting between my legs in the bilge. A puff of wind worked its way across the pond, wrinkling the water as I slipped the tie line off the pillar at the dock. With Dolly in the stern, I settled to face her on the middle seat. I flipped up the chocks on the gunwales and dropped an oar into each. Then, slicing the water with my right oar, I pulled it hard, spinning the little dinghy toward the center of the pond. Dolly ducked under my seat and scuttled to the bow, where she looked out ahead, panting and sniffing, standing up like a sentry with her front paws on the gunwale.

Eyes half closed, I rowed lazily out into the pond, going nowhere, really, just idly paddling around and around, relaxing, attempting to empty my mind and catch a breeze to cool my skin. I gazed down into the water, trying to catch a glimpse of a fish or two. *No luck.* Even with my sunglasses cutting the glare, the murky pond water appeared almost black, with little sparkles of sunlight dancing on the tops of the wavelets.

C'mon, Eva, you've got to deal with Dex.

Finally, I slipped the oars up, out of the water, and across my lap. Looking skyward, I leaned back, closed my eyes, and inhaled as the flowery breeze kicked up again. The little boat turned in the wind, and I heard tiny waves licking the rocking hull. Then a gust blew from the other direction. The boat briskly spun around and pitched side to side as Dolly scrambled toward the opposite side of the bow, sniffing and whimpering. With one hand over the oars in my lap, I grabbed the gunwale with my other hand and steadied myself, still with my eyes closed, still determined to bask *thoughtlessly* in the sunlight. I inhaled the scents of sugary flowers from Daphne's garden behind my cottage mingled with the wet, earthy detritus around the pond. A shadow crossed over us as the buzzard circled overhead.

That's when I began recounting the night before.

"Can you believe it, Dolly?" I said. "There he was. Dex. Standing in the house where I'd grown up. Grinning at me, like we were still friends. Like nothing had ever happened between us. Like it hadn't been sixteen or seventeen years since we'd last seen each other. As if he'd never . . . Oh, never mind."

I remembered how Daphne'd told me that Dex had specifically asked to sleep in my old bedroom. Of course, not having any idea who he was, or that he'd even known me before stepping onto the plantation that day, Daphne had happily assigned him my old room. Why wouldn't she?

Eghh.

"Ironic how after I'd left him, I'd never run across him during all those years in New England. I'd never even thought about him. Then, I'm back home no more than a couple of months, and *bam*! Here he is. Out of nowhere. Like a bad penny. My worst nightmare."

I groaned. Dolly sniffed the air and yipped.

"Why did Dex come to Abundance, Dolly? I never wanted to see him again. Surely, he must know that. And why are he and the others calling themselves 'bird-watchers'? I recognize every single one of them. Bird-watchers? Really?"

Hardly.

Dolly barked. I opened my eyes just as she jumped upright, knocking the dinghy around, placing her front paws on the gunwale. Looking across the water, she barked again.

And again.

"Shhh, Dolly!"

Squealing and shaking excitedly, with her attention fo-

cused on the far side of the pond, Dolly would not stop barking. I sat up.

"Dolly, stop!"

Bark. Bark. Bark.

"What is it?"

I tried to follow her gaze. She kept barking and whimpering, scratching at the side of the skiff. And then, finally, I saw
something. It was way across the pond. In the tall weeds.

"What is that, Dolly?"

Afraid she'd jump out of the dinghy, I grabbed my pup and
pulled her back between my legs. I slid my oars into the
water, spun the boat around, and started rowing toward the
brown clump in the weeds on the other side of the pond.

"Is that *fur*?"

Dolly barked again.

The wind blew, and the brown thing bobbed, making ripples in the water. I squinted to see. Still, I couldn't make it
out. So I rowed faster. Honestly, if Dolly hadn't barked and
put on such a fit, I'd never have noticed whatever it was. At
first, it looked just like a brown patch of thatch.

Cattails?

No . . . I decided it looked just like a clump of random
weeds. Then, not so much. As I rowed closer, the random
weeds began to look more like fur.

"A beaver? Groundhog?"

Is it moving? No . . .

"Ugh. Must be a dead animal."

Dolly squealed as I pulled the oars harder and faster
through the water, spinning to look over my shoulder as we
neared the floating blob.

Dolly made a shrill whining noise, y*eee-ow, yeee-ow!* Her
tail wagged furiously.

"Are there beavers around here?"

That made sense, I thought. A beaver. No. A *dead* beaver.
That explained the buzzard.

Gross.

I pulled the oars through the black water again. And again.

And again. We closed in on the brown thing. I rowed on. Pulled harder. Still between my legs, Dolly was near frantic. A hard knot grew in my stomach as I rowed nearer to the brown clump.

Something isn't right.

Squinting, looking over my shoulder again, I slowed my rowing as we drifted nearer to the mass in the weeds and grasses. I pulled hard on the right oar, spinning the skiff around to see . . .

In a barking frenzy, Dolly shot from between my legs. At the same moment, with a terrible start, I yelped. Instinctively, my body flew up and backward. My hat flew off. The oars slid from my grip and into the water. I almost fell out of the rocking dinghy.

Finally, I had a clear view of the brown clump.

Floating in the tall weeds was a mass of hair.

On a man's head.

Drifting faceup, with chiseled features and eyes as black and lifeless as the murky water around him, the man with fine, sun-bronzed skin was most definitely . . . naked.

And, most decidedly, dead.

Worse still, I recognized him.

Once upon a time, we'd been engaged.

CHAPTER 2

"Eva, what do you mean, you were engaged to him once? Babydoll, this isn't your Boston weatherman . . . is it?" His low, sotto voce voice was smooth as silk, with a distinctly Southern drawl.

Standing on the end of the pier, tanned, tall, rock of a man Sheriff Buck Tanner was calm but clearly puzzled as he stared at me from behind his dark aviator sunglasses. In his late thirties, Buck raised a big farmer's hand, raking strong fingers through his close-cropped dark brown hair. Even in all that summer heat, he looked cool as a cucumber.

Buck's white, short-sleeved, button-down uniform shirt precisely fit his immensely muscled chest and shoulders. On one shoulder he wore a large patch and bars that denoted his rank. Small gold pins with the letters "ACSD" embellished his lapels. A gold badge with an encircled star was pinned to his right chest pocket. A heavy-looking black belt with pouches all around holstered a large gun over his hip. Buck's mouth was tight as he shoved his phone back into his uniform pocket.

The dimples weren't smiling. Buck was all business.

I looked away, scanning the scene as blue and red lights flashed from vehicles up in the yard—SUVs, ambulances, fire trucks. Parked down at the pond, there was a truck with a trailer that had carried the small boat that'd been launched into the water to retrieve the body. It'd seemed a bit over the top to me . . . I mean, from where the body'd been, a tall person probably could've reached him with a pair of waders. Or certainly, they could've used my little rowboat for retrieval. *But no.* Apparently, this type of water retrieval doesn't happen much in Abundance County. The rescue team must've been eager to use the new aluminum rescue boat that a Samaritan had donated. All around the little pond, people in uniforms hustled about, barking orders, writing notes, taking photographs, measuring . . .

Watching the scene from the top of the hill near my cottage were three men and one woman, all about my age—in their late thirties or early forties. I recognized each one of them: pinched-looking, blonde Claudia Bacon Devereaux; geeky, spectacled Spencer Andover Fisk; burly, bearded John Cabot "Wiggy" Wigglesworth; and boyishly handsome Norcross Cooper "Coop" Tarbox the Second.

The rest of the crowd from Boston.

Outfitted like a crew from the L.L.Bean catalogue, they were all friends of the deceased and, like him, all worked for the Perennial Paper Company in Boston. Ostensibly on vacation, they were dressed in brand-new hiking clothes and were wearing binoculars around their necks. Returning from their guided nature walk somewhere off the plantation, the group remained up on the hill after the deputies cautioned them about coming any nearer to the pond. I looked down at the water.

"Eva?" Buck asked again.

A soft breeze made little wavelets on the pond. Standing alongside Buck, I got a whiff of the warm, honeyed scent of his skin mixed with something powdery and soft with spice, sandalwood and a hint of patchouli. His scent was comforting and familiar. Safe. And something else. My mind flashed to the last time he'd touched me—kissed me, with quite a bit of gusto, I might add—right here at the plantation, just a few weeks earlier. Thinking about it, the back of my neck flashed hot and got a little tingly.

Still, where'd Buck been lately?

I felt my cheeks flush.

A vehicle door slammed somewhere in the yard. I looked up to see Buck staring at me, waiting for an answer.

"No," I sighed. "It's not Zack Black . . . the Boston weatherman," I said finally. "And he wasn't *my* weatherman," I added sarcastically.

My sensational broken engagement to the popular weatherman Zack Black months earlier had been tabloid fodder all summer long. I'd become known all over the country as the kooky jezebel who'd run off from Boston's—the nation's, really—best-known and beloved celebrity weatherman on our highly publicized wedding day. Then after I'd ditched my wretched ex-fiancé, he and his TV station PR pundits had dredged up and publicized my runaway bride "history," making it look like the wedding-day blowout in Boston had all been *my* fault. Since I'd ditched another fiancé at the altar eighteen years earlier, *I*—the chronically disturbed runaway bride—was the problem, not Zack Black, everyone's favorite weatherman.

Of course, it was all bunk. I'd had good reason to run from Zack. Regardless, I couldn't match the television station's PR machine, and by week's end, the bad publicity about me had ruined my reputation as well as my PR business in New England. Not long after my aborted wedding day, with no clients and no income, and no place to live—*note to self, never share a condo with your fiancé, because if it doesn't work out, you'll get locked out and lose all your stuff*—I ended up hightailing it back to my hometown of Abundance, Georgia, after eighteen years away and plans to never return.

Never say never.

Then, right after I'd returned home, I'd had to face, for the first time in eighteen years, the *first* man I'd ditched at the altar.

Sheriff Buck Tanner.

That had been awkward, to say the least.

Then, there was a murder at our plantation. And then, a man suffered a heart attack and died. And then, there was *another* murder.

Now this.

I glanced over at the other side of the pond. *What happened to Dex?* Then the realization hit me.

I'm going to have to tell Buck the truth. All of it . . .

Like the other two times that I'd been engaged—before Dex to Buck, and after Dex to Zack Black the weatherman—I'd broken my engagement to Dex suddenly, and then I'd run away. It'd made perfect sense at the time. To me, anyway. Looking back on it, I should've handled it differently.

All of it.

Regardless, unlike the other two very public wedding-day routs with Buck and the weatherman, this broken engagement, the second of three, was something that no one knew about. Except for a few people from Boston—Dex's closest friends— no one had even known that I'd been engaged to Dex in the first place, including my family. I hadn't even told Daphne that I knew Dex when I'd discovered him and his cronies seated at the dinner table up at the big house the night before. My two older sisters and my dad were bound to be shocked and hurt about all the history that I hadn't shared with them.

And now, making things worse, those few in the know from Boston were standing on the knoll next to my cottage. Staring down at me. And they were pretending, for some unknown reason, to be bird-watchers. Here in Abundance.

And Dex was dead in my family's farm pond.

I looked up at the small gathering on the hill.

I felt sick.

Someone was approaching from the other side of the pond. Tall, slim Deputy Pierce. I recognized the young, hazel-eyed deputy from the last murder investigation. He ambled over to his boss and whispered in Buck's ear. Something about Dex's eyes. And then something about Dex's clothes. Buck nodded, without taking his eyes off me. Or at least I thought his eyes were on me . . . I couldn't see Buck's gorgeously chocolaty peepers because they were concealed behind his dark aviators.

"Go on, Eva," Buck ordered as his deputy took out a notepad. "You were telling me that you were engaged to the man you found in the pond?"

Deadpan. He could've been ordering a pizza.

"Yes. We knew each other a long time ago. His name is . . . Dex. Well, technically, Dudley Dexter Codman the Third. He was an acquisitions manager for the Perennial Paper Company. In Boston."

"And you say that you were *engaged*?"

"Yes. I said that. Engaged. To be married."

Duh.

"And when was that?"

I looked down. "About sixteen, no, maybe seventeen years ago." I felt my cheeks flush. Big-time. An urge to puke was hard to control.

Buck was silent. Didn't take a genius to figure it out. I'd broken off my engagement with Buck eighteen years earlier and run off. Then I'd broken off another engagement with Dex, not too long after that. Although I'd never admitted it to a soul, anyone with half a brain could figure out that it'd been Dex with whom I'd run off when I'd left Buck at the altar.

"Could you spell this fella's name, Miss Knox?" asked young Deputy Pierce, jotting something down.

"The last name is Codman. Like the fish . . . C-O-D-M-A-N. Just like it sounds. It's an old Boston Brahmin family."

"Brahmin . . . ?" The deputy furrowed his brow.

"I'll explain later," Buck said quickly. "Just think, 'old money.' Upper class. *Hah-vard.*"

The deputy nodded. "Got it, sir."

"Well, that's a bit coarse," I said. "And oversimplified. The Brahmins of Boston are an elite and integral part of the New England establishment." I turned to the deputy. "Oliver Wendell Holmes Senior first used the term 'Brahmin' during the late nineteenth century to describe a group of wealthy, educated, high-society families living on Boston's prestigious

Beacon Hill. The Boston Brahmins preferred to remain relatively private, both in their day-to-day life and in their wealth. They still do today. However, most continue to be extremely generous philanthropists."

Okay, so I was rambling, ad nauseam. Even I couldn't bear to listen to myself lecture the poor deputy like some uppity schoolmarm. Still, I couldn't help it. I was anxious. Worried. The blathering just tumbled out.

Buck cleared his throat. "Thank you for the history lesson, Professor Knox. Now, do you know where we can find Mister Codman's family?"

"He doesn't have any that I know of. His parents perished in a boating accident about twenty years ago. Dex is . . . was . . . the last of the Codman line. At least this particular Codman line."

"Wife?"

"Doesn't appear to have one," I said.

And he sure didn't act like it last night.

"No sisters or brothers?"

I shook my head.

"Kids?"

Again, I shook my head.

"You're positive he isn't married?"

"Not that I know of. Look, I'm sure Daphne has all his home information up at the big house. Or you could check with the people he was traveling with."

I waved toward the Boston crowd on the hill. Clustered in a tight circle with their heads bowed down, they appeared to be studying some sort of big map that they held between them.

"They're all his close friends and business associates from the Perennial Paper Company," I said, nodding toward the group.

"Why would a group of paper company people come all the way down here from Boston?"

"We were told it was for a bird-watching retreat. It *is* Peeps Week, after all. Why don't you ask them?"

"I plan to. However, right now, I'm asking you."

That was cold.

Buck continued. "Any idea what this guy was doing down here at the pond, or when he came down to the pond?"

"No. It looked like . . ."

I felt weak remembering Dex's body. It'd been ghastly-looking with his black eyes staring upward as he floated, bloated in the water. He'd had the most clear, smooth skin, refined features, and beautiful icy blue eyes when he'd been alive.

Well, they'd been beautiful until he got angry, that is.

"It looked like he'd been floating for a while . . ." I finally said.

I felt the blood rush from my head.

"Ma'am, you look kinda pale. Can I get y'all some water?" asked the deputy.

"He's been in the water several hours," said Buck, ignoring his deputy. Buck was all business despite my blanching. "Did he know how to swim?"

"What?"

"You were engaged to him, Eva. Surely, you know . . . was your *Boston Brahmin fiancé* a decent swimmer?"

Is there a hint of irritation in Buck's voice?

"Yes, he could swim," I answered. "Not competitively, like you . . . I . . . uh . . . He kept a Hinckley Sou'wester sloop on Cape Cod. It used to belong to his parents. It was a beautiful boat. A classic . . . wooden sailboat . . . you know?"

The corners of Buck's mouth tightened. He looked ever-so-mildly irritated.

"Get to the point, please, Eva."

"Oh. Yes. Sorry. We used to sail and swim off his Hinckley in Nantucket Sound all the time. I mean . . . What was your question?"

"Was your fiancé a good swimmer?"

"*Ex*-fiancé, you mean. Yes. To answer your question, Dex was an excellent swimmer."

"Was he alone here at the pond late last night or early this morning?"

Buck looked straight at me. Deadpan.

"I don't know. I never saw him here late last night or this morning."

"But you *did* see him . . . right?"

"Yes, but that was last evening, up at the big house."

"Let me get this straight. You're making a distinction between 'evening' and 'night'?"

"I guess so. Yes. 'Night' is *later* than 'evening'—"

Buck shook his head as he interrupted me.

"You never came down here to the pond with him? Or saw him come down here?"

"No." I glared at Buck. I'd already answered the question. *Buck is double-checking me.*

"Why are you asking me so many questions? This was an accident. Right?"

Buck didn't answer. "So, the last time you saw your . . . *ex*-fiancé, Mister Codman, was last *evening*?"

"Yes. In the big house."

"And can you be more precise about the time?"

"After dinner we had an olive oil tasting party."

"And who was at the party?"

"Well, Dex and the other four from Boston, Claudia Bacon Devereaux, she's Dex's assistant; John Cabot Wigglesworth—everyone calls him 'Wiggy'—he's an acquisitions manager; Coop, er, that is, Norcross Cooper Tarbox, the corporate lawyer; and the company numbers guy, Spencer Andover Fisk."

"Go on."

"They'd invited a few folks from the Abundance Bird Club to join them."

"Including?"

I sighed. "I'm not sure I can remember, really . . . It was the club's executive committee, I think."

"Try."

"Violetta Merganthal was there. She brought her daughter, Maisy, who I doubt is the least bit interested in birds. Daphne's theory is, now that Maisy's graduated from community college, she's husband shopping, so she won't have to get a job. Daphne says that Violetta brings Maisy anywhere there's a chance of meeting up with a man."

"Go on."

"Let's see, Millicent Page—you know, the librarian—

came. She drove old-timers Eunice and Eugene Ord, who apparently never miss a bird club meeting despite the fact that neither one ever goes on bird walks anymore."

"I should think not," said Buck. "Neither one can get around without a walker or a wheelchair."

"Right. Well, during the tasting, Eugene spent most of the time in the bathroom—citing prostate issues—and because Eunice forgot her teeth, she dribbled more olive oil down the front of her dress than she was actually ever able to swallow. It was a mess. Plus, I doubted either one could hear anything that anyone said. Poor Millicent had her hands full with those two."

"Who else was there?"

"Bernice Burnside came with Beula Beauregard."

"If I remember correctly, our timber heiress, Bernice Burnside, joined the bird club years ago while she served on the Georgia House of Representatives, to counter the public's perception about her anti-nature-loving timber business."

"That's what I heard. And philanthropist Beula Beauregard just loves birds and dumps a pile of money into the organization every year."

"Anyone else?"

"Tree hugger Zippy Grann, along with Fern Taylor, Tweets Buckingham, and Tallulah Hayes were all there. And, Dilly Willard. That's it, I think."

"All locals. No one we don't already know. Okay, I'll talk to them. How late did they stay?"

"I'm not sure. Once I finished my tasting spiel, which only took about forty-five minutes, I left before they did. Why are you asking me about all this?"

"What time did you leave?"

"I left at maybe eight thirty or nine, I'd say."

"And then what?"

"I went to bed."

He can find out about the argument between me and Dex from someone else.

I didn't need to make the situation any worse than it already was. Maybe no one would say anything about the argument,

I reasoned. After all, Dex's death was clearly just an accident. Although, really, I couldn't imagine what had happened. Remembering Dex, I felt the blood drain from my head again. I reached out to grab something, but there was nothing to grab.

Buck had an extraordinarily good poker face. And he could be impossible to read, especially when he was on the job. Still, I knew him well enough. Better than anyone, I'd wager. And I couldn't help but feel the ice behind his stare. He wasn't helping me.

That's fine, I thought. I steadied myself.

Given that I'd run off and left Buck with no explanation all those years ago, I owed Buck that much. Still, I was horrified to have to face him with the truth, even after all these years. Especially like this. He hadn't deserved it then. And, as it'd turned out, I'd made a huge and painful mistake. *Painful for all of us.* And foolishly, once I'd moved on, I'd blithely gone through life, assuming it was all water over the dam and I'd never have to own up to what I'd done to Buck. I'd imagined my history with Dex would never come out.

Wrong.

"Can you be more specific about the circumstances between you and Mister Codman last *evening*?" asked Buck.

"Dex and his business associates checked in yesterday afternoon while I was out," I answered, matter-of-factly. "I first saw him when they came down to dinner. The twins had the night off, so I filled in as server . . ."

Buck held his hand up. Without waiting for me to finish, he turned to Deputy Pierce. "Did you say you'd found his clothes?"

"Yes, sir, on a rock over there . . ." The deputy pointed to a big boulder in the grass on the other side of the pond. "Looks to me like Mister Codman mighta been skinny-dipping and drowned. Maybe he was drunk? Or he hit his head on something?"

"Thank you, Deputy Pierce. I've seen Mister Codman and have my own idea about what happened," said Buck. "I want to get the doc's report before we jump to conclusions. You can go, Deputy. I'll catch up in a few minutes. I want to take another look at the body."

"Okay, sir." The deputy closed his little notebook and ambled over to speak with an EMT.

Buck pulled his aviators on top of his head and stared at me, hard, hands on his hips. His chocolaty eyes simmered. There was an awkward silence. I crossed my arms and looked away, staring across the pond. Then Buck sighed and dropped his arms. Leaning in, he touched me on my elbow, speaking softly.

"So, do you mind telling me why your former fiancé decided to show up here, to little backwater Abundance, Georgia, all the way from Boston to go for a skinny-dip in your daddy's farm pond right behind your cottage? Did he follow you here? Were you together down here at the pond last night?"

I was pretty sure no one else around us could hear him.

"No!" I cried, a little too loudly.

Buck's eyes darted around. Still, no one seemed to notice my outburst. I lowered my voice.

"Look, I have no idea why he came here. Like I said, when I first saw Dex, I'd been told that he'd come for a bird-watching vacation and that it'd been a coincidence that he'd turned up at our place. Apparently, he and his friends first arrived in town late Wednesday night and were staying somewhere else—a bed-and-breakfast, in town. Then yesterday while they were out on some sort of nature jaunt, they passed our place and stopped in to check out the plantation and ask about putting together an olive oil tasting party.

"According to Daphne, they said that they hated the B&B where they were staying. And as it turned out, this was the only open week we have until after the New Year. As you can imagine, Daphne was all too eager to accommodate them. Heck, she probably did somersaults in front of them to get them to stay here. And whatever she did, it worked. She assigned them rooms; they settled in immediately. They never even went back to the other place to get their stuff; the B&B owner had to make two trips to get all their things over here.

Until the moment when I stepped into the dining room to serve dinner last night, I had no idea that the people I'd be serving were the same people I'd known once upon a time in Boston. Daphne had no idea, either. She still doesn't."

I decided not to muddy the waters, so to speak, by mentioning the fact that Dex had requested my old room. No need to rub Buck's nose in the fact that the man I'd jilted him for had come to town and slept in my childhood bed. Besides, it was creepy. I was still hopeful that by not acknowledging certain facts pertaining to Dex, all my troubles would somehow wash away . . .

Fat chance.

"Then after dinner," I continued, "they had this party with the local bird people. Even though it was last-minute, Daphne *insisted* that I host the olive oil tasting for them . . . like the one I did a few weeks ago for your mother and the ladies club. *And you know Daphne.*" I rolled my eyes. "There were no ifs, ands, or buts about it. So I did the tasting party. And that's it. That's all I know. Before yesterday, I hadn't seen Dex Codman in years."

Buck raised his eyebrows. He didn't look convinced.

At all.

"Eva, this pond is a stone's throw from your cottage. And you *never* sleep. Are you asking me to believe that you had no idea that this man, *your former fiancé,* was down here last night? And that you weren't here with him?"

"No. I mean, yes!"

"A man whom you were once engaged to? A man who came here—from more than a *thousand* miles away—was down here, at the pond, right behind your cottage, naked, and you had no idea he was out here?"

"Exactly."

"You actually went to bed shortly after nine o'clock and didn't hear or see *anything* unusual?"

"Nope. I slept like a baby."

Buck looked at me sideways.

"You're honestly telling me that you had nothing to do with his being here . . . that he just *happened* to stumble upon

Knox Plantation, the very place where his ex-fiancée grew up?"

"It's true!" I cried. "I had no idea Dex was in town! *Why* do you keep insinuating that I had something to do with whatever happened here?"

"Am I insinuating something?"

"Yes!"

"So, we're to believe that you had no other dealings with him last night except to *serve* him?"

"Yes. Believe me, Dex Codman is the *last* person I'd ever want to see again. Let alone someone I'd be skinny-dipping with!" I actually managed to laugh. "And it took all the professionalism I could muster to *serve* him, as you say. From the ill-mannered way he and his cronies behaved last night, he hadn't changed *one bit* from the way I remember him."

Buck's eyes snapped. He held up his hand. I knew I'd said too much. I bit my lip.

"Don't say another word, Eva. Right now, this looks like no more than an unfortunate accident. Still, I'd like it if you don't go anywhere today. I'm sure I'll have more questions for you." Buck stepped off the pier. Then he turned back. "I always do."

Striding briskly across the grassland, Buck headed toward his deputies on the other side of the pond. I watched as Dolly skittered down the hill from the cottage and trotted after him.

She always did.

CHAPTER 3

Standing together at the top of the hill, enjoying their cold drinks—evidently our "hostess with the mostess" Daphne had provided her guests with sweet iced teas, although under the circumstances, a round of bourbons, neat, might've been more appropriate—Dex's cohorts from Boston were hardly a picture of grieving friends who'd just lost their steadfast companion of twenty years. In fact, if it hadn't been for the flashing lights, emergency vehicles, and grim-faced rescue people dashing around the yard, looking at the four of them you'd be hard-pressed not to think that Claudia, Wiggy, Coop, and Spencer were merely looking for a spot to pull up some lawn chairs for an afternoon of socializing. Or bird-watching.

But, then, wasn't that the idea?

Still, when a juvenile bald eagle—the holy grail of North American birds—let out its distinctive high-pitched, piping cries from a tall pine tree down by the pond, none of the Boston crowd even blinked. In fact, they didn't even look up when the bird sailed overhead, with its characteristic, squeaky cries.

No doubt about it, I thought. *Our Boston birders are a sham.*

I'd been right all along to suspect them of being up to something. Still, what was it?

Overlooking the dismal scene as Dex's covered body was loaded up and onto a stretcher while a deputy bagged Dex's pants, the Bostoners tittered to one another, as if they were standing at a cocktail party. Or at a gallery opening. Not at all how you'd expect them to react, watching their dear friend get hauled off to the coroner's freezer.

As I hiked to the top of the hill from the pond, I heard Coop, the paper company's corporate lawyer, laugh. Then he said, "Spencer, looks like you've just kissed good-bye the fifty grand that you loaned Dex."

Tall, with dark hair and tanned skin, the boyishly hand-some Coop laughed again as he ran his fingers through his bangs, brushing them from his forehead.

"Looks like he screwed more than just one of us."

Spencer, a small, weedy man with bad skin, greasy black hair, round black glasses, and a red bow tie (of all things), said in his high-pitched voice, "Yeah, looks like it. Still, you know what? I don't even care, 'cause payout from his share will more than compensate my loss."

What?

"*Que sera, sera*," chuckled Wiggy, the burly, brown-haired, bearded acquisitions asset and operations manager—a fancy title that meant he was the guy who took charge of a property, just after it'd been purchased by Perennial Paper. He was dressed in a brown safari shirt and shorts. *Most likely new purchases from L.L.Bean*, I thought. I chortled. He looked like Smokey Bear.

"Do you know what happened to Dex?" I asked the group. "Did you all have a party down at the pond last night?"

No one answered. Wiggy smirked. Then he handed his iced tea to Dex's right-hand gal Claudia, the only woman in the group, before tucking a paper map under one arm. He reached into his pocket for a lighter and his meerschaum pipe.

While I waited for someone to say something, I saw that the map under Wiggy's arm was an Abundance County tax map . . . not exactly the kind of map you'd expect a group of "bird-watchers" to be poring over.

Wiggy puffed quickly on his pipe before answering with a sneer, "Why, Eva, aren't you a sight for sore eyes in your little baby blue bathing suit." He slid the lighter into his pants pocket. "Shows off your titties real nice."

Trying not to let my expression show my utter mortification, I crossed my arms over my chest as he puffed a couple more times. *Typical Wiggy*, I thought. *Crass to the max.* The pipe smoke billowed up in my face. It smelled like cherries.

I remembered the time when Dex had given Wiggy the pipe, a collectible antique, not long after Dex had returned from a business trip to Turkey. Dex'd given Coop and Spencer each a leather vest, and Claudia had gotten a small, hand-woven Turkish wool rug. Meanwhile, I'd received a macramé key chain with an evil eye charm on it, along with some soap and shampoo that Dex'd stolen from his hotel.

I should've known then . . .

"I'm so sorry to shock you, Wiggy," I said, waving the smoke away with my hand. "When I set off for my relaxing afternoon at the pond an hour or two ago, I hardly expected to see anyone, let alone Dex floating dead in the water, followed by the entire Abundance County rescue squad here in the yard. Not to mention the likes of *you*," I said sarcastically. "I'll dress more appropriately next time."

I'd let Wiggy's pompous attitude get to me. I shouldn't have.

He laughed. "Well, well, well! Looks like our little Southern belle has found her big-girl voice. Of course, you certainly had your say last night . . ."

He puffed contentedly on his pipe.

"Forgive me," I said. "It's been a stressful day. I don't mean to sound sharp." I made no apology for the previous night.

I turned to go.

"Can't go anywhere without making a scene, can you, Eva?" Wiggy shot back. "Although, I must say, I meant to tell you last night—before you left the party so *abruptly*—that you're much more womanly and interesting to look at than you were when you were Dex's little puppet all those years ago. Now that Dex is outta the way, if you want to get a taste of what it's like to be with a *real man*, stop by my room later."

Claudia stifled a gasp.

I turned back to roll my eyes at him. He leered.

Wiggy hadn't changed a bit in the one and a half decades since I'd last seen him. Always trying to get a rise out of people. Catch them off guard. Make them feel uncomfortable. I'd decided long ago that he played his mental games to buoy his own low self-esteem.

So much for my apology.

I turned to Coop, the boyishly handsome lawyer.

"I thought you all had an appointment to go on a nature walk this morning. Didn't anyone *miss* Dex when he didn't show up for the walk? Was he at breakfast?"

"To tell you the truth," said Coop with a wicked smile—his baby blue eyes twinkled—"we figured that ol' Dexter was with you this morning." He looked at Wiggy and winked. "Especially after all that *sexual tension* between the two of you during the party last night. We assumed you two must have been snoozing in after some sort of *explosive* encounter down at the pond, working out your years of pent-up frustrations." The men chortled.

Claudia made some sort of grunting noise.

That was tactless, I thought. Especially for Coop. Somehow, he'd become more jaded in the years since I'd known him. More like Wiggy. Like Wiggy, Coop was dressed in a safari shirt and matching shorts. Except the brown was closer to tan and the styling was a bit better. I wanted to tell him that he reminded me of a faded UPS driver.

I held my tongue.

Coop had always had a cheeky way about him. Born with the proverbial silver spoon in his mouth, like Dex and the others, he was a Dartmouth College grad. And the Boston Brahmin had been the consummate playboy when I'd first met him at my Mount Holyoke College friend Bibi's fancy wedding in New York. That was the same wedding where I'd first met Dex. Then later, shortly after I'd left Abundance and arrived in Boston, New England socialites were shocked when bad-boy Coop married a working-class girl named Heather, from Boston's Dorchester neighborhood. They moved into a refurbished row house in Boston's prestigious Back Bay. An attractive art gallery manager, Heather was a smart, funny redhead who'd worked hard to get where she was in society. She'd gone to Wellesley College on a full scholarship, and in her own words, marrying a rich Brahmin like Coop had been quite a coup for someone with her working-class background. Some of the cattier women I'd known had even accused Heather of being a gold digger.

Anyway, Dex had always wanted us to spend "couples" time with Coop and Heather. They were Boston's ultimate young, up-and-coming power couple, he'd said. He'd talked about them incessantly—*Coop and Heather did this; Coop and Heather did that . . . Coop and Heather bought this; Coop and Heather bought that . . . Let's get a car, like Coop and Heather; let's get a town house, like Coop and Heather; why can't you be more like Heather . . .*

"You're ridiculous, Coop."

I turned to look at the third man on the hill, Spencer.

Standing next to Wiggy was his sidekick, geeky numbers guy Spencer. With his iced tea on the ground next to him, the little greasy man seemed to be playing some game on his smartphone, which he held up in front of his face as his thumbs bounced over the screen.

He must have sensed that I was looking at him.

Spencer pulled the phone away from his face and winked, pointing a little finger at me. Then he fingered his glasses up his nose while he made a *click-clicking* sound with his tongue and cheek.

Like he was übercool.

Only he wasn't even close.

"We knew better than to disturb the mighty Captain Ahab while he was busy spearing his mighty whale last night," he chirped, elbowing Coop good-naturedly.

I shook my head as he pointed a finger toward me.

"That'd be *you*, you little hotheaded hussy."

He winked. Then he held the phone back up to his face and began playing the game again.

The guy had *never* had any social skills. Whenever he opened his mouth, no doubt trying to be like Wiggy—it baffled me why *anyone* would want to emulate Wiggy—it always went wrong. He said the stupidest things. I couldn't even take his intended insults seriously.

I laughed.

Standing off to the side holding two iced teas, Claudia gave Spencer a dirty look as the men chortled again.

"You guys are gross," I said, turning to Claudia. "I don't know how you can stand them, Claudia. If you had three hands you'd be holding three iced teas. And none of them would be yours."

Claudia's pinched expression matched her gaunt features. The straw-haired blonde with high cheekbones had once been a lovely beauty . . . Dex used to brag that he had the most attractive assistant in the entire company working at his side. However, standing on the hill, the Smith College grad appeared so thin and worn that she was a mere shadow of the luscious, elegant woman she'd once been. And the impression was made worse by the fact that her new outfit—a one-piece safari-style, short jumpsuit that was more like a romper, really—hung over her like it was three sizes too big. Of course, it probably was. I doubted they made many safari jumpsuits in size zero. She opened her mouth to say something, but Wiggy interrupted.

"Don't get mad at us, Miss High and Mighty," said Wiggy. "When Dex didn't come to breakfast, it was natural to figure that he'd overslept, after 'making up' all night long with his dear, devoted, long-lost fiancée." Wiggy laughed. "Are you telling us that you and Dex didn't [*he used a profane word*] last night?"

"Don't be such a pig," Claudia hissed. "Even if they did it, you don't have to shout it out to the world that way. It's disrespectful to *Dex*." She glared at me. "Get out of my way, you slut," she seethed. The iced teas sloshed wildly as she marched up the hill.

I held Wiggy's eyes as I yanked up my baby blue swimsuit by the straps and stuck out my chest.

"I assure you, *boys*, that I was not with Dex last night. In fact, he'd be the *last* man on earth I'd *ever* be with. Except for the three of you, of course."

Wiggy threw his head back and laughed again. I pointed to the binoculars hanging around his neck.

"Nice prop. Wiggy, you're the same egocentric, pompous ass you always were," I said.

Wiggy raised an eyebrow, then he laughed some more.

I spun to face the other two men. "Spencer, congratulations, you're as obtuse and out of the loop as ever. And Coop, I don't know what happened to you. Heather must be completely fed up with you by now."

Coop made a croaking sound and he had an odd, surprised look on his face, like someone had just smacked him. Wiggy and Spencer burst out laughing.

Finishing the laundry will be a pleasure, I thought, marching off toward the big house.

"Don't sweat it, guys." I heard Wiggy whisper loudly from behind me. "Dex didn't tell her, so she doesn't have a clue. It'll just end up being more for each of us."

CHAPTER 4

I never managed to have a decent working relationship with *any* copy machine. Regardless what size, what brand, or what specific type of machine, it always managed to break down mid-job. So, of course, that's exactly what happened when I was using the copy machine in the library at the big house.

It jammed.

Larger than most home-use machines, this one sat in the corner of the library, against the floor-to-ceiling bookshelves next to a great big oak desk that had been Granddaddy's. The gray, industrial-looking machine was in stark contrast to the tattered books and worn, traditional furnishings in the room. Daphne'd gotten a deal on the copy machine after it'd been reconditioned following years of use in the local school. She'd purchased the bigger-than-needed machine because she wanted a "reliable workhorse" for our own business use, but also so that visiting guests could use it, as well as the computer on Granddaddy's desk. That's why the machines were in the library, which was off the main parlor room, always open to guests.

I looked down at the copier. Sitting on four wheels, it was nearly as tall as my chest. It featured two drawers, low down in front, to store stacks of paper. And up top, it had a sorter. You could either feed the paper via the tray at the top of the sorter, or open the sorter and place your original on the glass platform. I shook my head as the obnoxious red ERROR light on the front panel flashed on and off . . . on and off . . . on and off . . .

Of course, I followed all the instructions—opening this door, then that door. Checking this paper feed, then that paper feed. Taking out the stacked paper. Fluffing the stacked paper. Searching for the problem so that I could rectify it.

And as always, it was all for naught.

The machine hated me. There was no paper jam. There was no part in need of replacement. The ink was fine. The toner was fine. Nothing appeared broken.

Not yet, anyway, I thought.

No matter what I did, the blasted blinking light on the machine wouldn't shut off. And the machine wouldn't copy.

A little bell tinkled from the kitchen.

"Eva," Daphne's voice trilled, "are y'all nearly done? I'm in *dire* need of those copies, please."

I knew quite well that Daphne wasn't in any sort of "dire need." The copies were to be of her handwritten calligraphy menu for the evening's "special" dinner. When they showed up for work—*if* they showed up for work, that is—the twins, Darlene and Charlene, would place one copy of the menu, along with a purple-beribboned olive sprig, at each guest's place at the meticulously set antique dining table in the formal dining room.

Daphne'd announced that she wanted dinner to be extra-special that night, "an exemplary experience," to make up for Dex being found floating dead in our farm pond. Of course, I'd said, if she'd *really* wanted to host an "exemplary" experience, Daphne should've handwritten a separate menu for each guest, rather than having me make copies. Daphne'd retorted that she didn't have time to write individual menus because a dead man had turned up in the pond, completely ruining her precisely planned schedule for the day.

Fine.

Of course, Daphne's notion that a dining experience of any

kind, let alone an "exemplary" one, could somehow wipe away the shock and grief of a dead friend seemed completely harebrained to me. However, it wouldn't be the first time that I thought a notion of Daphne's was ridiculous. Nor would it be the last. And it really didn't matter, I reasoned. Dex's longtime coworkers and friends hadn't seemed to miss him much, anyway.

And what was that Wiggy had said . . . about "more for each" of them?

There was definitely something fishy going on.

Meanwhile, the hubbub outside at the pond had mostly subsided—I'd slipped into my cottage and changed into a tee and cutoffs before returning to the big house, where I'd basically hidden out in the laundry room so I didn't have to see or hear what was going on from my cottage overlooking the pond. Or run into the Boston crowd. Finally, Daphne'd announced that the Bostoners had gone to the Palatable Pecan in the village for a late lunch. And that's when she'd handed me the menu to copy.

"Eva? Do y'all hear me?" called Daphne from the kitchen.

"Be right there," I called back from the library.

Shoot.

I kicked the stubborn copier.

That's when the behemoth machine rolled just a couple of inches back toward the bookshelves. And I discovered a paper on the wooden floor, peeking out from under the machine.

I reached down and picked up the paper.

What's this?

It looked like a legal document of some sort. PERIENNIAL PAPER LLC was printed at the top.

Suddenly, I heard footsteps behind me, and before I could turn, someone bumped me from behind, snatching the paper out of my hands.

"You!" screeched Claudia Devereaux. "How did you get this?" She studied the paper in her hand.

"It was—"

"This document is *proprietary*!"

Claudia waved the paper in the air, shaking it with her

bony fist. Her watery blue eyes bugged out from their sockets. Without mascara, her pale eyelashes were barely visible, and she looked like an angry flounder.

"You have no business with this! What are you doing?"

"I—"

"Are there *more* papers here?"

She didn't wait for me to answer. Like a mad person, Claudia started clawing at the machine, opening and slamming all the drawers and doors.

"Claudia, I assure you, I was just trying to make some copies when I found a page on the floor—"

"Shut up. Do you hear me? Just *shut up*."

She jerked the machine away from the wall and checked the floor.

"Really, Claudia, I'm sure you're upset about Dex. Especially since you've been with him all these years at the paper company. I understand—really, I do. It must be quite a shock. I'm so sorry. Everyone is sad and upset. Still, there's no need for—"

"What do *you* know about it?" she snapped. "You didn't give a rat's ass about Dex. I know all about it. You *never* did care about him. And you humiliated him in front of *everyone* last night! I *know*. You didn't just run away from Dex all those years ago. You *hated* Dex!"

She was positively seething. Then she shoved her face right up to mine.

"And I know why!"

I opened my mouth to respond, but she'd already turned, and her scrawny legs were fast-walking out of the room. Flapping from one fist, the paper Claudia'd snatched from me was a wrinkled mess.

She slammed the library door behind her. I was amazed it even latched. It'd probably been a hundred years since the last time anyone had shut that door.

The good news was she'd somehow managed to reset the copy machine. The ERROR light was off.

CHAPTER 5

"Here are your copies, Daph," I said, handing the menu papers to Daphne in the kitchen.

Daphne was seated in one of the Larkin chairs at the round oak family table. A steaming teapot and an empty teacup and saucer with tiny pink flowers patterned on them rested on the table in front of her. Daphne lifted the teapot and poured the amber liquid into her teacup before she grasped the cup by its delicate handle. With her manicured pinkie pretentiously extended, she raised the antique vessel to her lips. Then she stopped.

"Silly me. I forgot to ask. Would y'all like some tea, Eva?"

"No, thanks."

"Are you sure? I've made some olive leaf tea. It's full of antioxidants."

"I'm sure."

I pulled out a chair and sat down at the table.

"Daph, I thought you said that all the guests had gone out for lunch."

Daphne sipped her tea before answering.

"Mmm, this is yummy," she said to herself. Then she

looked up at me and smiled. "Yes. I did. I saw their rental car pull out a while ago."

"If you were counting heads, you missed at least one person. Claudia is still here."

"Oh dear! Do you think Miss Devereaux would like some lunch? Precious isn't here right at the moment. Still, I should go upstairs and check."

Daphne's delicate teacup *tinked* as she set it on the saucer.

"I wouldn't bother, Daph. I didn't get the impression that Claudia is hungry," I said. "Not at all, actually."

"Hmm. Alright, then. Perhaps she needs some alone time. I hear she was the poor dead man's assistant. She must be in shock."

"Must be."

"Perhaps I'll send up a fresh steaming pot of olive leaf tea for her . . ."

"Really, don't bother. She's not the tea type."

"A good, strong cup of olive leaf tea with some milk and honey might relax her . . . Don't y'all know it, a shock like that can *really* kick the stuffing out of a person."

I rolled my eyes.

"So I've heard."

Claudia's screeching was still ringing in my head. Shock or not, something about the whole library episode wasn't right . . . Still, I couldn't put my finger on it.

Daphne took another dainty sip of her tea, pausing for a moment as she considered the taste in her mouth. Then she set the teacup down on the saucer again.

"Eva, I need you to go to town for me this afternoon. With all that's happened, finding that *poor Mister Codman* in the pond and all"—Daphne shuddered—"I wasn't able to take care of a few errands that I'd planned for today. And now, now that everyone has *finally* left, I've *got* to prepare for this evening. Besides, it'll be good for you to get off the plantation for a while. Clear your head. You must be in shock yourself . . . finding *another* dead person, like that."

I nodded.

So much for my afternoon off.

"I've called Precious. She's comin' over from Greatwoods. She's got some errands in town, and she'll be here any minute now. Y'all can go to town together."

I'd wrecked my own car earlier that summer. And because I'd forgotten to pay my auto insurance, I'd not been able to replace my totaled car. So when I wanted or needed to go anywhere, I was forced to beg, borrow, or steal vehicles from family and friends. Unless Daphne arranged a ride for me.

Eye roll.

"And where, exactly, will I be going?"

"I need you to drop off some olive leaves and bark to Joy Birdsong at the Birdsong Botanicals shop on Main Street. It's all packaged up, waiting for you on the wicker table out on the back porch."

"I'm curious: Why am I delivering tree bark and leaves to Joy Birdsong?"

"Joy's agreed to sell our dried olive leaves in the shop, as well as our new olive leaf tea, once I get the pricing and packaging figured out, of course. But also, she suggested we come up with some olive leaf and herb tea *blends*. You know, like a blend of olive leaf and chamomile, for relaxing and bedtime. She's going to try some different combinations for me and then suggest a recipe or two."

"I see . . ."

"She's just a whiz about ethnobotanicals and all the like. She's even earned a master's degree in ethnobotany—did y'all know that?" Daphne picked up her cup and inhaled the steam coming from the tea inside the cup. "Although, I suspect most of her knowledge about such matters comes from her family."

She took another sip.

"Her family?"

"They're all Cherokee."

I shook my head. "Gosh, Daphne, good to know you don't stereotype people."

"Why, of course I don't."

I shook my head again.

"Okay. Olive leaves to Joy Birdsong, got it. Where else am I going?"

"I've made up a pretty basket with our best olive oils, plus some handmade olive oil soaps and bath oils. Please bring it to Pottie Moss Diggs at the Naturist B&B in town. Do you know where that is?"

"I think I can find it."

"Good. She won't be expecting you."

"And why am I going to surprise Pottie Moss with a basket of our best olive oil products?"

"Her establishment is where our guests were staying before they decided to jump ship and stay with us yesterday. Although I was delighted to take our new guests' money and fill our place up for the week—of course, I'd no idea that one of them would up and *die* in our farm pond—I don't relish that I poached these guests from another local business. So, I'm sending you over with a peace offering . . . the basket. Hopefully, Pottie Moss will forgive me for stealing her guests. And Eva, Miss Devereaux said that accommodations over there were positively *appalling*. I'd love to know what you see."

"Okay. Got it. Deliver olive leaves to Joy. Then, deliver guilt basket while spying on Pottie Moss's operation. Anything else you want me to do?"

"Yes! I almost forgot. There's a big box of used corks that need to go to the hardware store. Although they always collect corks and send them off to be recycled, they've been having a special cork recycling contest this week, and I promised Merle Tritt that I'd bring the corks to his store before the contest ends this weekend. So, it's *got* to be done by close of business today! I promised him. You can pick up the box of corks at the warehouse before y'all go to town."

"Got it. Olive leaves. Guilt basket. Corks."

"That should be it. Oh, and Eva, please don't forget that you agreed to help the Abundance Garden Club members during our annual village *refresher* tomorrow afternoon. It'll just take a couple of hours. I signed you up to do brush pile cleanup. It'll be fun!"

"Gee, thanks. Whenever I think of fun, I always think of cleaning up piles of brush."

"Please don't be sarcastic, Eva, dear. It's all for a good

cause. Daddy's leant us a tall ladder, and we've even managed to borrow a couple of chain saws from folks, to remove some of those dead and low limbs on the trees in the boulevard median. They're *such* an eyesore! The limbs, not the chain saws." Daphne giggled. "And I daresay, those big tree limbs are a potential danger. Remember after that dreadful storm a few weeks ago? When that giant limb fell onto Louisiana Heenehan's Mercedes while she was gettin' a perm in the beauty parlor?"

I started to say, that's what Louisiana gets for patronizing Tammy Fae Tanner's beauty salon. Still, I held my tongue. After all, Shear Southern Beauty was the only beauty parlor in town. Tammy Fae never forgave me for leaving her only son, Buck, at the altar, and since my return home that summer, she'd done her darnedest to besmirch my name in the community. Of course, operating the only salon in town, she had the ear of nearly every woman in Abundance, and a bunch of men as well. I heard that just since my return home that summer, she'd dredged up and disseminated every scandalous thing she could about me, and then some. What gossip she couldn't turn up, she'd made up.

"Why, poor Louisiana Heenehan is *still* fighting with her insurance company!"

"She can afford the repairs, I'm sure," I said.

Longtime local farmer Louisiana Heenehan was making a fortune in her new role as the self-published author of a scandalous book series of erotica, written under the pen name Kitty Kipple.

"Don't be cruel, Eva. That lovely Mercedes convertible was Louisiana's pride and joy. Before that, all she and her husband owned were farm trucks and used Chevies. We should all be happy for her success. Although, I'm sorry I didn't think of the idea to write steamy sex stories based on folktales and nursery rhymes myself . . ."

"Omigosh."

"They're quite titillating, actually. Perhaps you should read one? Especially while you're without a squeeze . . . I have a copy in my room."

"No! Please. Anything but that."

"Oh, Eva, *dahhwr-lin*, y'all are such a stick-in-the-mud. Why you'll *nevahh* get married if you keep carryin' on this way."

"Stop. Please. Respect my man moratorium."

"Oh, *fiddle-dee-dee*. Are we still talking about that nonsense?"

"Yes. Only it isn't nonsense. I have come to fully understand and appreciate the fact that when it comes to men, I am positively clueless and inept. Therefore, I am respectfully abstaining from any relations with the opposite sex. At least until I figure men out."

"Eva, women have been tryin' to understand men since the beginning of time. Y'all need to quit procrastinatin' and find yourself a nice, eligible, *trainable* bachelor. One with looks, good genetics, and enough charm to keep you swept of your feet. *Literally*. And lots of money, of course."

Daphne let out a snigger . . . Clearly, she'd amused herself. I shook my head and rolled my eyes.

"Please, Daph, enough. It's not the day for it."

Daphne prattled on. "Also, on Monday, don't forget that you're skipping our usual jujitsu class . . ."

That would be the weekly class that Daphne *insisted* that I attend with her. I'd actually enjoyed learning jujitsu, although I'd never let Daphne know.

"Instead of jujitsu class, you're going to help the twins set up a special picnic dinner on Alligator Island for our guests during their swamp tour with Skeets Diggs—that's Pottie Moss Diggs's brother. She'll probably be helping him on the trip as well. I hear she does that. And that's *another* reason I want to send Pottie Moss the basket today. We can't afford to have her deep-six the picnic because I stole her guests. Anyway, Precious will have everything for the picnic prepared, packed, and ready to go. All you have to do is accompany the Boston folks on their swamp tour. Then once you get to Alligator Island, you're to set up the picnic and serve the food and beverages. The twins will help you. It should be *easy peasy*. I'm told that there's a picnic site with tables and barbecue grills permanently installed there."

"Really? On Alligator Island? That's new."

Alligator Island was a decrepit little island located right in the middle of the Big Swamp. Growing up, the uninhabited island had been a "secret" scary hangout for kids, a favorite haunt for hunters, and a popular hideout for lawbreakers. Now, apparently, like most everything else in the county, it'd been transformed into a tourist destination.

"Yes, well, a lot has changed since you ran off eighteen years ago."

I'll say.

"It's not like *you* were here the entire time, either, Daph! Have you completely forgotten about moving to Atlanta, getting married, taking exotic vacations, having five kids, getting divorced . . ."

Daphne ignored me.

"So, back to our guests. On Monday, they've requested alcohol for the swamp trip, and since the twins are *just* of age, and quite immature if you haven't noticed—"

"I've noticed!" I grimaced. "Believe me, I've noticed."

"Well, at any rate, I don't want the twins pouring liquor. I don't think they know much about alcoholic drinks. I want *you* to manage the situation. And if the picnic somehow goes to hell in a handbasket, by all means, start pouring drinks. The more the better. I want our guests to be happy, happy, happy. Which reminds me, Skeets agreed to take our guests on a very *special*, *custom* swamp tour. Y'all will be leaving from the old Taylor Farm, taking Snake River, which runs behind the Taylor property to the Big Swamp, instead of Skeets's usual jump-off point at the Big Swamp dock over by the chemical plant."

"Taylor Farm? Oh gosh, I remember that place! I haven't been there in years, of course. Buck used to take me to the farm pier on Snake River to watch his friends shoot off fireworks from Alligator Island. It was all so romantic . . ."

Daphne's eyebrows pinched together. She puckered her mouth, like she'd eaten something foul.

"I'm sure that whatever Buck Tanner and his hooligan friends were up to was all *quite* illegal."

"Now, now, Daph," I chided. "You used to like Buck yourself, remember . . ."

Daphne threw her hands up in protestation.

"*If*, at any time in my life, I had *any* proclivities toward Buck Tanner, it was only because I was young and foolish."

"And horny!" called out my middle sister, Pep, as she trotted into the kitchen. The porch door slammed behind her. She broke out into peals of piglet snorts and giggles.

CHAPTER 6

"Heavenly day, Pepper-Leigh!" Daphne let out a big sigh. "You positively *shock* me with your vulgar language. What a terrible thing to say. Besides, it's not at all true. And, what on *earth* are y'all wearing today? *Good gravy!*"

Grinning, Pep ran her hand through her spiky, short-cropped platinum hair. At five feet two inches, with flawless porcelain skin, a pert little nose, and seductive gray eyes rimmed with some thick, smoky liner, Pep was a bit shorter and distinctly curvier than either Daphne or I. She wore a black tee shirt with ripped-off sleeves that read ROADHOUSE CREW in metallic sequins across her chest. A bronzy, skull-shaped earring dangled from one of her ears, and the leather-spiked collar around Pep's neck matched her spiked black leather wristband. She wore a leather miniskirt, black leggings, and combat boots. Her lips and short nails were painted purple.

"Ha! Terrible thing to say?" Pep asked. "Maybe. But y'all *both* know it's true." She laughed, stepping into the big-house kitchen. "Daph, you've always had the hots for Buck Tanner. You might as well give up denying it."

I stood from my chair at the table as Pep reached around my shoulders and gave me a hug and a peck on the cheek. Her jammy perfume smelled like velvety old-garden roses, with a dash of musk, pepper, and spice.

Decadent.

"Hi, Eva, hon. I didn't mean to ignore you. In fact, you're the reason I stopped by," said Pep. She reached up and adjusted her spiked leather choker.

Daphne remained seated, sipping on her olive leaf tea.

"What the heck happened here today?" asked Pep. "Eva, I heard you found a floater in the farm pond! Gosh, that's terrible. That makes four guys who've kicked the bucket here, just this summer! And you've found every single one. Imagine that. Must be some kinda record or somethin', don't ya think? Anyway, how are ya feelin', sweetie? Are ya alright?"

"Yes. I'm fine."

"Good. I'm glad to hear it. So what happened?"

"We don't know, really. It just looks like he drowned last night . . . sometime after the olive oil tasting party up here."

"And the stiff was one of the new guests? Part of the group that arrived yesterday, right?"

"Right. Daphne *stole* them from Pottie Moss Diggs."

"Stole them? Good goin', Daph. Way to smoke the competition." Pep made a face and blew a kiss to Daphne. Then Pep gave me another squeeze before she turned back to Daphne.

"So why were y'all talking about Buck Tanner when I came in?"

"We weren't," huffed Daphne.

"Oh yes, you were!" Pep laughed, then she winked at me. "Daph, why don't you just climb down off your high horse, *for once*, and admit that you had an itch to be with Buck Tanner so bad after Eva ran off that you could barely stand it, just like every other woman in this town. Y'all know I'm right. Remember, Daph? You . . . Buck . . . the two bottles of champagne? Do we *really* need to go there again?"

"I hope not," I said.

Daphne pursed her lips.

"I didn't think so."

"Oh *puh-leeze*, both of you," said Daphne, setting her teacup down. "Even if I were to think that Buck Tanner has *any* redeeming qualities aside from looking buff and solving crime, he certainly shot *that* silly notion all to pieces when he started dating Debi Dicer."

Pep let out a big snort. "Speaking of which, a bunch of the guys down at the Roadhouse were talking about *Debi's* 'redeeming qualities' last night at the bar. I think the deputies are all jealous of Sheriff Buck."

"Oh, Pepper-Leigh." Daphne made a big, exaggerated sigh. "I swear, working at that tawdry bar has absolutely ruined you . . ."

"I heard one deputy report that he heard Debi has mastered *all sorts* of 'skills.'"

Pep tittered.

"Skills?" I asked.

"You know, Eva. *Skills!*" Pep raised her fingers to make air quotes for the word "skills" when she said it. "Get it? The kind that aren't discussed in *polite* company."

"Pepper-Leigh!" Daphne shook her head.

"Really?" I asked.

I couldn't help myself. Debi Dicer treated me so badly every time she saw me—I swear, she'd even tried to kill me once by mowing me down with her Cadillac Escalade—I admit, I was eager to hear anything and everything scandalous about the woman. After all, it was only fair play . . .

"Tell me," I said to Pep. "Like what sorts of *skills*?"

I gave Pep an evil grin.

"Just about anything you can imagine. Dillard Coleman—y'all know him, he's the pig farmer livin' next to Putt Nutz Mini Golf—he said Debi knows how to please a man 'a million different ways' in the bedroom."

Pep snorted.

Daphne let out a disgusted gasp.

"Well, Debi *is* awfully good in jujitsu class . . ." I said with a giggle.

"Exactly." Pep grinned. "I bet she can twist herself into a pretzel if she wants to . . ."

"Pepper-Leigh," Daphne interrupted, "bein' a pretzel hardly has anything to do with jujitsu and y'all know it."

"And, Pep, Daphne knows *all* about it," I said, laughing, "because she reads Kitty Kipple books!"

"No kidding!" cried Pep. "I hear the Humpty Dumpty one is a hoot. Really *egg-cellent*!"

"Please, Pep, don't *crack me up*!" I said with a silly smile.

Pep and I broke out into peals of laughter. Daphne blushed. Then she cleared her throat.

"My point is, you two, any man who is interested in that sort of woman—a woman with *talents*, like Debi Dicer—is no more marriage material than she is. And Eva, forgive me, but you need to be hitchin' yourself to some man's wagon, real soon. Forty will be here before y'all know it, and you'll be an old maid! I simply can't have a sister who is an old maid. It's . . . depressing. Certainly, if we cleaned you up a bit, did something with your hair—"

"Why are you always picking on me about my hair?"

"It's just that you don't *do* anything with it. Like I've said before, you need to stop pulling it back in that silly, girlish ponytail. Instead, spend some time and *style* it once in a while. Wear some makeup. Go and get yourself a mani-pedi . . . a makeover!"

"Well, given that Tammy Fae's is the only salon in town, *that's* not gonna happen."

Pep snorted. "That's for sure. Plus, be real, Daph. Even if there *was* another salon in town, Eva still wouldn't go . . ."

I grinned.

"Eva, I'm serious. And I'm lookin' out for your best interest. We need to find you a man, right quick. No woman worth her salt is still single in her late thirties, livin' in a one-room cottage behind her family's big house. And you can do a lot better than the likes of Buck Tanner."

"Did I say I was interested in Buck Tanner?"

"You didn't have to," sniggered Pep.

"Oh, come on!" I cried.

Daphne shook her head. "Eva, I realize that with all this dead-body business, you *are* required to have some conversations with the man. After all, he *is* the county sheriff. And you *do* seem to have an innate talent when it comes to attracting . . . *dead* men. And, I recognize that Buck Tanner *has* helped us out of a few jams regarding all the bodies y'all have kept turning up this summer."

"That's for sure," said Pep. "Although, Daph, I'm disappointed not to have seen how you'd have managed wearin' an orange prison jumpsuit, if Detective Gibbit had gotten *his* way. You owe Buck for savin' you. After all, orange isn't your color." Pep snorted a bunch of giggles.

"That's for sure," I said.

Pep and I high-fived each other.

Daphne pursed her lips, slipping us a sideways glance.

"Well, I'll grant you, dealin' with Buck Tanner is better than dealin' with Detective Eli Gibbit. Goodness knows, given the chance, ol' Eli would throw *all* of us in jail, just for the sport of it."

"That's all we need . . ." I said, sighing.

"And whose fault is that? Daph, maybe y'all shouldn't have teased and made fun of Eli back in grade school," Pep said.

"What sort of a person holds a grudge from *grade school*?" I asked.

"A sniveling worm with a persecution complex, no personality, and no friends," Pep said. Then she broke out into more piglet snorts.

"Eva, after this nightmare is over, please promise me that you'll stay away from Buck Tanner socially. You have your reputation to think about. And of course, I don't have to remind you that what you do reflects upon our *entire* family," said Daphne.

"Righto." Pep slammed her hand on the counter. "We can't have our *fine* reputations soiled, now, can we?" She laughed. "I hate to clue you in, Daph; however, methinks it's a bit too late to worry about that! Let's see, mother abandoned us when we were kids . . . *that* certainly took a bite out of the family's good name. Then, Eva ran away from the altar, *twice*."

I winced. It was really *three* times; my sisters still didn't know about my engagement to Dex.

"Your big-time husband got caught cheating, and *you* got divorced. Then you had a scandalous affair with a famous chef just before he was found murdered—"

"It was *not* an affair! And *you*, Pepper-Leigh, *you* grew up acting like a *boy*, and now you work in a wretched bar and dress like a character from *The Rocky Horror Picture Show*."

Daphne's face was flushed. She rarely let her guard down to show her real feelings. Still, Pep always had a way of punching Daphne's buttons. Of course, I'd chimed in as well . . .

Clearly miffed, Daphne kept going. "And *your* lazy musician husband, Pepper-Leigh, gambled your life savings away and had an affair with the local lingerie merchant, who is still whoring all over town, even after your husband has flown the coop and run back to his mama in Alabama! If *that* doesn't give somethin' for folks to talk about, I don't know what does. We Knox sisters can't be the laughingstock of the town anymore. It *must* stop."

Daphne crossed her arms.

"Well, we do have the business to think about . . ." I said.

Pep laughed.

"Pepper-Leigh, I'm quite serious," Daphne scolded.

"Don't we know it? That's what's so scary about you, Daphne. You're always 'so serious' about the stupidest things. I gotta go to work now . . ."

"We need to come together as sisters and keep a lid on things," Daphne called out.

"Get real! Life happens, Daph. We can't always 'keep a lid' on everything that comes our way. I'm off to work."

The porch door squeaked open. Pep shuffled out. Then, there was a distinctly different, heavy footstep inside the house.

"Nice to see ya, Miss Pep. You're lookin' fine as frog's hair this afternoon. I'm diggin' those goth earrings," said Precious from the doorway.

"Howya doin', Precious?" called Pep from the porch. "Wish I could stay and visit with y'all a bit, but I'm off to tend bar at the Roadhouse."

"Well, it's been real nice seein' ya, just the same," said Precious. She sashayed into the kitchen.

"Hiya, ladies."

Precious gave us a big smile. Her impeccably made-up face flattered her flawless skin and dark, almond-shaped eyes. Towering over us, she wore a bright red dress with butterflies and flowers patterned on it. And her high-heeled Louboutin pumps were red, to match.

I heard footsteps out on the porch again. Pep pulled open the screen door and stuck her head inside.

"I'm sorry, Daph, I didn't mean to sound so wretched before. Really, I didn't. It's just that you set yourself up for it and I can't help myself sometimes. If y'all get a chance later, the Crop Pickers are playin' at the Roadhouse, and they're a killer band. Why don't y'all c'mon down tonight and relax for a few hours. Drinks will be on me."

"Not for me, thank you, Pepper-Leigh," said Daphne with a sniff. "I'd rather eat glass."

Pep snorted. Precious shook her head. I shrugged. We all knew that it'd take a while for Daphne to cool off. And really, I doubted she'd ever be convinced to step foot in a place like the Roadhouse.

It just wasn't *couth*.

"Well, *I* might just take y'all up on that, Miss Pep," said Precious brightly.

"Great!" said Pep. "Bring Eva." Pep stuck her arm through the open doorway and cocked a thumb toward me. "She looks like she could use a picker-upper. Or at least a cold beer." She pulled her head back outside and the door slammed. "Lemme know when you find out what happened to the dead guy," she shouted from the porch. "Tootles!"

"I'm not going!" I called after Pep.

CHAPTER 7

"I've just *got* to do somethin' about that slammin' door," mused Daphne.

Precious clomped across the kitchen floor to stand next to the farmhouse sink. She folded her arms and leaned against the red laminate counter, smiling. Her big, gold hoop earrings glinted in the sun that gleamed through the kitchen window behind her.

"I take it there's no new news about the dead guy in the pond?"

"No, I'm afraid not," Daphne said.

"Oh well. Miss Daphne, I gotta run a few errands in town for Mister Collier, so I'll take Eva with me now, if y'all don't mind."

"That'll be just fine, Miss Precious. I do appreciate y'all takin' Eva with you. I'm sure it is inconvenient."

It was like they were talking about a small child or a pet . . . except it was *me*. And I was right there. Finally, Precious turned to look at me.

"Sunshine, we gotta leave now. And we can't dawdle once

we get downtown 'cause I gotta be back to Greatwoods before four thirty."

"I'm ready when you are, Precious," I said, standing up from the table.

"Oh, Precious, I nearly forgot to thank you for tidying up the kitchen this morning," said Daphne. "It certainly was a mess! I can't imagine what happened. You always leave everything so pristine before leaving in the evenings."

"Yes, ma'am. I gotta admit, it looked like a small tornado'd spun through here this morning. Must've been one of your guests helped himself, or herself, to a late-night snack. There was olive oil spilled everywhere! On the counters. On the floor . . . And salt! Y'all shoulda seen the piles of sea salt that I swept up. Not to mention all my settings on the toaster oven were messed up, and there were crumbs and toasted bits of my fresh-made sourdough bread everywhere. Plus, I found a pile of smashed garlic cloves and skins . . ."

"Sounds like *fettunta*," I said.

"*Fe*—what?" asked Precious.

"*Fettunta*. It's Italian for a greased slice of bread. Dex used to have it all the time."

"Dex?" asked Daphne. "What do you mean *Dex*? Do you mean *Mister* Codman?"

"The guy in the pond?" asked Precious, raising her eyebrows. "The *dead* guy?"

I sighed.

"Yes. The same Dexter Codman from the pond. Our guest. I used to know him. Back in Boston."

"Is that why he asked to sleep in your old bedroom, Eva?" asked Daphne. "Because you two knew each other? Heaven forbid. I had no idea."

"That's freaky," said Precious.

"I thought he'd just read about you in the gossip papers and wanted to experience a little *celebrity*," said Daphne.

"There's more," I said.

"More?"

"Don't tell me you and him were doin' the dirty deed last

night!" Precious's eyes got big. "Were y'all skinny-dipping in the pond? Did ya boff the life outta him?"

"Precious!"

"No! Of course not."

"Then what . . ."

"I assure you both, I didn't see Dex at all after last night's olive oil tasting party. However, just so you know, Dex and I did . . . er . . . *date* each other for a while. It was a long time ago."

I just couldn't admit we'd been engaged. I knew it'd kill Daphne to hear it this way. Especially after all these years. I'd tell her later. Once she'd had time to process the fact that the dead guy in our pond had been one of my boyfriends. Maybe in a year or two I'd say something . . .

One step at a time.

"*Dated?*" cried Daphne. "When did this happen? Was this Dex fellow the reason you broke it off with the weatherman so suddenly? Why didn't I know about this person? Did Pepper-Leigh know about him?"

"No. No, nothing like that, Daph. My break with stupid Zack the weatherman this summer had *nothing* to do with Dex, I assure you. Like I said, Dex and I knew each other *a long time ago*. And, Daph, just so you know, Pep didn't know anything about Dex. She still doesn't. You're the *first* one in the family whom I've told."

"Oh. I see. Well, that's good, I suppose . . ."

Reassuring Daphne that she was *first* to know seemed to calm her. Good, better, *best*.

"Before yesterday, I hadn't laid eyes on Dex in years," I said. "Anyway, he often used to make himself *fettunta* at night. It's just sliced bread rubbed with fresh garlic and salt. Then it's drizzled with olive oil. Dex told me once that he first had *fettunta* in Italy. You won't find it in restaurants, he'd said. It's something folks eat at home. Just like no one dips bread in olive oil in restaurants over there, either. Dex made his own version of *fettunta* all the time. I bet he was the one in here last night."

I was racking my brain to try to piece together everything

the Bostoners had said on the hill earlier. Had anyone mentioned being with Dex? Or being in the kitchen late last night? *No, quite the opposite, actually.* They'd assumed that he'd been with me. Or at least they'd said so.

"Well, at least the poor boy ate well before he croaked," said Precious. "They all seem to eat real good here before dyin' . . . The last one, your chef fella, Miss Daphne, he had that yummy peach bourbon ice cream, remember?"

Daphne furrowed her brow and frowned, big-time.

"Precious," I said, quietly, warning . . .

"Oh yeah. Sorry," she said with a knowing nod. "Not to disrespect the dead or nothin'. Sorry, Miss Daphne. I know the chef was special to you." Precious gave Daphne a soft pat on the shoulder. "Okay, so Miss Eva, we got to be going now. Already, I'm runnin' late, and Mister Collier don't tolerate lateness."

"I'm ready."

"Wait! Eva! Surely, y'all are not goin' to town lookin' like *that*?" cried Daphne.

"Like what?"

"Like a street urchin! Surely, you can find something else to wear in public besides a tacky tee shirt and those ratty cutoff shorts! I bet they're twenty years old."

"Sure wish I could wear *my* twenty-year-old stuff!" Precious laughed. "Although, come to think of it, I sure wouldn't want to be wearin' *now* what I wore *then*." She shook her head. "*Nuh-uh.* I had no class back then. Like I do now, don't y'all know it?"

Precious threw back her head and laughed merrily as she headed out the back door and across the porch to the stairs.

"C'mon, Sunshine. We ain't got time for you to change clothes," she called to me. "Sorry, Miss Daphne!"

Daphne groaned as I followed Precious outside. The kitchen door slammed behind us.

CHAPTER 8

A bell on the door jingled as I entered the tiny Birdsong
Botanicals shop in the village. The shop smelled of sandalwood incense, and lots of it. New age music warbled softly
from speakers in the ceiling from which dream catchers, wind
chimes, and colored glass ornaments hung on long strands of
translucent fishing line.

Right away, a tall, noble-looking woman came out from
behind the counter to greet me. She was well tanned with
jet-black eyes, high cheekbones, and straight gray hair worn
loose, down to her waist. Most likely in her sixties or early
seventies, she was simply attired in a gauzy off-white caftan
worn over black leggings and thong sandals with shell accents. Handmade-looking silver earrings dangled from her
big ears, matching the stack of silver bangles on each of her
wrists.

"Greetings!" she said. "Welcome to Birdsong Botanicals."

Her tiny shop was filled, floor to ceiling, with rare and
exotic dried plants, seeds, and herbs. They were showcased
in shelves chock-full of boxes and bags as well as glass and
wooden bins set up around the store. Moreover, one wall was

covered with shelves of self-help and informational books about holistic health, natural healing, herbs, botanicals, seeds, plants, and natural gardening. Also, there were handmade soaps, bath oils, breath mints, lip balms, lotions, shampoos, conditioners, toothpastes, healing stones, and more.

"I'm Joy. You must be Daphne's little sister, Eva," Joy said with a toothy smile. "I can tell from your hair. It's just as pretty as your big sissy's hair!"

I laughed. "Thank you. It's a pleasure to meet you."

I held out my hand and Joy clasped it firmly.

"Your sister Daphne has told me so much about you."

"I'm not sure whether that's good or bad!" I joked. I handed Joy the package of olive leaves and bark. "Daphne tells me that you're going to come up with some new olive leaf tea blends. How exciting!"

"Yes, already, I have a few in mind," said Joy. "One with chamomile, rose petal, and passion flower, for a more calming blend. And then, perhaps another more invigorating blend with ginger, peppermint, and lemon."

"Daphne's thrilled to have you working on this. She speaks so highly of your knowledge and experience."

"I'm delighted to do it. It's always good to help out another local business. Besides, it's good for my own business." She set Daphne's olive leaves and bark down on the counter. "Your sister brought over some dried tea leaves last week and, look, already I'm sold out." She pointed to an empty spot about halfway up a shelf in the middle of the shop.

"Great!"

"Now that y'all are producing olive oils," Joy continued, "word is getting around about the many healthful benefits of the olive tree plant. I've had quite a few requests for more olive products. Did you know that folks as far back as the ancient Egyptians used olive leaf tea for medicinal purposes?"

"Please, tell me more."

"Perhaps you already know that the unprocessed olive leaf contains oleuropein, an antioxidant responsible for most of its health benefits, as well as several other polyphenols and flavonoids that help lower bad cholesterol and blood pressure.

Also, oleuropein has been proven to help prevent cancer, protect against oxidative damage, and slow cognitive decline."

"Yes, I talk to people all the time during my olive oil tasting events about polyphenols."

"Did you know that in one study involving animals with tumors, after scientists introduced oleuropein to the animals, within a matter of just two weeks the tumors in the animals completely regressed? Some disappeared entirely."

"Wow."

"And I have a couple of folks who stop by regularly to purchase olive leaf extracts to help fight diabetes."

I raised my eyebrows.

Joy continued. "Studies with both rats and humans have demonstrated that when fed olive leaf extracts, metabolic abnormalities associated with the disease can be countered."

"No kidding! I didn't know that."

"Yes. It's all very exciting. Your family's timing, getting into the olive industry now, couldn't be better. All sorts of studies are coming out showing that extracts from olive leaves have tremendous potential to lessen, or even prevent, serious health conditions such as heart disease, hypertension, diabetes, cancer, stroke, Alzheimer's, and even arthritis. Did y'all know that after drinking olive leaf extract infusions, people suffering from AIDS have reported surprising results in their fight against immune disorders and infections?"

"I had no idea."

"It's true. Although, for medicinal purposes, tea must be made strong, and that usually gives it a bitter taste, which is a shame, really, because with a light steeping, olive tea normally has such a distinctive, mellow flavor. Still, some lemon, mint, or ginger, as well as milk, sugar, or other flavorings, helps mask any bitterness."

"I'm so impressed by all this. Really, I knew the stuff was healthful; however, obviously, I'd not studied up enough."

"I can't keep supplies on the shelf. I'd love to have a regular, local supplier."

"Well then, please, count us in!"

"I'm looking forward to it. Tell Miss Daphne that I'll get back to her in a day or two about the tea blends."

"I will," I said, heading toward the door.

"Say, I'm curious," said Joy, "did you have any trouble parking in the village? It's the Peeps Week parade today, you know."

"Actually, a friend dropped me off. She's meeting me in another half hour or so. However, I did see folks beginning to line up outside. I suppose it's almost parade time?"

Joy checked a clock on the wall.

"Yes, they must be about ready to start. Although, I've heard from some folks in town that it's not expected to last long. There aren't many participants. It's only the second year they've held the parade."

CHAPTER 9

Right after Precious had dropped me off outside Joy's shop in the village, she'd taken off in her red Corvette to do her own errands. Our plan had been for Precious to return and pick me up thirty to forty minutes later, just down the boulevard outside the hardware store, where I'd be delivering Daphne's corks. Then Precious and I would go together to the bed-and-breakfast, where we'd deliver Daphne's guilt basket to Pottie Moss Diggs.

However, just as I hit the brick sidewalk after leaving Joy's botanicals shop, I realized that the plan wasn't going to work at all. That's because in our rush to get to town so that Precious could be back at Greatwoods by four thirty, we'd both completely forgotten to stop at Daddy's warehouse to pick up the box of used corks. Worse still, even as we'd made plans and discussed how she'd pick me up outside the hardware store, neither Precious nor I had even realized our silly mistake. Nor had we remembered the parade. And of course, after leaving Joy's shop, when I'd finally realized that we'd forgotten the corks and I didn't have my phone with me—I never carried my phone—I couldn't call Precious to confer.

I was destined to fight the crowd, hoofing it up to the hardware store in the blistering, midday summer heat, for nothing. And with the parade happening, I'd no idea whether Precious would even be able to get back into the village anytime soon . . .

Sigh.

Main Street was positively busting with tourists. In the parklike center of the boulevard median, folks crowded together on wooden benches, many of them snacking in the shade, while others pointed at and photographed the long cascades of Spanish moss hanging from the gnarled live oak trees above them.

Along both sides of the bustling boulevard, under the shade of colorful and perky striped awnings suspended from the Victorian buildings, people ambled along brick pavers dotted with giant pots planted full of greenery and flowers, while others stopped and admired enchanting window displays enticing them to enter cute specialty shops nestled within the picture-perfect buildings accented with gingerbread trim. On the far side of the boulevard from me, I could see that popular stores like Gifts Galore, Clayworks Pottery, the Kibler Gallery, and Buy the Book were absolutely jammed with gawkers and shoppers.

On my side of Main Street—the side the parade would be following—outside the old-fashioned movie theater the sidewalk was nearly impassable as a long line of people waited to get into the next matinee. A vendor was selling balloons from a cart. Another cart vendor hawked ice cream, another had cotton candy, and a fourth vendor sold smoothies. The curbside village information booth was mobbed with tourists demanding maps, directions, and free advice.

"Anyone know where we can get a good meal?" shouted one man.

"Across the street. That way," answered someone. "The Palatable Pecan."

"Try the Roadhouse," shouted someone else from the mob. "It's cheaper. Although it's not in the village . . ."

"Yoo-hoo! Eva Knox, is that you, *dahhwr-lin*?"

Waving frantically to catch my eye as she hustled up the jammed sidewalk, about half a block away, Daphne's book club friend Doocey Cronk was all smiles. From somewhere up Main Street behind her, in the direction of Town Hall at the top of the boulevard, I could hear the thumping of drums. A band was playing. Already, the Peeps Week parade had begun. It was headed our way.

I hope Precious can get back into town . . .

Stretching and peering down the boulevard to catch a first glimpse of the oncoming festivities, folks crammed themselves along the curbside.

"Why, I just *knew* it was you!" Doocey exclaimed breathlessly.

The sharp-nosed, curly-haired brunette grasped my shoulders, greeting me with an unexpected air-kiss. Her oversize straw bag swung wildly as she pulled me toward her. The bag *fwapped* me on the hip.

Normally, Doocey wouldn't have given me the time of day.

Stepping back, she propped her cat-eye sunglasses atop her head. Instantly, the glasses disappeared in her curls as she squinted in the sunlight.

"Hi, Doocey. It's lovely to see you," I said.

I doubted that the forty-something banker's wife believed my sentiment any more than I believed it when I'd said it. Still, politesse *is* the Abundance way . . .

"I heard y'all had some more excitement at your place today, Miss Eva. Do tell! What *happened*?"

Digging for gossip.

"Well, really," I said with a courteous smile, "Doocey, there's not much to tell, I'm afraid. We don't know what happened other than to say one of our guests accidentally drowned in the pond."

"Sounds positively *dreadful*! I heard the man wasn't very old. And was quite handsome. From up North, folks are saying. When I spoke with your sister this morning, she said that *you*, Eva, had found the body."

She shook her head dramatically. I said nothing. She carried on.

"Poor dear. And after *all* the other dead people you've stumbled over this summer, you must feel *terribly* distraught." She rested her hand on my forearm, as if her touch would somehow comfort me. "Tell me, Eva sweetie," spoken with all the sugary politeness she could muster, "what did the dead man *look like* when you found him?"

She smiled sweetly, as if it were the most normal question in the world to ask.

"He looked dead," I said flatly.

I wasn't at all in the mood to feed the local gossip mill. Especially when it called for describing a dead person. Let alone a man whom I'd known intimately.

"I'm sorry, Doocey," I said with as much of a smile as I could muster. "I'm afraid that I need to get going. I'm scheduled to meet someone at the other end of town. In fact, already, I'm late. Will you please excuse me?"

Without waiting for her to respond, I left Doocey with her mouth gaping open as I turned on my heel and pushed my way through the crowd. People were still jostling for position as the parade drew nearer. Just a block away, I could see the high school color guard twirling and tossing their flags, followed by the marching band. After that, a big road tractor towing a float kept blasting its noisy horn.

"Hey, you! Eva Knox!"

I recognized the harsh voice. It was local reporter, and thorn in my side, Pat Butts. Like everyone else, she must've been waiting for the parade. And like everyone else, she was always sniffing out a juicy story, especially when it centered around Abundance's most scandal-ridden resident: me.

"I heard y'all fished out another stiff at your place," she cried out over the crowded noise. "Can ya tell me what happened?"

I walked in the other direction, quickly heading toward the back of the crowd under an awning over the entrance to the Abundance Package Store.

"Hey! Eva Knox! Come back!" shouted the nosy reporter. "I have *questions*!"

"Take a number!"

No doubt, she couldn't hear me as I scrambled through the crowd. Changing direction again, I was jammed amidst the mob in front of the theater. Just then, a swarm of moviegoers pushed their way out onto the sidewalk. The first matinee show was over. That's when something neon in the crowd flashed and caught my eye.

Oh no.

Atop a white-trimmed neon orange and green Lilly Pulitzer sundress, I recognized the bleached blonde inverted bob hairdo. Buck's new squeeze, my old nemesis, the oh-so-flexible Debi Dicer was headed right for me. Distinctively tall and slender, and by all accounts quite attractive, people gave way as she marched through the crowd.

Trying to ignore her, I put my head down, hoping to pass unnoticed.

No such luck.

"Eva Knox, what are *you* doing here? Don't y'all have some more dead bodies to bury?"

Standing in front of me, blocking my way, Debi crossed her arms and stood stock-still. Her freshly painted and manicured hot pink nails glistened in the sunshine. The temples of her pink sunglasses featured interlocking double "G" logos. *Gucci.* Somehow, even in the crush of the crowd, no one bumped into her. It was like she had this invisible shield . . . People just steered clear.

Except the men, of course.

"Afternoon, Miss Debi," said an attractive young man wearing jeans and a flannel shirt.

Flannel? It's nearly one hundred degrees out here!

He winked at Debi as he sauntered by.

"Why, hello, Landon. Lovely to see you today."

She reached out and patted him on the arm as he passed her. She was all sweetness and honey. I stepped to the side and started to walk away; however, Debi suddenly grabbed my arm, squeezing it tight.

"Wait," she said through clenched teeth.

To anyone passing, it looked like she was smiling, I'm sure.

"Debi," said an older, well-dressed fellow with a beard. He smiled and nodded as he approached us.

"Kurt Morris," she said with a flirty smile, "why, I haven't seen you since Dickey and I sold your farm last year. I've *missed* you, sweetie!" She was positively gushing.

"I've missed you, too, darlin'," Kurt gushed back. He squeezed Debi's elbow as he strolled past us and melted into the throng.

Apparently, I was invisible. Again, that day.

That's when I saw the Bostoners, Wiggy, Coop, and Spencer, just down the block, with another man . . . Debi's real estate magnate brother, Dickey Dicer. Dickey's dark hair was slicked back, and he wore a red-collared jersey. They were a couple of buildings away . . .

"Debi, let go," I said. "I need to go."

From what I could see, it looked like Wiggy, Coop, and Spencer were arguing with Dickey. Everyone's hands were flapping angrily. I wanted to hear what they were saying. Puffed up and red-faced, Wiggy looked positively infuriated as he waved his cigar in Dickey's face. Dickey was nodding and holding his hands out, as if to say, "Stop!" He looked abashed. I needed to get closer to hear them.

Debi still clutched my arm. "Hold your horses, *Miss* Eva, I'm not finished sayin' what I've got to say . . ."

"Debi, please. Not now!"

I threw her hand off my arm and watched as Wiggy poked his finger into Dickey's chest. Then someone stepped in front of me, blocking my view and my exit away from Debi. Debi grabbed me again. This time, she pulled me right up against her side.

Still "smiling," she dug her nails in my arm and whispered in my ear, leaning in so close, she nearly bit my ear off. The noisy marching band, playing an ear-shatteringly discordant version of the tune "Rockin' Robin," was passing us in the boulevard, making it nearly impossible to hear. A block away, the road tractor following the band blasted its horn.

"It's obvious, honey bun, that y'all don't know the first

thing about men, or you never would've let Bucky get away all those years ago."

There she went, calling the sheriff "Bucky," like she always did.

How embarrassing . . .

With a goofy grimace, I shook my head.

"But you did," continued Debi. Her nails dug deeper into my arm. "And, goodness knows, I don't know why you're back in town now. Trying to reel Bucky back in, after all your other relationships have belly flopped, is my guess. But I've got news for you, sweetheart. I'm onto you. And I'm watching you. You hear me?" She was nearly shouting in my ear, trying to be heard above the band. "You keep coming on to Buck, or meeting up with him late nights the way I *know* y'all have been doin' all this summer, and I'll make sure you never meet up with Bucky, or any other man, again. You got it, sister? Whatever y'all *think* you got goin' on with Buck Tanner stops right here."

She smelled like sweet, intense tuberose with melon, coconut, and musk—kind of like sweetly scented flowers making whoopee. Was her perfume Carnal Flower? *How perfect,* I thought. Her breath smelled like cheap candy. I yanked my arm away.

"So, Debi," I said hotly, "let me get this straight . . . Are you telling me that *the Buck stops here*?" I snorted with a laugh as I put my hands on my hips. "Get a life." I had to shout to be heard over the parade noise. "The man has a mind . . . and a heart of his own. Don't come threatening me and blaming *me* just because *your* tricks in bed aren't enough to satisfy him. If he's not home at nights, that's on *you*. Not me."

People in the crowd tittered. No doubt they'd heard what I'd said. I didn't care. But Debi did. She was beet red with anger. She snatched at me, seething with anger, before she spit out her final words.

"Listen up, pretty pants. Just as soon as he picks out a ring, I'm going to marry Sheriff Buck Tanner. And there's not a damn thing you can do about it. Already, I have his mama's blessing . . . something you'll *never* have!"

"Omigosh, how will I *ever* sleep at night?" I shrugged.

The yammering crowd on the sidewalk, thunderous roar from the approaching parade trucks, and clanging band instruments in the street were sure to have my ears bleeding at any moment, I thought. I tried pulling my arm away from Debi. She clenched my arm harder, yanking me closer as she hissed again in my ear.

"After Bucky and I get married, right here in town in front of God and everyone, we're gonna make babies. And *lots* of 'em. In fact, I'm gonna keep that man so busy makin' babies that he won't have time to think about you, or anyone else in this town. And then we're gonna raise those babies together, Bucky and I. After that, we're gonna be grandparents. So, hear me, sweetness, I'm *deadly* serious when I say Buck Tanner and I are gonna live happily ever after. And whether y'all remain here *on this earth* to see it all happen, or not, is up to you."

"Is that a threat?"

"Just friendly advice. Take it any way you want it, darlin'." Debi smiled sweetly.

"Give it your best shot, Debster."

I smiled back.

Debi was forced to let go of my arm when the crowd on the sidewalk surged between us, as folks tried to get a better look at the act that brought up the rear of the Abundance High School marching band. In the road, a group of octogenarians from the nursing home, seated in wheelchairs, honked, tooted, dinged, and banged their handheld instruments while staff dressed in nursing uniforms pushed them along the parade route. The crowd on the sidewalk went nuts, cheering and applauding the old band members and their helpers.

To get away from Debi as quickly as possible, I decided to walk along the edge of the road, bypassing the near-impassable crowd on the sidewalk. As I started to step off the curb, I glanced down at my arm. She'd actually bruised it with her nails!

Damn her.

Someone shoved me hard from behind. Pitching forward,

I lost my balance. As I snatched at air, I managed to spin around just in time to see Debi in her bright neon colors vanish into the mob.

Did she push me?

It felt like slow motion as I continued falling backward into the street. There was nothing to stop me. The giant road tractor following the octogenarian band blasted its deafening horn. At the same time, I heard the growl of the truck and the loud *pssssshhhttt* of air brakes. As I smacked the pavement, the big truck's chrome bumper was nearly overhead.

"Get up!" I heard a woman shout from the curb. "Get up! *Get up!*"

CHAPTER 10

He literally snatched me out from under the oversize bumper of the road tractor. I'd been just inches away from one of the truck's huge, oncoming tires.

The crowd on the sidewalk cheered.

"Eva, are ye okay?"

His brogue was distinctly Scottish. With soft vowels. Hard consonants. Softened double letters. Gently rolled "R"s. It was my neighbor from Greatwoods Plantation, Ian Collier.

My gobsmackingly gorgeous knight in shining armor.

As always, Ian smelled divine. The fresh, clean smell of his starched shirt mingled with his usual seductive, manly woodsman cologne—a pungent, musky scent of earthy oakmoss, vetiver, and leather, set off with a faint smokiness. I inhaled deeply.

Heavenly.

"Eva?"

"Of course. Um. What?"

"We need to get ye to a doctor," said Ian. He was still holding me in his strong arms, pressed securely against his muscular chest. "Ye smacked yer head pretty good on the pavement."

The goggling crowd parted quickly as ruggedly handsome, forty-something Ian—several inches over six feet tall, with wavy, dark hair, broad shoulders, and a slender waist—cried out, "Make way, folks."

He carried me through the throng and toward the movie theater. Someone threw open the theater door, and a *woosh* of icy cold air washed over us as Ian walked us into the majestic, air-conditioned lobby. Decorated floor to ceiling in red velvet and gold leaf, the place smelled like popcorn and sticky sweet candy. I felt instantly better. Maybe it was the cool air. Maybe it was the popcorn.

Maybe it was Ian Collier.

"Please, I'm fine," I said.

The theater lobby was packed with noisy people lined up to buy movie tickets and snacks. Ian set me down on an old Victorian fainting couch in the corner. Like everything else, it was upholstered in plushy red velvet fabric.

"Sit," he ordered. Ian was dressed casually but neatly, with tan slacks, a leather belt, and a bright white long-sleeved shirt with the sleeves rolled up. And he wore pricey, well-worn loafers. No socks.

"I was just comin' from the surveyor's office up the street when I saw ye fall," he said. "What happened?" He brushed his dark, wavy hair from his smooth forehead.

"I must have slipped off the curb. Thank you for rescuing me."

His eyes flashed bright with alert intelligence. They were the dreamiest deep green, set between long, thick lashes.

"Slipped off the curb?" He furrowed his brows, giving me a quizzical look.

I nodded. "Um-hmm."

"I swear, girl, we're going to have to wrap ye in Bubble Wrap. Good thing I was walking the road and not the sidewalk . . . I'd have never gotten to ye in time. Are ye sure yer okay? Do ye need a ride home?"

"I'm fine. Really. And no, I don't need a ride. Thanks. I'm supposed to meet Precious at the hardware store in a few minutes."

"Precious?"

"We split up . . . doing errands. We've got just one more place to go and then she'll take me home. I know you need her back at Greatwoods by four thirty."

"Aye."

Ian raised a brawny arm and looked at his wristwatch. An old Patek Philippe. Simple but elegant. Probably mid-century.

"Which reminds me," he said, "I've got to be getting back to Greatwoods myself. Are ye sure I can't give ye a lift, now?"

"I'm sure."

"And yer alright?"

"I'm fine. I just slipped, that's all."

"Yer head is feelin' okay?"

"My head is okay. I'll take some ibuprofen when I get home. Promise."

"Okay, then. Yer on yer own. Tell Precious I'll be looking for her when she gets back home. And I'll be wanting a full report on how ye've fared. I don't like leaving ye here like this."

"I'll tell her. Thank you again, for picking me up. Literally." I giggled.

Idiot schoolgirl!

"Sure, Eva."

Ian bent down, gently putting a big, soft hand on each of my shoulders. He moved in close, transfixing me with his seductive, intense, woodsman scent. Pressing his warm lips firmly onto my forehead, he let his kiss linger just . . . ever so much. Afterwards, I felt his day-old beard as it brushed against my cheek.

My insides flipped. My cheeks flushed hot.

"Ye know I'm always here, looking out for ye," he whispered hoarsely. Then he chuckled before mumbling, "Goodness knows, ye need it, darling." His green eyes twinkled and he gave me a wink.

Then Ian stood and turned, before walking briskly through the crowd and out of the theater.

I could still smell his seductive, earthy scent all around me. The kiss on my forehead lingered, feeling just slightly warm and damp. I didn't dare move, for fear I'd melt it away.

CHAPTER 11

The Peeps Week parade turned out to be one of those blink-and-you-miss-it events. There was the high school band and color guard followed by the octogenarian wheelchair band. Then came the big landscaping road tractor that almost crushed me. It was towing a big forest-themed float. There were a bunch of landscape trees set up on the trailer to make a "forest" that "hid" the owners' kids dressed to look like woodland animals. Then came some scouting troops—the girls dressed like birds; the boys marched as trees. A float sponsored by the local chapter of the National Audubon Society featured folks dressed to look like wildlife. Loudspeakers broadcast various birdcalls to the crowd. The Abundance Naturalist Society passed out flyers and candy; members of the Abundance Swamp Huggers pulled wagons decorated to look like big alligators—one was supposedly a male alligator called "Suitcase"; the other was a female alligator called "Handbag." Suitcase and Handbag were two iconic legends supposedly inhabiting our Big Swamp. And there were smaller wagons decorated as baby alligators named "Wallet" and "Belt."

A few folks from the Georgia Wilderness Society marched and carried signs about saving the trees, and members of the Georgia Nature Photographers' Society walked the boulevard behind a giant banner depicting a wide-angle photo of our Big Swamp. Georgia Power had a small, well-decorated nature-themed float featuring giant papier-mâché butterflies, frogs, and birds. There was a person dressed like the Georgia state bird, the brown thrasher. A couple of clowns juggled and squirted water, and some kids on horseback rode the parade route as well—everyone cheered when the ponies pooped in the road.

Also, a couple of representatives from the Georgia Ornithological Society marched along, giving out pamphlets; there was a random park ranger from somewhere; and standing on a large trailer pulled behind another big truck, members of the Abundance Bird Club dressed themselves as various bird species, whistling and making birdcalls while throwing little packets of birdseed to the crowd.

Swamp tour owner Skeets Diggs drove down the boulevard in his pickup, towing a huge, flat-bottomed airboat, with a humongous fan spinning in the wind. His boat was covered with hand-painted signs advertising his tour service. Folks cheered when the giant fan in the stern got caught up in some low-hanging branches, causing Spanish moss to rain down on the boulevard. After that, Abundance Fire and Rescue made a showing with several emergency vehicles and blazing red fire trucks, blowing their horns to indicate that the parade was over.

Like I said, the parade was short. Describing it as I just did probably took longer than it'd taken to watch it pass by.

After Ian'd left me at the theater, and I'd watched the tail end of the parade, I figured it was just about time to meet Precious, so I headed toward Abundance Hardware. I'd have to give my apologies to store owner Merle Tritt for forgetting the corks that Daphne'd promised him.

Just a couple of doors up the street, dreading another confrontation with Debi Dicer, I ducked my head and fast-walked through the crowd past Dicer Realty, which was right next door to Abundance Hardware. Dickey and the Bostoners were nowhere to be seen. Even so, just outside the hardware shop, I ran into a different kind of trouble.

Beauty shop owner Tammy Fae Tanner put on a big smiley-smile when she stepped onto the sidewalk from inside the hardware store.

"My heavenly days! Eva Knox. Aren't y'all a *sight* . . . as usual, *tsk tsk*." She shook her head as she gave me a once-over. "Really, dear, I'd be happy to work you in for a beauty consult. A gal like you shouldn't be too embarrassed to ask."

A former beauty queen and sitting president of the local ladies club, Buck's mother was pretty and petite with big, brown cocker spaniel eyes, a turned-up nose, and curled, shoulder-length, whiskey-colored hair. Carrying a little paper bag from the hardware shop, she wore a simple sleeveless cotton blouse over a fitted black skirt. Her thong sandals were faux alligator, and her toenails were painted cherry red, to match her fingernails and lip color. Tammy Fae put an arm around my shoulders and gave me a too-tight squeeze.

"After all," she said in mock earnest, "that's what *friends* are for!"

"I'll pass. Thank you, Missus Tanner."

"Well, hon, if I may, here's a piece of friendly advice . . . Y'all will *never* land yourself a fella looking like this!"

She stepped back and gave me another once-over.

"A single woman your age must put in a little *effort*, don't y'all know it? After all, look at Debi Dicer . . . She takes *care* of herself and *she* got *her* man. And, I daresay, my son is the biggest catch in the county."

"By hook or by crook."

I smiled.

Tammy Fae leaned in and whispered loudly into my ear. "Bless your heart." She smelled like beauty salon chemicals. "Don't y'all know it, Buck just thinks Debi's the cat's pajamas! I've seen how my handsome son can't keep his paws off her. Mark my words, they'll be makin' babies, just quick as a bunny. I just know it."

Obviously, Debi and her hopefully-future-mother-in-law had discussed Debi's baby-making scenario.

"Does your handsome son know about his role in this imminent baby-making scheme?"

"Sugar pie, men never do."

Tammy Fae gave me a fat-cat grin.

A voice boomed from behind me. "Miss Eva, you ready to head outta here?" It was Precious.

"Precious!" I turned to smile at my friend. "It's so nice to see a friendly face." I turned back to address Tammy Fae. "I'm so sorry, Missus Tanner, no time to chitchat today. Perhaps another time."

I gave her the same sort of insincere smile that she'd given me earlier.

"No problem," said Tammy Fae with a little wave. "Have a lovely day, ladies. Oh, and Miss Precious . . . I'll see *you* next week, for your regular appointment!"

"Yes, ma'am," said Precious. "See ya."

I opened my mouth to chastise Precious for going to Tammy Fae's place. Before I could speak, she grabbed my arm.

"C'mon. Let's scram. I got the car parked in the lot behind Duke's Donuts. Got a box of donuts, too. Oh, hey. And I got *news*!"

"News? What kind of news?"

"Tilly Beekerspat called me. You know, she's my friend who works in dispatch. Anyway, she told me that our dweeby detective was jumpin' the gun again. He's looking to get a *search warrant* for all y'all's place. I figure that can't be good news, 'cause we all know his little brain rattles around like a BB in a boxcar!"

CHAPTER 12

The massive Diggs homestead wasn't hard to find. Tucked down a side street, not far from the village center, the rambling, asymmetrical High Victorian was painted gray with white gingerbread trim. There was no grass out front. Instead, the small yard was a tangle of overgrown trees, shrubs, and perennials. Curbside, there was a black post with a tasteful hand-painted sign that read, THE NATURIST B&B.

Riding in her red Corvette convertible, Precious and I hadn't said much since our discussion about Detective Gibbit's search warrant, which hadn't been much of a discussion, really, since that'd been all the insider news that Tilly Beekerspat had known before calling. Precious and I'd speculated a bit about what the detective was thinking. Then, as Precious careened down one narrow street after another, I'd sat brooding in the bucket seat until our arrival at the Diggses' place. Precious passed the drive that went up the side of the property. Instead, she parked on the street, in front of the long walk to the front porch.

"Gosh, this place sure could use a face-lift," said Precious. "It's pretty desperate for some paint."

"And a new roof," I said, noting the missing shingles on the red roof as I stepped out of the car.

"And a weed whacker. If ever there were a time to use a machete, it'd be now!"

Precious laughed and hustled around the Corvette to catch up with me as I hefted Daphne's basket of olive oil goodies up the front walk.

"Looks like someone had a green thumb . . . a long time ago."

Actually, I was thinking that the place looked a lot like every place in Abundance had looked, before the Internet had come to the community's rescue. It was tired, run-down, and in need of restoration. Or a wrecking ball.

No wonder Dex and his friends left this place for Knox Plantation, I thought.

Birds and bugs in the great trees in the yard squawked and sang in the shade. Leaves and weeds tickled our ankles as we picked our way up the overrun front path, headed toward the front door that was set under a three-story tower that protruded from the front façade. The entry porch underneath the tower was connected to an enormous wraparound porch—at least ten feet wide—that featured beautiful, intricately designed gingerbread trim. Or rather, it would've been beautiful, had it not been in disrepair.

"Looks a lot like our place before Daphne rescued it," I said. "Only, this place is bigger, and Daddy never stopped taking care of the plantings. He'd have died if the weeds had ever taken over like this!"

It was a reminder that there were Abundance folks still struggling to make ends meet. Turning the Diggs home into a hospitality business had been more about survival than it'd been about getting ahead.

The old wooden floorboards creaked as we stepped up the front porch stairs.

"Watch out," Precious warned from behind me. "This rickety stair railing ain't attached real good."

Still, someone cared. There was a pretty floral wreath on a freshly painted black door, and a hand-painted sign over the doorbell read, WELCOME GUESTS. Followed by, COME AS YOU ARE. We could hear classical violin music coming from inside the place.

Precious reached around me and pushed the doorbell. We waited thirty seconds or so before she pushed the bell again.

"Precious!"

"What? I ain't got all day to stand here. I might fall through this old floor . . ."

Suddenly, the front door flew open. I nearly dropped Daphne's basket.

"Lord have mercy," Precious whispered.

"Hi, folks! Welcome to the Naturist B&B. Whatcha know good today?"

Standing before us, a rotund woman with a too-tight perm and home-dyed brown hair with gray roots smiled and raised her arm, swishing it gallantly through the air, as she motioned us to step inside.

She was naked as a jaybird.

CHAPTER 13

"Come in, come in! May I offer y'all some sweet tea? It's hot enough to roast a lizard today."

Pottie Moss Diggs was just as gracious as she could be.

Even in her birthday suit.

"Please, y'all just call me by my first name," she'd said, scuttling away from the entrance as she welcomed us into the great Victorian foyer. Mingled with furniture polish, there was a musty smell to the place. "All my guests call me Pottie Moss," she continued. "Miss Diggs is too formal for my taste."

"How about Miss Pottie?" asked Precious.

She'd said it with a straight face.

"No. I'm afraid that won't do," said our hostess, smiling. "That'd be like calling Mary Ann, Mary. Or Betty Sue, Betty. It's Pottie Moss."

"Of course," I said.

I gave Precious a warning look.

I forced myself to look discreetly around us, mostly so as not to gape at the portly, sagging, naked woman. On either side of the wallpapered foyer were wide casements leading to giant sitting rooms crowded with Victorian furnishings, most likely all original to the house. The furnishings looked worn but well-kept.

In front of us, opposite the front door, was a double-wide curved staircase, anchored with a dark wooden newel post. Next to the grand stair, a wide archway led to a room in the back of the house where a pair of French doors opened to reveal a sunny patio with a gurgling pedestal fountain. Also on the patio, I could see lounge chairs and a dining table with chairs and an open umbrella for shade.

Apparently, I'd stood gawking too long. Precious stepped up and grabbed Daphne's gift basket from my arms.

"Um, ma'am, we can come back at another time, if ya need to . . . uh . . . finish what y'all were doin' . . ."

"No, *noooo*! No need. No need at all." Pottie Moss smiled. "I see that I've caught you off guard with my . . . appearance." She giggled. "No matter. I'm used to it. I catch folks off guard all the time."

"Really?" I said.

I figured that I had to say *something* . . . Still, I couldn't find words.

"Yes. You see, like the sign says out front, we're the Naturist B&B. And don't y'all know it, a 'naturist' is a nudist, not a nature person. That'd be a 'naturalist.' Folks make the mistake all the time, thinkin' we're a 'naturalist' place for nature-lovers, 'cept, we're *naturists*, not *naturalists*. Get it? We love nature here, but in a healthy, fun way . . . the way we were born into this world . . . without our clothes."

She giggled again, shaking the fat around her belly.

"I see," I said, looking quickly away.

No wonder Claudia insisted they leave!

"Silly us." Precious raised her arms and laughed, feigning some sort of relief.

"I'm sorry if you were caught off guard. I assumed y'all knew about us bein' nudists and y'all were here about renting a room or two. And if y'all are, and even if y'all aren't into nakedness, you're in great luck. I just happened to have some rooms free up after some tourists ducked out on us unexpectedly. I guess it's for the best. This one woman was positively screeching at me the entire time she was here . . . about *every-thing*. I couldn't do enough to please her. Then when she left, I had to personally pack all her stuff and deliver it to her at another place outside town. How tacky is that? I even had to come back to fetch her forgotten shopping bag full of silly touristy junk—tee shirt, sunscreen, maps, postcards, pens, some local oil and honey, and even one of those tacky peanut-shaped brass paperweights." Pottie Moss waved her arms dramatically and her face and neck blushed as she spoke. "I mean, you can go out and buy most of that crap in any ol' grocery store. And who the heck wants a stupid peanut paper-weight anyway? Really, except for the crazy-ass peanut—which nobody should want—it's not like the junk wasn't easily re-placeable! But *nooooo*, she had to have it *all*, and right away."

Precious and I nodded, sympathetically.

"Still, I hated to see the group go. We need the income, you see. Times have been tough. And my brother, Skeets, he can't do much since he's *got the sugar* real bad . . . you know, diabetes. It's so bad, he's insulin dependent. And he's afraid of needles, so I'm always givin' him his shots. Dealin' with Skeets and his diabetes, it's hard for me to get away from this place anymore. Actually, I'm thinking now that it was truly a blessing not havin' to be at that Yankee woman's beck and call. She nearly ran me ragged. *Nothing was right*. And I don't understand that, you see, because I pride myself on treating our guests right . . . That's why I was excited to see y'all here today, not that I'm *not* excited to see y'all, mind you . . ."

I was distracted from Pottie Moss's ramble when I spied a middle-aged man and woman walking hand in hand outside near the backyard fountain. Like Pottie Moss, they were com-pletely naked. Of course, completely oblivious to the fact that I wasn't listening to her, Pottie Moss chattered on. By the time I turned back to listen, I'd missed a whole chunk of what she'd said.

". . . That's why if y'all are here for a room, I can offer you a tremendous savings today! I have two singles, nice and bright. Or, if you prefer, I've got a *very private* suite with a king-sized bed . . ."

"Um, actually, Pottie Moss, that's why we're here today. About your vacant rooms," I said, looking her straight in the eye.

"Wonderful!" She clasped her hands together in delight. "Let's get you registered. I just need a credit card . . ."

"No. I'm sorry. You don't understand."

That's when I introduced myself and apologized for Daphne, about taking in the Bostoners.

"Oh . . . *Oh.* I see. Yes. I should've recognized y'all." She frowned for a moment, as if she was trying to get it all straight. Then she smiled. "Eva! That's it. You're Robert Knox's youngest girl. The one who keeps running away and finding dead people, right?"

I nodded.

"Well, well! *Do* come in and sit down! Please!" She turned toward one of the sitting rooms. "You, too, miss," she said to Precious. Like everyone else that day, it seemed that once she realized who I was, she couldn't wait to hear the gossip about the dead man.

"*Soooo*, I heard y'all found *another* dead person at your place! What happened? Does the sheriff know anything yet? Was it another murder? Do tell me *all* about it!"

I handed Pottie Moss the basket filled with olive oil from Daphne.

"I'm afraid we don't know anything yet. Just that a man appears to have drowned in the pond last night."

"A man, you say? It was a *man* who died? *Another* man? And *you* found him? Isn't that right?"

"Yes."

"Well ain't that the butt end of a dirty hog. Another dead person. A man. Why, I bet your guests are fit to be tied!"

"Actually, they're taking it all in stride."

"Even that impossible-to-please skinny gal? Why, I heard her screeching at one of her men friends from here to Sunday the other night."

"Really?" I said. "Which man was that, do you know?"

"Afraid not. They was all together in one of the rooms, acting real secretive. I knocked once to offer them some tee shirts—they got I'D RATHER BE NEKKED printed on the front—and that bitty woman nearly tore my head off, sayin' they didn't want to be disturbed or nothing. She sounded real upset."

"Excuse me, Miss Pottie Moss," Precious said abruptly. "We've gotta be going now. I got somewhere to be by four thirty and we're runnin' late."

"Oh yes," I said. "Thank you for reminding me, Precious. Pottie Moss, Miss Daphne packed all sorts of our olive oil goodies in the basket for you. There's some soap, bath oil, and fresh olive oils—"

"Oh, great day! Thank you. I'm all out of olive oil. You know, like I said, my brother Skeets is diabetic, and since we've changed up his diet and he's been usin' *lots* of olive oil, he's actually been able to reduce his insulin dependency by a whole lot. Since we've started on the olive oil diet, I probably give him half what he used to get. Oh, and I see y'all have brought me some olive *tea* as well! I just bought out the last box in town down at Joy Birdsong's place. You ever been there? Birdsong Botanicals? Why, Miss Joy is a whiz when it comes to natural remedies. She's taught us so much to help with Skeets's diabetes. This olive oil is like *liquid gold*!"

"As a matter of fact, I just came from Joy's place."

"Aha!" Pottie Moss cried, pulling a bottle of olive oil from the basket. "Just like I said: liquid gold!" She read the label on the dark green bottle. "I see, we got some Knox Liquid Gold Extra Virgin Olive Oil. I'll be sure to put it to good use, y'all hear! Thank you kindly."

Just then, there was a huge crashing noise outside. We all ran to the front door to see that Skeets had pulled into a drive on the side of the property in his truck, towing the trailer with the big airboat. Only, he'd gotten the huge fan at the stern of the boat stuck on a low-hanging oak tree branch.

CHAPTER 14

After Precious dropped me off back home, I was eager to return to the village and deliver the corks to Merle Tritt at Abundance Hardware before he closed the shop at six. So, I hustled in our Kubota RTV—something akin to a souped-up, heavy-duty, all-terrain, oversize golf cart with mini dump bed behind the covered bench seat—to Daddy's warehouse, where I abandoned the Kubota. I tossed two crates of used bottle corks into the bed of Daddy's old Ford F-250 pickup, and I hopped up into the cab.

That's when our farm manager, Burl Lee—a brawny fellow with muscled arms the size of telephone poles, an easygoing style, and a smile to match—ambled over from the big John Deere 4850 tractor he was repairing to warn me about taking the dilapidated F-250 onto the road.

"This ol' biddy never leaves the farm," he said, shaking his head. He slapped a bear-sized hand on the once-red, now-faded orange truck hood. "Tires are bad. Plus there's something hinky about the transmission. You'll never get her out of second gear."

"That's okay . . ."

"It ain't okay if you want to go much over twenty or twenty-five miles per hour, all the way to town."

He had a point. Going to the village normally took fifteen to twenty minutes or more, and that was going fifty.

"I don't care," I said. "I need to get to the hardware store before six. I'll barely make it as it is. Are the keys inside?"

"Sure are," Burl said, shaking his head with a shrug.

He patted me on the shoulder as he instructed me to be sure to carry my cell phone. Then, he added that he'd try to send someone to pick me up after they were done with work at six or six thirty, when I'd be *sure* to call him saying that I'd had enough, or wrecked the truck, whichever came first.

He got a big laugh out of that.

Of course, I figured he was kidding. And anyway, that never would've happened, because when I pulled out of the farm drive and onto the main road, I realized that I didn't have my phone with me. *No matter.* I grabbed the black plastic knob on the truck's manual gearshift and stepped onto the squishy accelerator pedal. The old truck lurched forward with a big jolt.

BANG!

The exhaust backfired as I pressed down on the rubbery clutch and shifted into second gear.

"Here we go!" I cried.

The hard plastic steering wheel burned my hands. The backs of my legs stuck to the piping-hot vinyl bench seat. The truck had been parked, unused, in the blazing sun outside the warehouse for weeks. As it lurched and bucked down the main road toward the village, I hand-cranked the window down. The hot breeze offered little relief to the sticky, stifling interior of the cab.

BANG!

I glanced in the rearview mirror to see a cloud of black smoke poofing up behind me. Bucking and farting down the twisty country road, Daddy's decrepit pickup groaned as I pressed down on the rubbery clutch and tried to wrangle the stiff gearshift into third.

BANG!

After a half mile or so of gnashing and grinding, bucking and farting, still no luck. I was stuck in second. Just like Burl said I'd be. The motor whined as I kept my foot on the accelerator pedal, pushing second gear to the limit. The truck hobbled past an old farmhouse and an antique barn set amidst flat, sandy crop fields. Behind the farm was a stand of fast-growing loblolly pines. Out front near the drive, someone had posted an auction sign.

"Well, that's new."

I wondered what had happened. I remembered the place growing up. Early Daze Farm had been one of the busiest short-day onion producers around.

"Huh. Times sure are changing . . ."

Still squealing at the high end of second gear, Daddy's rust bucket lurched under a shady tunnel of moss-covered oak trees. I kept my sneaker pressed on the accelerator pedal and slammed my other foot down on the squishy clutch pedal as I tried to shift into third gear. I wrangled with the gearshift a bit, and then I gave the accelerator as much gas as I dared . . .

The engine wailed, then with a giant jolt, the truck slammed forward as the transmission finally caught.

"Hooray for third!" I shook a fist in the air to celebrate my victory. "Wait till I tell Burl!"

Moving along at nearly forty-five miles per hour, my mind raced about Dex and the others. I still had no idea what to think. All I knew was that Dex and his Boston friends had shown up completely out of the blue, and then Dex had acted like his old jerky self and we'd argued in front of everyone, and then shortly thereafter Dex died. *Really,* I thought, trying to comfort myself, *it was all no more than a strange coincidence.*

But, what had happened to him?

I wondered. And what about the search warrant that Precious's friend had mentioned? Was it possible that someone had actually murdered Dex? Or was it just another one of Detective Gibbit's crazy fishing expeditions? Both Pottie

Moss and I had witnessed Claudia's over-the-top nervousness and wrath. *What was that all about?* And who had she been yelling at behind closed doors at Pottie Moss's place?

At least I'd discovered why the group had abandoned the B&B. *Naturists.* I cringed, remembering Pottie Moss and her guests in their birthday suits. Knowing prudish Claudia, I was surprised she'd even lasted one night there. Although, Dex and the men had probably loved it. Daphne would get a chuckle when she learned about the nudists.

Or, maybe not.

The truck lurched forward unexpectedly and careened to one side. I gripped the faded steering wheel with both hands as I pressed down on the accelerator.

I'll be damned if I'm going back into second gear . . .

Still, why was the group from Boston in Abundance in the first place? I knew darn well that Dex Codman remembered that Abundance was my hometown. Plus, he knew Knox Plantation was my home; he'd even proven it when he'd asked Daphne to sleep in my old bedroom.

Hope he liked the pink wallpaper.

Also, I knew that he and the others in the group—Claudia, Spencer, Wiggy, and Coop—were no bird-watchers.

So, what had they been up to?

Or more precisely, I thought, what *are* they up to?

Daphne'd reported she'd heard that because Dex had no family, and apparently, Coop was the executor of Dex's estate; already they'd made plans to ship dead Dex back to Boston while they stayed on for another week.

Not only was that weird; it was cold.

Very cold.

Regardless, whatever it was that had first brought the group to Abundance was still *keeping* the group in Abundance.

All at once, I had a vision of Dex, floating in the pond. He was grinning and reaching out to me. I closed my eyes and shook my head, trying to rid myself of the ghastly image. I couldn't shake it . . .

When I opened my eyes, I was passing another real estate sign on the side of the road. And I saw something metallic—

was it blue?—flash from deep in the bushes. But I'd seen it too late to take it all in, and since I'd already passed by whatever it was, I couldn't make it out. Quickly, I turned to look.

BANG!

I jumped in my seat. I tried to settle myself. But I kept seeing Dex's ghastly image. I pressed down on the accelerator pedal and focused on the road ahead for a mile or more. I was approaching Benderman's Curve.

I'm staying in third . . .

I barely pushed on the brake as I entered the near-hairpin turn. I should've downshifted—any normal person would've—except that I'd been so distracted I hadn't thought it all through. Besides, I was worried about getting the dang transmission back into third gear again. So I held on tight to the steering wheel as I accelerated around the curve, without downshifting. The old truck tires screeched as they slid over the pavement . . .

WONK!

Three-quarters through the turn, the right rear tire blew out. The unweighted back end of the truck swerved right and left, out of control as shredded tire spewed about the pavement. Still negotiating the curve, I tried to correct, but the truck just kept skidding, making this terrible high-pitched screech of rubber on asphalt as I skidded wildly across the pavement.

Everything flashed by in slow motion, asphalt, trees, telephone poles . . .

Finally, the truck stopped with a thud. The back end had slid deep down into a roadside ditch.

CHAPTER 15

With no spare tire, no jack, and no help getting the back end of Daddy's beater truck out of the ditch, it was pointless to even try to figure out how to fix it. Without a cell phone, there was only one thing to do.

Hoof it back home.

Burl Lee would never let me hear the end of this. I could expect a lifetime of "I told you so."

Still, I hopped out of the cab and circled around the truck, just to properly inspect the situation. Deep in a ditch, the truck bed was several feet lower than the cab, which was still on the edge of the road. There were skid marks and little bits of tire scattered all across the pavement. And the air was filled with a pungent burnt-rubber smell. Of course, as I'd known right off, there was nothing I could do by myself. It'd take a tow truck or a tractor to pull the flat-tired rust bucket from the darned ditch.

I kicked a tire.

It didn't make me feel any better.

So, I kicked it again.

Maybe someone will drive by and give me a lift, I thought hopefully.

I reached up into the cab and turned on the hazard lights. Ten minutes later, as I stomped down the blistering pavement, not a single vehicle had gone by in either direction. And it was hotter than hell on that road. About a mile or so after that, I was decidedly hot and sweaty, and the bottoms of my feet hurt from pounding the pavement. Several minutes later, I spied a real estate sign stuck in the ground in front of some piney woods. It was part of the old Twiggs Creek Farm. I remembered seeing something flash by, not long before I'd hit Benderman's Curve. *Was this it? Hadn't what I'd seen been something bigger?* Regardless, I was sure the sign was new . . . Like the auction sign farther down the road, I'd not noticed a sign at Twiggs Farm before that moment.

When I got closer to the sign, I wrinkled my nose. It read, LAND FOR SALE. 2,250 ACRES. RIVER FRONTAGE. DICER REALTY. There was a phone number and a photo of brother-and-sister real estate team Dickey and Debi Dicer. Just seeing Debi's smug, perfectly made-up face and her bleached blonde inverted bob hairstyle made me frown. I stood for a moment and studied Debi's mug on the sign. Then I imagined her making babies with Buck.

Blech.

I kicked the sign.

"Ouch!"

I wondered just how the lovely Debi and her big brother, Dickey—who was equally smug and arrogant, and according to my sisters, *slippery as a wet eel*—garnered all the important real estate listings in town. Surely, there was at least *one* other real estate agent in the county?

The Dicers smirked at me from their metal sign.

I swiveled and took in the property behind the sign. Alongside the road it was scruffy—crappy pine trees, some shrubs, grasses, and tall weeds, mostly. Behind that, down a slope, was a flat, grassy field.

Once a working farm, in recent years the fields had been

left to the wild. Across the field, maybe half to three-quarters of a mile or more away, there was some forested land, like a small island in the middle of miles and miles of grassy fields. After that, lower still, were more fields shrouded in a thick mist. Locals called it the Foggy Bottom. A river, Twiggs Creek, ran somewhere behind the bottom.

"Nice place," I mumbled to no one. *A shame it's all gone to pot during recent years*, I thought.

Then I saw it.

The big metallic thing I'd seen earlier when I'd driven by. It was down a little slope to my left, stashed in shrubby undergrowth below some pine trees. And it *was* blue. Dark blue. I left the road and headed toward it to investigate. It only took me a moment to recognize Ian Collier's navy blue Hummer.

CHAPTER 16

I'd know his distinctive silhouette anywhere. I initially caught sight of him after I'd made it across the first big grassy field.

Cheeyoo-cheeyoo-cheeyoo, cried a red-tailed hawk.

Stopping in the forested stand of trees between the fields, I looked up and around, trying to catch a glimpse of the bird. That's when a fresh breeze whistled through the pine trees above me.

Then I heard the voices.

They were faint but unmistakable. Coming from the Foggy Bottom, I heard the low drone of men talking. I looked out on the open field before me. Even late in the day, the grassy land was covered in a thick mist. And even through the heavy mist, I recognized him.

Ian Collier.

My drop-dead gorgeous Scottish neighbor was holding something long, like a shotgun or rifle, under one arm. Standing next to Ian was another man dressed in hunting gear with a dark cap and a long gun held crosswise in his arms. He leaned against a four-wheeler that looked to be painted in camouflage colors. I didn't recognize the man like I did Ian.

And I was somewhat astonished to realize that even though the two men were the better part of five hundred feet or so down the field from me, I could hear their voices. A cloud of mist rolled between us, and I lost sight of the men for a minute or so. Still, I could hear them.

How can this be?

I remembered a time when Dex and I had been sailing in New England. A heavy blanket of fog had rolled in, and we'd gotten lost in the shallows of Nantucket Sound. Then we heard the familiar *gong-gong-gong* of the bell buoy that marked the entrance to the harbor. The sound was coming from somewhere off to starboard. Only we were headed east, and according to our compass headings, the bell buoy should've been somewhere off to the port side of the boat. In the end, Dex had stayed the course, ignoring the bell sounds, following the compass settings, looking for the buoy to appear on our port side.

He'd explained that the moist atmosphere had impacted the bell's sound waves, bending the waves in an arc that rose up and over us. When the sound waves came back down to where we could hear them, they appeared to originate from somewhere to starboard.

It's one of Mother Nature's clever tricks, Dex had said.

And on that score, at least, he'd been right. When the fog finally cleared, Dex and I could see the buoy . . . to port, exactly where the chart and compass headings indicated it should be.

So, as I listened to Ian and the other man, with the heavy mist shrouding the field, I credited what I figured were bendy sound waves in Foggy Bottom. More importantly, I was happy to have run across Ian. No. Ecstatic, actually. *Surely, he'll not object to giving me a ride home.*

I imagined the heavenly scent of his manly cologne, mingled with the fresh starch in his custom-tailored shirt. I could see his gorgeous green eyes, feel his long fingers on my skin. I remembered his lips, *that kiss*, on my forehead . . . I hadn't even gotten close to the man yet, and already, my heart pounded. My insides fluttered.

Stepping through the foggy open land, the growth was nearly waist-high. I parted the grass with my hands as I made my way toward Ian and the other man. With their backs turned to me, they were down the field a bit, to my left. Closing in on them, I could see that their bodies were taut. Their movements sharp. They'd taken no notice of me as I stopped every few steps, trying to make out their words.

I heard Ian say, "Ye've got no business here." He was uncharacteristically sharp. "It's *my* land now."

There was more conversation, but I couldn't hear it.

Then I heard the other man say, ". . . This land's been in my family for generations."

It must be Elrod Twiggs.

As far as I knew, after his twin brother Elroy had shot himself to death accidentally, Elrod was the only Twiggs left. For as long as I could remember, his deceased brother, Elroy, had managed the land and lived in the main house, while Elrod—a sort of social misfit with a penchant for hunting, drinking, and drugs—lived in a small shack somewhere down by the river.

As I drew nearer, Elrod's voice disappeared for a few moments. Then, waving his rifle, I saw him step closer to Ian.

". . . poaching . . ." said Ian. I couldn't catch the rest of his words.

Next, just as clear as day, I heard Elrod say, "Funny thing, you threatenin' me. Ain't no one but us and the animals in this field to know what might end up happening here today. And *my* gun's loaded."

Ian laughed. "So, I'm to end up like your brother . . . just a victim of another hunting *accident*?"

"Yeah, somethin' like that, smart guy. People disappear around these parts all the time. No one's gonna miss another sorry, meddlin', son-of-a-bitch bastard from outta town, like you . . ."

I gasped as Elrod raised his gun, pointing it directly at Ian. The end of the barrel was just an inch or two away from Ian's chest. Shocked, I froze still.

"I wouldn't be too quick with that," said Ian calmly. He

never moved, leaving his own rifle pointed toward the ground and tucked under his arm.

"Oh yeah? And why's that? Ain't like there's anyone around to see me . . . 'cept *you*. And the likes of you ain't gonna be seeing *nothin'* much longer . . . like I said. This here is *my* land!" He raised his rifle, and this time, he pointed the barrel right at Ian's face. "My stupid brother had an untimely *accident*. But you . . . you're just gonna disappear, my friend."

Elrod spit on the ground before letting out a phlegmy chortle.

Then, the sky ripped apart with an explosive cracking sound. Instinctively, I hit the ground just as Elrod's cap blew off his head.

CHAPTER 17

I didn't dare move. I was sure something deadly had just whizzed past my right shoulder.

Rifle shot?

Crouched in the tall weeds, I peeked in the direction of Ian and Elrod. They were still standing.

Thank goodness.

Ian hadn't moved. His rifle was still tucked beneath his arm. Elrod, on the other hand, had dropped his own rifle and thrown himself around to the other side of the four-wheeler.

This doesn't make sense.

Shaking, I tried to catch my breath.

"I wouldn't be too sure about ye and me being the only two blokes out here," said Ian quietly. "And I'd sure think twice before ye go off threatening me again. See this?"

Ian pulled something small out of his pocket and held it up with one hand.

He continued. "My buddy, over there," he nodded toward somewhere behind me, "he can shoot this itty-bitty tube of lip balm from more than one thousand yards away . . . if I want him to. Ye see, losing yer cap was just his warning shot.

He'll be sure not to miss yer head next time . . . if I want him to."

I felt the blood drain from my head.

The bullet couldn't have been more than a few inches away when it whizzed past me!

Elrod cursed as he stood up and scampered around the four-wheeler, headed toward his rifle on the ground. He hucked a giant gob of spit toward Ian before reaching down to grab his rifle. Except before he could pick it up, Ian planted his foot on the gun.

"Ye'd better be hauling yer dirty ass off my land," warned Ian. "Or I might just let the sheriff know that ye confessed to murderin' yer own twin brother. Or I might just let my buddy over there take his one final shot. After all, yer *all about* disappearing bodies down here now, aren't ye?"

Ian tucked the lip balm back into his pocket. Then he picked up Elrod's rifle and tossed it into an old milk carton strapped to the back of Elrod's four-wheeler.

"Yer choice."

Without another word, Elrod jumped onto his vehicle, fired it up, and took off quickly. He charged across the field in a cloud of dust, before disappearing into the fog.

Still shocked and confused, I was suddenly afraid to show myself. I remained hidden in the weeds.

Ian strode across the field, heading right in my direction. I could hear my heart pounding in my ears. A moment or two later, I heard Ian's voice.

"Ye can come out now, Eva," Ian said calmly. "The coast is clear."

Good grief! How long had he known that I'd been there?

CHAPTER 18

Ian always made my heart race. Probably, he made *every* woman's heart race.

Still, this time, my heart was racing for a different reason. For one, I'd nearly been shot to death. The bullet that blew off Elrod's cap could only have missed me by a foot or so, maybe less. And also, Ian had shown me a side that I'd never known before. Something kind of smouldery and dark. Plus, he'd caught me in the middle of my impromptu recon mission. *Awkward.*

I didn't know what to think as I stood up slowly from my hiding spot in the weeds. Still, as Ian drew closer, swooping through the grasses with his gorgeous frame and unmistakable long, swinging strides, I could feel a smile growing on my face. I couldn't help it. Despite everything, I was relieved to see him. I marched across the field to meet him, replaying it all in my head—Ian's curt dismissal of Elrod Twiggs's very real threat with a rifle. Ian's obvious and meticulous preplanning for the perfect setup—with his accomplice at the ready. Ian's accusation about Elrod murdering his brother, followed by his ballsy warning. It all made Ian Collier seem even more complex and mysterious than before.

The guy could've been a freaking James Bond.

As the two of us strode across the meadow—each step bringing us closer and closer together—I imagined we were in some sort of cheesy scene from a spy movie where the two star-crossed spy-lovers finally come together in one climactic, steamy embrace . . .

"Ian! What are you doing here?"

Despite my earlier misgivings about the rifle shot, I was suddenly, completely nonchalant about the rifle incident. Sometimes, even *I* can't explain what I'm doing, or why.

Silly schoolgirl with a crush.

Facing each other for the second time that day, this time in waist-high timothy grass and chickweed (well, waist-high for me; not even hip-high for Ian), we'd stopped just as the red-tailed hawk with its distinctive *cheeyoo-cheeyoo-cheeyoo* cried. I looked up, hoping to see it soar above us, except the air was blanketed in white mist.

"I should be asking ye the same question," Ian said. And it seemed that he was being as unexplainably nonchalant about the awkward incident as I was.

Fine, I thought. *We'll just go with it. Maybe he has the same movie in mind.*

"What are ye doin' out here in the wilderness, Eva? Surely, yer not all by yerself? Are ye feeling alright . . . after hitting yer head earlier?"

When he said the word "wilderness," it sounded more like "welderness."

Even in the middle of the "welderness," his pricey slacks remained perfectly pressed. The button-down collar of his crisp, custom-tailored cotton shirt framed the flawless skin on his tawny face. Ian's strong jaw was tight as his deep green eyes flashed concern.

God, he's a hunk. How can a guy this amazing still be single? Must be some fatal flaw . . .

"Eva?"

"Sorry."

I'd let my mind wander and neglected to answer the man. *Idiot!*

"I'm fine. Really. I got a flat tire. I was walking home on the road when I saw your Hummer in the bushes. I thought I'd come and find you."

Ian frowned and gave me a serious look. Gently, he touched my chin with his long fingers. They felt soft and warm. Strong. Again, I smelled his musky bouquet of earthy oakmoss, vetiver, and leather. There was a hint of pine in his scent, with lingering pungent smoke. He smelled every bit the wealthy outdoorsman that he appeared to be. And every bit as damn sexy as he looked, too.

Just like always.

My insides flipped.

Ian tipped my chin up with his hand.

"Ye got a flat tire? Where? Are ye alright, girl?" His deep green eyes flickered as he drew himself near, studying my face. "Ye haven't answered me. Are ye all alone here?"

I sighed. "I'm just mad at myself, that's all. Burl Lee warned me that Daddy's old truck wasn't roadworthy, but I went ahead and took it, anyway. I blew a tire out on the other side of Benderman's Curve."

"Blew a tire? At Benderman's Curve? Again, at that *same* curve? Are ye dotty?"

I shrugged and made a ditzy face as Ian frowned, dropping his hand from my chin.

"That damn curve in the road doesn't like ye very much now, does it?"

He was referring to the fact that Benderman's Curve was the *exact* spot where I'd totaled my car earlier that summer. And afterward, it'd been Ian who'd come to my rescue. In fact, he'd come to my rescue more than once. It was becoming an all-too-regular thing, this knight-in-shining-armor stuff. Still, as long as I didn't kill myself crashing and falling, how could I possibly mind being rescued by one of the sexiest, most intriguing men alive?

From somewhere behind us, I heard an engine start. It sounded like a motorcycle. It roared off.

"Mister Lurch," said Ian, reading my mind. "My partner in crime." He gave me a mischievous look.

So, Ian's manservant, Mister Lurch, is more than butler and chauffeur. He's a damn sharpshooter! Holy smoke.

Still, neither one of us mentioned what'd just happened with Elrod and the rifle shot. It was like, we had some sort of unspoken *understanding*.

"Did ye call for help?" he asked.

"What?"

"I said, Eva, did ye call someone for help? After ye broke down in the curve?"

"No. I don't have my phone with me."

"Not carrying a phone with ye? Again? I swear, girl . . ."

Ian whipped out his smartphone from a vest pocket and punched in a single number. Then he handed me the phone.

"What's this?"

"Ye can't just leave yer truck on the side of the road . . . People will come lookin' for ye. And ye need to let the authorities know that we're gonna get it towed right away. Or they'll tow it for ye and yer gonna have to pay to get it out of the slammer."

"*You* left *your* Hummer up there."

Why I argued with the man, I'll never know.

"I left my Hummer *off* the road. *Hidden* in the bushes. Or so I thought it was hidden. I didn't count on old eagle eye here findin' it."

He tapped my temple with his finger, teasingly.

"Hello?"

I heard a familiar voice on the other end of Ian's cell phone. Realizing who it was, I shook my head and tried to hand the phone back to Ian.

"Hello?" The drawl was low and smooth, distinctly Southern.

Ian crossed his arms, refusing to take back his phone.

"Ye got yerself into this one; now ye need to take care of business," he said. "*This time*, I'm taking ye home. And I'll arrange to get yer truck out. *After* ye talk to yer man . . ."

"Ian?" called out the voice on the phone. "Ian, is that you?"

"Go on," ordered Ian.

I held the phone to my ear.

"No, Buck," I said, with a sigh. "It's me. Eva."

Ian nodded his approval. I rolled my eyes.

"Eva? Why are you calling me on Ian's phone. Is he alright? Are *you* alright?"

"Yes. Yes. We're fine."

"Then, what is it? What's going on? Oh, wait. Please, don't tell me you've gotten yourself into more trouble . . ."

Ian flashed an all-knowing smile and shook his head.

"I left Daddy's farm truck down in a ditch near Benderman's Curve. There's obliterated tire bits all over the road. I'm just calling at Ian's insistence to let the local authorities—that's you, apparently—know that there were no casualties or fatalities and that the truck will be removed . . ."

"Within the hour," whispered Ian.

". . . within the hour."

"Okay, I'll let the guys on patrol know." There was silence for a moment. "Christ, Eva, did you say you were in your dad's old farm truck? *The rust bucket?* I can't imagine what you were doing in that death trap. It wasn't road safe twenty years ago; it certainly isn't road safe now. What the *hell* were you doing in that *relic*—"

"Right. Got it. Bye now." I clicked off the phone and handed it back to Ian.

"Well, that's a dandy way to treat Abundance's finest." Ian chortled, shaking his head in mock disgust.

"I didn't know you and Buck were so chummy as to be on speed-dial terms. Live and learn."

"Aye. Live and learn." Ian smiled. "Yer a mite cheeky this afternoon, Mistress Eva, aren't ye? Especially given the day ye've had. I didn't know when I'd seen ye at the parade that there'd been another accident at yer place."

"Accident . . . ?"

I was so focused on Ian's sexy form and sparkly green eyes that I actually had to think for a moment. It wasn't the truck he was talking about . . .

Oh yeah.

Dex.

"Oh. *That,*" I said, trying to sound casual. "Yes. All in all, the day's been pretty awful, actually." *And it'll probably get worse.* "How did you hear?"

"Precious. She's like communications central. Ye know how the folks in town just love to blether."

"*Blether?* I'm afraid it's kind of an Abundance ritual."

"Precious doesn't miss a beat of it, mind ye. Best estate manager a man could have. Friend, too. Anyway, she told me all about yer unfortunate discovery earlier today. Seems that ye knew the bloke?"

"Something like that." I bit my lip. "A long time ago. I hadn't seen him in years."

"Aye." Ian nodded. "I'm sorry fer yer loss."

Ian studied me. I tried to give away nothing. Still, as he looked me over I realized that he was staring at my fists. Without realizing it, I'd clenched them when we'd started talking about Dex.

After a long moment, Ian smiled and said, "Shall we head back?"

"Sure. As long as I haven't cut short your visit here."

We started walking. I nodded to the fancy rifle he carried under his arm. It looked antique. Only it had a modern, big, fancy scope mounted on top of it.

"Are you hunting?" I asked. It was a loaded question, of course.

"Nah. 'Tisn't the season fer it."

I pressed him. "I'm not into guns, at all. Still, it's impossible not to notice your fancy rifle. Really, I've never seen anything like it, with double triggers and all!"

Ian stopped and held out the piece so I could get a better look. It really was a marvelous firearm. Almost like art.

"I love all the hand engraving on the bolt handle and knob. And all the floral and tendril engraving on the wood," I gushed as I turned over the old firearm, examining it more closely. It really was spectacular. "Wow . . . there's engraving *everywhere* . . . on the wood, the silver . . . the checkered panels with fleur-de-lis accents. And the engraved silver on the floor plate . . . Is that a woodland scene, with a stag and deer? This is a gorgeous piece."

"I'm glad ye appreciate it. I've a wee collection of antique firearms back at home. This is one of my favorites. It's a prewar custom Sempert & Krieghoff. German."

"So if you weren't hunting"—I raised my eyebrows— "then . . . ?" I handed the gun back to Ian.

"I was just enjoyin' the afternoon, roamin' the land, and havin' a look-see."

"A look-see?" I teased. "Is that Scottish for snooping around? Are you thinking about buying Twiggs Creek Farm? Is that why you were chatting with Elrod?" *Good one, Eva. You're oh-so-clever, calling their slow burn of a conversation "chatting."*

Ian looked thoughtful as we began walking across the field again. Still, he didn't answer.

"It's certainly lovely out here," I added, for good measure. *Isn't anyone going to mention the rifle shot?*

Finally, Ian laughed. It was a great big laugh. In that moment, it occurred to me that Ian's expressions usually weren't indicative of a happy, laughy person. Instead, he often appeared . . . troubled. Distracted. *Intense.* Some might even say broody. Almost never lighthearted or content. And yet, when he wanted to, he had such a wonderful sense of humor. *Just like all those irresistible Bond types.*

"I was wondering when you'd find the nerve to ask," he said with a smile. He reached out and held some thistle aside as I passed through the prickly weeds. "I'm here because I saw on my night cam some folks running about here during the night. And I thought I'd come down here today for a look-see, to figure out what they'd been up to. I'm carrying the rifle because there's been reports of a mama bear and two cubs runnin' about these parts. A person can't be too careful, ye know. Besides"—he tapped the big fancy scope mounted to the old rifle—"the scope is handy. Lets me see far away. That's how I knew it was you, comin' down from the road, before I met up with Elrod."

His answer sounded like a plausible reason to be carrying

a rifle with a monster scope in the open wilderness when it wasn't hunting season. Still, why would Ian Collier have a night camera on the Twiggs property? And still, there was the whole, as-yet-unspoken-about incident with Elrod and Mister Lurch. I looked up at Ian's ruggedly elegant face.

Do you think I didn't notice that my head almost blew off?

I tried to keep up with him as he strode quickly across the field, heading toward the road. Of course, what Ian was doing there wasn't any of my business. Still, being my nosy self, I figured it couldn't hurt to be direct and ask. Besides, someone had shot a rifle that could've easily *killed* me. Unspoken understanding or not, I deserved an explanation.

Anyone would.

"Wait! What *about* Elrod?" I asked, trotting to keep up. "The rifle shot!"

Ian kept walking.

"Ye were always safe, Eva. Mister Lurch is a dead-eye shot. I'm sorry if we frightened ye. He and I just needed to sort out a few things with Mister Twiggs. That's all," he said. After a moment he continued. "Elrod Twiggs has been poaching and running stills on this land for years. I grant ye, he's even got a marijuana plot out here somewhere; I just haven't found it yet."

"Yes. That's what I've heard. Still, I don't understand," I said. "Isn't this *his* land? Elrod's, I mean. After his brother died, didn't Elrod inherit everything? I remember he used to have some sort of shack down on the river, right? And why would *you* have a night camera out here?"

"Yer right, this land always belonged to Elrod's brother, Elroy. He was a good man. And we had an arrangement. The place officially became mine last week."

"So *you* own the Twiggs place now?"

"Aye, I do."

"I see." I thought for a moment as we continued walking. We were in the island of shaded forest between the fields. "So, I guess the Dicers just forgot to remove their for sale sign out on the road after you bought the farm?"

Ian stopped. "Elroy and I'd had our agreement in place

before he died. Regardless, Elrod decided the property was his to sell. It wasn't. Most likely, the Dicers are pissed at me for owning property they thought they'd be selling for an absurdly inflated price to someone from overseas, earning themselves a fat commission."

"I see."

"Determined to squeeze whatever they can for themselves, no doubt, they're now determined to at least have folks *believe* they're in on the deal. *My* deal. They'll leave their sign on the road until I toss it. Which will be momentarily."

"Right. No love lost between you and the Dicers . . ."

"Don't get me started."

Ian set his jaw as we marched through the trees. Finally, I said, "I'm just grateful to have found you out here. It'd have taken me an hour or more to walk home."

Ian stopped and turned to face me. His expression was completely matter-of-fact. With his rifle tucked under his arm, he grasped both my hands and held them tight within his big hands, close to his chest.

"I'm sorry, Eva, we frightened ye earlier in the field. Ye know I'd never let anything happen to ye."

I nodded.

"Now, ye won't need to mention to anyone what it is ye saw happen out here today. About Mister Lurch and all, now, will ye?"

"Of course I won't say a word," I said. "Besides, I get it. This is your property now. I'll just think of it like . . . Vegas."

"Las Vegas?"

"Yes, you know, like the city's marketing slogan: 'What happens in Vegas stays in Vegas.' Get it? From now on, we'll just say, 'What happens on Twiggs Creek Farm stays on Twiggs Creek Farm.'"

Ian laughed as he put his free arm around me and gave me a warm bear hug, nestling me in the crook of his arm.

"Aye, Eva. Sounds like a plan."

I let my head fall against his chest and inhaled his seductive scent for just a moment too long. My insides did a few excited flips as he let me rest there for a moment or two—I could've stayed there forever—safe and warm, before Ian pulled me away and surprised me by pressing his lips against my cheek.

"'Tis a right bonnie place out here, isn't it?"

I nodded.

"It'd be a shame if it were to fall into the wrong hands."

I nodded again. Although I had no idea what he was talking about.

Wrong hands?

Ian held me another moment as he took in the field behind us. I spun around to see that the fog was beginning to lift.

"Now let's get ye back on home before that ol' mama bear catches a whiff of us."

CHAPTER 19

Clearly, my sister Pep was in her element. Holding court behind a bar made from old railroad ties covered with about fifty layers of varnish, Pep chitchatted and flirted good-naturedly with patrons while serving them drinks. Wafting through cigar and cigarette smoke, I detected an underlying odor of old fruit, damp wood, and liquor-soaked bar towels. Not that my sister didn't keep her workspace spic-and-span. She did. It's just that decades of booze and food spills were ingrained in every soggy nook and cranny of the joint.

I can't believe I let Precious twist my arm into coming here tonight.

Seated at the very end of the Roadhouse bar, waiting for Precious to return from the ladies' room, I'd been amusing myself by eavesdropping on other people's conversations as I twizzled a little red stirrer in my iced cola.

Pep turned and reached way up to a top shelf in front of a mirrored wall that was jam-packed with booze bottles. After grabbing an unopened bottle of Pappy Van Winkle's Family Reserve 15 Year Old Kentucky Straight Bourbon Whiskey, she quickly opened it before slamming a speed pourer into the vessel. She upturned the pricey bottle high into the air, and amber liquid streamed from the speed pourer. My sister's big, soulful gray eyes sparkled under the spotlights as she moved the upturned booze bottle over four shot glasses and set one next to the other in a semicircle on a cork-lined tray. She never spilled a drop. All the while she kept one eye on the crowded, smoke-filled barroom around us. With her humor and quick smile, not to mention her curvaceous little figure, she was every man's dream . . . at least for that Saturday night.

And she knew it.

Next to me at the bar, a group of dusty "regulars" seated on bentwood stools ogled their favorite platinum blonde with her short, boyish haircut, as she worked the drinks *and* the crowd.

"Ooooh-weee!" cried a man on the other side of the empty seat next to me. Wearing jeans and a tattered long-sleeved shirt, he set his grimy baseball cap, riddled with dirt, on the bar near his arm. Pointing a calloused finger to the bottle of Pappy Van Winkle's bourbon, he grinned. "Sure ya don't wanna give ol' Pervis Jessup a little taste, Miss Pep? Just to make sure it's not gone bad, of course . . ."

Pervis, probably in his sixties, winked as he and his friends seated alongside him rubbed elbows and laughed together.

"I'm a beer man myself, but that bottle there must be something," cried the weatherworn farmer seated next to Pervis. "It's *some* pricey stuff, I hear!" Small and scruffy-looking, the farmer wore tan Carhartt overalls. He swigged the last drops of beer from his bottle.

"Pervis, I'd be happy to give y'all the whole bottle," said Pep with a laugh, "if I thought you'd pay for it. The tip alone might buy me a new air impact wrench. Still, I know better, sweetheart."

She patted Pervis on the hand before moving down the bar to grab a fresh pile of cocktail napkins. Seated about halfway down to my left was a big man with a white beard dressed in a worn plaid shirt and overalls—I likened him to a farmy

Santa Claus. He let out a big belly laugh as he slammed his beer down, leaned over the bar, and pointed to Pervis.

"Pervis, you'll never get a lick of that stuff, 'cause you're tighter than a bull's ass at fly time!"

"And ya still don't have a pot to piss in, or a window to throw it out of!" shouted a tidy fellow in pressed jeans and a faded chambray shirt, seated between the Carhartt man and Santa Claus. He *hee-hawed* a laugh as Santa Claus smacked him on the back.

"You got that right, Jimmy Ray!" said Santa Claus between chuckles.

The men roared together, slapping their hands on the bar before playfully whacking one another on their shoulders. Pep grabbed a handful of beer bottles from the cooler behind her, snapped off the caps, and placed a fresh beer in front of each man.

"Miss Pep, I *love* ya, darlin'!" purred Pervis.

"I love you, too, Pervis. Now drink up, hon, so I can afford to buy me a Millermatic 252 MIG welder for Daddy's old Farmall M tractor. I'm aimin' to fix it up, and you're gonna help me do it, sweetcakes."

"Your daddy always told me," said Pervis with a wink, "that if something needed fixin' on the farm, his daughter Pep was the man fer the job!" He took a swig of beer and laughed at himself.

"You get yourself a fancy welder like that, sweetheart, you let me know. I'll have you busy as a beaver over at my place. I got tons of equipment that needs work," said the farmy Santa Claus.

"Me, too," said Pervis.

"Boys, it's a deal," said Pep, laughing. "Now drink up!"

Pep patted each man on his hand before slapping her pile of napkins on the tray with the four shots of bourbon. She picked up the tray and rounded the end of the bar, passing me, on her way to a table buried somewhere in the boisterous crowd behind me.

It was about nine thirty on Saturday night, and the Roadhouse was rocking. Decorated with dark-stained wood and railroad memorabilia, the dingy establishment was full up with folks seated on cheap bentwood chairs around sticky, carved-up wooden tables. Just down the road from the chemical plant, on the seedier side of town next to some abandoned railroad tracks not too far from the Big Swamp, the local watering hole was located inside a defunct railroad station. Suntanned farmers and laborers in grime-infused jeans and overalls wearing ball caps and long-sleeved plaid and chambray shirts mingled with women and men dressed in casual business attire—village retailers, most likely—along with folks in blue uniforms sporting Climax Chemical Company logos, as well as the younger set of social "movers and shakers," out on the town for a Saturday date night.

Really, almost everyone in town stopped by the Roadhouse at one time or another. Except my sister Daphne, of course. She'd rather have her fingernails pulled out than step foot in a "dive" like the Roadhouse.

Still, for the rest of Abundance County, the Roadhouse was *the* place to be and to be seen, especially on weekends. Mostly because of the music. Not to mention the fact that it was the only bar in town. And as the favorite haunt for Abundance County's sheriff's deputies, the official late-night closing hours per county regulations were often . . . *overlooked* on weekends.

Serving simple tavern-style meals and late-night takeout, as long as you didn't mind a little grease with everything, the dive was never busier than on weekend nights when there was a live band in the house. In one corner of the smoky room, on a small plywood stage, a trio of men with tattooed arms and footlong beards, dressed in black jeans and cowboy boots, worked to set up their instruments—I saw an electric guitar, a bass, one man carried a fiddle case—behind big speakers that read PEAVEY. A fabric sign that read THE CROP PICKERS hung crookedly on the wall behind the band as they crawled around the tiny stage opening cases and plugging in cords.

"Y'all are mighty chipper tonight," said Pep, returning to

the men at the bar. She gave me a wink. "Peanut, are y'all doin' some celebratin' or something?"

Peanut—the man who looked like Santa Claus—gulped the last dregs of his beer before slamming the empty bottle on the counter. After exhaling with a satisfied sigh, he wiped his sleeve across his beard.

"I reckon we are, darlin'. Aren't we, boys?"

The other two men—like Pervis and Peanut—appeared to be in their sixties, or maybe even well-preserved seventies. They nodded in unison, before downing the last of their bottled beers.

"Yep."

Beyond Peanut, a bedraggled mechanic, not much older than I was, with muscular shoulders, sinewy hands, and a grease-stained tee shirt, grabbed a worn cocktail napkin. He wiped a dribble of beer from his weathered lips before tossing the napkin on the counter.

"Ya see, Miss Pep," said Peanut. "Jimmy Ray, here, just closed on his farm. Three generations and one hundred years of hard work . . . a lifetime . . . all gone. Sold to some foreigners. Ain't that right, Jimmy Ray?" He whacked Jimmy Ray on the back again. "How do ya feel, buddy?"

"I feel rich, that's how I feel," Jimmy Ray said with a silly grin, wiping a hand on his Carhartts.

"Sold your pappy's farm?" Pep interrupted.

Jimmy Ray belched. Seems that was enough of an acknowledgment for Pep.

"Well, congratulations, Jimmy Ray," said Pep. "I didn't know you were plannin' on retiring, hon. How 'bout a round of drinks, on me? Since this is an extra-special occasion, how 'bout some shots of Savannah 88 bourbon? Sound alright?"

The men at the bar mumbled and nodded in unison.

"Oh, waitron!" a man barked from the far corner in the room.

Pep grabbed several glasses and the Savannah 88 bottle from behind the bar and began pouring.

"Waitron!" shouted the man from the corner again. Even

in the crowded room, his voice cut through the noise. He had a distinctly Northern accent. "Another round! And make it pronto!"

That was rude . . .

I started to turn when someone tapped me on the shoulder.

"The ladies' room is a pisser!" cried Precious, sliding onto the barstool next to me. "Every time I come to this joint I forget how nasty it is. I must be dumber than a sack of hammers 'cause I keep comin' back for more." She rolled her eyes. "Why, it was so dark in there that I could barely find myself in the mirror. Naturally, touching anything was *completely* outta the question . . ."

"Sorry about that, Precious," Pep said from the other side of the counter. "I gotta double as waitress for another hour or so. Nettie Perle had to take her granddaddy to the hospital tonight. His heart ain't right again. She's comin' in late. Until then, there's no one here to serve tables or tidy up the ladies' room 'cept me . . ."

Precious started fishing for something inside her purple alligator purse.

"Hey, did y'all hear about the Twiggs place . . . It's sold!" someone down the bar said.

"No kidding!" said Pervis.

"And I hear that Taylor Farm might be goin' under contract . . . any day now," said Jimmy Ray.

"Sure ain't gonna be like it used to be around these parts . . ."

"Here ya go, gentlemen," said Pep. She slid the Savannah 88 shots in front of the farmers at the bar.

"Hey, you! Waitron!" shouted the gruff voice from the corner.

This time, the voice sounded familiar. My stomach churned. I didn't dare look.

Surely, it can't be.

"We need another round . . . and before *tomorrow*!" he boomed.

I started to turn again to look, when Precious grabbed my hands, pulling me around, toward her.

"Here, Sunshine," said Precious. "You mind holdin' this stuff for a sec? I don't dare set it on the bar, on account of all the germs."

"Hey!" cried Pep. "I heard that."

Precious wasn't listening. She was too busy shoving half the contents of her purse into my hands . . . purple alligator wallet, sparkly smartphone, reading glasses, embroidered linen hanky, lipstick, address book, sewing kit . . .

"*I swaney!* Where is my compact? It's like I'm a blind dog in a meat house," she mumbled.

She kept jamming the contents of her purse in my hands.

Smiling, Pep set four shot glasses on her tray. Then she grabbed the Pappy Van Winkle's bourbon. Again, she raised the bottle in the air and poured out four perfect shots. She grabbed the tray of bourbon, holding it high with one hand as she headed to the end of the bar. Tapping me on the arm, she rounded the end of the counter and tipped her head toward my watered down cola.

"I'll be right with ya in a sec."

I nodded.

"No prob," said Precious, yanking out her sparkly compact. "We got *all* night. Don't we, Sunshine?" She grinned at me. It'd been a statement, not a question. That's because Precious had the car.

CHAPTER 20

I rolled my eyes.

A full foot taller than I was, even seated, I had no doubt that Amazonian Precious was the biggest person in the bar that night. If she'd been a man, no doubt she'd have shopped at a big-and-tall store. That is, if they'd carried designer clothes.

For an estate manager, she sure makes a pile of money.

Precious tugged at her screaming yellow silk skirt. Then she flipped open the glittery compact from her purple alligator purse and checked herself in the teeny compact mirror.

"It's actually brighter out here at the bar than it was in the ladies' room. A ladies' room needs to have decent lighting."

"Precious, this is the Roadhouse. We're probably lucky there are any lights at all."

Satisfied, Precious snapped the compact shut and dropped it back into the bag on her lap. She fanned her coppery face with a well-manicured man-sized hand.

"Um, Precious," I said. Pointedly, I looked down at all the stuff from her purse, still piled in my hands.

"Oh, sorry, Sunshine."

She grabbed the pile and crammed everything back into the purple alligator bag on her lap.

"Boy, seems like I ain't been to this dump in ages," she said, looking around the dingy watering hole. "And I mean it in a good way. Although, I forgot how smoky it gets in here. Oh, wait . . ." She reached into her bag and pulled out her smartphone in the glittery gold case. "I'm shuttin' off my phone tonight. I don't want anyone to interrupt our girls' night out!"

"Why bother?" I asked. "I don't know how you could hear a phone in here, anyway . . . it's so noisy."

"Noisy?" asked Pep as she crossed back behind the bar. "Ha! Hon, you ain't heard nothing yet. Just wait until the band starts."

Precious lifted a tree-trunk-sized leg to show off a spiky purple linen Louboutin pump. "Ugh. These shoes are *brandee*-new! And already they're sticky on the bottom. I hate sticky shoes."

"No worries!" cried Pep. "Just like it'll kill the germs on the bar"—she winked—"alcohol will help anything that ails ya. Drink up, Miss Precious, and you'll never notice your sticky shoes."

"Ha!" Precious laughed.

"So what can I get y'all? Eva, darlin', you look like you could use something extra stiff. That cola you've been nursin' sure ain't gonna do the trick. Not after the day you've had. Findin' that stiff in the pond . . . yikes! Only you, sweetie. Only you."

"Your little sister's bottom lip is poochin' out so far, a whole flock of turkeys could set on it," said Precious to Pep. "That's why I insisted our Little Miss Sunshine come out with me. Pining away in that dinky cottage of hers, moping after findin' another dead man and blowin' out a tire on her daddy's truck ain't solvin' nothing."

"Precious has a point, Eva. You're turning into a hermit. Y'all need to get out more often. Why don't ya give Buck a call, hon?" She raised her eyebrows and lowered her chin, making a smarty face. "A little nooky can't hurt a girl."

"Very funny," I said.

"Ooooh, yes! Why not call Sheriff Sexy Pants for a date! I've seen the way he looks at you . . . That hunk of burnin' love lusts for ya big-time! I just know it!" Precious looked from side to side, like she had a big secret. Then she whispered, "I can see it in his peepers." She winked.

Pep let out a big snort. "Buck's always had the hots for Eva. I think he's just doin' Debi Dicer to keep himself in shape . . . for the time when Eva comes to her senses."

"Mmmm-hmmm." Precious nodded in agreement. "And don't he have the most pinchable butt!"

"Stop it, you two. Pep, don't mention Debi. Ever. She makes me crazy. And both of you, I'm not interested in Buck. Or any man these days. Remember my man moratorium? I haven't exactly had a lot of success with men, you know."

"Yeah . . . well, we all make mistakes," laughed Pep. "Look at me and Billy . . . he's run clear off to Alabama to hide out with his mommy after cheatin' on me." Abruptly, she frowned. Then she flapped her hand and smiled. "So, what'll y'all be havin' tonight?"

"I'll have another one of your badass pierced fuzzy navels, Miss Pep," said Precious, holding up her empty glass. "Grey Goose vodka, please. Heavy on the peach schnapps. Thank you."

"Hear, hear!" cried someone down the bar.

Pep grinned as she flipped a switch on the wall behind the bar. Up high on the wall, a toy train started up, slowly chugging its way around a near-ceiling-height track encircling the room. As the toy engine *toot-tooted*, the men seated down the bar suddenly stopped talking and chugged their drinks all at once.

Pep watched me, watching the men. "Tradition," she explained. "When the train toots, folks take a shot."

"Good golly gosh, girl." Precious slapped me on the shoulder. "Where y'all been hidin' all your life? *Everyone* knows that!" She laughed.

I rolled my eyes. "I'll just have another cola," I said.

"Party pooper," said Pep. She made a mock sad face.

"Ya know, Sunshine, I think a better idea is for me to buy you a shot of what *those* folks had."

Like Precious, I spun around on my barstool to look across the smoky room. Precious nodded toward the dark corner where a small group was talking animatedly around a big, round table. In front of them were the four shot glasses of bourbon that Pep had recently poured and delivered.

"Oh God," I said, quickly spinning back to face the bar.

The Boston crowd.

They were the *last* people I wanted to see. Especially on this night. Hadn't the day been bad enough? Apparently, I hadn't noticed when they'd entered the place and seated themselves at the table in the far corner. They'd been the group who'd ordered the Pappy Van Winkle's bourbon. Seeing them confirmed my worst fear. It'd been Wiggy calling *waitron*.

I groaned.

"How'd *they* find out about this place?"

"I told them," Pep answered brightly. "I ran into the big guy with the beard, the one who looks like Yogi Bear—"

"Wiggy," I said.

"Right. Well, I ran into him earlier today, and he asked me if I knew any place in town where he and his buds could drown their sorrows about their dead friend. I suggested they come here, of course."

"Crap." With my elbows on the bar, I put my head in my hands. "Just crap."

Nodding to Pep, Precious pointed to the Pappy Van Winkle's bourbon.

"I figure anything you got stashed high up on a shelf like that is either real bad stuff or extra-special stuff. And judgin' by the gleam in your little eye, I'm thinking this is the extra-special stuff. Plus, the group you've been servin' it to looks real happy, even after their friend croaked in the pond today. So I'll have me some, please. Pour Miss Poopy Pants one, too. My treat."

"Miss Precious, unless you've won the lottery lately, you

may want to rethink that notion," said Pep. "That particular vintage of Pappy Van Winkle's retails for more than thirteen hundred dollars a bottle."

"What?"

The farmer seated next to Precious whistled.

Pep smiled coyly. "The group from Boston said they wanted somethin' to commemorate the passin' of their friend. And they said that money was no object. Who am I to say no? I poured out the priciest bottle in the house."

"To Dex!" roared the Bostoners from their table in the corner.

Watching in the mirror behind the bar, I could just barely make them out. Holding their drinks high in the air, they clinked their glasses together before throwing back their heads to chug the pricey booze.

"Heavens to Murgatroyd!" Precious gasped. She snapped open her alligator purple purse. "Thirteen hundred dollars? Why, that's enough to buy a pair of Louboutins!"

"Sure is," agreed Pep. "Or a six-and-a-half to seven-and-a-half-inch truck suspension lift kit."

"I got no idea what that is, Miss Pep. Still, the point is, thirteen hundred dollars is a whole lotta cash to piss away," chortled Precious. "And I mean that literally."

"You're right about that, hon!" Pep snorted little piglet giggles. "Still, the fifteen-year Pappy Van Winkle's bourbon is cheaper than Pappy Van Winkle's *twenty-year* reserve. A bottle of *that* costs nearly *two thousand* bucks. And the *twenty-three-year* reserve is closer to *three* thousand! Alas, we don't carry it, or I would've served it to the folks from Boston." She broke out into little piglet snorts again.

I shook my head. "I'll stick to cola."

"Suit yourself," Pep said with a shrug.

Precious slapped a hundred-dollar bill down on the bar.

"Since the bottle's already opened, pour Miss Sunshine a shot of Pappy Van Winkle's thirteen-hundred-dollar bourbon. Me, too. Neat. No need to let it go to waste." She looked over her shoulder and frowned. "Or to waste it all on a bunch of rude folks from up North." She slapped a second hundred-dollar bill on the bar. Then a third. "Keep the change." She snapped her purple alligator purse shut.

Pep squealed, "Thanks!"

At the same moment, I moaned, "Are you kidding?"

Before Precious could change her mind, Pep grabbed the pricey bottle of bourbon along with two shot glasses and poured our drinks, sliding one small glass with the potent amber liquor in front of each of us. Precious raised her shot glass, waiting for me to pick up mine.

"C'mon, Sunshine. If ever someone needed a shot of bourbon, it looks to be you. You sure know how to rack up a pile of dead men. Not to mention vehicles. Drink up!"

"Fine," I said. "But only because I've never tasted a fifteen-year-old bourbon before. This is a learning experience."

Pep snorted a laugh as she flipped a switch under the bar and the toy train *toot-tooted*. The old men at the bar next to Precious raised their drinks.

"Here's to mud in your eye!" cried Precious.

"Cheers!" cried the men.

Together, Precious and I, along with everyone else sitting at the bar, tipped our heads back and guzzled our drinks.

"Mmm," said Precious with a big grin. "Warm and smooth as silk. I might hafta get me a bottle of my own to take home! Although, come to think of it, maybe Mister Collier has some of this . . ."

"And what was it you said your boss does?" I asked. The bourbon made my eyes water.

"Now, Sunshine, you know right well that I never said what it is that Mister Collier does. And I ain't planning to say it, neither, even to you. He's a private person, and he pays me real good to keep my mouth shut. And as much as I love ya more than bacon, I'm not singin' till the day I die."

I shook my head.

"Miss Pep," called Precious with a grin, "don't forget my pierced fuzzy navel!"

Pep laughed as she made her way to the other end of the bar. "You're a woman after my own heart, darlin'. Comin' right up."

"I need a cola chaser, please," I said.

"Oh, waitron!" Wiggy shouted from the table in the corner. "Another round!"

Pep smiled and gave the loudmouth a wave. "I'll be right with y'all in a minute, hon," she shouted across the room. I doubted he could hear her.

I peeked over my right shoulder. Wiggy was dressed in a polka-dot bow tie, oxford cloth shirt, and natty tweed jacket. *Looks like Smokey Bear got dressed at Brooks Brothers.* He pursed his lips together and puffed on his pipe.

"That fella's just plain rude." Precious huffed. "Even for a Yank. Do you think he murdered the guy in the pond?"

"I take it, by asking the question, that you think Detective Gibbit is finally right this time? About Dex being murdered?" I asked Precious. *Please no. Please no. Please no.*

"Looks like it to me," said Pep. "I mean, at your place, they usually are . . ." She rolled her eyes.

"Thanks for that." I let out an exasperated sigh. "Back to your question, Wiggy's always been a boor. He thinks his charge in life is to insult and order other people around. Still, could he have actually *murdered* somebody? Could any of them? It's certainly hard to imagine that anyone I know could do such a heinous thing."

"You *know* him?" interrupted Pep.

"I know *all* of them. We socialized from time to time when I dated Dex, years ago."

"So, then, I'm guessing that the big, fat argument I heard you had last night at the big house with the dead guy was *old* business," said Pep. "What gives, sis? Why all the secrets?"

"Looks like our Little Miss Sunshine has quite a few secrets up her sleeve, huh?" said Precious.

"I guess you're not the only one keeping a few secrets, Precious. You harbor all kinds of information about Greatwoods that you don't share," I shot back. "Besides, I already came clean. I told you and Daphne earlier today that I knew Dex."

Precious frowned at me.

"You didn't tell *me*!" cried Pep.

"That's not so nice, Sunshine," said Precious to me. "You know that I can't talk about my job at Greatwoods, or Mister Collier. It's not personal. It's work."

"Give me a break, Precious. I don't need to know all the gory details about the man; I just want to know *something* about him. After all, he *is* our next-door neighbor."

"Ha! More likely, ya want to know more about our next-door neighbor 'cause he looks tasty as gobs of butter meltin' on a stack of hot waffles!" Pep giggled.

"I already warned y'all: Stay away from Mister Collier. He's not up for grabs." Precious huffed. "Gobs of melting butter or not, y'all both need to mind your p's and q's."

"Speaking of minding one's p's and q's, Precious, how did you know this morning about the argument Dex and I had at the tasting party last night?"

"Aw, shoot. Everyone in town knows about that!"

"Everyone?"

"Heck, Sunshine. Beula Beauregard was at the tasting, and everyone knows she's got the biggest mouth in town. Anyways, I heard from Coretta Crumm that the dead guy pinched your butt and you didn't take too kindly to it. Then I heard that you called him a . . . what was it? Oh yeah. You called him a 'flipping ass.' Right there in front of *everyone*."

"That I did," I said. "Of course, I doubt Eunice and Eugene Ord heard any of it."

I rolled my eyes.

"I'm sure they were thrilled for the interesting pantomime . . ." Pep sniggered.

"Then, Coretta said that she heard the dead guy called you a tart and a tease, and a few other unflattering things, including a few curse words, and he said you wasn't worth a damn," said Precious.

"That he did."

"And then he grabbed your boob!"

"Yep."

"And after that, you slapped him on the arm when he tried to grab you again. Then you said some bad words and threatened him before you stormed outta the place."

"I'm afraid that's true."

"Damn," whispered Pep, tossing a paper cocktail napkin down on the bar. "Eva, that's not like you at all, hon. Here ya go, Miss Precious."

Pep set down a tall old-fashioned glass with a peachy-colored beverage inside topped with a peach wedge and mint sprig.

"Still no umbrella?" asked Precious.

"Sorry. This is the *Roadhouse*, Miss Precious. Not the Ritz." She looked at me. "Your cola chaser is comin' right up, darlin', although, the more I hear y'all talking, the more I think you need something with a bit more punch."

"Waitron!" cried Wiggy.

Precious frowned. "He's the kind of fella that gives all Yankees a bad name." She took a long sip from her straw. "Maybe all men." She sipped again. "I say he did it. Ummm. This tall, slender drink of peachiness is gooder than grits. Miss Pep, you're one talented barkeep!"

"Glad you like it," said Pep. "Here, hon." She slid my cola across the bar. "Looks like ol' Pappy Van Winkle may have done you a bit of good after all, sis. Already, you're gettin' a little color back in your cheeks. Sure you don't want me to slip a shot of rum in that cola?"

"I'm sure. Thanks."

"So c'mon. Quit holdin' out on me!" whispered Precious. She bumped my shoulder impatiently. "Tell me the details about the folks from Boston. Especially about you and the dead guy!"

"Waitron!"

Several people in the bar turned to stare at Wiggy and his table of Boston "bird-watchers." Then someone from the band hit a chord on the bass guitar, a speaker squealed, and the noise level inside the Roadhouse rose up a notch.

"They all work at the Perennial Paper Company," I said to Precious. "And they're all best friends. Or, at least they were when I knew them. All the men are Dartmouth College grads. Fraternity brothers. After he graduated, Dex became an acquisitions manager for the paper company. Wiggy got his job next, as the acquisitions asset and operations manager. He's always been rude and bossy. Across from him"—I nodded—"the greasy little one wearing a red bow tie . . ."

As the band struck their first chords, the crowd whooped and clapped in appreciation. I raised my voice so Precious could hear me.

". . . is Spencer Andover Fisk."

The band started playing the bluegrass tune "Rocky Top." I leaned closer to Precious so she could hear me.

"He's Perennial Paper's financial manager." Precious nodded as the band played on. "He's every bit the penny-pinching geek he appears to be. And coldhearted as they come. They used to call him the Slasher—to cut costs he'd recommend firing people right and left and never lose a bit of sleep over it. Also, he's completely devoid of any personality or social skills. And the guy next to Spencer is Norcross Cooper Tarbox the Second. He's a lawyer for the paper company."

"Norcross?"

"Everyone calls him 'Coop.'"

Precious cupped her hand to her mouth so I could hear her better. "And I thought we had crazy names down here in the South!" She threw her head back and laughed. "Folks don't give Northerners enough credit." She lifted her drink and took a long sip from her straw. Then she smiled coyly. "I could have me a slice of that hunka burning love. I kinda like those bad-boy types."

"You can do better, Precious. Coop was born with a silver spoon in his mouth. He's a trust fund baby and a total womanizer. Completely immature. I couldn't believe he was one of the first people in our circle to get married. No one could."

Precious nodded toward the skinny blonde woman at the table. "And the lovely Faye Dunaway look-alike?"

"Ha! That's a good one, Precious. She *does* look like a skinny Faye Dunaway. Acts like the actress, too . . . when Faye Dunaway plays an evil character, that is."

"So, I take it that you don't like her much?"

"Not much. But then, the feeling has always been mutual. Her name is Claudia Bacon Devereaux, acquisitions administrator for Perennial Paper. She works, or worked, directly for Dex and managed all his affairs—both in and out of work. He didn't step outside to pee and she didn't know about it . . . or plan it ahead of time."

"And she doesn't like *you* because—"

"I was close to Dex. In her territory. I always suspected that in addition to being his loyal assistant, Claudia held a torch for Dex."

"Makes sense."

"I can't imagine what she'll do without Dex now. She always worshipped the ground Dex walked on. He's been her entire life. And she'd kill anyone who crossed him. I mean that figuratively, of course."

"Of course. But then again, maybe not." Precious raised her eyebrows provocatively. "So, how did they all end up here? Did they come to visit you?"

Some of the barroom crowd began clapping, stomping, and singing along with the band.

"*. . . Good old Rocky Top, Rocky Top Tennessee . . .*"

I leaned in closer to Precious.

"Honestly, Precious, that's what I want to know. Last night at the tasting, Dex insisted that coming here and running into me had been merely a coincidence. They were just on a bird-watching retreat. I doubted his story then. And I doubt it even more tonight. I can't imagine a single one of them having an interest in birds, or nature. Unless it's to shoot something, just for fun."

"And I remember Miss Daphne said he asked to sleep in *your* old room. That hardly sounds like a coincidence to me."

"I agree."

"Okay. Still, you haven't told me about dating this guy. What was *that* all about? And, by the way, why are his folks staring at us?"

I turned to look at the group in the corner.

"They're staring at *your* screaming yellow skirt."

"No. They ain't. They're staring at *you*, Sunshine. What are you not telling me?"

"Yeah," said Pep, sidling up to the other side of the bar.

She never missed a word *anyone* said at the bar. "What exactly is it, Eva, that you're not telling us? There was definitely something fishy going on between you and this dead Dex guy. What gives? I'm getting the impression that he wasn't just some guy you casually dated a few times . . ."

"Good old Rocky Top, Rocky Top Tennessee!"

"I'm going to the ladies' room," I said, sliding off the barstool.

Precious and Pep shook their heads.

"We'll be waiting!" Pep called after me. "Won't we, Precious?"

"Sure will."

CHAPTER 21

It's always been a theory of mine that golf courses and bar-room bathrooms are information gold mines. And that night at the Roadhouse proved me right again.

I'd gone into the ladies' room and, basically, stood in a stall to gather my wits. I knew that I had to come clean to Pep and Precious, and, of course, Daphne, about Dex. *At least the part about our having been engaged.* Still, I worried that even my sisters would think the worst of me once they found out that I'd been secretly engaged to Dex, never told them, and then left Dex. Just like I had with Buck. And then later, Zack Black the weatherman. *I mean, who does that?* Even I knew how crazy my actions had made me look. Precious's plan to take me out to the Roadhouse to distract me from my troubles was backfiring. Big-time.

Like everything else in my life.

My mind was running wild with the thought that someone, someone whom I *knew*, might've actually *murdered* Dex, right on our plantation, right after I'd argued with him. *Talk about a freak-out.* Plus, knowing my history with Dex, I was beginning to seriously panic about my own role in all of this. If it really had been murder, could I be a suspect?

Of course I could be a suspect.

And with good reason.

Standing in one of the two stalls in the dark and dank ladies' room, I attempted to calm myself as I tried to figure out how best to present everything to Precious and Pep, without them thinking that I was a complete and utter jerk. Who wouldn't think I was a jerk? Even *I* thought I was a jerk. Still, admitting to Pep and Precious that I'd not just dated Dex, but that I'd been *engaged* to Dex, was bound to be a lot easier than telling prima donna Daphne. Regardless, it was bound to come out. After all, already, I'd told Buck that Dex and I had been engaged . . .

I dropped my head in my hands.

I'll just have to fess up, to everyone, once and for all.

I groaned.

Still, I need to come clean with Buck first. About all of it. I owe him at least that much . . .

That's when the ladies' room door flew open and the rowdy music from the barroom got real loud while two women stepped into the tiny room. One went into the stall next to me while the other waited by the sink.

"Did ya hear?" said the woman in the stall. "The Switzers sold their plantation. Ray Anne Bobbitt said they're movin' to Key West and buyin' a big place on the beach."

"No kidding?" said the other woman. "Waterfront property in Key West? That must take a *boatload* of money!"

"Sure does. And they got it, too. According to Ray Anne, they got enough money to burn a wet mule. Sold their place for more than three million bucks."

"Three million! For that ol' dump? Why, the house is a total gut job. The barns are barely standing. Fences are all torn up. And the fields are a mess. Who's got money to spend like that around here?"

"No one. I hear they sold it to some outta-towners. Dicky Dicer had some people . . . Chinese, I think."

She flushed the toilet. I heard the stall door squeak open.

"Apparently, they didn't care about the house at all. I even heard they might knock it down. Barns, too."

Water ran in the sink as she washed her hands, followed by the rackety rattling of the decrepit paper towel dispenser. Outside in the barroom, the crowd was clapping and stomping as the fiddler played "The Devil's Dream."

"C'mon, let's get back to the table. This is one of my favorite tunes," said the second woman.

Again, the ladies' room door opened and the bluegrass music filled the dingy bathroom.

"Excuse me," said the first woman.

I heard footsteps move across the floor. Then the door shut. I hadn't even used the toilet. I flushed it anyway. Then I pushed open the door and stepped out into the tiny sink area.

And bumped right into Claudia Bacon Devereaux.

Squinting into the dirty mirror over the pedestal sink, the frail, sinewy blonde was just finishing scrawling bright red lipstick across her lips.

"You!" she screeched when she spied me in the mirror. The bathroom was so small, just a few inches separated us. I could smell her flowery perfume. *Too flowery, too sweet*, I thought. Still, it smelled expensive.

"Hello, Claudia."

She spun around to face me. Clearly, she'd been drinking. She steadied herself with a hand on the cracked sink.

"*You're* the one to blame for all of this!" she seethed. Then she hiccupped. Claudia'd never been a big drinker. "If it weren't for you, Dex would still be alive. You know that? You *killed* him. And that's what I told the detective today. That somehow, someway, you were responsible for Dex's death."

Great.

"Claudia, I'm sorry that Dex is dead. But like I said in the library today, I had nothing to do with his drowning. It was a terrible accident. I've not laid eyes on Dex since I left him years ago. And if you think I knew anything about your coming here, you're dead wrong."

"Funny choice of words," her slurry voice squealed. "I'm

finding it quite remarkable that just hours after you and Dex had a most disagreeable fight, when you *assaulted* and threatened him—in front of *all* of us—he turned up dead. Just like you said you wanted him to be!" As she spoke, Claudia waved one arm, flapping her hand wildly, as she used her other hand to steady herself on the sink.

"Claudia, despite what I might have said in anger, I would never truly wish anyone dead. And I did not *assault* Dex. I defended myself when he reached out to grab me. Still, he grabbed my *breast*! Surely, if someone did that to you, you'd feel upset. Wouldn't you? It was humiliating."

Claudia's head started bobbing. "I get it now," she slurred. "You're the *real* reason Dex dragged us all down here to this Southern hellhole . . . Not land. Not trees! I should've known. Even after all these years, I should've known that he still carried a torch for you. What a fool I was not to see it sooner. That's what I get for going on vacation last month and letting that little sniveling twerp Ophelia Byrd in the office handle travel reservations. Wait till I get back to Boston . . . Her perky little ass is grass. That is, if I even *have* a job when I get back! Oh . . . my . . . God . . ." She started sobbing. "*My job!*" she wailed.

Claudia looked completely wild-eyed. Like a trapped animal.

"Claudia, I'm sure you'll keep your job—"

She wasn't listening.

"I should've *never* hired her in the first place!" ranted Claudia. "With a name like Ophelia Byrd, she was bound to be a ditz. Of course, if I'd handled the reservations *myself*, like I always do, I would've known this was the place where *you* came from. And I would've protected Dex from himself and stopped this little junket to hell before it even started. Now Dex is dead. *Everything* is ruined. All our plans! And clearly, you're to blame."

Red-faced and blotchy, Claudia checked herself out again in the mirror over the pedestal sink before turning on the water faucet. She was shaking.

"Claudia, I understand you're upset. We all are. Still, I

don't see how any of this was my fault. I didn't even know you were in town until you'd already checked in and were seated at dinner last night. Believe me, I was as shocked as anyone to discover you all here. And I'm sorry about Dex. I really am. I can't imagine what happened. Did you all go swimming in the pond last night after the tasting?"

Claudia cupped her hands under the running water.

"Like hell you're sorry. I heard him outside in the yard last night. He was out there, calling you like a crazy, deranged person."

"What?"

She splashed some water on her face as she kept talking, ignoring me completely. Mumbling to herself, I heard her say, "He sounded like he was out of his mind. Screeching out your name, singing . . . When I looked outside, he was dancing and skipping all around the place, like some kind of nutcase. And it was all about you. What did you do?" she shrieked. "Did you hold his head under the stinking, filthy pond water and *kill* him?"

She shut off the water and yanked a paper towel from the dispenser.

"Claudia—"

"If you didn't, you may as well have done it . . . It's all your fault! You should be *ashamed* of the way you treated him . . . running off and leaving him like that all those years ago. God knows, he wasn't perfect. He would've given you anything you wanted! All you had to do was stay with him! And then, after you dumped him, poor, poor Dex insisted that none of us ever mention you again, *ever*!"

She was quietly, somehow, screeching.

"Why, he still loved you. And he protected you!"

"Claudia, what on earth are you talking about?"

She shoved her face up to mine. "After the news came out that you'd dumped Zack Black the weatherman earlier this summer, Dex *still* protected you from all the media! He didn't tell anyone how you'd run off and left him . . . the same way!" She tossed the paper towel into an overflowing trash can. "Then we all found out in the news that you'd dumped some other poor fellow down here, years ago. So that means you left *three* men . . . on your wedding day! Is *no* man good enough for you?"

"Please, stop, Claudia."

"He kept his mouth shut, Dex did. Swearing us all to keep our silence about you. About your secret engagement. And about how you dumped him at the last minute. I even had to cancel your honeymoon reservations on Bora Bora." She turned and put her hand on the bathroom door. "Tramp."

That's it.

I reached around Claudia and put my hand on the door, pressing it shut.

"Did it ever occur to you, Claudia, that Dex didn't want anyone to know that I left him because I left him for a *good reason*? And it was that *reason* that he was afraid would become public, not the fact that I'd left him."

"I know everything there was to know about Dex Codman. None of it mattered. He loved you."

"Claudia, Dex was not the man you thought he was. And if you truly knew him, then you have no business criticizing me. Dex earned what he got. And in my case, that was nothing."

Claudia gave me a steely cold stare. Then very quietly, she said, "No one knew Dex better than I did. *No one.* He wasn't perfect. I know that better than anyone. He had his flaws. He needed someone who understood him. Someone to love him, accept him, no matter what. And he made it abundantly clear to me that person was *you.*"

"I don't understand . . ."

"And how *dare* you speak ill of the dead like this! Now let me out of here!"

Clearly even more upset than when she'd entered the ladies' room, Claudia took her nails and dragged them up my outstretched arm, scratching my skin as she swiveled and kicked me in the shin before yanking open the door and storming out of the ladies' room.

Believe it or not, my Roadhouse visit only got worse from there.

CHAPTER 22

I shouldn't have been surprised to discover the Saturday night barroom crowd had nearly doubled in size during the few minutes I'd been in the ladies' room. On weekends, most folks didn't show up much before the band started playing.

As I stepped into the crowd, I watched Claudia as she pushed her way through people, weaving and stomping back to the table in the corner where Spencer was holding his phone up to his face, no doubt playing some game. Puffing on his pipe, with a full shot glass and a fresh pint of beer in front of him, Wiggy studied the barroom crowd, while Coop chugged a beer from a bottle while a busty young woman wearing too-tight everything sat in his lap, giggling. I shook my head. It was Maisy Merganthal.

I wanted to warn her, but then, I knew she'd never listen to me. As I'd been once, she was just out of college. She knew it all . . .

I rolled my eyes.

I scanned the rest of the room. Except for my own seat next to Precious, all the seats at the bar were filled, as were all the tables. The place was mobbed.

Standing in the back of the room near the entrance, I was immersed in a crowd noisily chatting and drinking—giant mugs of beer, mostly—as they waited for seats that would probably never become available. Pressing through the drunken crowd, I worked my way along the back wall, headed toward the door, where a path cut through the roomful of tables straight to the bar.

A roar of cheers and applause erupted as the band strummed the first few notes of "Orange Blossom Special." People jostled around, trying to get a better view of the tiny stage in the corner. A big elbow knocked me hard.

"Oh, uh, sorry," said a tall, farmy guy in overalls.

His giant mug of beer toppled from his hand and sloshed all over me, before clattering to the floor. My white tee shirt and most of my black jeans were completely soaked through with beer. Moreover, the big galumph bumped me so hard that I lost my balance and smacked right into someone else.

Debi Dicer.

Crap.

I chastised myself for not noticing Debi's signature bleached blonde inverted bob ahead of me in the mob of people. How could I have missed her? Twice in one day was too much Debi, for sure.

Too late now.

Made up to the nines, as usual, Debi's bright pink lipstick and neon Lilly Pulitzer shift jarred against the tee shirts, jeans, and polyester suits in the dimly lit, grungy barroom. She smirked as she took in my beer-drenched shirt. Already it'd plastered itself to my skin.

That's all I need . . . to look like a wet tee shirt contestant.

And worse still, with her smug, delighted look, Debi hung off the forearm of none other than Sheriff Buck Tanner himself. Apparently, they'd just arrived.

As a couple.

I tugged at my soggy shirt, trying to pull it away from my skin.

No use.

Debi nuzzled at Buck's muscled arm and tittered.

"Heavenly day! Bucky, hon, look who the cat dragged into the Roadhouse tonight."

Buck, wearing black jeans and a black tee that showed off his massive biceps, turned to look at me. I thought there was a familiar flicker in his eyes for a second, as he stood motionless, taking me in. *All of me.* Then deadpan. He had no discernable expression. He didn't even crack a smile. Really, that wasn't the Buck I knew at all. The Buck I knew would've made some off-color crack about my wet tee shirt.

Not this time.

I tugged at my shirt again.

"Oh my!" Debi laughed. "Looks like you've had *another* accident, sweetness. Your second today."

Debi winked at me, with that sickly sweet—and totally insincere—expression she was so good at putting on as she ran her long, manicured fingers up and down Buck's arm.

"Miss Eva," Buck said finally. He gave me a polite smile and a curt nod. Nothing else.

That was a greeting? Seriously?

Buck's eyes were expressionless. He wouldn't even look me in the eye. Then I realized he was staring at my bruised arm. The one with the fingernail marks Debi'd left earlier during the parade. Now, of course, the same arm was covered with scratch marks, from Claudia.

"Sheriff," I said breezily.

What kind of game are we playing? Surely, it's a game . . .

I tried to be as offhand as Buck. Biting my lip, I gave up fighting my soaked shirt.

Already, he'd looked away and busied himself greeting other folks in the barroom. He was like a celebrity; folks were all-too-happy to schmooze it up with their sheriff. I was no more than a gnat that he'd thoughtlessly waved away.

Something is really off here.

I wondered, had Buck been playing me during the last murder investigation a few weeks earlier? I mean, he'd really planted one on and kissed me. Like . . . *kissed me.* The kind of kiss that made me feel all mushy inside. Also, he'd said things . . .

Remembering, I felt my cheeks flush hot.

And at the time of the kiss, I'd thought Buck had felt it, too. And, really, he'd *started* it. Could it all have been a game on his part?

Surely not.

Or maybe it had been real and now, he was just darned pissed at me for something? As if I didn't know what.

Dex.

Could that be what this was about?

Buck's coolness confused me. Moreover, as much as I tried to ignore it, I realized that despite trying not to care, my feelings were crushed.

Easy, Eva. This is why you have a man moratorium. You know nothing about men. Or relationships. Let it go . . .

"Surely, y'all are not alone. Where's your date, *sugar pie*?" Debi pressed me.

She reached up and fingered Buck's short-cropped brown hair and nuzzled him on the shoulder. Then she gave him a teeny bite on his neck.

Eghh.

He turned and gave her a peck on the cheek.

Omigosh! She bit his neck and he kissed her! Right there in the Roadhouse . . . He kissed skanky Debi Dicer! In front of everyone. Like a little puppy dog, eager to please his evil mistress.

"Well break my neck and leave me in heck," I said.

It was an expression that I'd heard Precious use once. It seemed to fit the occasion.

"I'm sorry, sugar, I couldn't hear you. Did *y'all* say something?"

Debi flashed me her sweetest, totally fake smile.

"No, I didn't. Excuse me."

I turned to get away. In all my living days, I'd never seen Buck behave like such a pantywaist. A scoundrel and a womanizer . . . yes. I'd seen that. Plenty of times. Yet, a dog on a woman's leash . . . no way.

What the heck was going on? Had Buck changed so much in eighteen years? Was such a thing possible? Had I not seen it during the few months I'd been back home? Certainly, I'd known Buck and Debi were an "item." Heaven forbid, Debi couldn't rub my face in it enough. Every time she saw me, she blathered on about how "Bucky" was about to put a honking engagement ring on her finger. Not to mention, there'd been all the baby-making smack talk that I'd gotten from her *and* Buck's mother, Tammy Fae.

Eghh.

Still, around me at least, Buck had always shrugged it off when I asked him about Debi.

"Don't worry about Debi," he'd said more than once. "She's not important."

I turned back to glance at Debi's left ring finger.

Still no ring.

"Oh, wait!" chimed Debi brightly.

She placed a cold hand on my shoulder and made a pouty face as she leaned in closer to me. "Surely, a woman of your *experience* can find someone to *escort* tonight . . . After all, even a blind hog finds an acorn now and then!" She tittered. "But then, given your reputation with men and, of course, *dead* men, perhaps all the available bachelors have figured it's not worth the risk sticking their toes into the Knox sister pond? Too bad. Of course, if I were you, I'd want to have someone by my side at all times. You know . . . just in case. Y'all wouldn't want to have another *accident*, now, would you?"

She plucked a strand of hair out of her mouth and laughed.

Another threat?

Chatting merrily with some old farmer dude next to him, Buck seemed completely oblivious to what Debi was saying. Turning his back on me like that niggled me even more.

I'd had enough.

"Don't pee on my leg, Debi," I snapped back, "and tell me it's raining. That old dog doesn't hunt with me anymore."

"Always with your panties in a twist," laughed Debi. "Maybe if you could stop chasing after *my* man, and find yourself your *own* man and *get* some . . . if you even remember how these days . . . you'd not be so surly all the time." She laughed again.

"Which is it, Debi? Am I *getting it on* with *your Bucky* when he's not at home at night with you, like you complained to me in town this afternoon? Or, am I so starved for some action that I need to *get some* with *anyone* . . . I wish you'd stick to one story. It can't be both, you know."

"Bless your heart."

I was on a roll.

"And it seems to me that *you've* had enough men for all of us. At least that's what all the men up at the bar say. Apparently, your skills are most appreciated. *And I don't mean your skills in real estate.* Excuse me."

I spun around to start working my way toward Precious and Pep at the bar. Out of the corner of my eye, I saw Buck turn back to where I'd been standing with Debi. His eyes flashed to me, then back to Debi. Her mouth had dropped open. She actually looked a bit shocked.

Good. Score one for me.

Then I heard Debi let out an exaggerated giggle before she cooed extra-loudly to Buck, "She's just like an old, broken down refrigerator . . . can't keep nothin'!"

I never heard Buck say a word in my defense.

Damn him.

CHAPTER 23

Settled into the tight black leather bucket seat of the late-model Corvette Stingray, I stared blankly out the window as Precious sped down the dark country road. Beside me, her man-sized hands gripped the leather-wrapped steering wheel.

"I dunno why you insisted on leaving. Things were just gettin' warmed up at the Roadhouse. I love the way the Crop Pickers play 'Orange Blossom Special.' That fellow with the nose ring plays a mean fiddle."

"I'm sorry. It's been a long day, Precious. I'm just tired. And if you haven't noticed, I'm soaked with beer."

Precious tightened her hands around the wheel. Looking at me sideways, she punched the accelerator pedal with her spiky purple Louboutin as she worked the stick shift in the center console. The car engine growled as we headed toward the village.

"You coulda borrowed a shirt from your sister. She offered."

"I wasn't in the mood to sit alongside a bunch of strangers with a sparkly skull and crossbones across my chest. Especially with the Boston crowd and Debi Dicer there."

"I figured us leavin' like someone shot us out of a cannon

had somethin' to do with her. I saw how she got you all bowed up when you were talking."

"C'mon, Precious. My wanting to leave wasn't just about Debi. I am *covered* in beer. Surely, you can't blame me for wanting to go home and get into some dry clothes."

"That tall bitch is slicker than snot on a brass doorknob. She'll say anything just to fuzz you up. Don't worry about it, Sunshine."

"I'm not."

"Yeah. Right." Precious rolled her eyes. "You look fit to be tied. Still, just you consider this, Sunshine. Her Nastiness wouldn't be so hell-bent on upsettin' you if she didn't know the sheriff on her arm had the hots for ya . . ."

"Stop. Please. He doesn't have the hots for me. And I don't want to talk about it."

"Have it your way. But you know I'm right."

"Not this time."

Precious snorted and shook her head. "For a Seven Sisters college–educated smart cookie, you sure don't have much man smarts. Like, none at all, I'd say."

"You can say that again." I turned to look out the window. "Welcome to my man moratorium."

We cruised under old-style streetlamps in the village, passing one picture-perfect Victorian with gingerbread trim after another. Most of the display windows in the shop fronts were lit, the wares in the shops behind them blanketed in darkness. The second stories of many of the old buildings were apartments. Most were lit inside. I even caught a glimpse of a couple of TVs as we swooshed past in the street below.

With her big head tilted to keep from bumping it into the roof of the little convertible, Precious hummed as we soared under a canopy of moss-draped live oak trees just outside the village. Ahead, all we could see was the dark road illuminated by the headlights. It was pitch-dark everywhere else.

I slid down in my seat as Precious downshifted, crushing the accelerator pedal with her purple Louboutin. We blasted around a curve. The tires squealed.

"Yikes!" I muttered.

"Speakin' of women who I ain't got no use for, you gonna tell me what happened in the ladies' room tonight with that uppity piece of work from Boston?"

"You mean Claudia? What makes you think something happened between me and Claudia?"

"I saw her come outta the ladies' room looking like someone'd just jerked a knot in her tail. And you looked like your feathers had gotten pretty ruffled yourself, following her out. I figured you two were havin' some sort of denouement."

"Denouement?"

"Yeah. You know, like, you was resolving some sort of old business."

"Ha! Hardly."

"You gonna tell me what *that* was all about?"

"Nope."

"Any reason why not?"

"No."

"Have it your way, then."

I gripped the door as Precious quickly accelerated. She drove the little car way faster down the narrow country road than I would—faster than most people would.

"Precious, maybe I should drive. After all, you did have a fuzzy navel and a couple of shots."

"Make that *two pierced* fuzzy navels, and more than a couple of shots. And I'm just fine to drive, thank you very much. It takes a lot more than that to take Big Precious down. Besides, no one drives my little 'Vette.' She's my baby."

"Right."

"When you were in the ladies' room all that time, *not* having your denouement"—she raised her eyebrows—"I heard folks at the bar calling your place 'Knox-Em-Dead Plantation.' Pretty clever, huh?" Precious slapped the steering wheel with a hand and chuckled.

"Clever." I rolled my eyes.

I gripped the car door as she downshifted and stomped harder on the accelerator pedal. We careened around another curve, rear tires skidding behind us.

"Hey, at least folks are talking about the place. That's what you and your sisters want, right?"

"I don't think the name 'Knox-Em-Dead' conveys the kind of image we had in mind, Precious."

I thought again about Dex and sank deeper into my seat.

"Why are ya groaning, Sunshine?"

"I'm concerned about what you told me earlier in town. About Detective Gibbit wanting a warrant for our place. If he gets it, what do you suppose he thinks he'll find?"

"Beats me, Sunshine. Anything to get himself a quickie conviction, I s'pose."

About a mile outside the village, we passed a white farmhouse with painted gnomes on a scraggly lawn with rosebushes. Mister Moody's place. Of course, it was late at night, and the old codger wasn't outside rocking in his chair on the big porch. I waved as we blew by, anyway . . . Habit.

We passed a few stately Victorian homes, set well back from the road. The motor snarled as Precious careened around a giant curve. I gripped the seat to steady myself, sure we were about to go off the shoulderless road into a ditch.

Screaming past some wilderness, the car jerked one way and then another as we jettisoned down the curvy country route. Several miles outside the village, we passed Georgian- and Federal-style mansions, each set far back from the road, featuring white fences, wrought iron gates, cobblestone drives, and well-tended gardens with flowering magnolias and roses. The rose-lined drive that belonged to Daphne's friend Bubbles Bolender was filled with cars. *The Abundance elite must be having a party*, I thought. Bubbles was president of the Abundance Garden Club and on the board of numerous foundations and conservancies. That reminded me, Daphne was making me go to the garden club cleanup in the village to pick up sticks the next day. There'd be more Debi Dicer.

Ugh.

I stretched my legs out into the cramped space under the dashboard.

We blew by Carter's Country Corner Store, the local convenience store, of sorts, and hangout for hunters and codgers. The place was just closing. *Must be eleven o'clock*, I thought.

Every now and again, there'd be a gate in front of a dirt drive that disappeared into the wilderness. *Hunting lodge*. Then before I could blink, it'd be gone. Then blurs of longleaf pine forests. Then we flashed by swaths of flat, sandy farmlands stretched out next to old, rambling farmhouses and barns. Precious slammed around a corner, nearly knocking my head into the car window. I hunkered down in the passenger seat.

I gripped my seat as Precious accelerated again.

Next time, I'm driving, I thought. *That is, if we make it home and there is a next time . . .*

We blasted down the twisty country road like a bat out of hell. I held tight to my seat and focused on the next upcoming curve in the road. At least it was a distraction from all my thoughts of murder, mayhem, and the group from Boston.

Why had they come here?

And what happened to Dex? Could I have somehow prevented his death? What if for once, Detective Gibbit was right and something nefarious had happened to Dex? Had there been a murderer at Knox Plantation? Again?

Suddenly, the little car shook. The ground shook. The *world* shook. Then, as if sucked into a vacuum, the car rocked violently to one side as Precious clung to the wheel and started hollering.

CHAPTER 24

"Holy . . . !" Precious shouted. A deafening *ROAR* drowned out the rest of her words.

I ducked down in my seat as a huge military-style helicopter with two rotors flew up out of the trees right in front of us, churning up a giant dust cloud of dirt and debris with its spot lamps glaring and deafening motors rumbling, as we hurtled by, no more than twenty or thirty feet underneath. I craned my neck around to watch as the behemoth chopper disappeared behind a stand of pine trees across the road.

"Woah! Precious!" I cried. "Look out for the curve!"

Precious had allowed the car to drift into the center of the road, right in the path of an oncoming pair of headlamps.

"Tarnation!"

Quickly, she jammed on the brakes, downshifted, and slammed the steering wheel hard to the right, wrenching the Corvette back into the right lane just as an old pickup screamed past.

"I need a distraction to calm myself," Precious mumbled. She reached out and turned on the stereo. Whitney Houston's voice boomed musically from the custom surround sound stereo speakers.

"If I should stay I would only be in your way . . ."

The saxophone accompanying Whitney Houston wailed over the sound system as Precious started humming nervously, and totally off-key, as we streaked down the road. Whitney Houston's voice warbled from the speakers, *"And I will always love you . . ."*

"What the heck is a military helicopter doing around here? And flying so low?" I asked, finally.

"I just ignore 'em," Precious said, shaking her head. "They ain't worth gettin' all bowed up about. Besides, they never stick around long."

"I hope life treats you kind . . ." sang Whitney Houston.

"You mean, this isn't the first time?"

"Nah. You'll get used to it."

"Why was it flying so low? We could've had an accident!"

Whitney Houston crooned from the speakers, *"But above all this, I wish you love . . ."*

"Don't you fret about it, Sunshine," shouted Precious over the music. She reached over to the dash and turned up the stereo volume until it was earsplittingly loud. "This is my favorite part!" she shouted with a grin.

Whitney Houston's fierce melody vibrated from powerful woofers and the car reverberated the music as we blasted down the road.

"And I-eee-I . . . will always . . . love you-ooooo!"

Precious sang along in terrible disharmony with Whitney Houston, stomping the accelerator pedal as we careened around another curve. The big engine roared as we whizzed past a white board fence embracing a peach orchard.

"C'mon, Sunshine. Sing along!" shouted Precious. *"I-eee-I will all-ways love you!"*

I put my hands over my ears. Still, Precious was so off-key that I just had to smile.

"I will all-ways love you-ooooooooo! I will always lo-uhve yoooooooo! I will always love YOUUU-OOOOOO! LOVE YOU! I will always love . . . you . . ." Precious howled.

I just shook my head.

"Beautiful song, ain't it? All about lettin' go . . ." Precious shouted. Then she reached over and shut off the music. "Let it go, Sunshine. Whatever it is. Let it go. And cheer up. You got your whole life ahead of ya."

"C'mon, Precious. Give me a break. We could've been killed out here tonight. Not to mention someone just died back at our place . . . *again*. Why does this keep happening? If you wrote this stuff as fiction, no one would believe it."

"I get it," Precious said, nodding. "You're upset. And especially this time, 'cause the dead guy was your boyfriend."

"*Old* boyfriend, Precious. It was a lifetime ago."

"Okay, sure. It was a lifetime ago. Still, you gotta learn to let stuff go, Sunshine. Stop pushin' it all inside an' hidin' from it. Ya *gotta* get it out!"

"I don't know what you're talking about, Precious."

"Have it your way. But you should mind my words."

"Do I have a choice?"

Precious laughed. "So then, not to change the subject or nothin', but when are ya gonna tell me the rest of the story about this dead Dexter guy?"

Precious glanced sideways at me, waiting for me to reply. I didn't. She held her look so long that I started squirming in my seat.

"I told Pep at the bar tonight that there was more to this guy than just bein' a boyfriend," Precious said. "She didn't believe me. She said if there'd been a story worth tellin' then she'da known about it."

I put my head in my hands.

"Why, ain't you *something*!" Precious smiled, like she was happy to have outsmarted my sister. "There *is* more to it! I knew it."

I looked up and gave Precious a weak smile.

"Y'all weren't together when he drowned now, were ya? Doin' a little skinny-dipping, for ol' times' sake? Maybe you an' he were fixin' to get together again? Ooooh, wait! Maybe y'all already did . . ."

"No!"

"I mean, I'd understand and all. Like the time my cousin Dewanna shot her husband when she found him makin' hanky-panky with the babysitter on the washing machine . . . Maybe this guy pissed you off and you pushed him into the water and he hit his head on a rock or something?"

"No," I said. "Now stop this!"

"Sunshine, accidents happen. You can tell Auntie Precious . . ."

"Please! Stop! I wasn't with Dex last night. I just saw him while I was working in the big house. And if the twins had shown up for work, I might not have seen him at all." Then I mumbled, "Really, I can't imagine what happened to him at the pond. I mean, I'm pretty sure it was him getting a snack in the kitchen last night. After that, who knows . . ."

"If you're in some kinda trouble, ya know Miss Precious has got your back." She reached over and patted me on the knee.

"Yes. I know that, Precious. Thank you. Still, there's no trouble."

Precious shrugged.

"I didn't *kill* him!" I cried.

"Aw, I know that! Musta been some kinda weird accident, I guess. Probably the guy got drunk and just drowned himself. Or maybe he choked on a garlic clove. Or, maybe he was allergic to garlic? You said he was snacking on garlic in the kitchen, right? That kinda thing does happen, I reckon. On the other hand, do ya think the whole bunch of them was out there last night?"

"Them?"

"The folks from Boston."

I shrugged. "Not according to Claudia."

"No matter. I figure we'll find out soon enough. Maybe they *all* killed the guy. Like Agatha Christie's *Murder on the Orient Express* . . . Love that one."

"Precious, we don't know that anyone killed him. At least not yet . . ."

"Maybe we'll *never* find out what happened," Precious

chortled, "because Detective Gibbit is on the case, and he's about as confused as a fart in a fan factory."

"Oh, right. The *case*. Let's see, most likely Detective Gibbit has made a 'case' out of this"—I held my finger in the air—"one, because there's nothing else going on in town." I raised a second finger. "Two, because it happened at our place and he can't stand *any* of us." I raised a third finger. "And three, because if he can land himself some sort of big, fat case—a murder, or something that *looks* like a murder—it would be perfect for generating publicity and kudos for himself . . . all helping him to usurp from Buck the job that he thinks Buck stole from him in the first place."

"He's sure proven himself to be bound and determined to make a name for himself with lotsa publicity and a snappy conviction. Another mysterious death at Knox Plantation would sure fit the bill."

I nodded.

"So, when are you gonna fess up and tell me about you and dead Dex?" asked Precious.

I sighed.

She pressed on. "You know you want to . . ."

"Not now, Precious. I admit it, you're right. We had more than just a few casual dates. We had a . . . *complicated* relationship. But it was a *long* time ago. And I had no idea he was coming here this week. Honestly. If I'd known, I would have gone away somewhere."

She gave me a sideways glance and rolled her eyes.

"It was that bad?"

"Precious, I promise, I'll fill you in. However, I need to talk with someone else first . . ."

I almost felt relieved to say it out loud. Although, after the awkward scene with Buck in the Roadhouse, I wasn't looking forward to facing him again. At all. Still, I owed it to him. No matter how he felt about me.

"Why do I think that there's *another* man involved?"

I shrugged. Then I thought I saw Precious suppress a smirk.

After that, racing past antique farmhouses and dilapidated barns alongside flat, sandy fields used to grow cotton, onions, soybeans, peanuts, pecans, and fruit, we hurtled along the twisty road in silence. Then Precious downshifted with one hand while she stomped hard on the accelerator pedal, and we ricocheted around a corner before shooting under a shaded tunnel of oak trees. Giant fingerlings of moss cascaded down over the narrow road.

"Holy smoke!"

I leaned over and looked at the speedometer. As was usually the case with Precious, we were closing in on seventy miles per hour. Sucking in my breath, I pressed my hand against the dashboard as Precious accelerated again. The big engine growled and revved higher as we careened sharply around another curve. Then, flying into the left lane, we passed a crawling John Deere tractor, yellow flashers warning us that it was a slow-moving vehicle.

"Crazy farmer . . . it's too late to be out on the road like that!"

"Gotta stay out in the field until the job's done," I said, repeating the words I'd heard my dad say a million times when I was a child on the farm.

"Oh darn. I forgot to turn on my phone," said Precious.

She threw her right hand up and behind her, reaching in between our seats, where she'd jammed her purple alligator purse. There wasn't much room to put a purse in a car like that. The car swerved left and right as she rummaged awkwardly inside her bag.

"Precious, can I help you?"

"No, thanks. I got it!"

She yanked her glittery smartphone from the bag. Without looking, she switched it on and set it down on her lap.

"So, Precious, what do you know about that helicopter that you're not telling me?"

Precious opened her mouth to answer me, just when singer Tina Turner's voice crooned, *"You're simply the best . . ."* from her phone. Precious grabbed the sparkly gold phone from her lap. She had a call.

At least she'll have to slow down, I thought.

She didn't.

"Oh, hi, Tilly. Whatcha know good?"

Precious's friend, Tilly Beekerspat, was calling with the latest installment of local gossip, no doubt. I figured they'd yammer on the phone until we arrived home.

"*No!* Y'all don't say!" Precious's eyes were as big as saucers. "Wait, hon. Hold on a sec."

Precious covered the microphone of her smartphone with her hand and leaned toward me. The car veered into the center of the road.

"Precious! Watch it!" I cried.

She jerked the steering wheel, and the car slammed back to the proper side of the twisty road.

"It's my friend Tilly," Precious said anxiously. "You know, she works at dispatch—"

"Yes, yes, I know," I said, waving my hand impatiently at Precious.

"She says she's been tryin' to reach me all night. She don't have any details yet, but Detective Gibbit definitely thinks your old friend in the pond was *murdered*!"

Precious never answered my question about the helicopter. And, after the news about Dex, I forgot to ask about it again.

CHAPTER 25

Dex and I were nose to nose. He was yelling. I was crying. It was snowing outside. He'd just brought me home from the holiday party.

"You whore!" he shrieked, ripping off his coat, dropping it on the floor. "How dare you stand in the corner and talk with Bud Crowninshield all night long! You're *my* fiancée, not his! And your job is to stand by *my* side, not his!"

I'd had too much to drink, and the apartment room was whirling around me. Still, I probably hadn't had as much to drink as Dex . . .

"I'm sorry, Dex!" I cried. I tried to pull off my scarf, except it wouldn't release from around my neck. "Really I am. I didn't talk to Mister Crowninshield all night. I did everything you always tell me to do. I made small talk with your boss, Mister Manley, about fly-fishing. Just like y'all told me to. I even complimented him on his ugly paisley tie. And I offered my cookie recipe to the human resources lady, Missus Featherstone." I wiped a tear before starting to unbutton my coat. "For twenty minutes or more, I listened sympathetically to your client from Michigan as he complained about his acid reflux! I even chatted about the pretty beaches on Martha's Vineyard with the guy from corporate headquarters. He said he liked my dress. And he invited us to visit his summer place! Isn't that what you want?"

"Stop it!" shouted Dex in my face. He grabbed my hands, pulling them away from my coat buttons. I snatched my hands back defiantly.

"Let go!"

"You weren't by my side, where you were *supposed* to be!" he shouted even louder. Spittle from his mouth hit me on the face. "Just like last time, you went off by yourself . . . to flirt! I watched you. You didn't think I noticed what you were doing. But I did! You're nothing but a cheap Southern tramp!"

As he stood nearly on top of me, tall and erect, Dex's normally handsome face was red and twisted. His steely blue eyes flashed fire. Backed up against the wall, I had nowhere to go. I looked down. Dex's hands were balled into tight fists.

"Please stop," I whimpered. "I wasn't flirting. I was being friendly. And I did everything you told me to . . ."

Every time I spoke, it only made him madder.

"Did I tell you to wander off by yourself? No!" he shouted. "Did I tell you to let Crowninshield peer down your dress? No! Did I tell you to accept drinks from other men? No! Did I tell you to laugh with Dick Coffin and look like you were having a better time with him than you were with me? No, no, no! Everyone warned me about getting tangled up with a Southern girl. But no. I didn't listen."

He was angry as sin. And I was, too. He was judging me unfairly and I knew it. Apologizing, trying to explain, arguing using logic, none of it had worked.

Finally, I couldn't stop myself. I looked up and the ugly words poured out . . .

"Yeah. That's right, Dexter Codman. I'm a cheap Southern tease," I said sarcastically, hands on my hips. "That's all I want to do. Flirt with your incredibly unattractive business associates. Especially with Bud Crowninshield who has dandruff, and a *terrible* case of halitosis. Quite the turn-on, don't you think? So, what are you going to do about it, Dex? Huh? Tell me! What are you gonna do about it *this time*? Push me down the stairs again like last time? Break my arm again . . . ?"

Dex roared as he held his fists in the air.

I kept going. "Maybe I won't cover for you *this* time. Maybe this time, all your friends will find out about you at work! What do you think everyone will say when they see me, again, all bruised and broken . . . huh? What do you think they will think about you then? You can kiss your fancy, high-paying career *good-bye*!"

There was a thunderous *CRACK*, and I was blinded for a moment. Then my face screamed in pain . . .

Suddenly, the scene shifted.

It was a summer night, and we were in the car, Dex's tiny Alfa Romeo Spider, his pride and joy. The top was down, and we were arguing as we flew down the Mid-Cape Highway. Dex had just hit a cat . . . and he hadn't stopped.

"Dex, please . . . That's someone's pet!" I cried. "Please, stop. We need to do something . . ."

"It was a stupid *cat*, Eva!"

"No . . . it was someone's beloved pet. I saw the collar. It had a *collar*, Dex!"

"Shut up about the damn cat, Eva. And leave me alone. I'm driving!"

"But Dex, maybe the poor thing was still alive . . . We've got to go back and see . . ."

"Jesus . . . I can't take any more of this!"

Before I could finish my sentence, Dex—still blasting down the highway—reached over and unhooked my seat belt.

"Dex . . . what are you doing!"

He swore at me. "You're nothing but an ignorant, spoiled little farm girl. Get out!"

"Wha . . . what . . . ?"

With his long arm stretched across me, he unlatched the passenger-side door of the tiny sports car.

"Everyone was right. I can do a helluva lot better than the likes of *you*, Eva Knox!"

"Dex! What are you *doing*?"

"Get out!" he shrieked.

"The car is still moving! Stop! This is a *highway*!"

"Get out, you silly bitch!"

Still maneuvering the convertible down the highway, Dex put his left foot on the accelerator pedal and swung his right foot over the center console and started shoving me with his foot and his free hand. Shocked, I didn't think fast enough to hold on. The passenger door was open and banging against the car, and although I was snatching at it, trying to close it, I couldn't get a grip on it, and Dex was kicking and pushing me out of the seat . . . I could see the highway pavement whizzing below . . . As inconceivable as it seemed, I was falling out of the speeding sports car . . .

I jerked myself upright, my heart thumping fast inside my chest.

Then my eyes flew open.

Sitting upright in my grandma's four-poster bed, I was covered in sweat, as tears poured down my cheeks. I heard Dolly whimper from her cushion on the floor below me.

"Bad dream," I said aloud, sobbing. "Bad dream."

CHAPTER 26

I knew better. I was kidding myself. It hadn't been a dream at all. It'd been memories. Bad memories of what had really happened with Dex all those years ago. I'd remembered the real reason I'd run off and left him.

If I hadn't, he surely would've killed me.

Remembering what I'd somehow managed to suppress for all those years made me feel sick. I threw off my bedsheet—it felt damp from perspiration—and I slid out of bed, still trying to hold it together as I caught my breath. I ran to the bathroom and stood over the toilet, gagging.

I heard Dolly woof quietly from her cushion, as if to ask, *Are you alright?*

I managed to regain my composure, and after a minute or so, I rinsed my face in the sink, before I went back out to Dolly. I sat down on the floor next to her bed and cradled her in my arms, hugging her close to me. Dolly's warm, soft body felt soothing. She licked me on the face.

"I'm alright, Dolly. I'm alright," I whispered.

A few minutes later, I set Dolly down and stood up. Opening my nightstand drawer, I grabbed a doggie biscuit and gave it to her.

"Just another bad dream, Dolly. I'm fine."

My nightie was drenched. I tried slowing my breathing. The air was muggy. As always, the useless cottage ceiling fan whooshed quietly overhead, barely moving the humid air. The black Victorian clock on the mantel across from the foot of my bed tick-tocked. It was thirty minutes after midnight. I'd probably only slept thirty minutes. Maybe fifty. In the yard outside, the leaves rustled in the balmy breeze as peepers sang their raucous songs in the trees.

Dolly chomped down the biscuit and waddled to the screen door. She put her paw on the edge of the door and pulled it open a crack. Wedging her body through, she wagged her tail on her way to the yard.

"Don't go far," I warned.

Keeping Dolly inside the cottage was a futile effort. Besides, she always returned. Although, I did worry about some of the wild animals in the forest.

I realized that I was crying again. *Really sobbing.* I just couldn't stop myself. Next to the door, I snapped on the switch that lit the antique cranberry glass lantern hanging over the dining table in the center of my cottage. The light gave the room a warm, rosy glow. I crossed to the center of the room, went behind the counter into the kitchenette beside the dining area, and poured myself a glass of water. Then I walked to the back of the cottage, into the bathroom a second time, where I soaked a washcloth with cold water and pressed it to my face.

A minute or two later, I plopped into my favorite armchair in the back of the room—it was the same chair that'd been in my bedroom as a girl, only Daphne'd re-covered it in a pretty floral chintz fabric. I picked up a cozy mystery from the shelf on the back wall and started flipping through the pages . . . trying to distract myself.

No use.

I kept seeing Dex and the angry look on his contorted face.

The storm in his steely blue eyes. His fists . . . I took a deep
breath.

"It's over. It's not my fault. It's not my fault."

It's not my fault.

It'd taken me years to realize Dex's abusive behavior toward me was all about him. Not me.

When I'd first left Dex, I'd felt embarrassed and ashamed.
I'd been sure that his anger had been my fault. After all, I was
the country bumpkin from Abundance, Georgia. He was the
worldly and wise Brahmin from Beacon Hill. Then later,
when I'd realized that I should've reached out for help, I'd
remained too embarrassed to tell anyone about what had happened. After all, I was an intelligent, college-educated, professional woman living in one of the world's greatest cities.
How could I have let this happen to me?

Of course, I should've left him the first time he'd hurt me.
Still, when it'd first happened, Dex had been so apologetic
afterward, promising never to hurt me again, I'd believed him.
He'd promised to love me even more.

Then the next time, he'd apologized again . . . He'd even
cried. He'd told me that our arguing and making up actually
brought us closer together, that it was natural for couples to
argue. He'd brought home expensive gifts. He'd touched me
tenderly, given me back rubs, run my bath for me . . . Dex was
the makeup king.

A classic abuser.

And I'd let him get away with it. Then afterward, after I'd
finally found the guts to leave him, I'd just tried to forget it all.

I let out a big sigh.

"It's water over the dam now."

Suddenly, I saw Dex floating in the pond. Bloated, eerily
off-color with black eyes, he looked like he was grinning
at me.

I shuddered.

And I had the sickening realization—the realization that
I'd tried to hide from myself right up until my dream came
along and smacked me in the face with it—that if anyone
knew my history with Dex, surely it would look damning for

me that he'd died just hours after I'd threatened him in front of a roomful of people. And already, Detective Gibbit had concluded that Dex had been murdered.

Lucky I never told anyone about the abuse, I thought. *Hopefully, they'll figure out what happened to Dex in the pond before I ever have to say anything.*

Maybe the detective was just on another one of his wild-goose chases when he'd asked for the search warrant. Maybe Tilly Beekerspat had gotten it all wrong. Most likely, Dex was drunk and just drowned, I reasoned. Everyone will find out that it was just a terrible accident.

That's it. I'm sure. A terrible accident. Eli Gibbit is wrong. Eli is always wrong.

I took a deep, slow breath. Trying to relax, I rested my feet up on the ottoman that matched the armchair. Then I just sat there. Lost.

Surely, there are hospital emergency room records. What if someone finds out what Dex did to me . . .

I jumped as I heard the terrible screeching of a night heron from somewhere in the woods. Then I heard Dolly barking. Already, it sounded like she was far, far away . . . maybe as far as the olive grove. Much farther than she normally went, especially at night. Usually, she stayed in the yard and came back inside pretty quick.

I got up and headed toward the front of the room, tossing the book on the dining table. Then I shuffled past the trunk at the end of the bed and pushed open the screen door. Stepping down the stoop, I walked into the yard, trying to breathe as I listened for Dolly.

The tree frogs and night critters were screeching in the yard. But there was no sound from Dolly. I called out quietly. I didn't want to awaken anyone across the lawn in the big house. It looked like all the guest cars were parked alongside the big house; the Bostoners must have returned from the Roadhouse.

"Dolly?"

Nothing.

She probably was *near Daddy's olive orchard*, I thought.

She liked it there. From the cottage, the quickest way to get to the olive trees would be to go down the hill and through the field around the pond, into some woods behind the pond, past Daddy's old hunting cabin, then down a path through the wire grass and longleaf pine forest for another five or six minutes. Eventually, that path would dump me out on the near side of the olive grove. If Dolly *was* way over there, I doubted she'd respond to my calling her from the cottage.

"She'll come back," I said to myself aloud. "She always does."

I was tired. I wanted to sleep. Forget all the mess about Dex. Quell my rising panic. *I'll deal with it in the morning*, I thought. I sat on the stoop and waited.

Five minutes went by. I stood up and went into the yard.

"Dolly!" I called out. I listened again.

Nothing.

I wandered toward the knoll and looked out over the moonlit pond below. The still water in the pond looked inky black.

Had it looked like this when Dex was down there?

My knees felt weak.

"Dolly?"

Eerie silence.

What if it hadn't been a night heron calling in the woods? Maybe it'd been a coyote?

I went inside and quickly changed into a black racerback yoga top and pulled on my stretchy black skort—my favorite one from Dick's. I shoved my bare feet into my cheapo sneakers and headed outside, quietly closing the screen door behind me. Then, remembering, I turned back, went inside, and rummaged through my sock drawer until I found my smartphone. The battery was at about twenty percent. Still, I grabbed the phone and flicked on the flashlight app as I started out again, headed toward the olive orchard.

CHAPTER 27

I felt pretty comfortable on our plantation trails, even at night. During the weeks I'd been back home, I ran for exercise every day, and my insomnia had driven me to take many nighttime treks on the trails with Dolly. I felt sure I could find her pretty quickly, even in the dead of night.

Deep in the forest on the other side of the pond, one hundred feet above me, the wind hummed through the tall, straight longleaf pine trees. Crickets and frogs chattered noisily in the brush and trees around me. Most of the trees were three hundred years old, or more. Alongside the worn woodsy path, the moon lit up multicolored little wildflowers that were scattered through the tall wire grass under the canopy of ancient trees. Every so often, I'd stop to listen for Dolly.

Nothing.

I heard an owl *hoot-hoot* a couple of times, but other than the blustery wind in the trees and the squealing and trilling of bugs and amphibians, that was all I was able to discern.

"Dolly!"

Still no bark.

Several minutes later, I stepped out from the noisy, dark

forest path onto open sandy soil. A breeze blew, and the narrow sage green leaves on Daddy's young olive trees shimmered in the clear moonlight. Except for the *shisshing* of the olive leaves in the wind, the open one-hundred-acre grove seemed quiet, especially compared to the raucous forest behind me. I snapped off the light on my cell phone and looked around as my eyes adjusted to the moonlit darkness.

In an area that had been cut out of old forest, still surrounded by pine trees, Daddy's orchard was filled with young Arbequina trees—a Spanish olive variety known for producing a mild, buttery-tasting oil. The olive trees were planted in compact, super-high-density rows—nearly seven hundred trees per acre. It was a vineyard-style planting system, as opposed to the way traditional European-style olive groves are managed with large trees, more like the stand-alone olive tree near the pond. In addition to the Arbequina trees in Daddy's grove, every twelfth tree in a row was a super-pollinator Arbosana or Koroneiki variety.

I picked an olive from the first Arbequina tree at the end of a row. Examining the fruit between my fingers—it was smaller than the fruit from the big olive tree near the pond—the hard, apple green olive was not even as large as the tip of my thumb. The Arbeq   riety produced small olives compared to other varietie., and each olive had a lot of pit for the size of the fruit. These were not table olives. Instead, they were perfect for making smooth, mild, buttery-flavored olive oil. The flesh from each Arbequina olive produced quite a bit of oil, especially for its diminutive size. I looked at the tree in the moonlight. Most of the fruit was apple green; some blushed a rich eggplant color. A few were already ripened brown.

Starting down one of the twelve-foot-wide swaths of soil between the rows of young trees, I stopped, listening for Dolly. That's when I caught a whiff of something unusual. I couldn't quite place it.

Smoke?

Spinning in a circle, I didn't see anything strange. And the scent disappeared.

Must've been my imagination.

Around me, the young trees—about six years old—were positioned on land that sloped slightly north to south, allowing a maximum amount of sunlight to reach each tree canopy. Drip irrigation hoses ran down each row, under the trees, a line secured to each side of the slender tree trunks. Grown in a series of hedgerows, the slender-trunked trees—not much bigger than large bushes, really—were staked with bamboo and trellised with twisted wire, grown much like grapes in a vineyard. Young trees were pruned each year to increase the fruit yield, regulate flowering, and shape the plants in order to maintain good air circulation around each tree, reducing fungal disease. Also, keeping the trees to no more than ten feet tall allowed Daddy's over-the-row harvester to fit above the plants.

During harvesttime—which was only a few weeks away—beginning in the wee hours before daybreak, the huge harvesting machine would roll through the hedgerows, straddling each row of trees with giant, man-height tires. Slowly, the harvester would pass over each row of plants while "fingers" inside the machine beat the fruit off the trees and into a large bin. Much of the fruit would still be green at harvest. For oil products, the fruit doesn't need to be fully ripened. Then at the end of each row, the fruit would be collected in plastic bins before the huge harvester would turn and the process would begin again with the next row.

Because olive fruit perishes quickly, the olives would be processed into oil on the very day of harvest. In our case, the fruit would be driven to the nearest processing plant, all the way in Texas. Daddy was working on building our own processing plant on the plantation . . .

Wait! What's that?

I smelled smoke.

CHAPTER 28

I inhaled deeply. Yes, it surely was smoke that I'd smelled earlier, when I'd first stepped into the olive grove. However, the smoke had a sweet, fruity scent to it that reminded me of my grandfather's pipe.

Cherries.

Then the wind changed, and I heard voices. They came from just two, maybe three rows away from me in the olive grove.

I froze, realizing at once that the cherry smoke *was* from a pipe. Of course, it wasn't from my grandfather's pipe. Instead, it came from the pipe that belonged to someone else.

Wiggy.

I stood stock-still, listening.

"Well, you should be happy, Coop, after what he did to you and Heather." It was easy to recognize Spencer's whiny, high-pitched voice.

"Yeah, payback's a bitch," said a pleasant-sounding voice. It was Coop, the lawyer. "Still, even though I still hate Dex's guts for that, I'll miss the guy."

"Not having to deal with Dex and his continuing crises with women definitely makes things easier," Wiggy said. "I mean, we really don't need him at this point. He was a liability to the operation."

"Damn. Last night at the tasting I thought he was going to blow this whole deal sky-high," said Coop.

"Well, we don't have to worry about it anymore now," growled Wiggy. "Dex's role was negligible at this point, anyway. And we'll all be stinking rich before you know it. Spencer, you got all the offshore accounts set up?"

"Geez, Wig, who do you take me for?" whined Spencer. "A friggin' neophyte? I took care of all that a month ago. We're good to go. All we need is for Coop to close the deal."

"Yeah, well, about that. Apparently, the same person who scooped the Twiggs property is bidding on the other one we're looking at," said Coop.

"Who?" asked Wiggy.

"I haven't been able to find out yet. I'm working on it. Just stay cool."

"We've come this far; we can't let this thing fall apart now," said Wiggy.

"I'm on it," said Coop. "I won't let this happen a second time. But you gotta remain cool, Wiggy. Got it? We can't afford to have people talking about us, especially when you make a big scene downtown yelling at the local Realtor."

"That guy pisses me off," growled Wiggy. "He lost us that place. And we're in it so deep now there's no turning back. And I'm not about to go to jail, dammit. Are we sure there's not another real estate agent in town?"

"I'm sure. Besides, we don't want to rock the boat now," said Coop.

"Do you think Eva suspects something?" asked Spencer. "Or worse, do ya think Dex clued her in before . . . you know . . ."

"I don't know. She certainly didn't seem convinced that we were here on holiday. She's not nearly as stupid as most of the people in this backwater place," said Coop.

You got that right, I thought. *But then, none of us are "stupid" here in Abundance. I'd like to see you operate a combine . . .*

"She's a woman," chortled Wiggy. "If she keeps up her attitude and acts up, leave her to me. She'll never say a word."

"And if she does?" asked Spencer.

"We'll just have to shut her up. Permanently," said Wiggy.

"What about Claudia?" asked Coop.

"I dunno. She's awfully wound up about Dex," said Wiggy.

"Think she can keep it together?" Spencer asked.

"I sure hope so. We need her. At least for now. She's the only one with all of Dex's codes and passwords. If we're going to pull this off, we'll need to access his accounts," Coop said.

"What if she cracks?" asked Wiggy.

"Yeah, she's kinda unstable, don't you think?" added Spencer.

"I don't know. She didn't used to be this way. At least not when we first knew her. Remember? Something happened," said Coop.

"It was after she and Dex came back from that trip they took to Zermatt," said Wiggy.

"Zermatt?" said Spencer.

"Sure, don't you remember?"

"No."

"Sure you do. A long time ago. Remember, she had some sort of ski accident in the powder," Wiggy said.

"I remember," said Coop. "She was in a cast for months. Dex used to complain because he had to make his own copies."

"And he had to fetch his own coffee. Still, right after that, Dex gave her a big raise," said Spencer.

"And she's been up to her eyeballs in his business and over-paid ever since. She screwed up something a few years ago, big-time. I told him to fire her. He wouldn't hear it. Said he couldn't function without her and that was that," said Wiggy.

"So, what do you think she'll do now, without Dex? Surely, no one else is gonna pay her like he did. Do you think he was doing her on the side?" asked Spencer.

Slimeball.

"Who knows," answered Wiggy. "But we need her for now, to get us through this. After that . . ."

Coop said, "I'm pretty sure they had something going . . . you know?"

"Really? When?" asked Spencer.

"Between Eva and Heather," said Coop.

What?

The time between Eva and Heather? Heather is married *to Coop! What are they talking about? Heather was never with Dex . . .*

"He was a sly one, alright," said Wiggy.

They laughed.

"Well, if Claudia can't toe the line, then we're gonna have to do something about it," said Coop.

"You mean . . ."

"I mean something permanent. *After* we get all the files, codes, and passwords," Coop said.

"Of course," said Wiggy.

"She keeps blubbering about losing her job now that Dex is dead," said Spencer.

Coop yawned before saying, "Wouldn't make me sad to see her go."

"Let's head back. I'm getting tired. We've got a big day tomorrow. I need to scout a few more places," Wiggy said. "There's some kind of 'hawk watch' going on over near the river. That's a place to start. I've discovered these bird-watching types are quite chatty, after they've been in the field for a few hours. They know all sort of details about the properties around here."

"Wiggy, you remember the way?" asked Coop.

"Sure, just follow the path. It's a couple of rows down, over there," answered Wiggy.

"Okay, we'll follow you. And keep your eyes open. I don't want to run into any surprises."

"Me, neither," said Spencer.

"You guys are wussies." Wiggy chortled.

"Well, I'd rather be a live wussy than a dead man!" said Coop.

The three men laughed.

CHAPTER 29

I heard Dolly bark. She was in the woods on the Greatwoods Plantation side of our property. After hearing the three men from Boston talking in the olive grove, I didn't dare call out. And although I wanted to follow the men back to the big house and try to hear more, instead, I hid under the canopy of an olive tree until I was sure they'd left the orchard and were headed back down the wooded trail to the big house.

One thing was for sure: As I suspected all along, they were *not* in Abundance to watch birds. It seemed pretty obvious that they were on some sort of land-grabbing expedition. But, was it something to *kill* for? Certainly, they didn't seem all-too-sorry that their old friend and cohort Dex was dead. Maybe the detective was actually right this time. Maybe one of them had murdered Dex. Or, like Precious had joked earlier, maybe they'd *all* done it.

Could Dex's closest friends have *killed* him?

The thought gave me the creeps.

Was that why Buck had been asking me so many questions at the pond? Had he suspected right off that Dex had been murdered? Had Buck considered *me* a suspect when we'd first spoken?

*I've got to figure out what happened to Dex before some-
one seriously thinks I had something to do with his death.*

Still searching for Dolly, I was on a narrow trail, surrounded
by wire grass, deep in the longleaf pine forest. Listening for
my wayward pup, I tried to remember everything I'd heard the
Bostoners say.

All merely suggestive. Nothing concrete.

I replayed what I'd heard in my head. Thinking about it
all made me even more determined to find out why they were
in town.

Ten minutes later, I hadn't come up with any answers. And
I hadn't heard or seen a single sign from Dolly. I decided to
continue following the trail that headed in the direction of
Greatwoods Plantation. Compared to many of the paths in
the longleaf pines, it was more of a "main" path, and Dolly
and I followed it quite often during our daytime walks.

"Dolly!" I called. I was pretty sure the men had made it
back to the big house and wouldn't hear me calling.

I continued sorting through everything I'd heard the men
discussing.

It all sounded so nefarious . . .

I jumped as something fluttered above me. Stopping to
listen, all I could hear was wind high in the trees and the
screeches and tweets of tree frogs and bugs. I pressed on,
making my way through the wire grass under the pine trees
on either side of the narrow trail.

Fifteen or twenty minutes later, still with my light on, I
came to see a barbed wire fence. It was the Greatwoods Plantation boundary line. The trail I'd been following turned
sharply to the left, running alongside the fence line for a bit,
before the trail and fence parted ways when the trail went left
and the fence veered to the right and disappeared in a thicket.
Somewhere in the distance from the other side of the fence,
I heard a low *coo-coo-coo*.

Probably a screech owl.

Then, from somewhere in the woods on the other side of
the fence, I heard barking.

"Dolly!"

I held up my smartphone, trying to shine the light into the dark wilderness on the Greatwoods side of the barbed wire barrier.

"Dolly!"

The light app was handy for seeing close-up, but it was impossible to see anything more than several feet away. I flicked off my light, hoping my eyes would quickly adjust to the darkness. I stared. I listened. Nothing. All at once, the night had become eerily silent.

"Dolly?"

Still nothing.

Precious had mentioned once that there was a "secret" way to get to Greatwoods Plantation from the woods at our place. Except after she'd blurted something about it and I'd asked her to explain, she denied saying anything in the first place. She was weird that way. Always protecting her boss, Ian Collier.

What was all the mystery about?

Regardless, if there was a "secret" way to get to Greatwoods, so far I hadn't found it. Still, I knew that Ian Collier had been able to get over to our place on horseback . . . more than once. *So, there must be a passage, somewhere,* I thought. And it had to be of significant size; after all, Ian's big mare fit through it. Dolly'd surely discovered the secret passage. Still, it remained elusive to me. If I was going to find Dolly, I was going to have to scale the blasted barbed wire fence.

"Dolly!"

I abandoned the trail on the Knox side of the fence and thrashed through the briars and wire grass, following the fence, hoping to find a place that was easy to cross. After several minutes, I saw a huge live oak tree, right in the middle of the forest. One massive limb hung over the Greatwoods side of the barbed wire fence. I figured that if I climbed up the tree, I could make my way down the big limb across to the Greatwoods side and then jump down.

Perfect.

I tucked my smartphone into a back pocket on my skort. I dragged an old, dead log to the base of the tree. Then another. And another. I piled them up so I could get as high a start up the tree as possible. I couldn't think of any other way to reach the first branch. I only hoped there wasn't any poison ivy or poison oak nearby.

It wasn't pretty, but after several tries, I managed to scramble up and hoist my way up into a crook of the gnarled oak tree. Then I climbed up to the biggest limb. It wasn't nearly as easy as I remembered it being when I was a teenager—it'd been easy to climb up and down the tree near my bedroom window when I'd sneak out at night and go on long walks with my boyfriend . . . Buck.

I shook my head.

From the trunk, the massive branch was bigger around than my thigh. I lay down on the branch and shimmied my way out toward the end, heading over the barbed wire to the Greatwoods property. By the time I'd wriggled to a point above the barbed wire, the limb had narrowed. I felt it bounce a little with my weight. About ten or twelve feet in the air, I kept slithering toward the end of the branch, trying to get all of me clear above the barbed wire fence below.

Of course, when I heard the crack beneath me, it was too late to do anything about it.

The limb snapped clean off.

CHAPTER 30

As the limb from the great oak cracked off the tree, I plummeted straight to the ground.

Despite the ten- or twelve-foot drop, I managed to tumble just the way I'd practiced in the jujitsu class Daphne'd insisted I attend every Monday evening. It worked. The soft forest floor, covered with years of decayed growth and leaves, made for a gentle cushion. For once, I thought, I'd managed to fall and land relatively unscathed. Better still, I'd made it to the Greatwoods side of the fence.

Bark. Bark. Bark.

It was Dolly. Still, she sounded to be quite a distance away. I imagined that she was quite close to Ian Collier's mansion. Once I caught up with Dolly, it'd take me nearly an hour to walk back home in the woods from Greatwoods, and that was assuming that I could even *find* Dolly. How we'd get back over the fence together would be another matter altogether.

I decided that I'd deal with all that after I found Dolly.

I picked myself up, brushing off the dirt and pine needles. Pulling briars out of the fabric of my skort, I listened for Dolly, trying to pinpoint her location. Then I headed in the direction where I thought Dolly and the Greatwoods mansion would be. It was only a minute or so later when I stumbled onto a narrow trail that wound through the trees.

"Thank goodness!"

Relieved to have found a path, I followed it for several minutes.

Then, off in the distance behind me, I heard a low rumble. I realized that it was a helicopter.

I wondered if there'd been an accident. Abundance was such a rural place, often helicopters were used to transport accident victims to the hospital in the next county. I turned my head and listened again. It was headed in my direction. I waited to see it. Except, this bird sounded different than the helicopter used to transport patients and accident victims. The drone was louder. Lower in pitch. In fact, it sounded just like the big chopper that had passed overhead when Precious and I'd been on the road.

Military?

I looked up to the sky to see the chopper's lights as it approached, but there was nothing. The big bird was coming closer, but it remained cloaked in darkness. Then suddenly, when it got to about five hundred feet from where I stood, a bright spotlight blazed from the chopper, lighting up the forest. Instinctively, I jumped into the wire grass and made my way to a huge pine tree trunk, pressing myself against the bark on the far side from the chopper's approach, trying to hide under the pine boughs.

At least I wore black, I thought. *What the hell is going on?*

The ground shook and the woods filled with the deafening engine noise as the chopper flew closer, skimming just atop the tall pines. The bright spotlight seemed to follow the general direction of the little path that I'd been on, and it lit up the woods as if it were daylight. Sheltered under the tree boughs as they twisted and twirled in the wild chopper wind, I pressed myself against the far side of the tree and held my hands to my ears as the noisy bird approached. It was a big military-style helicopter, for sure. With two rotors. The kind that transported troops.

A Chinook.

I shrank from the brain-rattling noise and my whole being throbbed as the chopper hovered momentarily overhead.

Are they looking for someone? Something? I couldn't imagine what was going on.

Like a tornado, dirt and detritus filled the air around me as I pressed myself into the tree trunk.

Then, as suddenly as it'd appeared, the monster bird moved on, traveling to my left. I waited a moment or two after it disappeared, before racing back onto the path, trying to follow the shining light illuminating the ground up ahead. I was able to follow it only briefly; all at once, the noisy aircraft jutted farther to the left and quickly disappeared from view.

Too many trees.

The droning engine and blade noise continued for several minutes, got quieter, then got louder again. Briefly, I saw the spotlight light up the sky to the left before it and the big, dark bird disappeared from sight. The noise diminished as the helicopter moved away into the night. Eventually, maybe three or four minutes or so later . . . I couldn't hear the Chinook anymore.

The aircraft had come and gone all inside of just a couple minutes.

Then I had a sickening thought. What if they were looking for an escaped prisoner? After all, there was a prison on the other side of the county, past the chemical plant. But then, would they use a big Chinook for that? Maybe not . . .

Really, I was scared. Maybe it'd been the noise. Maybe just being alone on the unfamiliar Greatwoods property. Maybe I was just tired from all the stress and lack of sleep. Whatever the reason, I wanted to turn back and go home. Yet, I was actually closer to Ian's mansion than I was to my own place. And I'd come so far . . . I was determined to find Dolly.

I shrieked as a bat flew toward me and nearly hit me in the face.

"Ugh."

With my heart racing, I switched on my flashlight app and hurried down a narrow, twisty trail to who-knows-where.

Then, a few minutes later, I realized that I'd lost the dinky trail. I tried to go back and find it. But it just made matters worse. Thrashing around in the briars and wire grass, I'd been out more than an hour, perhaps closer to two hours, since I'd left home. Really, I had no idea anymore where I was. It was about time to have a good cry . . .

I heard a twig snap.

"Dolly?"

Like lightning, someone behind me wrapped a strong arm around my chest. Then a hand clamped over my mouth.

CHAPTER 31

My heart raced as I struggled and fought hard to get free. I tried biting his hand. Kicking him in the shins. The groin. Grabbing for his ears, his neck . . . face . . . But he was strong as a bull, and his grip around me was ironclad. He'd been so quick and forceful that I wasn't able to use any of my jujitsu moves. I tried. More than once. It was futile. He'd snuck up and grabbed me before I even knew he was there. And he was able to counter every move I made. Like he knew jujitsu himself. Still, something was familiar . . .

"Shhh, Babydoll," whispered Buck in my ear. "Shut off that light! Of all the times to remember your damn phone," he mumbled. He took his hand away from my mouth.

"Let go!" I screamed.

He clamped my mouth with his hand. "Shhh! Dammit, Eva, I'm not kidding. This is serious. Give me that light."

Just then, the light on the smartphone in my hand went out. The battery had died.

Buck whispered, "If I take my hand away from your mouth, will you promise not to make noise?"

I nodded. He took his hand away. Still, he kept his other arm wrapped tight around me.

"What are you doing?" I asked angrily. "You nearly scared me to death!"

"Shhh!" he whispered again. "C'mon, I've got to get you out of here. Oh, Christ, you're shaking. Are you alright?"

"What are you talking about? I've got to find Dolly."

I shoved my phone into my back skort pocket.

"She's at Greatwoods," Buck whispered, finally releasing his arm from around me. He grabbed my hand and pulled me up and behind him as he started running through the brush. "How do you think I found you? Hurry. This way."

He led me through solid wire grass and pine trees.

"Greatwoods? Dolly's at Greatwoods? Ow!" I cried. The grass and prickers scratched my bare legs.

"Shhh!"

"What . . . is . . . going . . . on?" I asked, trying to talk and breathe as we raced through the brush. "Ouch! Why . . . are . . . you . . . here? Stop!"

Buck looked back at me and hissed, "Hurry up!"

"Ow!"

"Shhh!"

"My skort is caught . . ."

I pulled back with all my weight, my sneakers skidding into the dirt, prickers tearing at my skort. I wasn't going anywhere like that. Buck hustled forward and nearly pulled me over. Our hands jerked free.

"Babydoll, no!"

I stood my ground. Buck walked back to me, and as he looked over my shoulder he started to say something, but I interrupted.

"I'm not going another step until you tell me what the hell is going on out here," I said, hands on my hips. "And why were you so crappy to me at the Roadhouse?"

That's when, like a powerful cat, Buck sprang into the air and took me down. We landed in a thicket of prickers. Before I could move or utter a word, he pressed his body on top of me, his hand clamped over my mouth again.

CHAPTER 32

We lay in silence for a minute or two—it seemed like forever—Buck on top of me, his hand covering my mouth, in the pitch-black brush of the Greatwoods forest. Honestly, I was so stunned at first that I froze, my face in the dirt. Then I felt Buck nudge me. He raised up a bit to let me lift my chin. Not far from where we lay, I saw men in military fatigues moving stealthily through the forest.

I just got a glimpse before they stepped out of my sight. There were two, moving together. Then a minute or so later, there was another pair. Then maybe three or four more teams of two. With Buck still on top of me, I couldn't see well enough through the scrubby brush to know for sure. The men had hats and camouflage-painted faces, and they carried large weapons that looked like some kind of rifles as they moved silently through the forest, just about fifty feet from where we hid. They were completely silent; only their equipment jingled and clattered as they passed by. They signaled one another with their hands, cautiously surveying the woods around them. How they missed us—other than the fact that

Buck and I were both dressed in black, doing a face-plant in a thicket of briars—I'll never know.

I couldn't imagine what was going on. Were we in mortal danger? Were the guys in military fatigues hunting for *us*?

Still pressed on top of me, I could feel Buck adjust himself as he tried not to squash me. Somehow, he supported himself while still covering me with his body. It must've taken incredible strength. We lay that way in the brush, without a word whispered between us, for what seemed like fifteen minutes or more. I felt Buck's every breath as his chest heaved above me, his puffs of expired air tickling my ear. I remembered the way he used to tease me when we were in high school, blowing in my ear because he knew it made me crazy.

As we lay that way, I realized that despite the danger, I'd nestled comfortably under Buck's muscled warmth—his smooth, honeyed skin mingled with whatever that scent was that he wore; it was a mix of powdery freshness and Oriental spices. Wearing a tee shirt and jeans, he felt good against my skin. No, he felt great. And I couldn't help but think about how happy we'd been together long ago. I'd never been happier.

And I'd tossed it all away for Dex.

I felt a hot tear pool out of my eye before it hit the dirt beneath me.

"I'm sorry," I whispered.

Buck bent his head close to my ear and whispered, "You don't have anything to be sorry about, Babydoll." I felt his lips brush my ear.

Had he kissed me? My heart thumped. Something low in my abdomen flipped as I felt Buck tighten his hand softly around my wrist.

"No," I whispered, "I mean, I'm sorry that I left you."

"Left me?"

"At our wedding."

Buck tightened for a moment. *Maybe not.* He put his mouth to my ear and whispered, "Forget it."

"It was . . ."

"Shhh," he whispered close to my ear.

I knew that Buck was watching, scanning the woods around us for more military men. Clearly, he knew what was going on. Why were they there? Maybe we'd never come out alive. It seemed as good a time as any to finally come clean.

I have to tell Buck what happened.

"Remember when we were engaged, and I was in college . . . the time I went to Manhattan to be a bridesmaid in Bibi's wedding?"

Bibi Bambolari had been my roommate at Mount Holyoke College. Her father owned the Bambolari fashion house in Italy.

Buck put his head down close to mine. Then he whispered, "Wedding in Saint Pat's Cathedral. Reception at the Pierre."

"Everyone who was anyone in the fashion world was there."

Buck nodded. Then he whispered, "You came home and couldn't stop talking about it. You beamed for days."

"There was a guy in the wedding party. From Boston. He liked me."

Buck nodded again. "Of course he did. Here." He got up off me, offered me his hand, and pulled me up off the ground.

"Is someone going to shoot us?" I whispered.

"I hope not," he whispered back, dragging me through the woods behind him. He moved like a cat between the trees. I stayed close to him and kept whispering in his ear.

I have to tell him.

"We were paired up at the wedding—just as friends. He knew that I was engaged."

Buck nodded as he pressed on into the woods. He seemed to know where he was going. I stayed as close to him as I could, almost pressing myself against his back as we scurried through the trees.

"Except he kept in touch afterward. Kept asking me to come visit him in Boston."

Buck wasn't looking at me as he pressed on. Still, I knew he was listening.

"His family had horses and sailboats. And he traveled for work. He sent me gifts—perfume from France, silk scarves from Japan, chocolates from Belgium. He even invited me to Paris."

"Paris?"

I nodded, oblivious to the fact that Buck couldn't see me behind him.

"Let's make a run for it," Buck said, tightening his grip on my hand. And he took off even faster. Quickly, I charged behind Buck as he sprinted through the woods, zigzagging this way and that, between the trees and bushes. It was all a blur as the briars tore at my legs. Just inches behind him, I simply focused on and followed his hard-bodied form as he glided stealthily and easily through the thicket.

Buck moved like a panther through the trees.

A few minutes later, I was huffing and puffing when we reached a gravel path. As we pressed onward, I noticed the landscape changing. Soon, it became more open. And there were fewer longleaf pines and more hardwood trees and shrubs. Here and there were some boulders. Finally, Buck slowed to a jog, and we followed the gravel path to a high stone wall with an open black iron gate. I noticed a security camera mounted high up on the wall. With Buck still holding my hand, he led me through the gate.

On the other side, it was like the world opened up into a fairy tale. Buck closed the gate, and we faced acres and acres of majestically landscaped lawns and gardens, which flanked the magnificent, French chateau–styled Greatwoods mansion, sitting high on a knoll.

"Glad to see you've kept in shape, Babydoll," said Buck. Then he started running toward the mansion.

"Wait!"

I wasn't finished. I hustled right behind Buck. Even though I was an experienced runner, it took all I had to keep up with him as he raced up the knoll toward the great house.

"Listen!" I cried. "I'm not finished. I . . . must . . . explain. Please! Being with him . . . with Dex . . ."—I huffed—"made me . . . realize . . . how small-town, how ignorant . . . I was. There was a whole world out there waiting for me. I didn't want to come home and be a farmer's wife . . . not then, any-way. But it wasn't about you . . . really . . ."

Buck turned and started to say something, but I raised my hand and kept yammering as we scampered over an immac-ulately manicured, lush green lawn.

"For the first time . . . I realized . . . how sheltered I'd been . . . I wanted to see more . . ."

I was having trouble breathing while running and talking. Still, I was determined to get it out.

Once and for all.

"I was just . . ." I jogged a few more steps as Buck kept moving like a panther—quick, smooth, and sure—up the hill toward the formal gardens and terrace. ". . . a small-town farmer's . . . daughter from . . . the boonies. Other than college . . . I'd never been anywhere . . . dated . . . or been with anyone . . . other than you . . . It made me feel . . . unsure . . . of who I was . . . what . . . I wanted. How could I . . . commit . . . to you . . . when I felt . . . so unsure . . . about myself?"

I was completely out of breath.

"We can walk now," said Buck as he slowed.

I stopped, put my hands on my knees, and took in some deep breaths while Buck stood and watched me. Then I stood and took in the Greatwoods mansion. The place reminded me of the Rosecliff mansion in Newport, Rhode Island, which I'd often visited. Rosecliff was designed by architect Stanford White to resemble a small version of the Grand Trianon of Versailles in France. And like Rosecliff, Greatwoods was built in a similar vein during the Gilded Age of the late nine-teenth century by cotton magnate Duke Dufour and his rail-road heiress wife, Dina Abbot Dufour—the same couple who'd built the local library before donating it to the town. It'd been the summer playground, hunting retreat, and lavish party palace for some of the world's most rich and powerful people. In addition to the main mansion, the mega-thousand-acre Greatwoods Plantation had numerous hunting lodges, stables, guest cottages, barns, and more.

I wanted to stop and take it all in slowly—the stunning

mansion, the lawns, the topiary gardens—except, already Buck was walking.

I hurried to catch up.

Clad in white terra-cotta tiles, the residence was basically H-shaped with an arcade of arched windows and Ionic pilasters and columns that ran across a central loggia. There was a second story with French doors to balconies outside. A balustrade ran along the edge of the roofline. Much of the interior was lit that night—early morning, I should say. It all looked warm and glowy inside, including the space behind the loggia and some upstairs rooms.

Apparently, Ian Collier was a night owl.

Buck and I hiked toward a massive and well-lit stepped terrace with a huge pool flanked by big fountains, marble benches, lots of statuary, and well-tended gardens with topiaries. As we neared the back of the mansion, the flowering shrubs sweetened the summertime air. Fountains gushed water around the pool. It was easy to imagine the many exuberant and extravagant Gatsby-like parties that took place during an earlier, more extravagant era. The fresh scratches on my legs from the briars were beginning to bleed and sting.

"Remind me," I asked Buck, "why were we running?" I stopped atop the knoll, putting my hands on my knees. I bent over again, trying to catch my breath. My head pounded and my face was hot.

"No reason after we hit the gate," said Buck with a grin. "I just wanted to see if you'd keep up."

I smacked him on the shoulder. His arm was like a rock. "Ow!"

Buck huffed a little laugh. It made me mad that he wasn't even breathing hard.

We pressed on toward the Greatwoods residence, finally reaching the terrace steps. We climbed to the pool area. Huge marble cherubs danced around up-lit gurgling fountains. I felt so hot and tired—pretty gross, actually—it was all I could do not to jump into the crystalline water in the fancy tiled pool. Looking around, I couldn't imagine living in such luxury.

Buck strode across the terrace like he owned the place.

"Wait! I'm not finished!" I cried.

After eighteen years, I needed to get it all out. Finally.

"You don't have to explain," Buck answered with a wave of his hand.

"Yes. I do."

Buck stopped and took me in. I saw a flash of that keen look he gets when he's on a case. Alert. Cunning. Like a wild animal who hears something approaching. Then he nodded and motioned for me to follow him around the pool. We headed toward a lit area at the back of the building—what looked to be a service entrance in a corner of the mansion. Near the door was another carved marble bench flanked by two potted evergreens trimmed to look like stags. Buck motioned for me to sit down.

"I'm listening, Babydoll."

"Okay. Here goes," I said, seating myself.

Buck sat on the bench next to me.

"On that day," I continued, "the day we were to be married"—I hated the sound of my own voice— "the Boston guy called me."

"Dex Codman."

"Yes. Dex. He was several years older than me. A year or two older than you, actually. Anyway, he'd flown down from New England in his corporate jet and said that he'd come to 'save' me. He said I was too good to be a simple farmer's wife living in Georgia swampland. He'd show me a world that I'd never known. Never dreamed of. We'd travel together. Go to Paris. Milan. Hong Kong. There'd be a home in Chestnut Hill. A summerhouse on Martha's Vineyard. We'd host parties for some of the most influential people in the business world. And he said he'd support my dream to attend graduate school—I'd wanted to study art history, remember?"

Buck nodded. "And did he tell you that he loved you?"

"What?"

"Did he tell you that he loved you?"

"Of course he did. Well, I think . . . No . . . Actually, I don't remember. It was so long ago. I'm sure he did." *Had he told me that he loved me?* "He'd been like someone from a fairy tale, you know? Handsome, rich, powerful, educated. And I thought he made me feel safe."

"I didn't make you feel safe, Babydoll?"

"Of course you did. I was just . . . so young. And confused."

Buck nodded. "So you ran."

"Yes. I . . . I ran. Everything that he said made me doubt everything that I thought I knew about myself. About us. It was the first time that I could imagine a different sort of life. Something other than living here, in Abundance. I was so naive. I was in college. I thought that I knew everything . . ." I shook my head. "And I was blinded by his smooth style."

"And his money?"

"Yes. I admit it. Young and foolish, I was smitten by his money. I'd never imagined living the way he did. Traveling to the places he went. Possessing the kinds of things that he and his family had. They owned *racehorses*! But it was more than that. There was his education. And his Boston heritage. I was curious. I mean, the Brahmins were the people who started the Boston Symphony Orchestra, the Museum of Fine Arts, the Peabody Essex Museum, the Isabella Stewart Gardner Museum, WGBH public broadcasting . . . so many wonderful things and places! And I was hungry and greedy for all of it. And I guess, somewhere inside, I wondered why my own mother ran away from us when we were little. What had she known that I didn't? What had she discovered, out in the world away from Abundance, after she left us? Why had she never returned? Surely, I was missing something . . . great."

Buck just nodded.

"Of course, things ended badly, to say the least. And when I finally realized what a colossal mistake I'd made, after what I'd done to you, to your family, to my family, to *everyone*, I was too ashamed to come back and face you."

"So, you stayed in New England, all that time—for eighteen years—because you were too *embarrassed* to come home?"

"Yes." I looked at the ground. "And ashamed."

Now that I'd said it, finally, after all those years, I felt somehow greatly relieved and terribly sad and stupid at the same time. I heaved a deep breath. Something twisted and ached in my gut as I felt my eyes fill with tears. How could I have been so spoiled? So selfish? So stupid and uncaring? I was still embarrassed about how I'd behaved. How I'd hurt the people who loved me. And although I hadn't told Buck the *entire* story, I'd told him enough. At least for that moment.

"I'm so sorry."

Buck said nothing.

"I've never told anyone. Not even Pep or Daphne. Oh crappy," I said, wiping a hand across my face. I was embarrassed to be so weepy in front of Buck. *What a mess.* "None of them ever knew why I left you. And none of them ever knew about my relationship with Dex."

"Even after you were engaged to marry him?"

I shook my head.

"No. They still don't. It's . . . *complicated.*"

I'd said enough. I didn't want to say any more. Especially something that might implicate me in a murder. At least, not until I had more time to figure it all out for myself. Although, deep inside, I knew that I just wanted to bury all the bad things that had happened between me and Dex . . . forever.

"I feel terrible about how I treated you. I'm sorry. Really sorry," I whispered. "It was all a mistake."

I was trying desperately to hold back eighteen years' worth of tears. "I wish I could take it all back," I whispered.

"Babydoll."

I was making it all about me, and it shouldn't have been. For once, I needed to take Buck's feelings into account. Put him first.

Of course, I wondered if he still had any feelings left for me. Other than hurt, disgust, and disappointment. And then, of course, there was Debi . . . What the heck had been going on at the Roadhouse earlier? Why had Buck ignored me? And what was happening between me and Buck all these hours later? It was like he wasn't even the same person . . .

Buck let out a slow sigh.

"God, you're a mess, Babydoll."

When I finally turned and looked at Buck sitting next to me, studying me, his deep brown eyes appeared like soft pools of chocolate. This was the man I remembered loving. Not at all the icy cool man who'd been with Debi in the Roadhouse earlier.

Buck reached out and dabbed a bloody scratch on my knee with his hand. I caught a little whiff of his powdery, spicy fragrance. Then he smiled softly before he cupped his big hands around my cheeks and pulled my face toward his. He held me close. I could feel his eyelashes brush against my cheek. His muscled chest heaved in and out next to mine as his warm breath fell against my neck. Then slowly, he turned my head to face his, and with a fervency and tenderness I'd never known, Buck pressed his warm, wet lips into mine and kissed me, long and slow.

That's when my insides melted into a million pieces.

CHAPTER 33

The Greatwoods service door flew open.

"Well, well, well! Lookee who the wind blew in," tittered Precious with a silly grin. "At it again, you two?"

Precious laughed raucously. She wore a long silk kimono with multicolored butterflies and flowers patterned over it. And a multicolored silk turban on her head. And, yes, she was wearing Louboutins, even in the middle of the night.

Maybe she sleeps in them, I thought.

I pulled back from Buck and jumped up from the marble bench. Buck took his time standing, then took his finger and wiped the tear from my face before turning to face Precious.

"Miss Darling," Buck said too politely with an unfazed expression. "Miss Eva and I were just about to step inside. She's looking for Dolly."

"Uh-huh," Precious said with a wink. "It don't look to me like you two were about to step inside." Precious stepped back and gave me a look. "Lawdee, Sunshine, what happened to *you*? You two been makin' whoopee in the prickers?"

She roared with laughter.

I looked down. My arms and legs were covered with

bloody scrapes and scratches. And my poor skort was riddled with tears and pulls from all the woods. Buck raised his eyebrows and said nothing.

"Don't you ever *not* wear those ridiculous spiky shoes?" I asked Precious.

"Well, I don't wear 'em to bed, if that's what ya mean," said Precious. "Of course, if y'all weren't so rude creeping around the place all night long a person could catch up on her beauty sleep." She laughed, motioning us into the building. "Y'all know I'm just kiddin' with ya. Dolly's in the pantry. I gave her a snack. All we had was leftover filet mignon and lobster tails. Mister Collier and Doc Payne are still in the library. Y'all come inside to the air-conditioning now—it's too hot to be sittin' out here. Sunshine, you need a Band-Aid or something?"

"Not unless you have one big enough to cover my entire body," I said ruefully.

Buck chuckled.

"Nope. Okay, I'll leave you two alone. I gotta go check on somethin' upstairs."

By the time Buck and I had stepped into the massive kitchen, already Precious was hustling off somewhere through an interior door.

"Sheriff, you know your way around," Precious said with a wave of her hand before disappearing.

The Greatwoods kitchen was at least twice, maybe three times the size of my cottage, with a high ceiling, polished tile floor, black gas stove the size of a train, deep marble sink, baker's racks, and an antique butcher-block table. The eye candy of the room was the ginormous metal pot rack. Two or three dozen polished copper pots and pans hung over a massive open-leg, marble-topped wooden island that must've been at least ten or twelve feet long.

"Holy cow," I said, looking around. My voice echoed in the big space. Then, "Wait. I don't get it. About Dolly. Why would she come here?"

Buck pointed to a doggie door in the bottom of the service door.

"Her old stomping grounds," he said with a shrug.

Dolly must've heard my voice. I heard her feet skittering over the polished tile floor as she rounded a corner, coming from a room off the side of the big kitchen—I guessed it to be the pantry.

"Dolly!" I cried, happy to see her.

Dolly jumped up on my leg, all whimpers, licks, and wags. Then she went over to Buck and did the same thing. A moment later, she scampered back to the pantry . . . no doubt to finish her lobster and filet mignon. There was no denying it: My dog was spoiled. And a pig when it came to food.

"Okay, so there's a doggie door here," I said to Buck. "So what?"

"Don't you know?"

"Know what?"

"Dolly's mother is one of Ian's hounds."

"Are you kidding me? Dolly came from *here*? You mean, she was *Ian's*?"

Buck nodded.

"Why has no one told me this? Daddy, Daphne . . . they never said a word! How come you know and I don't?"

Daddy and Daphne had given me Dolly as a present when I'd first arrived home that summer. They thought a new puppy would help cheer me up after my heartbreak and all of the hullabaloo in Boston.

"You'll have to ask them. C'mon. Our host is waiting in the library." Buck turned to leave the kitchen.

"Just a minute!" I grabbed Buck's arm. "Did you forget the giant elephant in the room? Or rather, in the woods out there? What's going on? Why are military guys with guns crawling all over the place?"

"They're Navy Seals."

"What?"

Buck just lifted his eyebrows.

"Navy Seals? Here? In Abundance? Right in my backyard? *Why?*"

"Practice makes perfect, Babydoll."

"What?"

"You ever play capture the flag?"

"Yes, of course. We used to play all the time as kids."

"That's kind of what's going on out there. A big game of capture the flag."

"Okay. You need to do better than that. Explain." I crossed my arms.

"Sometimes military ops need a certain kind of terrain to practice and train for particular missions. Sometimes Abundance fits the bill. Ian lets them use Greatwoods."

"You're kidding?"

"I'm deadly serious."

"So the helicopter . . ."

"Was dropping off a special ops team. There were two drop-offs tonight."

"And they're all running around in the woods trying to capture one another?"

"Something like that."

"What if someone gets killed?"

"They won't. Not on purpose, anyway."

"Oh, that's reassuring." I rolled my eyes. "But they had guns. Big ones!"

"Some are paintball guns. However, those are the only things that aren't real for them. They would have found you— make no mistake, they would have—and you might've been detained for a bit. Probably would've been half a day or so before you'd have gotten out."

"Are you for real? They'd hold me *prisoner*?"

"No. It's just that they have a mission . . ."

"A *make-believe* mission."

"Not to them. Anyway, you would've been a complication, and complications can take time to rectify. They can't afford to have you compromise a mission."

"I thought they were trying to kill us! You're telling me now that it was all a *game*? You could have at least shared that with me while I lay in the woods thinking it'd be my last night on earth!"

"I explained . . ."

I raised my hand. "Stop! Never mind. I don't want to hear it."

Buck raised his eyebrows again. Then he smiled and brushed his hand across my cheek. I hadn't even realized a tear was there.

"Don't fret, Babydoll."

"I'm not." I bit my lip.

"Right. Anyway, when Dolly showed up here tonight, apparently, she popped straight through her old doggie door in the kitchen and made her way directly to us in the library, like she owned the place. I guessed you weren't far behind. So I went looking."

"And what if the Navy Seals had found Dolly in the woods?"

"She'd have been neutralized."

"No!"

Buck chuckled. "Nothing permanent. However, this is as close to real ops as it gets. So it's no holds barred out there."

"And you know all this . . . how?"

"I'm not exactly an impartial bystander. Let's just say that I've got connections. Besides, as the local sheriff, they have to coordinate the operation with me. That's one reason I've been hanging around here tonight. Just to be sure everything goes without a hitch."

"Connections?"

"Yes."

"You're not being very forthcoming here."

"It's not my place."

I sighed. "What does that mean?"

"It means what I said."

"Which is nothing."

"If you see it that way."

"Argh! I *hate* this. Why must you always play games with me?"

"I'm not playing games. You just don't have a need to know."

"Right. So it's 'need to know' only?"

"Exactly."

"That sounds like government clearance talk to me."

One of my public relations clients back in New England had been a government contractor. The company hired me to deal with the local community and media when they acquired a parcel of land and built a new facility to manufacture communications devices for the United States military. I'd actually been awarded a Secret government clearance. It wasn't very high up the totem pole, but it was enough to recognize some of the jargon when I heard it. It's also how I'd recognized the Chinook—not that there's much else out there like it.

"If you say so," said Buck.

"That's Buck-speak for 'yes.' Okay. I'm getting the hang of this now," I said, trying to coax more from him.

"You're not going to quit, are you?"

"No. Would you? You're all up to something, and I want to know what it is."

"Okay. Stop." Buck raised his hand, then thought for a moment. "So, I'm not saying this is the case; however, theoretically, sometimes the government doesn't exactly cut a person loose, when it appears that they have."

There was a beat while I let what he said soak in.

"You were . . . are . . . in the military? That's where you went when people said you left Abundance for all those years while I was away. The military?"

"I didn't say military. You did. Let's just call it 'protective service.'"

"What the heck is that?"

Buck shrugged. "Whatever you want it to be. You've got a Secret clearance. You figure it out."

"How do you know that? About my clearance?"

Buck smiled with those damned dimples. "A good operative never reveals his sources."

"This is surreal."

"Your words, not mine, babe. Shall we go to the library?" He gestured toward a door.

"You're not going to tell me any more, are you?" I remained planted in the kitchen.

"No." Buck kept walking toward the door. "And you're not

going to ask me any more or talk about it with anyone. Understand? The only reason I clued you in was because you stumbled into it. And I knew that you wouldn't let it go. So now that you know what it's all about, I'm telling you: Let it go."

This was the second man in less than twenty-four hours to tell me not to talk about what we'd just talked about. Or what'd just happened.

What gives?

"Still, theoretically," I said, ignoring what Buck had just said, "if someone were doing whatever it is they're looking like they're not *really* doing, why would they come back home to the middle of nowhere to '*not*' do it?"

"I can't answer that, other than to say that home in 'the middle of nowhere,' as you put it, would be the most logical place for a person to be doing what it appears he is not doing, if there were some reason to do it." Buck turned to leave the kitchen.

"What?" I needed time to process what he was saying. But as Buck started to leave, my mind flew elsewhere . . . "Wait!"

I grabbed the back of Buck's arm as he stepped away. My hand barely wrapped halfway around his muscled bicep. He turned to face me. I got another whiff of his damned captivating cologne. I felt paralyzed by exotic spices, patchouli, baby powder, something honeyed and warm . . .

I shook my head. "Why did you kiss me tonight?" I demanded.

"Talk about a non sequitur!" Buck laughed.

He took my elbows in his hands and leaned in close. He waited a moment before answering. The hairs on the back of my neck stood on end . . .

"Because I wanted to, Eva."

There came that devilish smile that I remembered from our early days. And again, somehow we were nose to nose. My insides flipped.

"And you didn't seem to mind," he whispered in my ear. His breath was warm. I felt his lips brushing against my ear.

Quickly this time, he pulled me toward him, wrapping his

arms around me as he planted a wet, wild kiss on my lips. I could feel the heat rise up the back of my neck. My cheeks flushed. My knees felt weak. And this time, I kissed Buck back. I put my hands around his neck, mashed myself into him, and kissed him long and hard. He was warm, soft. Familiar. I felt like I was seventeen again.

Young, happy, and blissfully in love.

It was the longest kiss ever.

I pulled back. Embarrassed. I stared down at the polished marble floor. Then I looked up. Buck's eyes were flashing.

"What about Debi?" I whispered, remembering how humiliated he'd made me feel at the Roadhouse. I took both hands and pushed Buck away.

"Debi? Debi Dicer?" Buck pulled me toward him again. "What about Debi?" he asked playfully. He gave my ear a nibble.

I put my hand up, and again I pushed back on Buck's muscled chest. He dropped his arms and stepped back.

"I mean, aren't you *engaged*?" I asked. I wiped my forehead and put my hands on my hips. "And why didn't you acknowledge me tonight at the Roadhouse? You made me feel like crap, by the way."

"I may not have spoken to you, Babydoll. However, I sure noticed you. Every man in the place was ogling you. Did you know, you look sweet as sugar all wet and covered in beer? It was all I could do not to grab you and kiss you all over. Actually, just thinking about it now . . ."

He stepped toward me, looking like he wanted to kiss me again. I put my hand out to stop him.

This is all play for him, I thought. It'd been stupid of me to kiss him. It was all a game for Buck. Probably all lies. *All of it*. Most likely the government stuff, too. It was just like my old prankster boyfriend Buck to have been pulling my leg the whole time.

Aw, heck.

I was a mess when it came to men. Always making the wrong decisions. I didn't know what to think. My heart was still racing.

"Are you telling me that you and Debi are *not* planning on getting married?"

"Engaged? Me and Debi?" Buck teased. "She's not really my type." He grinned and advanced toward me again.

I put my hand up again. He stopped.

"Not your type? Then why are you with her all the time? Goodness knows, she practically *lives* with you, from what I hear. And you kissed her on the cheek tonight after she nibbled on your ear . . . in public! Do you hear me? *Nibbled on your ear!* What were you thinking? You're the darned sheriff, for gosh sakes!"

"Really?"

"Don't play coy with me, Buck Tanner. You can't even look at me when you're with her. I'd say that's because you're guilty. For whatever reason—and I don't dare imagine what it is—you can't get enough of Debi. And just so you know, it irritates the snot out of me."

Buck laughed. "I'm happy to hear it. It irritates the snot out of me when I see every other man lusting after you. Especially when you're drenched in beer!"

"Don't play with me, Buck. I'm not going to let you, or any man, hurt me again. Got it?"

"Okay. I got it. Loud and clear. Seriously, let's just say Debi is no more than a means to an end."

"What does that mean?"

"It means you've got nothing to worry about, Babydoll. I'm all yours. Always have been. Now, c'mon." Buck took my elbow. "Dolly can stay in the pantry. It's late. Ian is waiting for us."

"But what does that mean? About Debi! A means to an end?"

Buck didn't answer as he pushed open the door and pulled me through.

CHAPTER 34

No doubt about it, I thought, *my life was becoming more bizarre with each passing hour.*

There'd been *another* death . . . my estranged ex-fiancé. And as it had been with earlier deaths that summer, the circumstances surrounding his demise had been odd, to say the least. Then I was pushed in front of a parade truck; then I crashed a vehicle, for the *second time* during that summer, on Benderman's Curve. And Ian Collier had come to my rescue both times. Except the second time, I'd interrupted him threatening a man in a foggy field and his manservant had nearly shot my head off.

At the Roadhouse, my conversation with Claudia had unnerved me. And Buck had ignored me while Debi insulted me. Then, Precious and I heard that my ex-fiancé was probably *murdered*. And the creepy conversation I'd overheard in the olive grove between Wiggy, Spencer, and Coop made me wonder even more about what, exactly, had happened to Dex. Had one of them killed him? And for what possible reason? Was it somehow connected to real estate in Abundance?

And at Greatwoods Plantation, mysterious helicopters

were dropping off Navy Seals who were running around playing capture the flag in the woods at night. Dolly had returned
"home" to her mansion where she was served filet mignon
and lobster tails. And, Debi Dicer and Buck were *not* getting
married, not even close, according to Buck, even though for
weeks Debi'd been by his side all over town, telling everyone
she knew that she and Buck were getting married and would
be popping out babies, *imminently.* Still, according to Buck,
Debi was merely "a means to an end." Was he talking
about sex?

Gross.

And Buck was, or *was still*, in the military—no, wait,
what did he call it? *Ahh yes.* "Protective service." Whatever
that was.

And Precious Darling wore Louboutin pumps twenty-four,
seven, except when she was sleeping, of course. But then, did
she ever sleep? By the same token, did anyone ever sleep at
Greatwoods Plantation? It was probably well past three in the
morning, probably closer to four, and the place was lit up like
a Christmas tree. Buck, Doc Payne, and Ian had been carous-
ing in the library . . .

Eye roll.

Weirder still, I thought, was the very fact that Buck Tanner
was hanging out with Ian Collier at all. And in the middle of
the night?

What gives?

Does anyone ever sleep around here?

Moreover, even as I pined away for Ian—I couldn't help
myself; by all accounts he was one of the sexiest men alive—
Buck, the *other* sexiest man alive, had just planted on me the
biggest, wettest, most swooningly wonderful kiss that I'd ever
experienced in my life, bar none. And much to my surprise,
I'd jumped in and kissed him back with every bit of heart and
passion that I had. And it'd felt good. No, it'd felt great. Maybe
even greater than great. It was insides-melting, knee-buckling,
earth-shattering, heavens-moving great. Afterward, Buck had
said, *I'm all yours.* Except, he wasn't all mine. Not at all. He
was with Debi.

Wasn't he?

Good thing I had my man moratorium going for me.

Yeah. Right.

Sure. I can handle this, I thought, as I followed Buck through the massive Greatwoods ballroom, a gape-worthy mini Versailles. *No problem.* Still, the thought crossed my tired and confused brain that perhaps being inside the mansion was the opportunity I'd been looking for. Perhaps, I might somehow be able to get some answers about what my mysterious neighbor was up to, besides hosting military games.

"Wait," I said to Buck.

I had to stop a moment to take it all in. It was the kind of place that I'd only seen in movies. Or while touring the great mansions of Newport, Rhode Island.

With French doors running the length of each side of the great ballroom, the furnishings were all Louis the Somebody or Other—Fourteenth or Fifteenth; I was too tired to keep them straight. Basically, it was lots of three-hundred-year-old furniture with cherub, botanical, ribbon, and curlicue motifs finished in gold leaf paired with elaborate silk and tapestried fabrics and rugs.

Although it was all in keeping with the architecture, the furnishings were definitely froufrou. Not the kind of style I'd have imagined a man like Ian would choose for himself. Although, I shouldn't have been surprised. A few weeks earlier, I'd wakened after an accident to find myself convalescing upstairs at Greatwoods and mistakenly thought that I was actually *in* Versailles . . .

Long story.

A massive marble fireplace was centered at each end of the great room. At one corner, there was a grand piano. Enormous gold and crystal chandeliers hung from the frescoed and intricately hand-carved ceiling that soared above us.

I followed Buck across the awe-inspiring space. At the far end of the room, Buck grabbed a lever and opened a French door to cross a threshold. I followed him as we stepped into a very large wood-paneled chamber filled floor to ceiling with hardbound books.

Ahh, I thought. *This is more like it.*

A man's man room.

There was a massive carved wooden desk and tall leather chair, a half dozen brown leather upholstered wingback chairs, a card table and chairs, some gun cabinets, marble busts and metal sculptures, hunting trophies, and dark green velvet drapes drawn across the massive arched windows—or French doors; I couldn't tell which. Rising nearly to the ceiling on the far side of the room, an immense, hand-carved, dark wooden fireplace surround with a high mantel showcased sculptural carvings of stags, foxes, pheasants, and local flora. The room smelled like wool and wood polish, and hinted of cigar smoke.

A massive grandfather clock ticked away in the corner. I'd been right. It was well past three o'clock in the morning.

Seated at a game table in front of a massive window, Ian Collier, the consummate moneyed outdoorsman, puffed on a cigar. My sexy and oh-so-mysterious neighbor flipped the cover closed on a hardcover book he was reading and rose from his chair. Buck and I stepped onto a ginormous Turkish carpet. If Ian had worn a velvet smoking jacket I wouldn't have been surprised. However, he wore his usual pressed shirt and khakis. Except his shirt was comfortably rumpled, his sleeves rolled up.

He looked good, rumpled.

"Eva, what's the craic?" Ian asked with a welcoming smile. Then he furrowed his brow as he looked me over. "Eva, girl, yer lookin' a bit worse for wear. Are ye alright?"

Ian looked to Buck, then back to me.

"I'm fine. Thank you. I'm afraid I got lost and the briars got the better of me wandering around stupidly in the woods."

A chessboard—game in progress—and a couple of empty lowball glasses on leather coasters sat on the table.

"Your move, Sheriff," Ian said to Buck, motioning to the chessboard. "Doc Payne's gone home."

Ian stepped over to me and gave me a hug and a peck on the cheek. His warm, woodsy scent wiped away the vestiges of Buck's heady powder and spice, which I'd been savoring since the kitchen. My senses, not to mention my heart, were in utter confused chaos. Still, my knees didn't go quite as weak as they usually did. Some part of my mind and heart was still wrapped tight around Buck. And I was still confused about the side of Ian that I'd discovered in the field hours earlier.

Why can't I just stick to my man moratorium!

"It's late. I'll pass for the night," answered Buck. He reached into his pocket and drew out his smartphone. It was vibrating. Someone was trying to reach him.

Ian motioned for us each to take a seat at the circle of four leather wingback chairs that were set around a large wooden coffee table with carved legs. Buck frowned as he studied his phone then put it away without answering. He waited for me to take a seat.

"Thank you," I said to Ian, who stood behind my chair as I sat down. "I'm sorry to bother you so late at night. I got worried when Dolly ran off, and I tried to follow her. I never imagined that we'd end up here."

"Yer always welcome here, Eva. Anytime," said Ian with a genuine smile. "Ye can even come up the drive, if ye like. No need to fight the woods each time ye come over. There's a button on the box at the entry gate. Ye just push it and someone will open the gate for ye." His evergreen eyes sparkled with mischief, as he looked me over. "The bloody prickers definitely got the best of ye this go-round."

He looked at Buck and they both chuckled.

I looked down at my scratched and bloodied legs. "Yes, well, I hadn't expected to be out so late . . . or be so far from home. I never realized what a jungle it is out there . . ." I covered my thighs, with my hands, trying to cover the scratched, bloody mess.

Ian laughed. Then he looked at Buck. "Any trouble?"

"No."

The way they looked at each other, it was like they had a secret code.

"I can have Miss Precious take ye to get cleaned up if ye like, Eva. Maybe some salve would help fix ye right up? Some tea, perhaps?"

"That's okay. I'm fine, thanks."

Liar! The bloody scratches on my legs were on fire. And I was dying of thirst.

Be cool, Eva.

Ian nodded. "Looks like it was good ye had yer man the sheriff to rescue ye."

Buck took out his phone again and sighed before putting it back in his pocket.

"Buck just told me that Dolly was born here. I had no idea," I said, changing the subject.

Ian chuckled. "Ye didn't know? Dolly and I are family, I guess ye could say. She's the illicit progeny of a shadowy tryst between one of my hounds and a visiting Romeo." Ian winked at me. "A Maltipoo, or some such thing. I assumed ye knew about me bein' Dolly's family."

I heard Buck's phone vibrate again. He ignored it.

"No. No one told me. Daddy and Daphne gave me Dolly shortly after I arrived back home. Still, they never told me from where they'd gotten her. Buck said Dolly's mother is a hunting dog?"

"Yer sweet Dolly's a mutt, I'm afraid," Ian said with a dramatic sigh. "Her mother is some sort of beagle cross. Someone abandoned her after hunting season. I rescued her on the road a while back. Her name is Daphne."

"Daphne? Did you say Daphne? Dolly's mother—the abandoned hunting mutt—is named *Daphne*?"

I heard Buck chuckle. "So good," he muttered.

"I daresay, we won't tell your sister the dog's name." Ian chuckled.

"No doubt. High Priestess Daphne Knox Bouvier would have a heart attack," said Buck with a grin.

We all laughed. After so much turmoil and stress that day . . . that night . . . it felt good to laugh.

Buck's smile faded when his phone buzzed again.

"Can I get ye something to drink?" said Ian, rising. "Sheriff, a refresher? More bourbon? Eva? Ye must be ready fer something?"

"I'd love a glass of water," I said. "I mean, if it's no trouble. Then I should get Dolly back home."

"I'll take you," Buck said quickly, stuffing his phone back into his pocket.

"Aye. Water's no trouble at all," Ian said, crossing the room. He picked up a decanter off an elaborately carved bar in the wall. There were several decanters and bottles of distilled spirits. "Ahh, bloody . . ."

The decanter was empty.

I heard heavy clip-clopping in the ballroom outside the door.

"Excuse me, Mister Collier?" Precious stood in the doorway. "You're needed upstairs. Right away."

She sounded serious. And she didn't look at me or Buck. I thought that was strange. Especially for Precious. Usually, we were close. Usually, she'd give me a smile. Or a wink. At least a nod . . .

Ian's expression clouded. He set the empty decanter down. "Excuse me," he said. Quickly, with long, swinging strides, Ian whisked himself toward the door. Buck gave him an odd look and a nod.

"We'll let ourselves out," Buck called after Ian.

Buck pulled out his phone again and sighed.

"I need to take this call," Buck said to me. "Then, I'll take you and Dolly home."

He stood up and left the room. I had the majestic Greatwoods library all to myself.

CHAPTER 35

I walked around Ian's manly chamber, his magnificent library, marveling at all the hardcover books. It was an extensive collection, with history and historical novels taking up the most shelf space. Moreover, there was everything from the oldest classics—*Beowulf, The Canterbury Tales*, Shakespeare—to Victorian romance novels, noir crime fiction, modern thrillers, all the definitive Russian titles, translations from French, Chinese, Japanese . . . tomes by the great philosophers, literary fiction, science fiction, travel, even poetry. Cozies? Yes. Even cozy mysteries. I snickered thinking of profound Ian Collier curled up in his manly mansion with a merry little cozy mystery.

I worked my way around the room until I got to the game table where I saw not two, but three empty glasses. *That's right.* I remembered Precious saying that Doc Payne had been here in the library. I spun, looking around the room, as if somehow I'd expected to find the old geezer, perhaps reading a book in the corner somewhere. *Someone said he'd left. He must've gone home while Buck and I were still in the kitchen*, I thought.

After all, it is very late . . . Er, early.

My heart flipped remembering Buck's kisses. Why the hell had I let myself do that? My emotions were completely confused. Could I believe Buck about Debi being just "a means to an end"?

What on earth did that mean?

And then I remembered Ian in the field, standing with his high-powered rifle. Sure, he looked sexy. Still, I didn't like guns. Ironic, as these two men both carried them: Buck for work, and Ian for . . . Why *did* Ian carry a gun? For *sport*? Protection? Enforcement?

Really, I didn't think he hunted at all. So, why did seeing him like that unnerve me? After all, I'd been taught to handle a gun myself. Daddy'd taught all us girls. After Mother left, he was worried about us being alone in the house during his long hours in the fields. We could all shoot . . . Daphne, Pep, and me. And I daresay, at one time I'd been the best shot of the three of us. But there'd been an accident. After that, I didn't want any part of guns anymore.

I looked back to the three empty glasses. *What an odd combination*, I thought: Ian Collier, Buck Tanner, and Doc Payne. Smoking cigars, drinking bourbon, and playing games in the middle of the night.

I smiled. Floyd "Doc" Payne was an odd sort of duck and well into geezerdom, easily twice the age of the other men. Since I was a child, Doc Payne had reminded me of photos I'd seen of Albert Einstein, with his wiry white hair and big, bushy eyebrows. Most of all, I always remembered his bad breath. *Worst ever.* Hard to imagine him "hanging" late at night with Buck and Ian. Although, when I thought about it, Buck and Ian seemed an odd pairing as well.

Outside the library, I heard the purr of Buck's smooth Southern drawl echoing in the ballroom. His low, sotto voce voice didn't sound happy. Just then, a freakishly tall, bald-headed manservant with sallow skin, a long nose, and black sunken eyes skulked silently into the library.

Mister Lurch.

Ian Collier's manservant.

The sharpshooter.

When I'd first seen him weeks earlier, I'd been dumb-founded to learn that the man's name was the same as the similar-looking character I'd watched as a child during Saturday morning reruns of *The Addams Family*. Except the make-believe Lurch had hair. This one didn't. I thought Ian's Lurch looked more handsome this way . . . no hair.

Ian's sharpshooting manservant shuffled in silently and placed a fresh decanter of water on the bar before mumbling something incoherent. I think I heard my name. He turned, and I tried to discern whether he had a gun tucked into his waist. He was wearing a vest. I couldn't tell . . . Maybe not. He shuffled from the room.

I picked up a cut-crystal highball glass and poured myself water. I guzzled it. Then I poured another and guzzled it as well. Then, I let my eyes roam over the room, to Ian's great carved desk.

Instantly, something caught my eye. I put the glass down on the bar and walked over to inspect. There was an oversize pile of papers atop the desk—Abundance County tax maps, to be more precise. The one on top was of Vanderbiddle Plantation. *Five thousand acres.*

I picked up the map and studied it for a moment. Then the one below it: Hickey Hills Plantation. Ten thousand acres. And the one below that: Sky Pines. Seventeen thousand acres. There were more. Cotton Ball Farm. Balmy Way Plantation. Bountiful Acres. I recognized some as having been recently sold. Had they *all* been sold? At the bottom of the pile, there was a map of the entire county. Each of the individual tracts of land that I'd surmised had been sold during the past couple of years—there were as many as a dozen or so—were outlined in red marker. Given the relatively small size of Abundance County and the high price tags of each property, it was a shockingly high number of sales within the span of just a couple of years. I picked up the county map.

A map like the one Wiggy had been holding on the hill overlooking the pond at Knox Plantation.

Alongside every red-marked property, there was a handwritten note penciled in that read, *Dicer*. And there was a number. The numbers were probably sales prices for each property. As I'd surmised, the prices were very, very high. Well beyond what anyone local could afford to pay. Maybe they were the asking prices, not the sales prices? Still, either way, the numbers were astronomical.

I stared at the *Dicer* notation beside each parcel.

Debi is a means to an end, Buck had said. It hadn't occurred to me when he'd spoken that he was talking about anything more than sex or good fun. Yet, seeing all this made me wonder . . . had I missed something completely? Something was going on with all this. *Something big*. And I was beginning to think it involved both Ian and Buck. Could it somehow involve the Bostoners, too? There was just so much *land* stuff going on. Could it all be a coincidence? As I put the papers down, another thing caught my eye.

Behind the desk there was a velvet curtain, drawn closed like the other curtains in front of the windows and doors. However, as I understood the space, the wall behind the desk was an interior wall, not one with a window or door to outside. And what caught my eye was the edge of a great gilded frame peeking out from one side of the dark green curtain. Of course, my former art-historian-wannabe self just had to see. I reached out to pull the curtain back . . .

"Alright, Babydoll," said Buck from behind me. I hadn't even heard him reenter the room. "Time to hightail it home." I dropped my hand and turned to see Buck, holding Dolly in his arms.

How could I not have heard them?

CHAPTER 36

Dolly sat on my lap, panting and drooling all over my legs. We hadn't even gotten to the main road when Buck said, "Our guy in the pond was your fiancé." It wasn't a question. It was a statement. Like some sort of delayed reaction to what I'd told him hours earlier, at the pond. "You left me for him."

"Yes. I left you at the altar to run off with Dex. And now he was found dead, in our farm pond."

"Anything else you want to tell me?"

"What?"

"I said, is there anything else you want to tell me, about you and your dead fiancé? Now would be the time . . ."

"No. There's nothing more to say. Other than it was all a huge mistake on my part."

Buck didn't look at me as we headed down the Greatwoods drive. I could tell his mind was racing.

I wanted to change the subject.

"What is Ian Collier doing with tax records for sold Abundance properties? Big properties?"

It was a guess about all the properties being sold.

"What are you talkin' about?" asked Buck. He had one

hand on the wheel of his SUV as we coasted down the cobble-stone drive, passing through a virtual tunnel of pink-flowering crepe myrtle trees.

Yes, Sheriff Buck Tanner is smooth, I thought.

I knew that he knew exactly what I meant.

"On Ian's desk in the library, there was a pile of tax maps," I said. "And one of the entire county."

"Really?"

"Yes. Really. Don't act like you don't know. All the recently sold properties were circled. And the selling prices were noted. Why does Ian care? What's going on? Did he buy them?"

Buck laughed. "Your next-door neighbor isn't going to be too happy to learn you've been snooping around his desk. That was hardly neighborly of you, Babydoll."

"Oh, come on! I wasn't snooping. I just happened to see the maps. They looked interesting."

"I'm sure. And you 'just happened' to be reaching to look behind a closed curtain when I came back into the library." Buck laughed.

"I was not."

I knew he'd known all along about the maps. He'd seen them as clearly as I had. And he'd caught me snooping about the painting.

"Ouch! Dolly, you weigh a ton." I shuffled in the seat, trying to get comfortable underneath my weighty pup. "No wonder you're so fat, Dolly. You've been dining on lobster and steak at Greatwoods. You eat better than I do! You're busted now, young lady."

With Dolly's extra weight, my dead phone had mashed into my butt. Leaning forward, I reached into my back pocket, took out my phone, and placed it on the seat near my leg. I was sure the phone imprint in my backside would be permanent.

"Babydoll, I know you better than that. Never kid a kidder. You were snooping, big-time."

"I was not snooping!"

"You were snooping. You stayed up North too long. A good

Southern belle would've never gotten caught with her hand in the cookie jar like that. You're out of practice, babe."

"You are too funny." I made a face. "So when are you going to clue me in about the tax maps?"

"Not my place to tell."

"Oh! So now all of a sudden, you *do* know what they're about."

Buck shrugged. "I wouldn't be much of a sheriff if I didn't know what's happening in my own county, now, would I?"

"I'm not sure that I believe you even *are* the sheriff. And if you are, then I wonder what sort of nefarious forces put you in place. It certainly explains why Eli Gibbit is so mad at you and determined to take you down. You disappeared after I left town, then waltzed back after a pile of years and got the sheriff's job that Eli Gibbit had worked to get during his entire career. From what I hear, everyone in town thought he'd be the next sheriff after Sheriff Titus retired."

"And would that have made you happy? Would you rather see Eli as your sheriff?"

"No. It'd be awful. He's a louse. And I don't think he is at all good at what he does. But still, it hardly seems fair . . ."

Buck let out a hearty laugh. "I love the way your little mind works." He tapped a finger on my temple, just like Ian had done earlier. "Always overthinking. And now, everything must be *fair*. It must be agony in there. Ever take a vacation from all that fret and bother?"

"You ever take a vacation from all that pompous hot air?"

Buck laughed again. "Lost your manners while you were up North, too, I see. We'll have to do something about that."

Dolly jumped off my lap and onto the vehicle floor to sniff under my legs. I looked out the passenger window and crossed my arms. We were at the bottom of the Greatwoods drive. In front of us, automatically, a pair of massive wrought iron gates slowly opened. Buck pulled out onto the main road. The gates closed behind us.

"You're so full of stories. I never know what to believe," I said.

"Likewise. But mark my words, I aim to get to the bottom of all *your* stories."

Dolly scrambled back up into my lap.

"Ugh, Dolly, come on!" We rode in silence the rest of the way home.

CHAPTER 37

Buck pulled into the parking area at the big house. In another hour or so, it'd be sunrise. Without a word, I flung open the SUV door, and Dolly hopped out, trotting across the lawn to the cottage. I jumped out and started to follow her. Then, about ten steps later, when Buck hadn't yet pulled away in the SUV, I decided to turn back. I could see that he was on the phone inside his vehicle. I went around to the driver's side where he had the window down.

"Hey," I said.

"I promise. I'll be there soon," he said on the phone before ending the call. He ran his hand through his short-cropped hair and shook his head. He looked tense.

"Yes?"

I banged my hands on the SUV door. "What about the tax maps!"

Buck stopped and shifted the vehicle into park.

"What about them?"

"Can't you tell me *anything*? After all, I've helped you solve *two* murders since I've been home this summer. Surely, that's worth something?"

"Why do you want to know so bad?"

"I don't know. I just do."

Pieces of the conversation I'd overheard in the olive grove just hours earlier filtered through my mind. Then I saw the maps on Ian's desk, with the red circles. And I remembered Ian standing in the field a day earlier.

"Look," I said, "I really want to know what's going on. This community means a lot to me; the fact that I haven't been around for years has made me realize what a special place this really is. Besides, if something is going on, maybe I can help."

"That's a nice thought. But there's nothing you can do."

I remembered the notations on Ian's maps.

"Does it have something to do with the Dicers?" I asked.

Buck didn't answer. However, I'd seen his eyes flicker. I knew I was onto something. I pressed on.

"Dickey?"

Buck shrugged.

"And Debi?"

Buck smiled.

"I knew it! Everyone says those two are up to something. But what is it?" I leaned my elbows on the window frame of the driver's door and stuck my head in Buck's open window.

"Babydoll, I haven't admitted anything."

"I know you, Buck Tanner. You don't have to *say* a word."

"Really? Perhaps then I need to brush up on my secret-agent skills. Anyway, given the maps are property maps, and the Dicers are in the real estate business, I'd say there's a natural connection."

"That's not what I mean. And you know it. There's something fishy going on."

"Leave it alone."

"I can't. Besides, would it change anything if I told you that I think Debi may be trying to kill me?"

Buck burst out laughing. "What on earth? You really *are* desperate for information. Debi's tough as nails, but she's not homicidal."

"You men are always the last to know."

I put my hands on my hips. Honestly, I didn't know what to think about some of the accidents I'd had that summer, but Debi'd known all about every one. And she'd sure made certain that I *thought* she'd been trying to kill me. Apparently, that notion was out of the realm of possibility for Buck. And for a moment, I wondered who was really a means to an end, Debi to Buck, or Buck to Debi . . .

Buck was still laughing.

"Just wait till she tells you she's pregnant." I crossed my arms and smirked. "She and your mother have it all worked out, by the way."

That'll give him something to think about.

Buck raised his eyebrows. "Well, I daresay, it wouldn't be the first time I've been hoodooed, now, would it?" He gave me a long, purposeful look. "Speaking of my being hoodooed, why don't you fill me in on your ex-fiancé . . . Mister Codman."

We'd circled right back around to where we'd started when we were in Ian's driveway. I didn't like it. I thought I'd finished it. And I was determined not to say any more. Dex was dead. What had happened between us was over. I *needed* it to be over.

All of it.

Did Buck consider me a suspect for Dex's murder? It would be just his style . . .

Had Buck been playing me all night?

Argh! I hate men!

"Tell me what you know about his business," Buck said. "What, exactly, did he do at the paper company?"

"Why?"

"Just humor me. You owe me that much."

"Maybe we can trade? I'll tell you about Dex's business if you tell me about the property maps."

"Alright."

"Promise you'll share?"

"Sure. I give you my word. Now, what can you tell me about his job . . . at the paper company?"

"Dex was Perennial Paper's acquisitions manager. Kind

of a 'front man' for procurements. Usually these were full-blown businesses, land for new operations, or investment properties."

"Go on."

"He'd first head up a market analysis study and work up growth potential studies for emerging markets. Then he and his team would identify potential acquisition locations. After that, he'd build an acquisitions team—like the group here, for example: Wiggy, Claudia, Spencer, and Coop. As far as I know, he was still doing that sort of stuff when he came here this week."

"I thought you said the group was here on vacation. You don't think the group was vacationing?"

"That's what they've been telling everybody. Still, I definitely do not think that's why they came here. Not a one of them is remotely interested in nature or bird-watching. In fact, it's so preposterous, it's almost funny."

"Almost."

"They're cutthroat corporate raiders. I'd venture to say that none of them ever stop working, let alone make time for bird-watching."

"Okay. So, what else?"

"Well, after building his team, Dex and his group would visit their intended targets and start building relationships with local communities, especially key commercial brokers, bankers, property owners, appraisers, lawyers, contractors, and the like. Dex used to brag all the time about how good he was at snowing unsuspecting 'marks.' People just loved Dex. He had this way . . ."

"It's called a con. Go on."

I furrowed my brow and gave Buck a look. "No, a con would be illegal. This was more like . . . what I'd call slick business."

"Slick business?"

"Yes. Sure. Anyway, Dex and his ground team would identify prospective properties, choose one if there was a fit, then submit a letter of intent to the seller. If the letter was accepted, a deposit was made before a six-month or more study period, during which time the team conducted inspections, surveys, audits . . . all that stuff. If everything worked out, the money deposit would go hard, and soon after, the deal would be closed. Perennial Paper acquired a new asset."

"For example . . ."

"A forest to cut trees for paper. Or land to build a processing plant. Or both. Land with river or railroad access is prime."

"So these people who came with Dex Codman—they all worked *for* him?"

"Claudia did. She was Dex's administrator and right-hand man, so to speak. And she was loyal as a mama tiger. In a sense, she really ran the show."

"I see . . ."

"No, really. She's the one who coordinated everything and pulled all the details together while Dex got all the credit. He was really more like the front man. I've always thought Claudia was the real brains behind his business team. It's just that no one has ever respected her enough to give her any credit."

"Got it. What about the big guy . . ."

"Wiggy. Er, sorry, John Cabot Wigglesworth. He's the acquisitions asset and operations manager. He worked *with* Dex, not *for* Dex. He reports directly to an operations director, but he was *assigned* to Dex. He's the guy who would take over and manage the asset after Dex and his team made the purchase."

"Okay."

"And in similar fashion, Spencer Fisk reports to a financial director. He manages all the finances leading up to an acquisition. And Coop Tarbox, that's Norcross Cooper Tarbox—"

"The Second. I know. I got that."

"Right. Well, he reports to the legal director, and he manages all the legal business for an acquisition."

"So, all together, the group would seek out and set up a property for the paper company to purchase, then afterward, once the property was acquired, three would move on and the Wigglesworth guy would take over operations."

"Right. At least for a while, anyway. Eventually, Wiggy

would turn the operation over to someone else, then he'd back out, returning to corporate to begin work on another acquisition."

"And you think your man and his team were up to some sort of acquisitions deal here in Abundance?"

"Please, don't call him 'my man.' And yes, I'd stake my life on it . . . They're up to something. Why else would they be here? Dex was the man who wanted to marry me because he needed a good-looking young woman on his arm and someone to hostess business parties for him. And he openly admitted it to me, thinking that was a perfectly acceptable reason to marry someone. He was *all business*. Cold as ice. He doesn't . . . didn't . . . take vacations."

Buck stared at me for a moment. I hadn't clued him in before as to Dex's motives for wanting to marry me. Even to me, when I'd said it out loud, it sounded preposterous. Still, Dex had said it, not long after I'd run off with him. And I'd almost taken him up on it.

Almost.

"Right," Buck said, finally. "Cold as ice. And why did he and his paper people come here, do you think?"

"I have absolutely no idea. It's a paper company. Abundance is full of trees. And compared to a lot of other places, land is cheap here. And we've got a river for processing. As well as railroad tracks that could be upgraded . . . all the kinds of amenities they look for in a property."

"I see. Anything else?"

"That's all I know about Dex and his business. After all, before this week, I hadn't seen him in sixteen years."

I shrugged. I wasn't sure what I wanted to say about the conversation I'd overheard in the olive grove earlier that night. I still wanted time to process it all. So I didn't say anything. And I wanted to change the subject before Buck could ask me more about what had happened between me and Dex.

"So now it's your turn. Tell me what you know. Tell me about the maps in Ian Collier's library."

"It's not my place."

"Oh, *come on*! You promised."

"Don't look at me like that, Babydoll. You know I can't stand it."

"Buck Tanner, you gave your word!"

Buck's phone buzzed. He looked at it and sighed before resting it on the seat beside him, unanswered.

"Christ," he whispered under his breath.

"Don't you need to get that?" I asked.

"It'll keep."

"It's probably Debi."

"Probably."

"You'd better answer it then."

"Why's that?"

"Because if you don't she'll come over here. I'm telling you, she's stuck a tracking device on your vehicle. You'll never get away from her. Maybe she wants to tell you she's pregnant. You'll have to marry her right away."

"You're very amusing."

"I'm serious. She's crazy jealous."

"I know that."

"Now that we've established that your girlfriend—or whatever she is—is a paranoid, conniving, homicidal nutcase, are you going to answer my question? What about the maps?"

"Okay." He sighed. "It somehow may all be connected."

"Or not."

"Or not. Still, consider these facts," he said. "Farm and open land in the United States has become a hot commodity not only for American businesses, but also for foreign speculators. Including many foreign entities who have no experience or interest in agriculture."

"Is this going to be complicated?"

I leaned in the SUV and inadvertently inhaled a whiff of Buck's spicy, powdery scent. His brown eyes took me in for a moment. They were all business, not the warm, melted chocolate I'd seen earlier. Still, he looked sexy as hell.

"Eva, you asked for this. I'm only going to spell it out once. So, listen up."

Elbows on the car door window frame, I put my chin in my hands. "Fine. I'm listening."

Buck's phone buzzed again. He glanced down at it on the seat next to him and then snapped off the ringer.

"*Someone* must be eager to talk with you . . ."

"Not now."

I raised an eyebrow and gave him a teasing look. He didn't crack a smile.

"GPS. GPS. GPS," I chanted.

"Okay. You want to hear it. Pay attention," said Buck. "Wealthy international investors and businesses are purchasing land in the United States at astronomical prices per acre," Buck said. "No local farmer has a chance to compete with these foreigners. And because no one local can afford to pay those prices, these transactions change our farmers from landowners to tenants."

"Not good, right?"

"Not good. Or in some cases," Buck continued, "foreigners are repurposing land altogether, so we lose out on cropland."

"What do these foreigners want the land for?"

"Different things. More than half the foreign-held land is in timber or forest. Other buyers want land for crops and pastures, often because their own countries don't have enough water to grow and sustain enough crops for their populations. This impacts our food supply, soil, and water tables. Also, crop- and pastureland is long-term leased for foreign-owned wind companies. And foreign banks and investment firms are buying land simply as long-term investments. They rent the land back to corporate farmers to cultivate and maintain their investment."

"Okay . . ."

"Skyrocketing prices for commodities like corn and soybeans have driven up farmland prices so that farms are worth around four times more than they were at the peak per-acre prices during the seventies and eighties. That was just before the big farm crisis."

"And Ian Collier is involved because . . ."

"Ian Collier is one of a handful of concerned citizens who believe that, if gone unchecked, these massive land grabs pose a threat to our national security, as well as our economy and food base. And Georgia happens to be one of the top states for foreign land investors."

"Really?"

Buck nodded. "Plus, some folks are convinced that there are a few factions out there who—on a much smaller scale— use the land for illegal purposes."

"Such as?"

"Cultivation of illegal substances."

"Drugs?"

Again, Buck nodded. "And there is worry about extremist cults and training camps."

"Training camps? You mean, like, *terrorist* training camps?"

Buck raised his eyebrows and pursed his lips.

"Here? In this country?"

Buck shrugged. "If not today, then tomorrow. If you hadn't been in the woods and witnessed the drop tonight, you'd never have known all those troops were out there, now, would you? Some terrorist training is no different than what you saw goin' on tonight. Just a different team. Although nowadays, all it takes is a big truck to terrorize innocent folks . . ."

I held up my hand. "Okay. So even if that's all true, what can Ian Collier do about it?"

"I can't really say."

"What do you mean, you can't say . . ."

"All I can tell you is that, among other things, your neighbor is 'connected,' as they say."

"Connected?"

Buck nodded.

"Like you? So, what does that mean?"

"I'm not at liberty to discuss it, except to say that he has a ton of money—"

"No kidding."

"And he knows powerful people in high places. He's one of the reasons I'm here."

"I'm lost."

"It's okay, Babydoll. I can't talk about it, anyway. Just know that Ian does a lot to monitor and protect what's around here as well as other places."

"Other places . . . ?"

"Other places."

"Argh! You are so frustrating, Sheriff Tanner!"

"Thank you." Buck grinned. Then he wagged his finger. "And you know way more than you need to know. So, I'm trusting you, Eva, to not say a word to anyone about this. This is *all* on the QT, got it?"

Again with not telling anyone.

I rolled my eyes. "It's not like you've told me anything that I couldn't learn on my own from Wikipedia."

I'd exaggerated, of course. Buck had told me more about Ian Collier than I'd been able to find out after weeks of online research.

"But then, how are the Dicers connected?" I asked. "Oh. Wait. I get it. They're the ones making all the land deals, right?"

Buck blinked. I took that as a "yes."

"But they're just the agents who make it happen. They're not really 'involved' more than that, are they?"

Buck shrugged.

"They *are*?"

"I didn't say that."

"But you didn't say no, either. Okay. So, wait a minute. I need to think." I walked around the SUV as I sorted through what Buck had told me.

"I gotta go, babe."

"Wait!" I walked another lap around the SUV. Then I mumbled to myself, "So, Debi is a 'means to an end.'" I made a third lap around the SUV. I could see Buck shaking his head as I tried to work it all out. Was he playing Debi—"the means"—to get close to the foreign real estate buyers—"the end"? Or, was Dickey "the end"? Whichever it was, Buck was *way* more than just a small-time county sheriff. And his relationship with Debi was more complicated than even she might suspect. I leaned into the SUV window.

But then, maybe Debi was just a means for sex, I thought. *After all, Pep heard all those rumors . . .*

"Hey, where did you get that?" I cried.

Buck munched on a Butterfinger candy bar.

"Well, I got hungry," he said with a mouthful, "just sitting here all this time while you marched around and around out there. You really need to step up your Southern hostess game, Babydoll. It's rude not to at least invite a person in for sweet tea."

"It's nearly sunrise!" I cried.

"Good manners never sleep," he said before taking another bite of candy bar.

"Give me that!" I said, snatching the final bite in the wrapper. Before he could grab it back, I popped the crispy peanut butter and chocolate confection into my mouth.

CHAPTER 38

I slept late the next morning. Later than I should have, for sure. And, as usual that summer, I woke up hot and perspiring. Even my sheets were damp.

Ugh.

After I bathed and dressed, I put fresh, clean sheets on my bed and tucked them in nice and tight before pulling up my white candlewick bedspread. And when I finally stepped outside into the bright midmorning sun and looked over toward the big house, I groaned.

"Might as well get this over with," I said to myself.

There were two vehicles I dreaded seeing. Debi Dicer's black Cadillac Escalade, because I was certain she'd used it to try mowing me down one night, and Deputy Eli Gibbit's totally nondescript four-door black sedan, because I'd seen his vehicle enough during the weeks prior to know that when *it* was around, *he* was around. And when *he* was around, then, guilty or not, no one was safe from being hauled off to jail. It seemed that he loved working overtime trying to pin evil-doings on me or some other innocent Knox family member.

I started hiking across the back lawn. Already, the temperatures were in the nineties. Dolly was out and about on her own, somewhere. Probably chasing squirrels.

Aw, heck, maybe she went back for more surf and turf at Greatwoods.

I glanced at the pond behind my cottage. Except for crushed and flattened grasses, and some tire tracks on the marshy side of the pond, the birds were flitting about, and it all looked perfectly normal. Peaceful. Like no one had drowned there and nothing bad had happened.

I shuddered.

Hopefully, I won't think of dead Dex every time I look out there for the rest of my life.

Then I thought about what Dex had done to me all those years ago. I stopped in my tracks and took in a deep breath. Then another.

It's okay, Eva. No one knows.

I took a few more deep breaths before I pulled myself together and headed across the lawn to the white clapboard big house. With its peaked red metal roofs and second-story balconies, the pre–Civil War homestead was an eclectic mix of neo-Gothic and Victorian architecture. And it was relatively modest when compared to most antebellum plantation homes. Our place had been built for a large working family that labored on farmland almost entirely without indentured laborers. As my family grew with the changing times, the house had been altered and added on to, many times.

Daphne's sweetly scented roses, lilies, hostas, and other perennials perfumed the warm air as I stepped along the path through her cutting garden. I climbed the wooden back stair to the big porch and pushed open the kitchen door.

"Mornin', Sunshine. You feelin' better today?" asked Precious.

Sunlight streamed through the curtained window over the farmhouse sink. Precious grabbed my favorite hand-thrown, glazed blue and cream coffee mug from the red laminate countertop. She upturned the full coffee carafe and poured me a fresh cup of coffee, handing me the mug as I pulled out one of the Larkin pressed-oak chairs. I plopped myself down and set my mug on the table.

"Oh, wait, gimme that. I forgot the milk." Precious snatched back my mug, grabbed a little pitcher from the counter, and poured milk into my coffee.

"Here, Sunshine. Just the way you like it." She replaced the mug on the table in front of me. "Milk. No sugar. Drink up."

"Thanks," I said. "To what do I owe all this service?"

"That ol' weasel, Detective Gibbit, is here. He's been talkin' to everyone—me, your big sis, and now the guests—for two hours or more. He asked me to summon you, but I figured if he wanted to talk with you, he could find you himself. Besides, I don't take orders from weasels."

"Precious, you don't take orders from anyone!"

"Sunshine, ain't *that* the truth." She laughed. "Anyway, drink up. I figure you're up next with the detective, and it can't hurt to get fired up with a little caffeine in your belly."

I took a sip. "This coffee is excellent."

Precious nodded. "Y'all ran out of coffee beans yesterday, and I forgot to get some new. I stole this from Mister Collier. It's Geisha cultivar. Pretty outstanding, huh?"

"Sure is. Can we get some?"

"Sure. But you'll pay a pretty penny for it."

"I'm sure Daphne will spring for it. Just tell her it'll impress the guests."

Precious chortled. "Sure thing. Hey, want some fresh-fruit pizza? Just made it this morning. I'm into out-of-the-ordinary pizzas these days. And they work real good with your daddy's olive oils."

"I think I'll wait until after the detective has his way with me."

"You sure? You might lose your appetite after talkin' with him . . ."

"I'm just not hungry now. Thanks, anyway."

"I tried to call you earlier. Tilly called me first thing. I wanted to warn you about the weasel bein' here. And also, there's big news! Although I doubt you'll want to hear it. Given your relation to the floater and all . . ."

"The floater?"

"The dead guy! Dexter Codfish."

"Codman."

"Whatever." Precious waved her hand. "Listen up. This is important. The whole town is talkin' about what happened here yesterday. I got *three* calls this mornin' before the detective got here. The most important call was from Coretta Crumm . . . you know, my friend who works at the bank? Remember, her brother, Bigger, works in the morgue? Well, it seems like your Codfish fellow died of . . ."

The door from the dining room swung open and banged into the counter.

"Ladies! Am I interrupting?"

"Would it matter?" snarked Precious, under her breath.

Detective Eli Gibbit ignored her. "Miss Eva Knox. I'm so glad to see you're here. Please, don't get up on my account. You and I need to have a little chat. Will you excuse us now, Miss Precious Darling?"

"You can't go somewhere else to grill your next victim? I got work to do . . ."

"It's fine, Precious. I'm sure Daphne won't mind if you take off a little early today. I'll finish the dishes," I said.

"Uh, sure thing. I got some coffee to buy anyway." Precious gave me a wink. "Sunshine, you just find your phone and call me if ya need anything. I'll be back in a couple of hours. I'd offer y'all some coffee, Detective, but we're all out." Precious snapped off the lever on the Bunn coffee maker. The carafe on the warmer was still half full.

I smiled as Precious clomped across the kitchen and out the back door.

Detective Gibbit sat himself at the table, took out a pen from his shirt pocket protector, and opened his black notebook. He was an odd little man, with a proven persecution complex, for sure. With big jug ears and buck teeth, the detective's adult-sized body parts hung awkwardly from his small, child-sized frame. And even when he smiled, he always had a peculiar sourball expression on his face.

I was pretty sure he was a miserable human being . . . always seeing the worst in people.

"Well, now. Let's just you and me review some facts, shall we?"

"This is your party, Detective."

"So, Miss Eva Knox, what happened Friday night? Folks have been telling me that during some sort of olive oil event you had an argument with the deceased, Mister Dudley Dexter Codman the Third, from Boston. Is that correct?"

"An argument? Well, really, I don't know if it was an argument. More like a difference of opinion, I'd say. But, I don't understand. What does my conversation with Mister Codman on Friday have to do with his drowning in the pond?"

"Yes, well. That's the thing, Miss Eva Knox." He looked up and grinned like a Cheshire cat, his little beady eyes glinting. "It seems that your old friend didn't drown at all. Well, at least it wasn't an *accident*."

The detective licked his lips and gave me a smirky sort of self-satisfied smile.

"It wasn't? I don't understand."

That wasn't exactly true, of course. I'd heard what Precious's friend Tilly had said. And I'd heard a lot of suspicious talk between the Boston men in the olive grove.

"Well, you see, my dear, Mister Dexter Codman the Third ingested a large amount of a substance called *Atropa belladonna*. Do you know what that is?"

I shook my head, no.

"Really?" He raised his eyebrows, making a point. "No matter. It's a plant. And quite poisonous, too. I reckon most folks around these parts just call it 'belladonna.' Sure you don't know it?"

I shook my head again.

"*Aaannn-yway*, apparently, a deadly dose of *Atropa belladonna* was delivered to Mister Dexter Codman the Third while he was right here, at your plantation." He smiled. "The poison was in the olive oil he'd ingested. *Your* family's olive oil. And didn't you host the olive oil tasting party? Now, shall we begin again? Why don't you tell me about that argument you had with the deceased?"

CHAPTER 39

My hour-long interview with Detective Gibbit hardly made for an ideal Sunday morning. It was anything but pleasant. But then, *every* encounter with Detective Eli Gibbit was doomed to be one of unpleasantness. It was just the way he was.

Unpleasant.

And of course, no one likes being investigated for murder.

Not that the detective had gone so far as to actually accuse me of murder. Not yet, anyway. However, even to me, it was perfectly clear that I could've easily done it. After all, I had motive—Dex and I had a history, and he'd humiliated and embarrassed me during the tasting party and we'd argued. The detective even pointed out that, "technically," I'd assaulted Dex when I'd slapped him. His public insults, slapping my butt, and grabbing my breast notwithstanding. And I had no alibi—I'd been alone, sleeping in my cottage during the time the murder happened. Moreover, I'd had access to both Dex, who was staying at the plantation, and the method of delivery for the poison—our olive oil—which was every-where at Knox Plantation.

However, two questions concerning my involvement remained unanswered. First, did I have access to the deadly poison? And, second, exactly how and when did I get the poison into the oil that Dex ingested? I believed that those two unanswered questions were the only reasons the detective hadn't hauled me into the station that morning.

And perhaps, perfectionist Buck had insisted behind the scenes that his loose-cannon detective dot all his i's and cross all his t's, as they say, before hauling me in as a suspect. The detective's quick-to-judge actions regarding suspects during two other murder investigations that summer had led to his red-faced admissions that he'd been wrong. Dead wrong.

Twice.

The only good thing was that I still had time on my side. So far, no one knew about Dex's abusive behavior toward me all those years ago. Still, I worried that once that cat got out of the bag, my ship would be sunk, so to speak.

Good thing Daphne knows a great criminal lawyer up in Atlanta.

Still, regardless of whether he uncovered the abuse or not, I knew that chances were almost one hundred percent that the detective would be back to question me. And next time, I'd be headed to the slammer if I didn't figure out who killed Dex before the detective returned.

I decided to spend the few free hours that I had before the garden club cleanup holed up in my cottage researching my old Boston friends on the Internet. My many years working in Boston-area public relations left me well equipped to dig into the online social and business strata.

So I grabbed one of the big ham hock bones that Precious kept stashed for Dolly, before heading across the lawn, back to my little cottage. Dolly lay under a great live oak in the yard, chomping on her prize, while I stretched out in a hammock next to my cottage and dug into the Internet via my laptop computer.

And as it turned out, my time investigating that morning was well spent. It wasn't long at all before I struck pay dirt.

CHAPTER 40

I'd grossly underestimated the size and popularity of the Abundance Garden Club. Arriving in the village for the afternoon cleanup, along with Pep—who'd also been wrangled, er . . . *volunteered* by Daphne to work—we were both surprised to see that nearly *everyone* in town had turned out to help beautify the village. Or at least, as Daphne said, *everyone who was anyone.*

"*Gir—rrrrls!*" cried Daphne when she caught sight of us crossing the boulevard. "Yoo-hoo! Over here, *dahl-ings!*"

She waved for us to join her, as she stood chatting with gardening friends in the boulevard median. There must've been at least fifty people on hand, and they all wore casual clothes—brightly colored short-sleeved tops, shorts, golf skirts and skorts—and gardening gloves, thank-you gifts from Abundance Hardware store owners Merle and Roxxy Tritt.

Oh crappy! I never got them the corks yesterday.

"Guess it's too late to turn back now," said Pep with a sigh.

Standing next to Daphne, her best friend, tall, brown-haired Earlene Azalea Greene—the twins' mother—welcomed me and Pep with a warm smile and a hug, as did longtime Knox family friends, poultry farmers Alice and Emmett Spencer. Sadie Truewater, Daphne's book club pal who worked in child protective services, gave us a friendly wave as she headed off, firing up her noisy weed trimmer.

"Hiya, girls!" cried jolly Violetta Merganthal. "Nice to see y'all this afternoon. Hope y'all can forget some of your troubles for a few hours . . . Your big sis has been fillin' us in on all the latest goings-on at your place since we left Friday night. Wowser! I sure wouldn't want to be in all y'all's shoes!"

She wore a purple sleeveless top over a purple and pink polka-dot skort.

"Break time is over now," she said. "We best be gettin' back to work."

She turned to a raven-haired, sloe-eyed, curvaceous young woman next to her wearing a too-tight tank top with the word GOSSIP printed across the chest over hot pink sweatpants with JUICY printed across the butt.

"C'mon, Maisy, we're off to the mulch pile. See ya, ladies!"

Violetta headed off while her husband-hunting daughter Maisy followed, chewing a wad of gum, pushing an empty wheelbarrow. Maisy looked totally bored, as if she wanted to be *anywhere* else but there, that afternoon.

"We're so happy to see y'all!" gushed Daphne, giving me an air-kiss. "Aren't we, ladies? Oh, and Emmett is happy to see y'all, too, aren't you, Emmett?" She tittered as she *fwapped* close friend Emmett on the forearm with her hand.

"Sure am," said Emmett. He tipped his cap.

"Girls," said Daphne, addressing me and Pep, "we've got your rakes and tarps all set up for y'all over there. Just rake up everything you see. What you can't rake just set on the tarps. Then wrap up the tarps and haul the waste over there, to the pickup. The boys will drive it all away."

"If y'all ask me, it sounds like prison work," huffed Pep. "Sure y'all don't have pretty orange jumpsuits for us to wear?"

Daphne tittered. "Oh, Pepper-Leigh, I just *a-dorwh* your sense of humor!"

"Yeah, right."

Although well-intentioned, the cleanup was all a bit ironic, because it had originally been scheduled to take place two weeks earlier, so that the village would be picture-perfect for the Peeps Week parade. Unfortunately, severe storms made postponing the cleanup a necessity, and the garden club folks weren't able to make it happen before the Sunday *after* the parade.

In the end, it all worked out, because there was an extraordinary amount of trash that had accumulated during parade day. The cleanup couldn't have come at a better time.

Most of the volunteers gathered in the boulevard's parklike center median. Some mowed grass, others trimmed flower gardens, while others pulled weeds or picked up trash. Still others wandered up and down the boulevard, emptying trash cans, sweeping the sidewalks, and watering, trimming, and repotting plants in the many planters and hanging pots up and down the street.

Looking around, it was obvious, as in most community organizations, that there was a clear hierarchy to the group. Longtime garden club leader Bubbles Bolender, who, by the way, was a dead ringer for Marilyn Monroe, sat in a high director's chair under the biggest live oak tree in town, smack-dab in the boulevard's median center. With an iced tea in one hand and a bullhorn in the other, Bubbles ordered everyone else around. And although using a bullhorn may sound a little over-the-top, it was an absolute necessity for Bubbles, because she not only looked like Marilyn Monroe, but with a soft, airy voice, she sounded like the famous siren as well. Without the horn, no one would have heard her instructions that afternoon. Not that anyone was really listening . . .

As non–club members and reluctant "volunteers," according to the hierarchy, Pep and I were ranked lowest of the garden club caste, hence our job reflected our station. For example, next down from Bubbles and her bullhorn were the social elite of Abundance, commonly referred to as the B6 group. The group included Cat Blankenblatt, tall and svelte with short, dark hair and exotic features that heralded her Cherokee heritage. It was Cat's job to pass out name tags, while her handsome lawyer husband, Ty, jotted the names of everyone who showed up.

How hard is that?

And peanut money heiress Asta Bodean trotted about in her signature white pants and caftan, serving everyone iced sweet tea in red plastic cups.

Again, how hard is that?

And if you wanted something with a little more punch than sweet tea, blonde, bug-eyed plastic surgery junkie and winery owner Bunny Bixby had a table setup offering wine . . . to purchase, of course. All proceeds to benefit the garden club. Timber heiress Bernice Burnside, who looked like a female Raymond Burr, ambled around giving photo ops and news interviews while occasionally stabbing at trash with a long spear, while her nephew Tommy, who ran the tee shirt place in town, walked alongside her, holding the trash bag.

Again, was that hard work?

You get the idea.

And it was no surprise to see redheaded gossipmonger Beula Beauregard huddled near a dogwood tree, pointing me out to her friends, as she, no doubt, filled them in on all the juicy details concerning what she knew about the latest man to turn up dead at Knox Plantation.

And to be fair, there *were* folks working quite hard. A number of new club members were on their hands and knees, happy, it seemed, to weed and plant. And there were people marching around blasting noisy weed choppers, grass trimmers, leaf blowers, and pushing mowing machines. Most of them were men, obviously thrilled to get out and play with their deafening equipment.

Of course, it was often the male club members or the husbands who handled the heaviest equipment. Except Debi Dicer. Apparently, she was queen of the chain saw.

"How appropriate," Pep laughed when she saw Debi arriving about an hour or so late, with her precious tool in hand. "A chain saw. The perfect device to cut folks down. Just what the she-devil needs!"

"She doesn't need a tool, Pep. She can slice and dice quite well on her own," I said.

"Well, I think it suits her."

"I don't disagree. Just stay out of her way."

We giggled as we raked up a massive pile of leaves and twigs probably left from fall the year before. That's because at the bottom of the Abundance social caste, we were the rakers and pilers, raking and picking up the debris that everyone else left behind—leaves, sticks, rocks, branches, dead shrubs, trash, and some darned heavy tree limbs. In fact, some of the tree limbs were so big and heavy that we should've had someone cut them up for us. But that someone would've been Debi, so we decided to drag the heavy stuff ourselves.

"I need a break," said Pep, after several hours. She plopped down under the shade of an old oak tree. An abandoned ladder leaned on the back side of the tree trunk.

"Sounds good to me," I said, dropping down next to Pep. The shade under the tree felt good. At least for a moment, anyway.

An older man operating a weed whacking machine walked past, spinning dirt and debris all around us. We were too tired to move. The debris stuck to our sweaty skin.

"Do ya think Asta Bodean will see us way over here and bring us some tea?" shouted Pep over the machine racket.

"Doubt it," I yelled back.

Pep cupped her hands. "I meant to ask you, how'd it go this morning with Detective Gibbit?"

"As well as it could've, I guess." The weed machine man moved away. I lowered my voice. "I mean, I'm not in jail. Not yet, anyway."

"So somebody really *killed* Dex Codman? Hard to believe another murder happened at our place."

"You're telling me. Still, I did some research this morning. Found out some stuff. I just can't put all the pieces together."

"What do you mean? Do you think you know who killed him?"

I waited to answer while a noisy lawn mower grumbled past us.

"Well, certainly, it has to be one of the people from Perennial Paper, right? I mean, who else would it be? It wasn't me. It wasn't you. Or Daphne or Daddy. Or Precious . . ."

"I get it. I get it. So, what are you thinking?"

"Well, I found out some stuff on the Internet this morning that I didn't know before. Like, the woman Coop married when I knew him—her name was Heather Tarbox—apparently divorced Coop to run off and marry *Dex* a few years ago! I found a wedding announcement in the *Boston Globe*. I also found a blog written by someone who said Heather cleaned Coop out, financially. Also, I saw a bunch of society page stuff about Dex and his wife, Heather Tarbox Codman."

"No kidding."

"And judging from a conversation I heard between Wiggy, Coop, and Spencer, Coop wasn't too forgiving about losing his wife to Dex."

"Can you blame the guy? One of his best friends obviously stole his wife . . ."

"Right. But then, apparently, Heather dumped Dex, too!"

"So, you mean he wasn't married when he died?"

"Nope."

"Did Dex have any kids?"

"Not that I can find."

"So, why did Heather dump him? Oh, I know . . . the second marriage never lasts."

"What?"

"It's true. Just ask anyone at the Roadhouse."

"Omigosh, Pep. That's ridiculous."

Pep shrugged. "So, it's like, this Heather babe cleaned out the first guy—"

"Coop."

"Then she cleaned out the second guy, our dead guy—"

"Dex."

"And she moved on, rich and free."

"Exactly. She married a retired bank executive and they moved to Brazil."

"So, what do you think . . . that the first husband, Coop, had it in for Dex?"

"Could be."

"Wow."

"And apparently, Heather cleaned out Dex, just like she'd done to Coop. Which is really interesting, because I heard Coop make some comment yesterday about how Spencer would never see the 'fifty grand' he'd loaned to Dex."

"That's a ton of dough to lose . . ."

"Sure is."

"So, the Spencer guy could've killed Dex because he didn't repay a loan?"

"Could be. But there's more. Dex's longtime assistant, Claudia, had a relationship with Dex after I was out of the picture. I heard the men mention that Dex took her skiing in Switzerland. But afterward, something happened. Like, maybe, he dumped her."

"And you think she might've killed him . . . because after they arrived here, he had the hots for you and she was jealous? I mean, he *did* grab your boob . . ."

"Please. Don't remind me. Maybe. She's definitely not completely stable, if you ask me. Still, it doesn't quite fit, because according to everyone else, Dex was paying her way too much for what she did for him at work. And her job with him was very secure. Now that he's dead, she's whining about how she'll never find another good-paying job . . ."

"So, in other words, why would she kill her cash cow?"

"Exactly. But then again, it doesn't seem like their personal relationship had been too solid."

Out of the corner of my eye, I saw Joy Birdsong coming across the grass.

"And what about the other guy . . ."

Joy looked to be finished for the day.

"Eva, are you listening?"

"What?"

"I said, what about the other guy? The big guy with the beard? What's his name, again . . . Uncle Wiggly?" Pep giggled.

"Wiggy. I'm not sure. However, listening to him, he doesn't seem at all upset that Dex is gone. In fact, he seems to think Dex was a liability . . . Dex's death seems to have had some sort of unburdening effect on Wiggy. And this is the part that I can't figure out. There's an important reason they're in town . . . except it is *not* vacationing or bird-watching, like they say. It's something to do with land—"

Just then, there was a crack above us, and a huge tree branch came crashing down, landing with an earth-shattering *WHUMP* on the ground, just inches away from me.

"Criminy, Eva! You could've been killed!" cried Pep, jumping up.

I took a deep breath. Then I heard a voice, above us. A voice I knew *all* too well.

"Oh gee, did that big ol' limb almost crush y'all? I'm *so sorry*!"

Overhead, Debi Dicer peeped her head around the oak tree and looked down at us. She was standing atop the ladder we'd seen earlier, leaning against the other side of the massive live oak.

"I gotta give the bitch credit," said Pep, looking up. "She's catty alright."

Debi hopped off the ladder and seated herself on a massive branch above us. With her legs swinging to and fro, she brushed the tree detritus from her neon, shorty-short Lilly Pulitzer skort.

Of course, the tree crap fell right onto our heads.

"My little ol' chain saw needed sharpening, so I took a break earlier," said Debi, smiling from the big limb above us. "Then when I got back from my break, I thought I'd just climb up here and *snake* myself around the tree to test the branch I'd worked on earlier . . . you know, just to see whether or not I really *needed* to haul my heavy ol' chain saw back up here again—it's just so *dangerous*, working with a chain saw, don't y'all know it? And after all, I'd nearly cut clean through the limb before my saw stopped working earlier. Plus, I saw y'all talking down there and I *hated* to disturb y'all."

Pep snorted. "'Snake' says it all for me . . ." She flicked tree bark from her hair.

"And do y'all know what?" asked Debi, still talking. "Turns out I *didn't* need to use the chain saw anymore, after all! Except, bless your little hearts, I forgot to call out to let y'all know I was about to push on the limb that was above your pea-pickin' little heads. I'm *so glad* y'all are okay."

Debi looked down at us, smirking. Like the proverbial cat that swallowed the canary.

CHAPTER 41

I didn't even care. It was almost as if Debi were some sort of cartoon character, always dropping anvils out of the sky, in hopes of landing one on me.

Really, she didn't faze me one bit anymore.

"Better luck next time, Debi," I said, pulling myself up from the ground. "I don't have time for you or your desperate, jealous antics today."

Really, my mind was so preoccupied trying to sort out all the details concerning Dex's murder, that when I'd seen Joy Birdsong crossing the grass a few moments earlier, all I could think was that I just needed to get to her.

"Pep, I'll be back," I whispered. "Debi is all yours."

I picked myself up, stepped over Debi's near-miss giant limb, and jogged away, leaving Debi high up in the tree overhead.

Pep will know exactly what to do with Debi, I thought.

"Hey! Where are y'all going, sweetness?" Debi shouted as I took off after Joy. Apparently, it wasn't enough for her to try to crush me with a humongous tree limb. She needed a bit of verbal sparring, as well.

She'd have to wait on that. Besides, I knew she'd have her hands full with Pep.

"Joy!" I shouted to the botanicals shop owner. "Joy Birdsong! Hello!"

I ran up to Joy and touched her lightly on the shoulder just as she reached out to her car, which was parked in the boulevard. It was a refurbished green Volkswagen Beetle that looked to be vintage seventies.

"Well, Eva Knox! Hello, hon. I see your big sissy 'volunteered' you to help out today! I hope you're enjoying the afternoon. It's always so refreshing to be outside in the clean air."

Like the day before, she wore a lightweight caftan over leggings. Only this time the caftan was coral colored and the leggings were green. And she wore a pair of big black rubber boots. She carried a worn pair of garden gloves in one hand.

"It's been an interesting afternoon, for sure!" I said. "And I'm sorry that I didn't see you earlier, Joy. I see you're on your way home. Please, do you have a moment? I have some questions, and I think you're just the person to ask."

"Sure, hon. Ask away." Joy motioned for me to join her on a nearby park bench. "Let's sit down over here in the shade, shall we?"

"Thanks."

"Do tell, what are your questions about?"

"Belladonna."

"The plant?"

"Yes. What can you tell me about it?"

"Well, now, let's see. It is a perennial herb, part of the nightshade family, native to wooded areas of Europe, North Africa, and parts of Asia—"

"But it's available here in the United States, right?"

"Oh yes. The scientific name for the plant is *Atropa belladonna*. It's also known as nightshade, deadly nightshade, black nightshade, sleeping nightshade, Barbados lily . . ." Joy turned her eyes skyward and looked thoughtful as she called out the long list of names for the plant. ". . . banewort, devil's cherries, devil's herb, dwale, naked lady lily, naughty man's cherries, witches' berry." She tittered. "Oh my! The list just goes on and on. There are a whole bunch of wonderfully descriptive names for it. Really, the plant is not too uncommon these days. It's sometimes planted as a flowering perennial in gardens, although it is often considered more of a biennial. Did you know that other members of the nightshade family include the potato, the tomato, and the eggplant?"

"So it could be growing here, in Abundance?"

"I know it is. In fact, I believe your sister has some at all y'all's plantation. I sold her some seeds a while back. I usually have some in the shop. Although, it *is* difficult to grow from seed. Oh dear, wait a moment . . . perhaps, I'm mistaken. Perhaps that was Bubbles Bolender . . . or Pickles Kibler . . . who has the belladonna. I'm sorry, I don't remember, really. Maybe it was Beula Beauregard?"

"That's okay. Can you tell me what it looks like?"

"Well, it's not terribly distinctive, I'm afraid. Around these parts, the bushy plants are usually about three to five feet tall, with dull green ovate leaves that are about eight inches long. Although, it does have pretty, bell-shaped, reddish bluish or purple flowers during summer. And, the flowers are followed by dark purplish or black berries about the size of cherries. It's still summer around here, so you may find some plants that continue blooming. Or, they may already be sowing berries. I'm not sure."

"Is it used for anything other than decoration?"

"Oh, goodness, yes! It's an ancient herb that's now cultivated for its medicinal alkaloids, mostly scopolamine and atropine, which are used in narcotics, diuretics, sedatives, antispasmodics, and the like. You can purchase it in pellet or tablet forms, as well as seeds, roots, or foliage to make your own liquid solutions, suspensions, powders, decoctions, tinctures, infusions, plasters, pills, or suppositories. Belladonna can be used alone and in combination with other herbs and medications. Although, some synthetics have been developed in order to bypass the terrible, undesirable side effects of the alkaloids."

"I'm sorry. All that means?"

"When used properly, belladonna can be an extremely useful medicinal plant for humankind, delivered to the human body in many ways. However, like its name 'deadly night-shade,' all parts of the plant are extremely toxic—leaves, roots, berries—to the point of being quite deadly. It must be used with extreme care. The roots are most poisonous; however, the pretty berries with their intensely sweet, inky juice are particularly problematic. They've killed many people accidentally, even unaware children. Just two berries can kill a child."

"And an adult?"

"Oh, ten or twelve would do it, I suppose. Thinking about it, I'd guess that those pretty yet deadly berries are one reason we don't often see the plant marketed to ornamental garden-ers. Plus, like I said, it's not a terribly easy plant to grow. Of course, it's less common to accidentally poison a person with the leaves, which have a bitter taste even when dried. It would only take one leaf to poison a person to death."

"Can you be more specific? About the poison, I mean. What happens?"

"Let's see . . . the alkaloids are anticholinergic, which means they block certain nerve impulses involved in the para-sympathetic nervous system that regulate certain involuntary bodily functions or reflexes."

"Such as?"

"I'm sure you've heard of atropine being used to dilate pupils. Also, belladonna can impact heart rate, secretion of glands and organs, the lungs, and the digestive tract. The plant relaxes smooth muscles of the internal organs and inhibits or dries up secretions. Still, we often see it used as a homeo-pathic remedy to treat symptoms like fever, nausea, delirium, spasms, flushed skin, and dilated pupils . . . basically, all the things that a belladonna poisoning might trigger."

"All those things?"

"Most definitely."

"And if someone were to take a deadly dose of belladonna, what would happen?"

"Well, the toxic alkaloids would target the nervous system,

causing the person's heart rate to increase while inhibiting skeletal muscle movement. Symptoms might include dilated pupils, sensitivity to light, increased heart rate, headache, hallucinations, and delirium."

I remembered how Claudia had said she'd heard Dex in the yard outside Friday night, calling me like a crazy, deranged person. And when I'd found him, he'd had no clothes on in the pond.

Had he been crazy with delirium from the poison?

"Delirium? Like a crazy person?"

"Yes. And these symptoms could last just for hours or for several days."

"And then?"

"Coma and convulsions, followed by death."

"Sounds grisly."

Joy nodded. "Yes, I suppose so. Still, if one wanted to do away with someone, belladonna would be an exemplary way to do it. It's been used as a poison since ancient times. For example, the Roman emperor Augustus was rumored to have been killed by his wife with the poison."

"Really?"

Joy smiled. "And, of course, author Agatha Christie used the poison to kill her victims quite a few times in her mystery books."

CHAPTER 42

Despite all the doom and gloom around us, Pep and I giggled all the way home that afternoon.

"Well, I'm glad I thought to bring my truck," Pep said. She let out a little piglet snort. "I bet Debi *still* up in that tree, hollerin' for folks to get her down."

"Oh, I don't know. Debi's probably pretty capable of slithering down a tree. She's like a snake—isn't that what she said?"

"She's definitely a snake, that one!" Pep guffawed. "Although I didn't notice anyone rushing over to help her before we left."

She grinned.

"Still, it was genius of you, Pep, to take the ladder while she was still standing on the tree limb."

"Well, it *is* Daddy's ladder! I nearly forgot that he'd leant it to Bubbles Bolender for the garden club event today. And when I remembered to grab it, I guess"—she rolled her eyes dramatically—"I didn't notice that Debi was still in the tree." She sighed. "Oh well. Too bad."

Pep turned and looked over her shoulder at the sixteen-foot ladder stowed behind us in the bed of her GMC pickup. A red bandana flapped off the end of the ladder hanging beyond the back of the truck.

We high-fived each other before breaking out into peals of laughter.

A few minutes later, after Pep dropped me off at home, I found Daphne on her knees under a big, floppy straw hat, cutting roses in the garden behind the big house.

"Oh, there y'all are, Eva, dear. Did you and Pepper-Leigh enjoy the afternoon? I know everyone in the garden club appreciates y'all joining us in the village today to help."

Not quite everyone, I thought, with a giggle. I was still embracing my image of Debi, stranded up in the tree, with no ladder to get down. As far as Pep and I knew, Daddy's ladder had been the only one at the cleanup that day.

Daphne stood up to give me an air-kiss on each cheek.

"Actually, Daph, despite my reservations," I said, "I have to admit that I thoroughly enjoyed the day. It was both informative and surprisingly entertaining."

"Well, that's wonderful, dear. Actually, you look . . . rejuvenated. It's lovely to see a smile on your face again. Now, if we could just find you some nice clothes . . ."

"Daphne, Joy Birdsong said she thought that you might have a belladonna plant around here somewhere. Do you know?"

"Belladonna? You mean nightshade? Let me think . . . I'm not sure. If there is one, it might be out behind your cottage, Eva. That's where most of the herbs and shade-loving plants are. Do y'all know what it looks like?"

"Kinda nondescript, five feet tall, with little bell-shaped flowers that turn into big purple berries—"

"Wait!" Daphne cried. She stood up and began heading down the walk, toward the lawn. "I think I know just the plant you're describing. Come with me."

A few minutes later, Daphne and I stood in the garden behind my cottage where most of the flowering plants soaked up the bright sunshine. Then Daphne pointed to the far side of the garden, over in the corner against the cottage, where there was a cluster of big, flowering crepe myrtles.

"There!"

In the shade of the tall crepe myrtles, there were low-growing shrubs and green-leaved perennial plants and herbs.

Dang.

No doubt about it, dead center in a cluster of shaded perennials under the biggest red-flowering crepe myrtle tree was a leafy plant that matched Joy's description to a T, deadly black berries and all.

CHAPTER 43

I groaned.

Finding the belladonna behind my cottage meant that I had motive, means, *and* opportunity to kill Dex. And since I was able to put together all those pieces, I knew that it wouldn't be long before Detective Gibbit would put it all together as well. If he hadn't already. It was only a matter of time before he'd return for me.

"Probably with a warrant for my arrest," I said to Dolly.

She yipped and wagged her tail as I threw her my last pizza crust.

I need to figure this out . . . and fast.

It was about an hour or so after I'd been in the garden behind my cottage with Daphne, looking at the belladonna plant. Sitting at my dining table inside the cottage, I popped into my mouth the last bite of a quickie dinner Precious had made for me—strawberry pizza, made with strawberries, fresh greens, and our olive oil and drizzled with balsamic vinegar; it'd been positively delicious. And Precious had bragged about how easy it'd been to make.

"I need to make strawberry pizza my regular Sunday evening meal," I said to Dolly. "That is, if I'm not eating prison food off a tin plate."

Dolly barked and spun in a circle.

"Dolly, Precious said the guests requested an early dinner. They must be in the dining room by now, don't you think?"

Dolly wagged her tail.

I got up and headed toward the cottage door. Then I stopped short. My smartphone was sitting on the antique trunk, at the foot of my bed.

Aside from the fact that I rarely used my phone, when I did use it, I never put it there . . . on the trunk. I always kept it stored in the top drawer of the Sheridan dresser, next to the cottage door. Of course, the phone was usually dead. I could never remember to keep the thing charged.

I picked up the phone.

Full charge.

"Huh."

When had I last used it? I couldn't remember. Still, it surely hadn't been charged up all the way . . . had it? My mind was on more important things . . . I couldn't remember.

I shrugged.

I shoved the phone in my jeans pocket and headed outside and across the lawn to the big house.

CHAPTER 44

I'd been right. According to Precious, the Boston crowd had just sat down to a fancy dinner in the big-house dining room. I grabbed the master key from the back pantry and hightailed it up the back stairs to the second floor.

"I don't know what kind of *business* you're up to, Sunshine," Precious whispered loudly from the bottom of the staircase, "but whatever it is, you'd better be lickety-split. I ain't never seen a bunch of folks eat as fast as these folks from Boston. They positively *inhale* their food!"

I turned to look down at Precious at the bottom of the stairs.

"That's because your meals are *so* delicious, Precious!" I blew her a kiss before heading down the second-floor hallway toward the guest rooms.

Okay. I only have a few minutes . . . Which room?

I decided to check out Wiggy's room first, because, clearly, he'd been acting as the group ringleader. I slipped the key into the door and stepped inside.

The room was decorated in elegant country style, with floral-patterned chintz curtains covering the bay window. The pretty bedroom was filled with antiques, including a king-sized four-poster bed, my grandparents' antique side table and drop-down

desk, along with some upholstered chairs. Over on an upholstered bench at the foot of the bed, Wiggy's hard-sided black
suitcase was left open. Quickly, I shuffled through the contents
of his suitcase . . . extra socks and underwear, mostly. And
some other random stuff. I checked the pockets . . . nothing
other than pipe tobacco. Then, I went over to the closet, quickly
yanking the doors open. Again, it was filled with Wiggy's
clothing. A tweed jacket—*what was he thinking? It's much
too hot down here for tweed!*—a lightweight seersucker
jacket—*much better*—some oxford cloth shirts, a few polo
shirts, and several pairs of khaki slacks. And, the stupid
safari-wear.

I stifled a laugh. The safari shirt and shorts *were* from
L.L.Bean!

Except for the extra pillows and linens, laundry bag, and
shoe-cleaning stuff on the top shelf, there wasn't much else. I
closed the closet door and scrambled across the room to the
drop-down desk where, quickly, I yanked open all the drawers,
rifling through the contents. Again, nothing except what we
normally left for our guests . . . pens, pencils, notepad, phone
directory, a promo card about our olive oils . . . that sort of
stuff.

There's got to be something somewhere!

That's when I spied a briefcase, nestled on the upholstered
bench, *underneath* Wiggy's big suitcase. I yanked the briefcase out from under the suitcase, careful to notice exactly
how it had been positioned and which side was up. It wasn't
locked. I opened the case and pulled out papers. There weren't
many, perhaps ten or twelve sheets or so. Mostly, the bag held
Wiggy's pipes and bags of tobacco. Plus his laptop and
charging cords were there. I thought about opening the laptop;
however, I didn't feel confident enough that I could get in and
out of it without my nosing around being discovered later. I
mean, it's not like I was a private detective or anything.

I took my smartphone from my pocket and, working as
quickly as I could, snapped a photo of every page from the
briefcase. Most looked like official Perennial Paper forms
and documents. Then I put it all back inside the case and slid

the case back under the big suitcase. After one quick look around, I hustled to the door, opened it, and peeked up and down the hall, before stepping out and closing the door quietly behind me.

One down.

I figured that I had time to check at least one more room. Maybe two. I moved down the hall to the next room. Again, I inserted the master key into the door and slipped inside the room.

It was Dex's room, done up in pretty Laura Ashley–style florals, wide pink and white stripes, and lots of antique furnishings. In fact, the room was my favorite, having been my own room as a girl. Of course, Daphne's renovation had made the place an absolute palace compared to what it'd been when I'd grown up there. And the little sewing room off the hall had been converted into a pretty pink and white bathroom with bronzed fixtures and a marble-topped sink, transforming the bedroom into an elegant suite.

Fit for a princess.

As far as I could tell, Dex's personal things had been left pretty much as they'd been when he'd been alive. If the detective and his crew had removed or moved stuff, I'd never have known it.

A brown Louis Vuitton duffel bag sat open on a luggage rack near the window. Quickly, I rummaged through it. Mostly underwear, socks, and phone and computer cables. And a book titled *Purchasing Your Own Private Island for Status, Privacy, and Wealth Management.*

An unusual choice for a man who was cleaned out by his ex-wife.

Most of Dex's clothes hung in the closet, along with a Louis Vuitton hanging bag.

On the marble counter in the thick-striped pink and white wallpapered bathroom, there was a leather dopp kit, containing all the usual items: razor, shaving cream, nail clippers, deodorant, cologne, hair product, hair comb . . .

Back in the bedroom, in a corner next to a tall Chippendale desk, I spied a shopping bag that read GIFTS GALORE on the outside. Inside there was a tube of sunscreen, a couple of maps, a brass paperweight shaped like a peanut, some local honey, some pens with ABUNDANCE, GEORGIA printed on them, and an extra-large tee shirt that read OLIVES on the first line, GROWN IN on the second line, ABUNDANCE on the third line, and GEORGIA USA on the fourth line.

I had to laugh. I'd designed the tee shirt myself, and had several hundred printed up at Tommy Burnside's Hot Pressed Tees downtown. Gifts Galore owner Soletta Overstreet had agreed to take a bunch of the shirts on consignment to sell.

"This is the shopping bag Pottie Moss forgot," I whispered to myself.

She'd been right. The bag was mostly touristy stuff.

I made one more pass around the room before I found Dex's briefcase, behind the drapes. It was unlocked and I opened it. Only to find it empty.

"That's odd," I said aloud. "Surely, he hadn't come to Abundance with an empty briefcase."

Did Detective Gibbit empty it? Someone else?

Worried about my time, I went to the door and pulled it open a crack and listened. I could hear the Bostoners downstairs, still talking in the dining room. I shot out into the hall, quietly closing the door behind me, and I moved on to the next room.

We called Claudia's room "the yellow room" for obvious reasons: The walls and furnishings were covered in cheery yellow-patterned papers and fabrics with bright white, lacy accents. The antique furniture was dark mahogany, and the star of the room was a queen-sized canopy bed. This time around, when I stepped into the room, I knew exactly where to go. Sitting on the tall, open-front Chippendale desk in the corner, Claudia had left a gray metal file box.

That's it.

I raced over to open the box. Only the lid was closed and the box was locked shut.

Of course.

I tried fiddling with the lock for a minute before giving up. Then I looked in the desk cubbies and pulled open all the desk drawers, hoping to find *something* to help me open the lock. I grabbed an antique letter opener. It'd been my grand-daddy's. Except it was way too big to do me any good with the tiny lock on the box.

How do they pick locks on TV? Paper clip, I thought. *But does it really work?*

Again, I scrambled around the desk, hoping to find a paper clip.

Not that I'd know what to do with it, even if I found one.

It didn't matter. There were no paper clips to be found.

I considered breaking the box open.

Stop, Eva. Think! If you were Claudia and had this key, and it wasn't with you—which, of course, is a distinct possibility—where would you hide it?

I looked around the room, considering everything I saw. Then it hit me.

Makeup bag.

I scurried into the cheery yellow and white bathroom. Behind a large ottoman with a fluffy sherpa top, the late-day sun filtered through lace curtains that were flanked with floral-patterned floor-to-ceiling drapes. The big ottoman was dual-purpose . . . it was both a seat and a storage container for extra towels and linens. Over at the sink, as expected, Claudia had left her makeup bag sitting on the marble countertop.

Inside her purselike red leather bag, there were several clear pouches chock-full of stuff—body cream, face cream, travel-sized shampoo and conditioner, deodorant, mascara, blush, eyeliner, a compact with eye shadow, nail polish, nail polish remover wipes . . . I kept looking through the pouches . . . aspirin, ibuprofen, acetaminophen—*won't just one of these do?*—allergy pills, blood pressure pills, insomnia pills, nail clippers, nail file, breath mints, tooth floss, brush, comb . . . it was endless.

Still. No key.

Then I noticed a zippered compartment on the *outside* of the bag.

"That's where I'd put it."

And sure enough, that's where it was.

I grabbed the little key and scurried back to the file box in

the other room. I stuck the key in the lock and unlocked the
box. There were ten or more files, stuffed with papers.

Argh! I don't have time to get through all these.

I was getting worried that the group would be finishing
dinner soon.

Quickly, I studied the names on the file tabs, searching for
one that looked most suspicious, or helpful, depending on
your take on things. Most were names of places I didn't recognize . . . then I saw ABUNDANCE written on a tab. Of course,
that's the folder I grabbed. There must've been forty or fifty
pages in the file.

I set the pages on the floor, took out my camera, and snapped
a photo of the top page; with a header that read PERIENNIAL
PAPER LLC, it looked to be some sort of legal document. I flipped
the page and snapped a shot of the second page. Then the third.
The fourth. The fifth. I kept going. Most of the pages appeared
to be legal documents, many from the Boston paper company.
Also, there were some that looked like land survey results.
Realty agreements. Others were related to banking. I noticed
some were from or about financial institutions that were outside
this country. Malaysia. The Cayman Islands. Switzerland. I
didn't have time to stop to read them all. More paper company
documents. Contracts. I just kept snapping away.

Then when I got to the end of the pile, I shoved everything
back into the folder and put the folder back into the file box.
Then I looked to see that the box looked just as it had when
I'd entered.

I must be running out of time.

I worried about Precious's warning regarding the group's
being fast eaters. Surely, by then, they'd had enough time to
eat a meal. Also, I was feeling pretty scared about what I'd
done. After all, I was fairly sure that I'd just broken the law,
breaking into and photographing, of all things, private papers.
Quickly, as I huffed and puffed, I shoved my phone into my
pocket and returned to the bathroom, carefully placing the
key back into the pouch on Claudia's makeup bag.

Phew.

That's when I heard the bedroom door open.

CHAPTER 45

Behind the ottoman in the bathroom, the toes of my sneak-ers stuck out underneath the floral drape. Still, I didn't dare move them to try to get more coverage. I sucked in my breath and held it, paralyzed with fear as I hid behind the yellow and white curtain.

At that very moment, Claudia was clip-clopping into the bathroom, just three or four feet from me. I didn't dare move.

Or breathe.

Of course, the ottoman could've saved me from it all. When I'd heard Claudia entering the suite, I *could've* just flipped open the top to the ottoman and grabbed some of the clean towels that Daphne always left stashed inside. Then I could've closed up the ottoman and walked out of the bath-room into the bedroom where I would've met Claudia and pretended that I'd just come into her suite to deliver fresh towels, and been done with it.

After all, it'd worked one time before.

Long story.

But in the split second I'd had to make my decision about how *not* to get caught, I'd figured Claudia wouldn't have gone for it. She was much too savvy. And paranoid. So instead, I'd hidden behind the curtain.

Of course, ten seconds later, I regretted that stupid decision.

What if she's in for the night? Even if she doesn't find me, I'll be stuck here!

Of course, I was sure she'd find me . . .

I had the overwhelming urge to itch my nose. I tried not to think about the itch. Or breathing.

A few feet away, standing over the sink, I heard Claudia turn on the water. Then she began brushing her teeth. Slowly, I let my breath out, trying not to move the curtain in front of my face. Then, I tried to inhale . . . silently.

Hopefully, the ottoman on the floor will hide my sneakers, I thought. The window behind me was open, and I felt a breeze. Next to me, a lace curtain between the drapes puffed with the wind. I listened, holding my breath, as Claudia finished rinsing her mouth. Then I heard her footsteps clip-clopping on the tile floor again.

Please, God, don't let Claudia come over to the window.

No luck. She was headed my way! I sucked in my stomach and tried to remain still. My nose itched like crazy. Then, suddenly, I felt an urge to sneeze . . .

A little musical tune played in the bedroom.

Claudia's phone.

The clip-clopping stopped. Then, it began again. Only this time, the clip-clops headed away from me and into the bedroom.

I let out a breath.

"Hello?" I heard Claudia say from the other room. "Yes. Okay. I'll bring them over. I understand. I'm on my way. Bye."

Claudia's shoes hit the tile in the bathroom again. She stopped for a moment at the sink. Then quickly, she left the room and went back into the bedroom. About thirty seconds later, I heard the bedroom door open and close shut.

She was gone.

After Claudia left the bedroom, I waited just a second or two before stepping out from behind the curtain. I bent over, exhaling a huge breath, before gobbling up more air. Then I opened the ottoman and pulled out a couple of clean, folded towels.

Just in case I get caught this time.

I headed into the bedroom. The file box was gone. I went over to the suite door. Waiting a moment, I figured I'd give Claudia extra time to go wherever she'd been headed, before I pulled open the door and peeked into the hallway.

All clear.

Quickly, still holding my pile of towels, I stepped into the hallway and quietly closed the door to Claudia's suite behind me.

Then I got the heck out of there.

Ten minutes later, as the sun set low in the sky outside I sat at my dining room table, flipping through all the photos I'd taken on my phone while Dolly gnawed on a giant bone at my feet.

Surely, I thought, looking through the photos, *there must be some sort of clue in here as to what they're up to. Or why Dex was murdered.*

Still, after looking at it all, an hour later my mind was mush. I was exhausted. So I drew myself a bath and took a long, relaxing soak. Then, I decided to climb into bed early, where I could continue studying the photos. Only when I turned down my sheets, I jumped backward with a scream.

There was a huge black snake slithering across my bed.

CHAPTER 46

Normally, I wasn't one to freak out over snakes. After all, my niece Amy had a pet snake, Noose. And when Noose got loose, as he often did—I was sure Amy let him out on purpose, mostly to freak out her mother—I was the one Daphne always sent to find and capture him.

Still, discovering a random snake in my bed like that undid me. Not to mention that the little beastie was nearly five feet long.

I remembered that my sheets had just been washed, and afterward, I'd made up the bed and tucked in my sheets—in fact, I remembered *distinctly* tucking in my sheets that Sunday morning, nice and tight, just like my mother used to when I was a little girl. Usually, the only time I'd tuck in my sheets was after I'd just washed them. Honestly, I was too lazy to do it the rest of the time.

So I was thinking, a snake wouldn't work its way under a perfectly made bedspread and then under a *super-tightly* tucked top sheet.

Someone must've put the snake in my bed.

Who would put a snake in my bed? And why? Could it be

one or all of the Bostoners? Had I unwittingly discovered something about what they were doing here? Dex's murder?

Wait a minute.

What was it Debi had said in the tree? Something about her being a snake? Or slithering? Then Pep and I had laughed. What was it, exactly, Debi'd said? I couldn't remember.

Then I remembered finding my phone, sitting on the trunk in my cottage. And it'd been charged. I was sure that I hadn't left it there. And I was surer still that I hadn't charged it. But then, when had I used my phone last?

I tried to remember.

I just couldn't. I was too stressed about everything else going on to remember a detail like that.

Still, it was clear: Someone had entered my cottage that day. And someone had tinkered with my phone. And someone had left a snake in my bed. Frowning, I looked around my little cottage. Had someone gone through my stuff? Opened my drawers? Taken or moved something else . . . ?

The thought totally creeped me out.

I felt violated.

Was it Debi who'd fiddled with my phone and put the snake in my bed? She'd been an hour or more late to the garden club cleanup . . . and with Daphne, Pep, and me in the village, no one would've been home at the plantation to see her.

Takes a snake to know a snake, I thought.

Swiftly, I grabbed the snake behind its head, went over and kicked open the screen door, walked behind the cottage, and chucked the big snake out back. Then, I returned to my cottage where, too tired to remake the bed, I pulled the bed-spread up and over the entire bed and lay down on top of it.

I didn't sleep a wink that night.

CHAPTER 47

Monday morning couldn't have come soon enough. All night long, I'd fretted, tossed and turned on top of my bed, and wished sunrise would hurry up and come. Then when the sun finally rose up, I hadn't even noticed. Probably no more than thirty minutes before sunrise, I'd finally drifted off to sleep.

Several hours later, I awoke with a start when a sunbeam streamed through my window and straight onto my face. Quickly, I jumped out of bed, washed, and dressed.

I had lots of investigating to do that day.

Opening the screen door, I let Dolly in—apparently, she'd let herself outside while I'd slept. That's when, while I was standing at the door, I recognized Buck's SUV parked up at the big house.

"C'mon, Dolly. Let's go see what's happening."

Only, when I started across the yard toward the big house, Dolly turned and ran in the other direction, heading down the hill to the pond, where Buck was working with his deputy. They were walking through the grasses on the side where Dex had been, looking down, as if they were searching for something.

I turned and hurried to the pond. Maybe Buck could help me figure out what the papers I'd discovered were all about. Although, I worried about telling Buck just *how* I'd actually come across the papers . . . After all, he *was* a man of the law.

Cheeyoo-cheeyoo-cheeyoo. Soaring overhead, a red-tailed hawk cried.

"Buck! What are you looking for?" I asked, walking up behind him. Bent over and walking slowly, Buck was moving the grasses this way and that with a stick.

He stood up to face me. Deputy Pierce was working several yards away, carefully combing through the grass where he was.

"Eva. What are you doing here?" asked Buck sharply.

Dressed in his uniform, Buck was all business that morning. He didn't even crack a smile.

"Why . . . What do you mean? I *live* here . . ." I laughed. "I'm just wondering, why are *you* here? Are you looking for something? Did you find out something about Dex?"

"As a matter of fact, I did." Still holding the stick, Buck placed his hands on his hips. "I found out that you lied to me."

"What are you talking about? I've never lied to you . . . about anything!"

"Alright then. You *kept information* from me. We've had this discussion before, Eva. Remember? Many times, in fact. Hiding important information from me, *during an investigation*, is the same as lying to me. I thought that I made that clear weeks ago. In fact, I *know* that I made it clear. And I was sure that you understood me."

"You don't have to talk to me like I'm a child, Buck Tanner. Besides, I don't know what you're talking about," I said.

I started to feel a sick, tight feeling in the pit of my stomach.

"You know damn well what I'm talking about. And do you want to know what really irks me, Eva?"

"No . . . not really . . ."

"What really irks me is that I asked you, time and time again, over the course of these past two days, whether or not you had *any more* to tell me about you and Dex Codman. And do you know what you said, *every* single time?"

"Sheriff . . ." said Deputy Pierce quietly.

"Eva! I'm asking you a question." Buck raised his voice. Buck never raised his voice. And he ignored his deputy. He never did that, either.

"No . . ."

"Sheriff Tanner . . ." the deputy said.

"Each and every time I asked you if there was any more to tell me about your relationship with your ex-fiancé, you said no. *No!*"

"Yes . . . I did."

That sick feeling in my stomach was growing by the moment. I felt the blood rush from my head. I thought that I might puke.

It's coming, Eva. He knows . . .

"You lied to me, Eva. Over and over again. You lied to the one person who could help you. The one man who has *always* had your back. No matter what. You lied."

"I . . . I'm not sure what you're talking about, Buck."

Liar!

Buck lowered his voice. All of a sudden, he was eerily calm.

"For one thing, you neglected to tell me that you and your ex-fiancé had an argument during the olive oil tasting party at the big house. A big argument. In fact, the argument was so *spectacular* that everyone—*everyone*—whom Detective Gibbit has interviewed mentioned it. And *everyone* said that you threatened to kill Dex Codman."

"I didn't threaten to kill him!"

I felt faint.

"Right. And do you want to tell me now just *why* you would say such a thing to Dex Codman, your *ex*-fiancé? Or even *hint* such a thing?"

"What do you mean?"

"I'm talking about the fact that your Boston Brahmin ex-fiancé Dexter Codman *the Third* abused you, Eva. He broke your arm. Then your nose. He bruised and cracked your ribs. Tell me *that* isn't the truth. Go ahead. Lie to me one more time. I've seen the doctor's reports. The X-rays . . . I've read the drivel of completely implausible excuses that you told the doctors . . . all of it! Did you think that by going to different hospitals around Boston, what happened to you would never be found out?"

"I . . ."

I was sobbing. After all these years, the truth was out. And Buck was furious. And honestly, I didn't know whether he was more furious that it'd happened, or about the fact that I'd lied to him. Or simply that I'd jilted him all those years ago at the altar, in favor of an evil, self-absorbed abuser named Dex Codman the Third.

"Tell me now *that* isn't the truth!"

I'd never in my life seen Buck so angry. He was quiet, but his eyes were flashing daggers, and he was positively trembling.

"Sheriff Tanner," said his deputy again. He'd crossed over to stand in between me and Buck.

I looked down. Feeling nauseous, I was frantic to get away.

"Did you *not* think that I would find out?" Buck said, quietly. He stepped around Deputy Pierce. "And given that this man was once close to you, did you not expect me to look into *everything*—especially his personal, significant relationships, which included you? Did you not think that I'd look even *more* carefully, given that he'd shown up here *to see you*, after all those years? I was worried, Eva, that he'd somehow put you in danger. And I was right. Only I was sixteen years too late."

"But he didn't show up for me," I whispered. "He showed up because . . ."

"Christ, Eva." Buck let out an exasperated sigh. "Just save it. You didn't tell me about him before because you were embarrassed and ashamed. That much you've admitted already. And although you hadn't come clean about what, exactly, you were embarrassed and ashamed about, I get it now. You were embarrassed and ashamed because *you think* that you *let* a man abuse you. Which is nothing, you hear me, *nothing* that you *let* happen, and it is nothing to be embarrassed about. Or ashamed of. Or something that should be kept a secret. *He's* the one who was messed up, not you. But that's neither here nor there, now. Still, what really tees me off is that after you found out he'd been murdered, you decided not to tell me because you knew it would 'look bad.' Because you *knew* it'd make you look like a prime suspect for his murder. And you know what?"

"What?" I whispered. Hot tears ran down my cheeks. I folded my arms across my chest.

"It does. It makes you the prime suspect for this guy's—this sicko abuser's—murder. And now, I can't help you. I'm too close to it. Too close to *you*. By not coming clean when you should've, you've tied my hands. So please, Eva, leave this pond, right now, and go find Daphne. Tell her to call her fancy lawyers up in Atlanta. I'm afraid you're gonna need one."

"Sir," said Deputy Pierce. "I think I found something."

"Go on, Eva. Get out of here!" Buck ordered.

Inserting a stick inside to pick it up, Deputy Pierce held up an empty dark green bottle of Knox Liquid Gold Extra Virgin Olive Oil.

"I bet that's it," said Buck.

"I don't know how we missed it the other day, sir. It was right over there, in those tall weeds next to the boulder, where I found the vic's clothes."

"Get out, Eva. This is a crime scene," Buck barked at me.

Buck turned and completely shut me out, busying himself with collecting evidence. I turned to leave him and Deputy Pierce. When I'd just gotten a couple of steps away, I heard Buck's smooth Southern drawl as he spoke to Deputy Pierce.

"This conversation is off the record," he said under his breath.

"Yes, sir," mumbled his deputy.

"No one hears that it ever happened, you got it? No one. Especially not Eli. It's his investigation. And I'm afraid he'll get to it soon enough."

"Yes, sir. You know that I always got your back, Sheriff."

"Yes, I do. Let's get back to work. Hopefully, we'll find something to incriminate someone else."

CHAPTER 48

After my argument with Buck, I was pretty shaken. And I had every intention of going back inside my cottage to lick my wounds and figure out what to do next. Detective Gibbit was sure to pay me a visit soon. Except, when I reached the top of the hill, there was a large U-Haul rental truck in the backyard, parked near the outside entrance to the big-house basement.

"Afternoon, Miss Eva!" called out someone from the other side of the U-Haul. "It's a gorgeous day today, isn't it?"

Alvin Winston rushed across the yard to embrace me. Alvin was a slender, fair-haired, fair-skinned fellow with smiling blue eyes and boyish good looks. He was dressed to the nines in pressed white linen slacks, a button-down chambray shirt, spit-shined penny loafers, and a cashmere sweater tied around his shoulders—despite the fact that temperatures were already in the nineties. He air-kissed me with great flourish. He smelled like a fresh ocean breeze.

"Alvin!" I cried. Quickly, I wiped my teary cheeks with the back of my hand. I took a deep breath. *Try to look normal, Eva.* "What a surprise! What on earth are you doing down here in Abundance? Can't take the big city in Atlanta any-more?"

"Why, my lovely, I'm moving into Knox Plantation, that's what! Your big sis has hired me to live here, full-time, in this fancy basement apartment of hers! I mean, when she told me that the apartment is right next to the wine cellar . . . how could I say no!" Alvin waved an arm toward the basement entrance below the big house. "Your sister has such *fabulous* taste in wine, and I'm sure she won't miss a few bottles here and there!"

He tittered a laugh.

Growing up, the basement had been no more than a dirt floor surrounded by rock walls—a homestead for spiders and crickets, snakes and rodents. It had been dirty, dusty, and mold infested. And the only electricity down there had been a little light bulb in the ceiling with a pull string. Accessed only by the exterior bulkhead, the basement had been the place where my family stashed decrepit tools, forgotten fur-niture, broken toys, and old lawn gear.

But when Daphne came back from Atlanta and renovated the big house, she changed all that the basement used to be. After excavating down and pouring new concrete floors, sta-bilizing all the outer foundation walls, adding new inside walls, ceilings, electrical, and plumbing, Daphne created a generously sized, slate-tiled mudroom, with cubbies, shelves, and hanging hooks, that led to a small but beautiful studio apartment with kitchenette and bath. Also in the basement there was a state-of-the-art, climate-controlled wine cellar, an exercise room, and a large storage area.

"Daphne, share her precious wine? Aw, Alvin, I wouldn't be too sure of that!" I said, teasing him.

In his late twenties and successful as a home decorator back in Atlanta, for several years Alvin had helped my sister and her Atlanta socialite acquaintances maintain their mansions in the up-to-the-minute style to which they'd been accustomed. Then, the economy crashed, and even my sister's wealthy friends couldn't afford to spend obscene amounts of money decorating their homes. Still, with a pro ballplayer's fat income to support the family, my sister remained loyal to Alvin and single-handedly kept his decorating business afloat. Then, about the time Daphne and Alvin had finished decorating and redecorating Daphne's Atlanta mansion, Daphne and her husband, Big Boomer, were well into their divorce. Alvin had been a lifeline and near-constant companion for my sister.

"I can't believe Daphne actually convinced you to leave Atlanta for Abundance." I shook my head.

"Well, you know I just *adore* your nieces and nephew. Being a full-time 'manny,' of sorts, will be loads of fun. Plus, your big sis convinced me that if I came down here, I could still be her personal designer and she'd find me some new clients as well—something about some B6 group needing help with their homes. Daphne said their interiors are just *so* passé! And best of all, your sis and I will be full-time shopping pals!"

"That's great, Alvin. I'm excited that you're here. Abundance sure isn't Atlanta, but it does have its own special charm. And the kids will be tickled to death. I know they all adore you."

"I can't wait to see the little monsters again! Now, enough about me. Miss Eva, *what on earth* happened to you, darling?" He put his hands on my shoulders and looked me up and down with an appalled look. "You didn't really *kill* that poor fellow I heard about, did you?"

"Of course not," Daphne answered for me. Striding across the lawn from the big house, Daphne's soft peach–colored chiffon dress swirled around her long legs, making it look as if she was floating across the lawn.

"Well, that's good to know!" said Alvin. Then he gave me a little hug. "Of course, you know I'm only kidding."

"Of course," I said.

Daphne handed Alvin an envelope.

"Here are the keys, Alvin. They're all labeled for you. One key is for the outside door to the basement; one is for the back door; one is for the front door; and another is for your apartment. Oh, and there's a key to my Buick inside as well. Welcome home, *dawh-lin*." They air-kissed. Then Daphne gave Alvin a big hug. "We're all *so* delighted you're finally here."

"I'm thrilled to be a part of the family."

"You always have been. Listen, I've got a ladies club meeting in town, so I've got to run. We'll talk when I get back in another couple of hours. The girls are all at school, and Little Boomer is at preschool. Missus Greene will drop him off. Then, we'll all get reacquainted this afternoon! Meanwhile . . . I'm off!" Daphne blew a kiss before she turned to hurry away. "Oh, and if you need help unloading, just ask Burl to help. He's over at the warehouse. Eva can help you find him!"

"No problemo!" Alvin called out with a wave to Daphne. Then he turned to me and said, "I'm too tired to unpack now. I'll wait until she gets back home."

"Alvin," I said, "I can't believe you actually suggested that I'd killed someone."

"Oh, sweetheart, y'all know I was just pullin' your leg. Although, if I do say so, you do look *frightful*. Is everything okay? Are you still upset about all that wedding business up in Boston? That was awful, it truly was. I'm sorry about the weatherman, and your wedding not working out and all."

"It's not that, Alvin. Goodness knows, I've finally come to understand that when it comes to men, I've absolutely no clue. I've actually declared a moratorium on men for myself."

"Well, still, sweetie, you should've figured that marrying a queen wouldn't work out. I mean, everyone in the gay community knew your weather guy wasn't straight . . ."

"Omigosh. Alvin! You know?"

"Why, of course."

"Well, I wish you'd told me! *I* didn't."

"Oh dear. I'm so sorry. I guess I just assumed that you knew. I mean, it was just *so* obvious, wasn't it?"

"Alvin, honestly, I had no idea. I thought Zack Black was the real deal . . . that he loved me. We even lived together for a year. I never had a clue that I was only a prop for his career and the television station. Some promotions person, or Zack's agent—or both—decided that Zack Black, everyone's favorite weatherman, needed to be married to pull in better ratings. And then, along I came . . ." I sighed. "The perfect mark. A naive Southerner from a backwater town who was desperate for love and attention."

"Well, it must've been a terrible shock when you found out." Alvin shook his head. "So, if I may ask, if you didn't know, what finally happened to make you run on your wedding day?"

"Minutes before our wedding was to begin, I went out in front of the church on Beacon Hill to pat the horse that was going to pull our carriage after the ceremony. I really had no reason to go out there, other than the fact that I like horses and I suppose I was nervous and just wanted to take one more look at the world before I became Mrs. Zack Black. Except when I was out in front of the church, the carriage driver gave me a weird look. And I heard noises from inside the carriage. That's when I threw open the carriage door and discovered Zack inside, being cozy with his male producer."

"How positively *ghastly*! I'm so sorry."

"Alvin, no one knows. Especially no one in my family. And the television station threatened me about spilling the beans, especially because no one in the public actually saw anyone else inside the carriage with Zack. The world just thinks I'm a nutcase. And really, I don't even care anymore. So please, I'm begging you, can we keep it a secret, just between you and me . . . and whoever else in your community knows?" I rolled my eyes. "I feel so stupid. As it is, Daphne bugs me every day about my need to catch a 'suitable' man to marry me. Already, she's calling me an old maid. She's driving me crazy. If she finds out that I cluelessly nearly got hitched to a gay man, she'll *never* give it a rest."

"Sure, hon, we can keep it a secret. And I'll even let some of my decorator buddies know, just in case they run into Daphne. No worries, Miss Eva. You can count on Alvin Winston. Mum's the word."

Alvin raised his hand and pretended to zip his mouth closed.

"Thank you. I really am glad you're here."

"Me, too."

Alvin kissed me on the cheek.

"Now, Eva, hon, is there a spa around here somewhere? You *really* look like you could use a day . . ."

CHAPTER 49

I was too tired, too upset, and, frankly, too stupid to know how to interpret the documents that I'd photographed in Wiggy's and Claudia's rooms. I needed help.

Except that Buck certainly wasn't going to help me.

So instead, I decided to take Ian up on his offer.

Yer always welcome here, Eva. Anytime, Ian had said. *Ye can even come up the drive, if ye like.*

Alrighty, then.

Who better to interpret a pile of legal and land documents than the multi-estate-owning, land-grabbing, wealthy Scot who was "connected" himself?

I was going to Greatwoods.

With a top speed of about twenty-five miles per hour, the Kubota RTV was nearly as speedy as Daddy's old F-250 farm truck. Only the Kubota was *way* more roadworthy. It had tough tires and a roll bar.

From our place, Greatwoods was in the opposite direction down the main road from the village, and I rarely traveled that way. Regardless, tootling along the road was actually quite pleasant in the Kubota. There was a roof over my head for shade, and seated on the vinyl bench seat behind the steering wheel with the wind in my hair, I enjoyed inhaling the sweet scents of summer.

Moreover, moving along at such a leisurely speed, I was able to take in roadside sights that I often didn't notice. Like the snapping turtle crawling in the wetlands growth, just off the road. And beautiful pecan trees that I spied in a field down a drive that I'd never known existed. And the barbed wire fence in the woods, on the opposite side of the road.

That would be Ian Collier's.

Of course, I was all-too-familiar with that danged fence in the woods. Even so, I'd never noticed the high fence from the main road before.

I continued on until the barbed wire changed to a very tall, black, wrought iron fence that continued running along the opposite side of the road.

Almost there.

Fifty feet or so later, across the road I saw a massive, black, wrought iron double gate hanging from large brick pillars, marking the entrance to Greatwoods Plantation. There was a camera mounted atop one of the pillars. I shifted to neutral and waited on my side of the road while a small pickup drove past in the opposite direction, followed by a sedan and then a fertilizer truck. Then I shifted into first, then second gear, and pulled across the two-lane road to the plantation entry. Inset from the road, the entrance provided enough room for a couple of vehicles to park in front of the gate while still being off the main thoroughfare. I parked the Kubota and stepped out onto the cobblestone drive, looking for the "box."

There's a button on the box at the entry gate, Ian had said. *Ye just push it and someone will open the gate for ye.*

"There it is."

A nondescript little black box was mounted to the left pillar at about shoulder height. I walked over and pushed the button. Nothing happened. I stood and waited.

Thirty seconds later, like magic, the huge wrought iron

gates opened inward. I ran back to the Kubota, climbed in, shifted into gear, and motored on up the shady, cobblestone drive. Behind me, the giant gates closed shut.

Huge, pink-flowering crepe myrtle trees lined the drive on either side. Honestly, the winding drive was probably a half mile long or more . . . and there were blooming crepe myrtles the entire way. Furthermore, every inch along the side of the drive was meticulously landscaped and managed. Under the crepe myrtles were sweet flowering lilies, hostas, gardenias—their scent was pure heaven. There were blooming roses, plus azalea bushes, rhododendrons, and more. The air smelled like sweet flowers and damp earth.

Of course, Buck had driven me down the drive once before. But that had been at night. Seeing the pink-flowering trees in the daytime, along with all the landscaping, under a bright blue sky, was quite another experience altogether.

In the woods behind the crepe myrtles were giant magnolia and holly trees, tall poplar and hickory trees. There were live oaks, red and white oaks, and probably a whole bunch of oaks that I couldn't recognize. Also growing were majestic pines, beautiful sycamores, hemlocks and cedars, maples, and even walnut trees. And some of my very favorite beech trees.

The place was a naturalist's dream. *Naturalist, not naturist*, I thought with a chuckle.

After a couple of minutes, I motored around a final corner, and the landscape opened dramatically to reveal acre after acre of pristinely manicured lawns dotted with perfectly trimmed specimen trees, shrubs, and topiaries, all showcasing the majestic Greatwoods Plantation mansion at the top of the hill. The fresh green grass scent of the clipped lawns was intoxicating.

I followed the drive to a large circular area in front of the building where a ginormous circular fountain gushed water. Clad in white terra-cotta tiles, the front of the mansion was every bit as stunning as the rear of the place, with the center loggia of the H-shaped mansion showcasing an arcade of arched windows and Ionic pilasters and columns, behind which, I knew, was the stunning ballroom.

Honestly, the understated front entry was almost a let-down compared to the rest of the façade. At one of the corner sections of the "H," up half a dozen wide marble stairs, underneath an intricately designed wrought iron sort of pergola, was a large black door. It was at the diagonal opposite end of the building from the kitchen entrance that Buck and I had used at night.

I parked at the base of the stairs and shut off the Kubota. Then I climbed the stairs to the door. There was no doorbell that I could see, so I reached up to an oversize bronze door knocker that was shaped like a stag's head . . . antlers and all. Before I even touched the knocker, the door flew open.

"Eva. What brings ye here?"

Much to my surprise, Ian opened the door himself. I guess I'd imagined that was the sort of thing Mister Lurch would do. Or even Precious. Regardless—looking as dapper as always, this time dressed in khaki shorts and his usual pressed and starched shirt with the sleeves rolled up and a pair of well-worn moccasins—Ian caught me off guard. Plus, I'm sure that he caught me staring . . . tanned, toned, and muscular like a runner's, Ian's long legs were gorgeous.

He smiled.

"Come inside, Eva."

His eyes twinkled as he looked over my shoulder at the Kubota in the drive.

"Ah, I see ye've brought yer chariot!" he said with a chuckle. "Is everything alright with ye?" He took me by the elbow and ushered me inside.

"Yes, everything is fine." *Well, not really.* "Thank you," I said, stepping over threshold. "I'm sorry to come unexpectedly . . . I guess I should've called first. Really, I'm here to ask a favor."

"Ye don't ever need to call first. Yer always welcome. What can I do for ye?"

In the huge entry, we stood before a ginormous, curved marble staircase, covered with red carpet. The kind of thing you see in movies. *Or Newport mansions.* Above us, a giant crystal chandelier was suspended from a frescoed ceiling that must've been thirty feet high, or more. There were marble pillars and walls that were rendered with beautiful three-dimensional carvings and sculptures of South Georgia flora and fauna.

"Can I get ye something to drink, or a snack, perhaps?" Ian motioned me to follow him. To our left was a door to the great ballroom Buck and I'd passed through before. We passed that door as Ian headed to the left corner of the grand stair, where there was a small passageway. To our right, behind and underneath the great stair, there was another door.

Ian must've seen the puzzled look on my face, because he pointed to the door and said, "Coat closet under the stair." Then he laughed. "And a mighty big one, too, I might add. This way."

Ahead of us, buried in the carved white wall, I finally saw the "invisible" door. Ian pushed something on the wall, and the thick door sprang open.

We walked through the doorway and into the corner of Ian's library. Like the wall next to it, the back of the door we'd opened was filled with book-laden shelves. The entry to the study from the ballroom—the way Buck and I'd come in the other night—was on the adjacent wall, just past the corner, on our left. The grand fireplace was at the far end of the room. Ian's desk, where I'd discovered the maps, was in the corner to my right. Behind it, next to the bookshelves we'd just passed through, was the mysterious green velvet curtained wall, where I knew there was a painting of some sort with a gilded frame that I was dying to see.

"Please, Eva, sit." Ian motioned to the same group of high-backed leather chairs in the center of the room that we sat on during my last visit.

"This is going to sound a bit weird," I said, seating myself, "but I've come across some documents, and I think there may be something illegal going on. Or at least something under-handed."

Ian raised an eyebrow but said nothing.

I continued. "The documents seem to be about transactions

involving land here in Abundance. And money. Big money, involving financial institutions all over the world."

Ian's eyes sharpened. Still, he waited.

"I'm not too knowledgeable about any of this sort of thing, and I was hoping you might be able to take a look at the documents, so you can explain to me what is going on."

"Of course. I'm happy to help ye. Where are the papers?"

"Oh, right. Sorry. They're on my phone." I pulled my smartphone out of my pocket. "I took photos of everything when I . . . um . . . kind of *stole* a peek."

"Ye *stole* a peek?"

"Yes, well . . . Look, I think this business might have something to do with the man who was murdered at our place, Dex Codman. And I'm pretty sure Detective Gibbit is about to arrest me for the murder. And I didn't do it! I swear. So I'm trying to figure it all out before I get arrested for something I didn't do."

"Eva, I don't doubt ye . . . I'm sure ye didn't murder any-body. It's definitely not yer nature. It's laughable, really. But still, if it's something illegal ye think is going on, then why aren't ye talking to yer man, Buck? After all, he's the law around here."

"Buck and I . . . we had sort of a falling-out. He told me that he can't help me."

"Did he now?"

"Yes."

"And why's that? It seems to me if there's something crim-inal going down around this county, the local sheriff's the man ye need to be siding *with*, not against . . ."

"He's angry because I hid some information from him."

"Did ye now? And why would ye do such a thing?"

"Look . . . it's complicated. I made some mistakes a long time ago, and when it was all over, I thought I could just sweep it all under the rug and no one would be the wiser. I was wrong. Now Buck found out about it, and he's angry with me. Really angry. And it involved Dex Codman, the man who was mur-dered. So now, Buck says I'm on my own. And he means it."

"Aye, that explains a bit of it, I suppose."

"I'm so sorry. I would never bother you like this, really. However, I've gotten the sense that you know an awful lot about all the land sales going on around here."

"Have ye now?"

"Yes. Like when I saw you at the Twiggs place. You were arguing . . . about the land."

"Well, I'm not sure it's the same sort of thing yer talking about, Eva. My beef with Elrod was about him leading everyone to believe that he found his brother Elroy dead after the poor man had shot himself to death by accident while cleaning his gun. I don't believe it. In fact, I found it quite odd that Elroy died just hours after he left me, after signing an agreement, turning over his place to me in order to ensure it'd never be developed. Our agreement gave him lifetime rights, but the place was to be mine, once the legal stuff was worked out. And I had the papers filed on that day. Later, I found out that even before Elroy died, Elrod had signed an agreement for big bucks to sell the land to a foreign client of Dickey Dicer's. The only way he could have accomplished that was if his brother, who owned the land, was dead. Clearly, as the last remaining Twigg, Elrod was counting on being the sole heir. Unfortunately, he hadn't counted on me already being the owner."

"You see, you *are* knowledgeable about this kind of stuff. And Buck told me that you're 'connected.'"

For a moment, Ian looked surprised before he quickly gathered himself again.

"Did he now?"

Too much information, Eva.

Quickly, I said, "He didn't tell me anything specific. Just that you were *concerned* about things."

"Things?"

"He described you as sort of an *advocate* for preserving land."

That's broad enough, I think, not to alarm him. I need his help!

"I see."

"I think, once you see these documents, you'll understand what's going on and you'll know what to do. And if you can help me understand what's going on, *maybe* I can figure out how Dex was involved and who really killed him and why, before Detective Gibbit arrests me."

"Don't fret, girl. Ye know I'm always in yer corner, happy to help ye, Eva. Always." He smiled.

"Oh good, I'm so glad! I'm thinking the easiest way might be for you to download my photos, right from my smartphone?"

"Sure."

I got up and handed him my phone. "Here. Don't worry, there's nothing else important on it."

Ian took my phone in his hand and stood up. "If ye don't mind, I'll take this upstairs to my office where I have a computer. I can download yer photos there. It should only take a couple of minutes."

"Thank you."

"I'll be back when it's done. Would ye like something to drink or a snack while ye wait?"

"No, thank you. I'm fine."

Ian took my hand, giving it a squeeze.

"There's no need to worry yerself. We'll get it sorted out."

He nodded before he turned and strode out of the room with my phone.

I sat still for a minute or so, taking in the manly library, this time in the daylight. Then, restless, I stood and started pacing around the room. The velvet curtain on the inside wall bothered me. I knew there was a painting behind it.

Why would someone cover a painting on a wall?

Maybe it was an important work of art. With Ian's knowledge and appreciation of fine things, a collectible painting wasn't out of the realm of possibility. Certainly, he could afford one.

Maybe it's a landscape painting? Like something from nineteenth-century Scotsman David Roberts. Or a big-time artist like Monet. Or even a Turner!

My imagination got the better of me. I couldn't stand it. I

walked up and grabbed the velvet curtain on the wall and yanked it aside.

Only, when I saw the painting, I nearly collapsed from shock. It wasn't a landscape at all. Instead, it was a portrait. Of a young woman dressed in an elegant bridal dress. Standing in the countryside, with a noble hound at her side, she held the reins to a beautiful white horse.

And except for her jet-black hair, the young woman was a dead ringer for me.

"What the heck have you gone and done now?"

It was Precious. She was standing in the doorway with a scowl on her face, her arms folded across her chest. And she looked angry.

CHAPTER 50

Precious wasn't angry.

Oh no.

She was *really, really* angry. So angry, in fact, that Ian rushed down from upstairs to see what all the commotion was about as Precious berated me for uncovering the portrait and being a "spoiled little busybody."

And if I thought Precious's reaction was weird, Ian's re-action to the scene was even more bizarre. When he walked into the library and saw me standing next to the uncovered portrait, he turned white as a ghost. He just stared at me, and then at the portrait. He didn't utter a word. Then he just turned on his heel and left the library.

"You see!" Precious scolded. "I told you to stay away from Mister Collier! Mind your p's and q's, I said. Why can't you *listen* to anyone? You're just messing up the poor man's heart."

I couldn't make heads or tails of what Precious meant, but in the next moment, Mister Lurch appeared, and without a word, he handed me my phone as Precious was busy hustling me to the front door. Next thing I knew, I was out on the doorstep.

"Mind your own business," Precious warned. Then the great black door had closed behind me.

I'd lost Buck. And now, after revealing a mysterious portrait of a woman who could've easily been me, I'd lost Precious. And Ian. And I didn't even know why.

It didn't matter. They were *all* mad at me.

Worse still, I was sure that I was about to be arrested for killing Dex.

"I give up!"

I just sat down on the steps, about to have a good cry.

Then I remembered the stupid swamp tour. Daphne was expecting me to go, in just a little while. It was the *last* thing I wanted to think about.

Then it occurred to me that having to go on the swamp tour that afternoon with the crowd from Boston would not only be a relief from all my own drama, but also, it would be a perfect time to question Wiggy, Claudia, Coop, and Spencer about what it was they were up to. Quite literally, there'd be nowhere for them to go or to hide while I asked them questions. And although I hadn't figured out exactly what they'd been up to, maybe I didn't need to. Certainly, I knew enough to fake it.

I was determined to get to the bottom of the mystery and figure out who killed Dex. Even if I had to do it alone.

Game on.

I wiped my tears on my sleeve and headed home.

CHAPTER 51

If I'd thought that nothing could've been more bizarre than my morning at Greatwoods, then I'd have been wrong.

We arrived at the Taylor Farm and were standing on the pier that jutted into the swampy Snake River. It was the same rickety old pier that Buck had taken me to years ago to watch the fireworks that his friends shot off from Alligator Island. I smiled, remembering the good times. Not much had changed at the Taylor place in all the years I'd been away, except someone had erected a roof over the length of the pier and added some steps at the end that went down into the water. That's where Skeets had tied up his three canoes.

"Where's the fancy airboat that we're taking?" asked Spencer. "I've always wanted to go out on an airboat." He held up his smartphone and snapped a selfie, standing next to the river.

"No airboat today!" Skeets answered breezily. He carried a machete and a small ice cooler into one of the canoes. "You folks asked for a *special* tour, so I'm givin' you a right up close and personal one. Airboat's too noisy to fully experience nature. Plus, it's too big to get down this little river, and you all said this is what you wanted to see."

I had a pretty good idea about what *really* happened to the airboat: Skeets Diggs had fatally damaged it when he'd run it into the tree limb outside his sister's Naturist B&B. So—as Skeets was unwilling to give up his one-hundred-dollar-per-person fee for the three-hour swamp tour—he'd *made do* by lashing three red canoes together.

Yup, he'd actually *lashed them together* to make a sort of canoe *raft*.

Then, much to my amusement, via a hand-built wooden bracket hanging off one side of the farthest canoe from the pier, Skeets mounted a 1938 Johnson Sea Horse 1.1 horse-power outboard motor.

That was how nine of us—Skeets and his sister, Pottie Moss, along with the four Bostoners, plus Charlene and Darlene and I—were to travel together down Snake River, out into the Big Swamp, and over to Alligator Island. In three fifteen-foot-long canoes, tied together, side by side, powered by an antique motor with as much juice as a kitchen blender.

I slammed my hand on my forehead, remembering the old *Gilligan's Island* television show theme song about a bunch of tourists stranded on an island after setting out on a quick three-hour tour. The ominous tune played in my head.

A three-hour tour . . . a three-hour tour . . .

"Load up, folks!" Skeets cried out merrily. "We ain't got all day! Only got three hours to get out, eat, and get back!"

A three-hour tour . . .

I figured it'd take us at least forty minutes, maybe an hour, to get to Alligator Island with the little putt-putt engine. And it'd take us an equal amount of time to return. That didn't leave much more than an hour for the picnic that the twins and I had to set up and serve. And, of course, it was super hot and muggy that afternoon, and the *bugs* were everywhere. I was happy I'd remembered to apply bug spray before leaving home. Regardless, it was going to be a killer afternoon.

Still, it was better than being arrested for murder.

I reminded myself that I needed to stay focused. My main

objective was to glean information about Dex's death, and whatever else I could about the land shenanigans. And already, I'd learned something. The Boston crowd had requested *specifically* to travel down Snake River. And I had the idea that it wasn't so much Snake River they'd wanted to see, but instead, the land abutting the river. And it just so happened that most of that land was part of the Taylor Farm. And, as I'd overheard at the Roadhouse, the Taylor Farm was for sale.

I remembered Pervis in the Roadhouse saying there was a contract coming in on the place . . . Could it be the Bostoners had already made an agreement? Or maybe it'd been Ian?

Don't think about Ian now.

Thinking about Ian—likewise, Buck and Precious—upset me.

Focus, Eva.

"Ma'am," said Skeets, reaching out to take Claudia's hand, "I'd like to have you sit in the center of the farthest canoe, the one with the engine."

"I can't do this," cried Claudia, grabbing her chest. "I can't swim. And I'm afraid of this place."

Apparently, unbeknownst to everyone until the moment she tried to step off the dock into the canoes, Claudia was deathly afraid of water. Of course, the giant orange life preserver she'd insisted on wearing should've been a clue. Still, even the life jacket she wore, like a giant, puffy vest over her safari suit, didn't calm her. Hyperventilating, she bent over, gasping for air.

Pottie Moss opened a small cooler at her feet and pulled out a paper bag, handing it to Claudia.

"I brought it for leftovers," Pottie Moss explained to whomever would listen. "I hear the chef at Knox Plantation is *a-mazing.*"

Immediately, Claudia put the bag to her face and began huffing into it.

"It's alright, darlin'," said Pottie Moss. She put a hand on Claudia's shoulder. "It'll all be over before y'all know it. I promise." Then she turned to the rest of the crowd and said, "And we ain't had a gator eat no one yet! Right, Skeets?"

Claudia staggered backward.

"You said it, Pottie Moss!" Skeets laughed.

Standing next to me, holding our own Knox Plantation coolers, the twins giggled. I shot them a quick look.

The twins, following Daphne's official Knox Plantation protocol, wore their Southern belle uniforms, the little black minidresses with crinoline skirts and frilly white aprons. I admit, acknowledging the complete inappropriateness for their swampy circumstances, the petite duo *was* darling as all get-out, with their matching long, dark hair, pretty heart-shaped, freckled faces, and healthy young bodies. Still, the shorty-short skirts and ruffled, off-the-shoulder tops exposed the twins' arms and legs to gazillions of hungry bugs and mosquitos. And apparently, they hadn't worn bug repellent. So the girls could barely function, as they kept kicking and slapping at the bugs on their arms and legs.

"Let's load up!" cried Skeets. With long jeans, boots, and a cap with an alligator motif on it, he wore a wifebeater-style sleeveless tee shirt that looked like it could've used some bleach during the last hundred washes. Still, it was probably comfy pulled down over his potbelly. I marveled at how the bugs didn't seem to bother him at all.

"There's more than four hundred different species of vertebrates, including more than two hundred varieties of birds and more than sixty different reptiles, livin' in this swamp. And we ain't gonna see any of 'em just settin' here on the pier. Let's go!" Skeets ordered.

"Okay, let's climb aboard, folks," said Wiggy. "Where do you want us, Mister Skeets?"

"It's Skeets. Just call me Skeets. And you, sir, are anchoring boat number two . . . right there, if you wouldn't mind just climbing in and taking the seat in the stern. Thank you, sir."

Wearing his Smokey Bear outfit, along with a pair of Top-Sider moccasins, heavyset Wiggy crashed down into the center canoe in the three-boat "raft," sloshing the river water and making waves.

"Oh my . . ." cried Claudia. She still hadn't stepped off the pier. "I'm going to throw up."

"Welcome, folks! Welcome to Skeets's Swamp Tours and the wonderful world of the Big Swamp, home of alligators, water moccasins, and black bears! We *promise* you'll see at least *one* of these majestic creatures, or you'll get your money back!"

Skeets sounded like a circus hawker.

"I just love nature," said Spencer, holding his phone up to his face. It looked like he was playing a game.

Pottie Moss gave him a funny look, as Spencer, never looking up from his phone, stepped from one canoe to the other, finally settling into the bow of the farthest boat.

"C'mon, Claudia," said Coop. "Man up."

"The swamp is also home to many species of birds, like the sandhill crane, anhinga, and osprey," announced Skeets. "Not to mention the barred owl, great blue heron, yellow-crowned night heron, red-billed woodpecker, great egret, and white ibis. You'll see many of these birds today. In fact . . . why, look, folks! There's a red-billed woodpecker right over there!"

He pointed to a tree on the other side of the narrow, murky river. No one looked.

As Skeets pointed and talked, the twins, Charlene and Darlene, were busy slapping themselves and helping me load the canoe closest to the pier with all the fixings and setup for the picnic supper on Alligator Island. We had several coolers, a case of beer, a box, two great big canvas bags, and seven bags of ice.

"C'mon, deary," Pottie Moss said to Claudia, "let's get you into the canoe over there. If you just step in, I promise you no one will ever ask you to do another thing today."

She chortled good-naturedly as she took Claudia's arm.

Claudia finally scrambled over to the last canoe and sat on the middle seat. Then she looked down at the water.

"Wiggy!" gasped Claudia. "I can't do this. Please, take me back to the plantation."

"Shut up, Claudia, and just sit still in the damn canoe. We all came together in one van, and we're not going back. Besides, we need to get going. There's stuff I want to see out here."

"Now, folks," said Skeets, "a swamp is a wetland habitat with large landmasses that are flooded with shallow water. There are freshwater swamps and saltwater swamps. This is a *freshwater* swamp."

Carrying a small cooler, Pottie Moss climbed into the first canoe and then into the second canoe. "I got your insulin, right here, Skeets. Don't let me forget to give it to you . . ."

"Alright, folks, looks like we're off!" In the stern of the farthest canoe, with Claudia in the center and Spencer in the bow, Skeets pulled on the recoil starter on the outboard motor. The Lilliputian engine started right up. It sounded more like a bug zapper than a boat engine.

"Here we go!" cried Pottie Moss from the bow of the center boat. Coop was in the center, and Wiggy was in the stern.

"Little lady," Skeets called to the twin in the bow of our boat, "if you just throw that line on the bow off the pier, we'll be off!"

"Oh no!" cried Claudia.

"Oh, Claudia, shut up," said Wiggy.

"We're in this together," cried Coop. "It's too late to turn back now."

Sitting in the center of the first canoe, with a twin in the bow and a twin in the stern, and picnic fixings in between, I pushed the canoe away from the pier.

I wondered whether Coop's advice to Claudia had been about the canoe ride, or something else.

CHAPTER 52

"Why is the water so brown?" asked Claudia.

"Tannins from rotting leaves leach into the water, causing it to become brown," answered Skeets. "Speaking of the water, folks, swamp water is characterized by stagnation. Very slow-moving swamp waters are often adjacent to lakes or rivers, like the little river we're in now. Pretty soon we're going to access the Big Swamp."

"Ugh," said Claudia. She swatted around her face. "So many bugs!"

Already, it'd been fifteen or twenty minutes, and we were winding down Snake River. At one point, the river'd been so narrow that I worried the three-wide canoe raft wouldn't be able to pass through. My canoe ended up scraping the vegetation on our side of the muddy riverbank, but we managed to eke by.

Claudia looked green. Spencer kept his face buried in his phone, while Coop and Wiggy surveyed the land around us and the twins slapped at bugs, as Skeets pointed out a number of snapping turtles, frogs, several wading birds, and even a few deer standing in a field on the left riverbank . . . probably part of the Taylor Farm, I figured. Coop and Wiggy took particular interest in that field. They even snapped a few photos with their cell phones. Also, Skeets showed us several narrow offshoots of the river, explaining that the narrow, slow-moving waterways were favorite hunting spots for water moccasin snakes.

Claudia started crying. She made this high-pitched wail that reminded me of nails on a chalkboard. Pottie Moss held her hands to her own ears and started chanting, "Lalalalala" ostensibly to block out Claudia's screeching. Spencer put earbuds in his ears. Coop complained. Wiggy cussed a lot. The twins thought it was all absolutely hysterical.

After Claudia finally stopped her boo-hooing, Pottie Moss pointed out all sorts of quirky plant life, including the carnivorous pitcher plant that ate bugs to survive, and the water tupelo tree, which, she explained, sometimes developed a hollow middle called a "chimney" that was usually a home to bats.

Claudia said she felt faint. Pottie Moss started talking about the bladderwort plant, with leaves that have small air sacs or bladders that trap small water creatures like larvae, nematodes, water fleas, protozoa, and small worms. Eventually the trapped creatures die and their bodies decompose, feeding the bladderwort. Claudia cried out that she had to "get out of this hell-forsaken place." She jammed her head between her knees to keep from fainting. And it struck me that Pottie Moss enjoyed seeing Claudia squirm. Certainly, I did.

Wiggy and Cooper, in the center canoe, continued pointing to the surrounding farmland and whispering back and forth. Wiggy even took out a map, and several times he asked Skeets to confirm where, *exactly*, we were on the map. Coop took photos of the land beside the river with his smartphone. Wiggy spouted off something about acreage, and Spencer made calculations on his phone, when he wasn't busy taking selfies or playing games, that is.

There was little doubt in my mind; for the Bostoners, the

swamp tour was not about nature. Not at all. No, it was about land . . . land with some sort of potential to make them money.

And lots of it.

If only I hadn't snooped at Greatwoods and gotten Ian upset, maybe I'd know what it was all about by now . . .

Claudia asked, "Do I dare ask why it's called the Snake River? We're not *really* going to see any snakes, are we?"

Skeets laughed. "Well, ma'am, we call it the Snake River for two reasons. First, because it twists and winds around like a snake. And second," he chuckled, "because there are more snakes out here than any other place in Abundance County. In fact, there are twenty-seven different varieties of snakes out here. The water moccasin is the largest and one of the most venomous."

"Oh my God," cried Claudia. "I *can't* do this. We have to turn back. If I see a snake, I'll *die*!"

"No goddamned snake is going to come anywhere near you," said Wiggy. "It'd be too damn scared."

Coop and Spencer cracked up. The twins sniggered as they slapped at bugs.

"Shh!" I warned them.

There was a low growling sound from somewhere behind us.

"What was that?" cried Claudia.

"Gator!" said Skeets. "Yee-haa! They've been so quiet today, I worried that we wouldn't see one out here. Normally, we'd have seen a bunch by now."

"No!" Claudia cried out. She put her head back down between her knees.

Skeets started reciting his gator spiel.

"Alligators are found in swamps and marshes all over South Georgia. A full-grown alligator is about fifteen feet in length and can weigh about seven hundred or eight hundred pounds. Of course, a bunch of gators have been found in these parts weighing as much as one thousand pounds or more. Like Rip. Know how he got that name?"

"How?" asked Wiggy.

"'Cause Rip is spelled R-I-P, which stands for 'rest in peace'!" Skeets slapped his knee and hollered in delight as Pottie Moss laughed.

"Rumor has it, Rip ate a Cherokee man who tried to wrassle him once," said Pottie Moss.

"Please. I need to go back . . ." Claudia's voice was barely more than a whisper. She sat clutching her hands in her lap.

"Anyways, moving on," said Skeets cheerily, "all alligators have massive tails that help them move and steer through water. And boy, oh, boy, they can sure be fast . . . whooo-wee . . ."

"Cool," said Spencer. "Do you see one now?"

He looked to his right and then to his left.

"Nope. But they're in the water for sure. Usually, there's a few sunning on the shoreline, over there." Skeets pointed to a low, marshy area with tall green grasses. "But I don't see any. Not sure why not. But their dark, blackish brown color helps them hide in the water, helpin' them to sneak up and kill other smaller animals. There's a bunch out here. They're probably all around us. We just can't see 'em."

There was another low bellow. This time it was coming from somewhere in the river ahead of us. Still with her head down, Claudia shrieked.

"Claudia, if you don't shut up, I'm gonna toss you into the brown water," said Wiggy.

"Gosh, woman, don't you *ever* let up?" said Coop. "I don't know how Dex stood you for all those years. He's probably glad he's dead."

For the first time on the trip, no one said anything. For several minutes, the only sounds we heard were the singing and screeching of birds, frogs, and bugs, along with the dinky engine pushing our canoe raft along the river. Because the engine was mounted off to one side, and no one except Skeets was using a paddle to steer much, the three-canoe raft traveled at a slight angle through the water.

There were more growls. Seated in the bow of my canoe, Charlene giggled.

"Sounds like burping to me." She slapped at her shoulder. Then, at her legs.

Behind me, her sister Darlene cracked up.

"No, no! It's farting!"

The two of them broke out into peals of laughter.

"Hi-dee-ho! There's one," said Skeets. He pointed out in front of us. "See him? Over there, by the bank? That's a bull gator croaking over there, for sure. Looks to be eight hundred pounds or more."

"Good God," whispered Claudia. She sat up to look around.

The river had opened up, and over in a marshy area of grasses and woody growth near the water's edge, we could see a large alligator very slowly moving toward the water. We'd never have noticed him, if he hadn't bellowed. Then, most silently, he slipped into the river, and with just his eyes and the top of his long body visible, he swam stealthily through the water, barely making a ripple.

Suddenly, there were low bellows and groans all around us. To me, they sounded like lions growling.

Everyone was silent. Except Claudia. She was whimpering.

After a while, Pottie Moss cleared her throat.

"As we get closer to the Big Swamp, you'll notice more cypress trees, with the beautiful Spanish moss hanging from their limbs. Cypress trees are quite common in swamp and wetland habitats. These trees are easily recognized by their woody 'knees' that stick up above the water, around the trees. The 'knees' bring oxygen to the roots of the trees."

"Also," said Skeets, "notice how our river has become more stagnant as we near the Big Swamp. See it ahead?"

The group all looked ahead, nodding and mumbling, to where we could see the river opening up to what looked like a lake. Except there was green vegetation and lily pads floating on top of the water. After a few minutes, we'd left most of the bellowing behind, and a few minutes later, we were out in the open swamp, surrounded by lily pads. Here and there, some grasses stuck out of the water. Alligator Island was just ahead.

Wiggy lit his pipe and puffed contently as he surveyed the land around the Big Swamp.

"Back in the old days, swamps like this were often drained

to provide land for agriculture," explained Skeets. "Also, to reduce the spread of diseases borne by swamp insects."

"Diseases?" asked Claudia.

"Swamp plants have flexible stems, floating leaves, or deep roots that grow underwater," said Pottie Moss, changing the subject. "There are even plants that grow and shrink according to the water level. There are water lilies, pickerelweed, and yellow-eyed grass. And we've got lots of shrubs and trees growing on floating mats of peat. We call 'em tree islands. Look, there's one over there." She pointed. "Of course, the Big Swamp has many dry islands with woody plants. Like Alligator Island. We're almost there," said Pottie Moss.

If we had a regular boat, we'd have been there thirty minutes ago, I thought. *Maybe forty.*

I rolled my eyes.

We chugged along silently for another few minutes. Then there was another alligator growl. And another.

"Oh, please, I don't want to see another alligator!" cried Claudia.

"Lookee over there."

Skeets pointed to a dark blob on the water, maybe twenty feet away. It blinked. Then it bellowed. Claudia gripped her seat and blanched.

"Cool," whispered Spencer. He raised his phone, ready to take a selfie, once the gator came into the photo frame with him.

"Hot diggity," said Coop. "Now *this* is worth the money."

The gator snorted again. Then it disappeared beneath the water.

"Sounds like it was a big'un, too," said Skeets, smiling. "Maybe it's Suitcase."

"Go on, Skeets," said Pottie Moss. "Tell the folks about Suitcase."

"Ol' Suitcase and I are longtime friends." Skeets held up his left hand. Most of his ring finger was missing. Claudia gasped. "Let me tell you, folks," Skeets continued, "I have a healthy respect for that gator. He got my finger and a good part of my arse!"

"I suppose you all don't have seasickness bags on board?" Claudia asked. She looked positively green.

"Give it a rest," Wiggy said. "I'm beginning to wish Dex had taken you with him when he left this world."

"That's a terrible thing to say!"

Skeets kept telling his story.

"There ain't nothin' much to wrestling a gator, as long as you keep your fingers out of his mouth. And I never mess much with small gators. They bite hard and spin fast," said Skeets. "So when I used to look for a gator to wrassle, I always went lookin' for the biggest damn gator I could find. And ten years ago, I found him. Suitcase.

"Even back then, he was a monster . . . about fourteen feet long and way more than a thousand pounds. I was over on the prison side of the swamp, hunting for snapping turtles, when I spied him. He was about thirty feet in front of me, in about twenty inches of water. I wanted to get on him from behind— never get on a gator from the side or the front; if you do, you're pretty much guaranteed to lose a nut or two."

Spencer made a choking sound.

"Anyway, I didn't have a buddy to distract him, and I didn't have a towel or a shirt to throw over his eyes so he couldn't see me coming . . . It was hot that day, and I wasn't wearing a shirt. So it was just me and Suitcase. I got a running start behind him, and with my hands out in front of me, I leapt low and deep onto him from the bank. I grabbed him around the neck with my hands between the back of his jaws and his front legs, except he took off, heading toward deeper water. Still, I pushed down on his neck as hard as I could to force his head under the water and to the ground. Just so y'all know, folks, by pinning his head to the ground, gator can't open his jaws 'cause they open their jaws just like a man does, meaning the bottom jaw moves—the top don't."

Everybody except Skeets and Pottie Moss started opening and closing their jaws.

"Anyway, I was up on old Suitcase's back, right behind his front shoulders, and I got my knees around him, squeezing his sides. I started to get my calves back to pin his hind legs when all of a sudden he starts 'death rolling' and I lost control of him as we started spinning violently.

"We went at it in the water for a while, thrashing around. And eventually, he dislodged me, and somehow the bastard bit me on the arse, barely missing my manhood," he laughed.

"Damn," said Coop.

"Eventually, we worked our way back into shallower water, and while straddling ol' Suitcase's back, I managed to get back on top and pin his mouth in the water with my right hand, thinking I'd put enough pressure on him to keep the ol' bugger's mouth shut. Only, when I reached over front of his snout with my left hand to muzzle him—that was my mistake 'cause I shoulda been using my more dominant hand—his jaws clamped down on all four of my fingers. We rolled in the water a good long time until I finally broke free. 'Cept about two inches of my ring finger was missing. Suitcase swam away; with two flicks of his tail he was gone. And I saw my finger floating in the water and grabbed it. Only, when I got to the hospital, the doc said it was too late to reattach it."

Pottie Moss was chuckling. "He used to joke all the time about how that ol' Suitcase just loved his finger food! Skeets has still got that finger, too, don't ya, Skeets! We keep it in a pickle jar on the kitchen windowsill."

Claudia groaned. "Now I am gonna be sick."

"Number one rule when you wrassle gators is not *if* you're gonna get bit, but *when* you're gonna get bit. Heck, I was pretty lucky. I've seen where entire limbs come off folks . . ."

Suddenly, when we were no more than fifty yards from Alligator Island, the little Sea Horse motor sputtered and died.

Skeets cussed.

"Don't tell me you ran out of gas, old man," said Wiggy.

"Naw, we got plenty of gas, see?"

To prove his point, Skeets held up a little plastic gas container attached to the motor with a black hose. He shook the container, sloshing the gas inside.

Less than ten feet from my canoe, another alligator popped his head above the water's surface. He growled big . . . like a lion.

Claudia cried out.

"That wretched prehistoric monster is as long as this stupid canoe," Claudia hissed. "Did it ever occur to you people that a beast like that could flip us over with one knock of his tail? I'm not kidding. I want out of this godforsaken place . . . Now!"

Unfortunately for Claudia, as bad as she wanted to get out of the swamp, it was impossible. At least until Skeets got his little Sea Horse engine running again.

We'd have to stick it out with the alligators.

A three-hour tour . . .

CHAPTER 53

After the Sea Horse motor died, we paddled the rest of the way to Alligator Island. It only took a few minutes. Honestly, we were faster moving through the water paddling than when we'd used the engine.

The minute we hopped onto the sandy soil, Claudia started shrieking that we needed to call someone to come pick her up, because she wasn't staying in the scary swamp one moment longer.

And that's when Pottie Moss told her, told everyone, that no one would be leaving until Skeets fixed the engine, because there was no cell phone service out in the middle of the swamp, so we had no way to let anyone know that we were stranded.

A three-hour tour . . .

"Quick, girls," I whispered to Charlene and Darlene, "we need to get the food ready ASAP before the group gets restless. Charlene, did you remember the booze?"

"Yes, ma'am. We've got lots of booze over here, in this carton."

"Good. Start setting up the bar."

"Miss Daphne told us to make it look like a tiki bar. We brought decorations."

"Why am I not surprised? Okay. So, in addition to corny tiki bar decorations, what've we got for actual *liquor*?"

"Miss Daphne told us to pack beer and bourbon. So that's what we did. Also, she thought it'd be fun to pass out Swamp Waters. So we've got stuff to make those, too," said Charlene.

"Swamp Waters?"

"Miss Eva, don't tell me you've never heard of a Swamp Water!"

Charlene sounded absolutely incredulous.

"No . . ."

"Well, there's a ton of different recipes," said Darlene. "Miss Daphne said we needed one that was simple and easy to make. So we googled until we found one. Our Swamp Water recipe is equal parts lime vodka and apricot brandy, plus sweet-and-sour mix and 7 Up. Got it all right here."

Darlene reached into a cardboard carton and pulled out a bottle of mixed sweet and sour. "We were gonna bring lemonade instead of the sweet-and-sour mix and soda, but we figured we could make Bourbon and Sevens with the soda, if the Swamp Waters bombed."

"Good thinking."

Note to self: Daphne need not worry about her young staff being naive about alcoholic beverages.

The twins and I quickly got to work unloading cartons and coolers of food and provisions on the picnic tables, so we could set up and serve the picnic as quickly as possible. Meanwhile, Claudia had completely run out of patience and was screeching, even more than usual. Finally, she insisted that the twins remain on either side of her—like human shields—throughout the duration of the picnic so no wild animals could eat her . . . at least not before devouring the twins first. She also refused to take off her life preserver. Her continued presence beside the twins didn't make our setup any faster, for sure; still, we got everything set up pretty fast, including Daphne's tiki bar.

And I got the sense that Wiggy and Coop were getting

fidgety, because everything they *really* wanted to see was back on the shore, not on the island. They really had no interest in Alligator Island. On the other hand, Spencer seemed delighted to wait for more gators to appear. He was ready with his smartphone camera.

Pottie Moss started pointing out plants and animals of interest, while Skeets got right to work on his disabled engine.

"Is there a bathroom around here someplace? I need to go to the bathroom," Claudia said.

"Uh-oh," whispered Darlene.

Pottie Moss told Charlene there was no bathroom.

"No bathroom? What kind of hellhole *is* this?"

"There's a bush over there," said Wiggy, pointing to a large shrub. "We won't look."

Coop chimed in, "God no!"

Claudia let out a wail.

The twins were on it, quickly adopting Daphne's standing advice that when stuff goes to hell in a handbasket, pour liquor.

Charlene said, "Miss Claudia, can we offer you a drink? A little Swamp Water . . ."

Pottie Moss held court with the men.

"During the early twentieth century, there was quite a bit of cypress logging going on in these parts," she said. "In fact, a bunch of logging companies ran railroad lines into the swamp until the nineteen forties."

"You don't say?" asked Wiggy. He seemed genuinely interested.

"Yes, sir. In fact, you can still see some tracks crossing the swamp waterways, if you go up that way"—she pointed to the opposite end of the swamp from where we'd come— "toward the prison and the chemical company."

"Huh," said Coop.

"An added perk," said Wiggy. "Let's go take a look."

"Certainly, a marketing plus," said Coop.

They wandered off, with Pottie Moss trailing after them, yammering away.

"Here on Alligator Island," she said, "there's some logging

equipment and other stuff left over. If y'all walk around, you can see it. I'm not exactly sure where it is. But I know it's out here somewhere. Believe it or not, some folks actually lived on the island for a time."

"No kidding," said Wiggy.

It was hard not to notice that Alligator Island held quite a bit more interest for Wiggy than it had just an hour earlier.

CHAPTER 54

A three-hour tour . . .

My plan to ply our guests with alcohol—loosen them up, so to speak, before asking them about Dex—was a good one. And it meshed perfectly with Daphne's hell-in-a-handbasket plan. In fact, it was *such* a good strategy that I didn't even need to set it in motion myself.

Five hours after our arrival, as the sun set over Alligator Island and it didn't appear that Skeets was any closer to fixing his stupid Sea Horse engine than he'd been when it'd first died out in the swamp—and Pottie Moss had *finally* run out of educational swamp drivel, and after a belly-full of Precious's delicious food and three or four rounds of drinks, and in Wiggy's and Coop's cases, more like six or seven rounds, because Charlene and Darlene had done a *masterful* job tending bar—my plan set sail on its own. No one even cared that we'd been out of ice for an hour or more.

"So, which one of you bastards killed Dex?" asked Claudia. With her fourth or fifth Swamp Water in hand, and the twins still flanking her, she swaggered over to the group of men who were sitting on the sand near the water's edge, watching Skeets as he fiddled with his motor. The men were smoking cigars and chugging beers. Except Spencer. He'd choked on the first few puffs of his cigar, then begged off the whole male-bonding smoking experience, saying he was "allergic."

"I thought we'd all decided," said Wiggy with a smirk. He took another swig from his beer bottle, then he waved the butt end toward me. "Our hostess here, *Miss* Eva, did it."

"I did not!" I replied hotly. I was sitting at a picnic table.

"I *know* you hated Dex," said Claudia to me. "She hated Dex," she insisted to the others.

Wiggy and Coop both smiled, puffing on their cigars.

"Claudia, I don't know why you keep saying that," I said. "I did not kill Dex. Sure, I didn't like him. Not one bit, if you must know. But I definitely didn't *kill* him."

Claudia let out a contemptuous sniff.

"However," I said, "at least one person here *did* kill Dex, and since we're not going anywhere anytime soon"—I looked over to Skeets who was knee-deep in Sea Horse outboard engine parts—"I aim to figure out who did it before we leave this island."

"Oooh, scary," said Spencer. He didn't even look up. He was playing some game on his smartphone.

"And if you're so certain there's a murderer within our midst," said Wiggy, wiggling his fingers in the air, "then shouldn't you be concerned about your own personal safety?" He raised his voice and said dramatically, "Shouldn't we *all* be concerned for our welfare? I mean, out here in this swamp, at night, all alone, with no cell phone service, no way to get off this damned little island . . . If the murderer really is out here, then who is to say we won't all end up dead? Or maybe, we'll just end up as gator bait." He chuckled.

"Well, technically, we *could* get off the island . . . All we have to do is paddle," said Coop.

"Over my dead body," said Claudia. She hiccupped. The twins held her up.

"Could be . . ." teased Wiggy.

The twins giggled. They led Claudia through the sand,

back to a picnic table they'd converted into the tiki bar, with a grass skirt around the edge, pretty orchids, wooden tiki sculptures at each corner, and plastic coconut-shaped drinking cups with straws. They didn't mind bookending Claudia, because apparently, she'd worn enough bug repellent to work for all three of them.

"I, for one, think how terribly convenient it is," snarked Claudia, plopping down onto the bench behind the bar, "that Dex's own killer says she's going to 'figure out' who killed him. I suppose you think you're being clever, Eva Knox."

The twins slipped onto the bench, flanking Claudia.

"I don't think I'm being 'clever' at all, Claudia," I said. "However, given what I know, I do think I'm being reasonable to assume that at least *one* of you killed Dex. After all, each of you had motive *and* opportunity."

"Well, aren't you a regular Nancy Drew," said Wiggy with a laugh. "Why don't you go ahead, then? Entertain us and share what you *think* you know."

"This should be enlightening," said Coop under his breath. He rolled his eyes and took a big swig of his warm Swamp Water.

"I told you Dex said something to her," whispered Spencer to Coop.

"Shut up, Spencer!" Wiggy ordered. He smashed his cigar butt into the sand. He looked at me. "Let's hear it, *Miss* Eva. What incriminating evidence have you possibly got on *me* that proves I killed your boyfriend."

"He's not my 'boyfriend.' Wasn't, I mean."

"Whatever. Spill it, sister."

"Alright, let's start with you, Wiggy. Clearly, you all are up to something that involves purchasing property here in Abundance."

"No," said Wiggy, "we're here on a bird-watching retreat."

"That's hogwash, Wiggy, and you know that I know it. You guys are the last people on earth interested in birds. My gosh, a bald eagle flew up in front of you yesterday, and not one of you noticed it . . . not one!"

"It did?" croaked Claudia.

I rolled my eyes.

"No, Wiggy. You're here on some sort of land-grabbing mission. However, there is something underhanded about it all, and I can't quite put my finger on it. Still, I've overheard you all talking enough to know that whatever role Dex had in the deal, he wasn't needed anymore. Perhaps you killed him to keep him quiet. Or maybe just to keep his share of the take."

"I see. And then just how and when did I kill dear old Dex?"

"After the tasting party. You poisoned him. In the kitchen when he made himself a snack with toast and olive oil."

"Really, and just how did I poison him?"

"Belladonna."

"Bella what?"

"Belladonna. It's a plant. You crushed the berries and put the juice into his olive oil."

"You're a loon. Even if I knew what you were talking about, I couldn't have done it when you said I did, because I wasn't at the plantation after the tasting party."

"Oh no? Then where were you?"

"Out looking at some property." He turned and glared at Coop. "Property that was already *sold.*"

"Aha! So you admit it then—you *are* here to purchase property!"

Score one for me.

"Thanks, Dex," said Coop sarcastically, glaring back at Wiggy. "I *told* you, it wasn't my fault. I'd no idea there'd been another buyer until after the fact. The real estate guy didn't know it, either, apparently. But then, you're already aware of that." Then he added, "And pray tell, Wiggy, what property were you visiting, without the rest of us, under the cloak of darkness? It wouldn't have been the Twiggs place, would it?"

Wiggy must've been the person Ian saw creeping around the Twiggs place on his night cam!

"Coop," I interrupted, "*you* could've easily poisoned Dex yourself."

"Really, my love? And why would I have done that?"

"Because Dex stole your wife, Heather, from you . . . That's why you all laughed at me when you were standing on the hill Saturday after I asked how Heather could still stand you all. Obviously, I hadn't known then that she'd indeed *already* left you . . . because she couldn't stand you. That joke was definitely on me. However, the joke was certainly on you when your wife ran off with Dex. Then she cleaned you out. Must've made you pretty mad."

"That's an understatement," said Spencer, looking up from his smartphone.

"Ah, Spencer, glad you could take time out from your game to join us for a moment. I've no doubt that you could've killed Dex. After all, I heard Coop say that Dex owed you fifty thousand dollars . . . He probably needed the loan after Heather cleaned *him* out. Smart Wellesley girl, that Heather."

"Oh, please, Spencer wouldn't hurt a fly," said Claudia. "He's too weak. We all know it was you, Eva, who killed Dex."

"Me? And why would I kill Dex, Claudia? You know, I've been wondering why you keep telling me you 'know' it was me, and you 'know' how much I hated Dex. And, for the longest time, I couldn't figure out what it is that you think that you know about me. Until I replayed the conversation I'd overheard about *you*."

"About me?"

"Yes. The gentlemen here were complaining about you, saying how you'd changed over the years. How the change occurred after a trip to Zermatt where you'd returned with a broken leg. And after that, Dex overpaid you to continue working for him. And you know what, Claudia? *I get it.* I totally get the fact that, like you've been saying, you were the only person who knew why I left Dex."

"I doubt that."

"Claudia, *I get it* because Dex did the same thing to you that he'd done to me. He hurt you physically. Perhaps not often. Maybe not even more than once. But he *did* hurt you on that trip to Europe. Dex was the reason you broke your leg, not some ski mountain. And he paid you extra money all these years to keep your mouth shut about it."

"No! Don't say that!"

"I admit, although it does seem odd that you might've killed your golden goose, so to speak, it could be that seeing Dex come after me the other night was all that was needed to tip the scales. I mean, forgive me, Claudia, but you do seem a bit 'emotionally challenged' these days. And, of course, you've been extorting money from Dex for years . . ."

"My, oh, my," said Pottie Moss. "This is better than Bravo TV. Skeets, hon, it's time for your insulin, sweetcakes. Don't say any more, folks, until I get back. I don't want to miss a word!" Pottie Moss went over to the farthest canoe and rummaged around for her cooler. "Wait for me! I don't want to miss anything. I'm coming right back!"

"The problem is," said Coop, "we all have alibis. Like I was 'entertaining' in my room after you left the party."

"Entertaining?"

"Why, yes. I met a lovely young woman at the party, and we had mutually satisfying relations in my bedroom."

"You did?" asked Spencer.

"Yes. All night long, as a matter of fact."

"And who was your lovely date?" I asked.

"The busty dark-haired girl at the olive oil tasting party. Let me see, what was her name? Do you guys remember?"

"Daisy . . . no, Maisy," said Claudia.

"You had sex with Maisy Merganthal?" I asked.

"Yes, I believe I did. Thank you for asking."

"Are you kidding? Why, she's just out of college."

"That's old enough for me."

"You're a pig, Coop. Where was her mother?"

"Why, I believe her mother was out waiting in the car all night. After all, it was *her* idea to hook me up with her daughter in the first place. Something about how I'd make the perfect husband for her sweet daughter . . ."

"Omigosh! That's gross. Don't tell me any more."

"If that's what you want."

"Okay, so, Spencer, where were *you* that night?"

"I was in the library, playing games on the Internet. That's pretty easy to check."

"Claudia?"

"I was in my room. Sleeping pills knocked me right out. That's what us emotionally unstable types do, you know. Take pills. Of course, I can't prove it, though . . ." She smirked.

Pottie Moss said from the canoe, "If y'all ask me, *she* did it! The woman always does."

"Wait a minute."

I was remembering something. Something that had been buried in my brain . . .

"Pottie Moss, when Precious and I were at your house, you said you'd had to bring a shopping bag to Claudia, but I found it in Dex's room . . ."

And at just that moment, the Sea Horse engine revved up.

"Wait!" I cried.

"Stop!" Behind me, the group jumped up and started yelling with me.

Pottie Moss and Skeets were in the canoe raft, and they'd left the beach! They were headed out into the swamp . . . without us. As I neared the canoes, Skeets raised his machete and brought it down hard and swift, cutting the lines that bound the three canoes together. He and Pottie Moss motored away in their single canoe as the other two boats drifted into the swamp.

"Wait!" I shouted at the top of my lungs. This wasn't about being stranded on the swampy island. This was about something else altogether. I knew if I didn't stop them, we might never see them again.

I *had* to stop them.

I ran full speed into the swamp and tried to grab their canoe. I just missed. They were just three or four feet away and pulling away faster and faster. Which wasn't really very fast, because they had an eggbeater for a motor; still, it was faster than I could wade through the swamp after them. I lunged forward and started swimming. Kicking and thrashing, not even looking where I was headed, all I wanted to do was grab hold of the red canoe.

Then, I couldn't believe it.

I hit the canoe with my hand.

Kicking hard, with the next stroke, I stretched as far as I could, and I was able to grab ahold of the pointed canoe stern. Skeets was smacking my hand as I threw my leg over the side. Then, I heard Pottie Moss tell her brother to stop.

"It's alright, Skeets. Let the poor girl up. After all, she's only trying to do what's right, aren't you, dear?"

Huffing and puffing, draped across the center seat in the canoe, finally, I caught my breath.

"Why, Pottie Moss? Please, tell me. *Why?*"

CHAPTER 55

All the light in the sky disappeared. In the middle of the swamp, it was pitch-dark. As the little Sea Horse engine puttered us farther and farther away from Alligator Island, Skeets, Pottie Moss, and I could still hear the group calling for us to come back and pick them up.

"Why?" I asked again. "Why did you murder Dex?"

"And what makes you think I did any such thing?"

"Nothing else makes sense, that's why. Because at your place on Saturday, you said there was a bottle of oil in the bag you'd delivered to Claudia, only when I eventually discovered the bag, it was in Dex's room, and there was no bottle of oil. That's because Dex must've pulled it out. And the bag must've been his, not Claudia's, as you'd thought."

"Why's that?"

"Claudia does everything for Dex. She'd probably done the shopping. Or carried the bag for him while they'd been shopping together. Oh, I don't know! Still, I know the bag was Dex's . . . the tee shirt inside was a size extra-large, and that's definitely not Claudia's size!"

"That's for sure."

"And I saw the sheriff and his deputy pull a bottle of olive oil from down in the weeds near the pond. And I know Dex was delirious after he had a snack in the kitchen that night and before he died at the pond. I'll bet the bottle of olive oil was the one from the shopping bag, and that he used it in the kitchen to get a snack. Which means he wasn't poisoned at all during the tasting party; he was poisoned *afterward*, with the bottle of olive oil that you somehow tainted with poison at your place before you returned it to Claudia. Only it was *Dex's* olive oil, not Claudia's."

Pottie Moss heaved a big sigh.

"Actually, if you must know, hon, it was a mistake," Pottie Moss said, calmly. "Pure and simple, I meant to kill that insufferable Claudia woman. That bitch is too damn big for her own britches. Always havin' a dyin' duck fit about everything. Why, she had me waitin' on her like she was the Queen of England! Ain't no other way to say it; she just made my ass itch."

"I don't understand."

Off in the distance somewhere, an alligator growled.

"Why does that not surprise me? You and your uppity sister Miss Daphne with all her money from her fancy *dee-vorce* up in Atlanta, y'all wouldn't know a damn thing about what it's like to struggle to get along and put a meal on the table. No, siree, y'all think nothin' about poaching another woman's payin' customers."

"That's not true."

"No? Did it ever occur to all y'all that me and Skeets, we *really* needed the money these obnoxious folks from Boston agreed to pay us? We needed it to eat. And Skeets has got *big* medical bills!"

"Now, Pottie Moss, don't go frettin' folks about our personal problems," said Skeets.

"Skeets, what the hell is wrong with you? I just told this woman that I murdered a person, and you're goin' on about lettin' her in on our *personal problems*?"

"Shoot, Pottie Moss, I just figured you were kidding . . ."

"Oh, *be quiet*, Skeets. This whole stinkin' mess is your fault, anyways."

"*My* fault?"

"Yes. 'Cause I have to stay home and take care of you and your diabetes all the time, I can't go nowhere, do nothing, or even get a decent paying job! Did ya ever think of that, little brother? Do you think that I *like* doing laundry and servin' naked strangers who come to my house and mess it up all the time?"

"Gosh, I'm sorry, Pottie Moss."

"Every time someone sets a naked butt down on my furniture, that's another time I gotta come back later and wipe it clean with a Clorox towelette. I'm *tired*, Skeets."

"Pottie Moss, you're not making sense," I said. "You said you wanted to kill *Claudia* . . ."

"Well, let me explain it to you, missy. That Claudia woman drove me insane, with her whining and complaining. Then she and the others just jumped up and left . . . to go to a *better* place. *Your* place. Knox Plantation. And as if that wasn't upsetting and insulting enough, she called and insisted that Skeets and I bring over their luggage, *all* their luggage, to their new fancy digs at Knox Plantation. And she said that we had to pack it all up, too!"

"That is pretty bad . . ."

"Plus, she said she was canceling the corporate credit card that was on account with us, and she wouldn't even pay for the time they'd already stayed with us if we didn't deliver the packed luggage right away."

"Wow. That *is* bad . . ."

Pottie Moss was waving her arms excitedly.

"So I packed everything up and hauled it over to your place. Only when I got there, the woman started havin' another hissy fit 'cause I forgot to bring some shopping bag she left in her room. So, back I went to my place, looking for the damn shopping bag. And before I even found it, the woman called me on the phone yelling about the way I'd packed her stuff. I hadn't folded her pretty panties the way she liked 'em folded, she said. And I'd mixed her dirty laundry with her clean laundry . . . blah, blah, blah."

Pottie Moss stopped for a moment and took a deep breath.

Skeets looked like he was as shocked and befuddled as I was about the whole story. Outside the canoe, alligators were snorting and bellowing all around us in the swamp. The group on the island had stopped calling.

Pottie picked up her story again.

"So then, after yelling at me, the woman hung up on me. *Rude*. So, I finally found the stupid shopping bag she wanted me to bring her. It had all sorts of touristy stuff from downtown. You know, junk, like we said before. And I saw there was a bottle of Knox olive oil inside the bag. And, don't ya know it, I went and got all mad again . . . Here I was, working like a dog, when you folks at Knox Plantation were gonna end up making all the dough, I thought. And, I was thinkin' that y'all would probably get another five-star review on the Internet, while I'd get squat. *Squat!* After all I'd done. Then, all of a sudden, I had this idea. I read about it in a mystery once. I could poison the bitch from Boston with one of your bottles of olive oil. She'd be dead, and y'all would take the blame. It was brilliant. I could kill two birds with one shot of poison!"

"I just can't believe I'm hearing this."

"Me, neither. You're real smart, Pottie Moss," said Skeets.

"Thank you, Skeets. So anyway, it doesn't take me long to figure out what to use. Belladonna. Agatha Christie used it all the time in her stories. Well, at least a couple of her stories. And I even had some nightshade growing in the yard. So I went out, grabbed a handful of the pretty berries, and used my juicer to squeeze out as much poison berry juice as I could. Then I took one of Skeets's syringes . . ."

Pottie Moss flipped open the lid on a little cooler, grabbed a syringe, and held it in the air. I was pretty sure the syringe was loaded . . . with something.

". . . and I loaded it up with the poison berry juice. Then I stabbed it into the cork in the olive oil bottle and pushed all the poison inside. Then, I pulled the syringe out and smoothed over the top of the cork, so no one would see that I poked a little hole in it. Then I delivered the shopping bag with the poisoned Knox olive oil to your place, and I went home and waited. I gotta tell ya, I was absolutely thrilled to bits the next day when I heard another person had died at your place. I mean, it could've been *weeks* before anyone'd opened the bottle of olive oil. I didn't know whether I'd be able to wait that long."

"And it could've been consumed by *anyone*!" I cried. "Did you ever think of that, Pottie Moss? What if an innocent *child* had ingested it!"

Not that Dex had deserved it, either . . . Oh, what's wrong with me . . .

Pottie Moss shrugged.

"That dead person was number four this summer for Knox Plantation. Wasn't it?"

"Yep," said Skeets.

"I was so happy. I knew that my plan had worked. The bitch was dead, and your business—my competition—would be down the drain in no time. Only later, I heard it was one of the *men* who'd died. Not the bitchy woman. *Dang*, I thought. I was real sad. Until I realized that I'd have another chance!"

"I don't understand . . ."

"I figured that I could get the bitch tonight. Only, she spent the entire time sandwiched between the Doublemint Twins, so I haven't been able to get a shot at her, *or* her drinks. And believe me, I've tried everything except . . ."

Pottie lunged toward me.

"This!"

She stabbed at me with the loaded syringe. I managed to grab Pottie's wrist, keeping the syringe in her fist away from me. We struggled, wildly rocking the narrow canoe back and forth in the water, nearly capsizing the boat. Still steering the little engine, Skeets was yelling something, but I couldn't hear what he was saying, because Pottie was yelling and swearing at me.

"I'll kill you all!" she shrieked. "I hate you skinny bitches! All of you!"

Pottie threw me to the bottom of the canoe, but I managed to kick her hard in the ribs as she bent over me with the syringe, poised to stab me. Still, I had a hold on her wrist, keeping her hand with the syringe inches away from me. With my other hand on the gunwale, I managed to pull myself up, and we thrashed violently around the little boat as I kept squeezing Pottie Moss's wrist, desperately trying to keep the poisoned needle pointed away from me.

With one hand steering the little engine, Skeets was batting me on the head with an oar as Pottie jabbed me hard in the stomach with her other fist, knocking the wind out of me. I fell backward, this time landing on the gunwale. Then, sitting on me, she was one-handedly wrapping a heavy rope around my legs—I think she was trying to tie them together—while I still clung to her wrist. I was half in and half out of the canoe when she finally wrenched her wrist free from my hand. Something knocked me hard in the chest.

Pottie lunged at me with the syringe. Only this time, I managed to roll away.

And down into the swampy water below.

CHAPTER 56

When I'd rolled off the canoe and into the swamp, I'd planned to grab ahold of the canoe and hoist myself back in. I hadn't counted on not being able to breathe. Or kick. Pottie really had punched the air out of me, and I couldn't get a breath. I couldn't even gasp. Plus my legs were tangled up in the big rope.

It was a terrifying feeling.

I was sinking. And under the water, I could hear the little Sea Horse engine as it moved farther away. There was another humming sound as well, but I couldn't place it.

It felt like time slowed down as I was dropping deeper down into the swamp. I was tiring fast.

Lifting my head up under the water, I did a two-legged butterfly kick once, as hard as I could. Then, with everything I had, I kicked again. Without air, I thought my chest would explode. My insides pounded. Then, just at the moment I broke the surface of the water, my lungs expanded and I was able to gasp for air.

My legs were still tangled in rope. And to stay on the surface, I had to keep butterfly kicking . . . hard. I'd soon be exhausted. Still, I'd made it without drowning. I kept gulping for air, pushing aside scores of lily pad plants.

Of course, I don't have to tell you what I heard next.

A big alligator growl.

And it didn't sound all that far away from me. Not far enough, anyway.

As my panic deepened, off in the distance, I saw a light. It was a bright spotlight, quite far off. Still, it was heading in my direction. And I heard the high-pitched hum of an engine.

A boat!

But would anyone see me in time? Or at all?

Kick harder, Eva! Harder!

There was another growl. Closer this time. And another, more like a roar, coming from behind me somewhere.

I kicked furiously, thrashing in the water, trying to get myself as far up and out of the swamp as possible. Waving my arms, I tried yelling as the boat quickly approached. Underwater plants and detritus brushed against my skin, freaking me out . . . I kept imagining the stuff was a hungry alligator, rubbing up against me.

"Help! Help me! Help!"

Yelling was probably completely ridiculous, considering whoever was inside the boat certainly couldn't hear me over the roar of the boat engine. Still, if I hadn't yelled, it seemed like I wouldn't have been doing enough to save myself . . .

"Help!"

I swallowed a big gulp of swamp. It wasn't long before I felt too tired to yell anymore. I simply couldn't get enough air. The boat was approaching at a shockingly fast speed. There was a splash in the water, off to my right. Did I see a tail? I wasn't sure which would be worse: getting eaten up by an alligator or chopped up by a propeller blade.

"He-elp!"

I kicked harder, still trying to lift myself out of the water as high as I could so whomever was in the boat would see me. Frantically, I flapped my arms. The high-powered spotlight was almost close enough to shine on me. I was sinking.

I gasped for air.

Did I hear another alligator roar?

Popping my eyes just above the water, I was blinded by the high-powered light. There was another big splash.

Please see me. Please see me. Please see me.

I closed my eyes, kicked, and waved like my life depended on it—it did. I knew the boat was close; the engine noise was very loud. Then all of a sudden, it stopped. There was no engine noise at all. I opened my eyes, just above the water, to see the spotlight swinging slowly back and forth, surveying the swamp around me. I kicked hard, trying to lift myself above the water.

"*Help*," I croaked. I could barely speak, let alone yell.

The light moved across the water until I was blinded again. I was dead center in the light.

Oh, thank heavens. I don't think I can kick much longer . . .

"Oh, Christ," I heard him say.

Please . . .

The rope around my legs was heavy. I was going down. I couldn't yell anymore. Couldn't kick. I was too tired . . . too tired . . .

The engine started up again. Actually, it sounded like two outboard engines. With the light still focused on me, the boat crawled in my direction.

"Babydoll, is that you?"

About ten feet from me, I heard the engines shift into neutral. Then they shut off. I kicked again, giving it everything I had, to raise my head above the surface of the swamp.

"Who else would it be?" I said hoarsely. My legs felt like jelly. I sunk down into the murky swamp water again.

Slowly, the midsize aluminum boat, painted in a green and brown camouflage pattern, drifted across the water to stop beside me. I kicked one more time, lifting my head out of the water.

"I can't . . . swim . . . Legs tied . . ."

"Give me your hand, Babydoll. It's alright. You're gonna be alright. I'm right here."

Buck reached over the side of the boat to grab me.

Suddenly, I felt a jerk from below. Next thing, I was underwater.

CHAPTER 57

It was all pretty much a blur after that. I remember seeing Buck's horrified expression as I gulped for air just before being pulled down into the muddy swamp. I remember a lot of thrashing, water churning, weird grumbling noises, shouting . . . then for a moment I was back on top of the roily water again. That's when I caught a glimpse of Buck in the boat, pointing a pistol in my direction.

I think I shouted, "No!" Still, maybe I only thought it. Whichever it was, I was certain of one thing: I was scared for my life.

There was more turbid water, bubbles, thrashing, churning, all sorts of crap under the water. I was going up and down, my head was above the water, then below the water, then above the water . . . but just for a moment. I saw Buck dive over my head into the swamp. And then I went down, finally realizing that the gator had a hold on the lines around my feet and was diving deeper. After that, I went down, down, down. It was noisy. Chaotic. I couldn't get any air. And I just don't remember any more.

CHAPTER 58

I heard night creatures. They were loud. Screeching all around me.

"Eva!"

I felt myself shudder. Then I choked and coughed up water.

"Oh God," he said, relieved.

I opened my eyes to see Buck bending over me. I heard water slapping the side of the boat as I coughed again.

"Don't *ever* do that again, baby. You hear me?" Buck whispered.

Water dripped from Buck's face onto mine. I'd coughed up a boatload of swamp. At least that's how it felt. He kissed my cheek.

"Christ, don't do that again," Buck mumbled to himself. He turned away for a moment, holding his hand on his forehead. He heaved a deep breath.

"I won't," I whispered. "I promise."

He turned back and smiled. Except, his eyes were worried.

"I was about to give you CPR."

"That sounds like it coulda been fun," I said weakly.

"Aren't you the comedian tonight. Here, try to sit up." Buck grabbed my shoulders and helped me up. Then, he moved around to sit behind me, wrapping his arms around me. He held me tight.

"You must be cold. We need to get you to the hospital."

We were in the bilge of his boat . . . or, I guess it was his boat. I'd never seen it before. But it was the one he'd been driving when he found me in the water. The one with dual engines. We were both soaked, floating around in the middle of the Big Swamp.

"I don't need a hospital. Did the alligator make it?" I asked. "You didn't shoot him, did you?"

"Actually, he did make it," he whispered in my ear. "And I never fired a shot. I figured it was easier to jump in, cut you loose, and get you out of the water and out of harm's way than it was to try to kill the bastard and have him die then drag you to the bottom of the swamp with him before I could get you free. Of course, he didn't like that idea, and I had to bop him on the nose a few times, just to let him know who was boss."

"But you let him go?"

"Yup. I already have a pair of alligator boots."

"That's good," I said.

Still holding me from behind, Buck bent around me so I could see his face. He winked. I tried to laugh. But I was too exhausted. And Buck still had that worried look in his eyes that I wasn't used to seeing.

"Babydoll," he said, taking my hands in his. "I'm sorry for the things I said to you this morning. It was wrong. Someone hurt you. Seriously bad. And instead of coming to you and offering my support, I yelled at you."

"No one hurt me. At least not recently. Unless you count the alligator . . . Do you think it was Suitcase?"

"Eva, I'm serious. I was so outraged when I discovered what Dex Codman had done to you, it didn't matter that it'd been years ago. For me, it was like it'd just happened. And it made me crazy. Frankly, the guy is lucky he was already dead."

He took one hand and caressed the side of my face.

"I get it. You had to do your job. And you couldn't do it being involved with me."

"No. I took it all out on you . . . the very reaction you feared when you decided not to tell anyone in the first place. I promise you, I will never, ever, put my feelings ahead of yours again. Look at me, Eva." He pulled my face around to his. "I will *always* keep you safe."

"Even when I do stupid things?"

"Even when you do stupid things. But what happened with Dex did not happen because you did something stupid. Do you understand?"

"Yes. If you say so. Still, I should've known better."

"Stop. It wasn't your fault. And you did the right thing when you left him. A lot of women, and men, never get to that point. It took guts to leave. I'm proud of you."

Buck squeezed me close to him. Even soaking wet, his skin felt warm.

"Now," he said, releasing me, "do you think you can stand up?"

I nodded.

"We need to get you out of these wet clothes." Buck reached into a locker box and pulled out a sealed plastic bag and handed it to me. "Here's a sweatshirt and some running shorts. Not your usual style, but they're dry. Put them on."

"I can't. I'm too tired. And we need to catch up to Skeets and Pottie Moss."

Hurriedly, I told Buck everything that had happened, about the group on the island—already, we could hear them yelling again—about Pottie Moss's confession, and about how she was getting away. And although cell phones didn't work on the swamp, radios did. Buck was on his radio calling for reinforcements before I'd even finished my story. Some of his deputies were to meet him at the Taylor Farm dock. Others were to get boats into the water at the main Big Swamp dock and start fanning out across the swamp, looking for Pottie Moss and Skeets.

When he put the radio down, we were headed to Alligator Island.

"Eva, I'm serious: Take off your clothes. Or I'll do it for you."

"That sounds like fun, too."

"Don't tempt me."

"Fine."

While Buck navigated the boat, I peeled off my wet clothes, tossing them in the bilge, before pulling on Buck's sweatshirt and shorts. Both had Abundance County Sheriff's Department insignias on them. And once I got into the dry clothes, I did feel better.

"Here. Eat this." Buck handed me a Butterfinger candy bar. "You need to get your strength back."

"Thanks."

At Alligator Island, we picked up the group and loaded up Daphne's picnic stuff. It seemed that all the alcohol had finally kicked in. Except for Claudia's whimpering, and a few giggles from the twins, no one said a word. We made it back to the Taylor Farm dock in less than fifteen minutes, where we quickly unloaded and met up with some of Buck's deputies. Buck barked out instructions to his deputies before he grabbed my hand and led me up onto the field where the vehicles were parked. In addition to the deputies' vehicles and the rental van we'd all taken from the plantation earlier that day, there was a big, shiny, chromed-out, one-ton white Dodge dually with clearance lights and a big brush guard around the grill guard, with an empty trailer hitched behind it.

"Yours?" I asked Buck.

Of course, I knew it was his before I'd asked. He nodded.

"Nice," I said.

"When Daphne called me saying you all hadn't returned home from the swamp tour, I decided to start where you had taken off. So I launched the boat here. Then, I just headed out to Alligator Island."

As we were talking, the group was loading the supplies into the van. The twins were slapping at bugs again.

"Wait here a minute."

Buck went to confer with his deputies while Wiggy, Coop, Spencer, Claudia, and the twins piled into the rental van. The driver's-side window in the van rolled down. One of the twins looked out.

"Miss Eva, are you coming?" asked Charlene. Or maybe it was Darlene.

"I . . . I . . ."

I didn't know what to say. Getting into the crowded van with the group from Boston somehow riled me. And for some reason, I really wanted to be . . . alone. Like, *totally* alone. I just wanted to sit for a bit and listen . . . listen to the bugs, the frogs, the night birds and creatures . . . all of it.

Buck was at my side. His deputies waited near the dock.

"Eva, are you alright, Babydoll? Do you need me to take you to a hospital? I can call Doc Payne."

"Oh, goodness, no, not Doc Payne!" I laughed. "His bad breath would surely kill me on the spot." I smiled. "No. I feel fine, really. Just tired. I can't explain it . . . I just want to be . . . alone. It's kind of like I need to push my reset button."

Buck patted me on the arm. "It's okay. I get it. Used to happen to me all the time. After a big mission."

He walked over to the van and told the twins to go ahead without me. As the van pulled away, Buck headed to the truck and trailer, released the hitch, and jacked up the trailer.

"What are you doing?" I asked.

Buck reached into his pocket. "Here," he said, tossing me the keys. "When you feel up to it, drive my truck home. I'll have one of my deputies bring me by later to pick it up. If you feel okay enough to drive, that is . . ."

"Yes. I'll be fine."

"Okay, then. If not, just stay here, inside the truck. And lock the doors. I'll come find you. Okay?"

"Yes."

Buck gave me a hug, pressing himself close. "Be safe," he whispered. "And don't worry. We got this."

Then he pulled away and started jogging back to the boat. "Come on, boys, we've got some catching up to do."

Buck hustled down to the pier and climbed back into his boat, along with a couple of deputies. He waved as the twin engines grumbled and the boat took off down the river. Meanwhile, the remaining deputies climbed back into their vehicles and fired up their engines. And they all left.

Without me.

CHAPTER 59

Sitting on the dock on Snake River listening to the cacophony of night creatures, I was totally alone. I must've sat there for thirty minutes or more, just thinking. I'd spent nearly half my lifetime running away from what Dex had done to me. Hiding from myself, really. And now Dex was gone . . . and my secret was out.

I wondered, had I changed? *Not really*, I thought. Still, I did feel stronger. More sure of myself. And I did know what I wanted from life. Still, I knew that I had more work to do on myself, before I'd be ready for a forever relationship with someone.

Finally, I stood up to leave.

Everything is going to be okay.

And that's when an engine roared as a pair of headlights came flying across the field, headed right toward the dock. I knew instantly who it was. And I had to laugh.

"A perfect ending to my night," I said out loud.

The black Escalade slammed to a stop. The door flew open, and out jumped Debi Dicer. Fists clenched, arms flapping, she stomped over to the dock.

GPS, GPS, GPS . . .

"Eva Knox! I warned you!" she cried, slamming her feet onto the pier. She was wearing a white linen shift with a big, bright pink beaded necklace and matching pink dangly floral earrings. The heels of her Tory Burch sandals click-clacked on the wooden planks.

"Where's Buck? *Buck!*" she called out. "Buck!"

To say that Debi looked upset was an understatement. Her normally pretty face was all knotted up. She slammed down to the end of the pier to face me.

"We were having a *date* when we got interrupted by a phone call. I just knew it was *you*, Eva Knox! Buck! Come out here! *Bucky!*" she screeched.

"And good evening to you, too, Miss Debi," I said with a smile. "*Bucky's* not here."

"What do you mean, he's not here? His *truck* is here!" She stepped closer. "And well, well, well, just *look* at you! Been doin' a little skinny-dipping in the river? Where are your clothes, Eva Knox? If he's not here, then what are *you* doin' wearing Buck's sweatshirt and . . . pants!" she shrieked. "Buck! Y'all come out here, right this minute!"

"Actually, since you asked, I did do a little dance in the swamp with a big reptile earlier. But I'm used to it . . . After all, I found a snake in my bed the other night, thanks to you."

Suddenly, Debi stopped spinning around, looking to catch sight of Buck. And she smiled.

"Ahh, so you *did* find my little gift. I thought it suited you."

"Yes. And I found my phone, too, so *thank you* for returning it. It was really very sweet of you."

"I'm always sweet, sweetness. I found it in the seat of Bucky's SUV. Should've been more careful, hon. *That's* how I knew you two were still sneaking around together. Well, I'm totally onto you now. As you can see. So your little nighttime nooky sessions are no more."

"Gosh, Debi. You're so smart."

"You think this is funny?" she said. "Watch this!"

Suddenly, she reached out to shove me hard, toward the edge of the pier. Except I was ready, and at the last moment,

I stepped aside. When Debi kept falling forward and lost her balance, I *might* have left my foot in the way, and she *might* have tripped over it, completely losing her balance. Of course, with nothing to hang on to, and no one reaching out to save her, Debi tumbled right into the muddy river.

"Enjoy your dip, Debi," I said, turning on my heels. "And watch out for Suitcase. He missed his first course tonight. He must be hungry, no doubt, for a *sweet Southern* dish like you."

CHAPTER 60

Later that night as I walked across the moonlit lawn to my cottage, I spotted Ian Collier sitting on the stoop with Dolly. When Ian saw me, he stood up.

"Eva, I hope ye don't mind my coming here this late at night," he said outside the cottage. "I figured I needed to apologize to ye . . . for the way I reacted this morning when ye found the painting."

"Hi, Ian. I'm so happy to see you. There's no need to apologize. Really. I'm so terribly sorry. I'm the one who should be apologizing. I was snooping around in your home, and I had no business . . ."

Ian stepped close and put a finger to my lips.

"Fiona," he said.

"Wh . . . what?"

"Fiona. The young woman in the painting. She was beautiful, full of light and life, just like you are standing here in this moonlight, even in . . . Wait!" Ian took a step back and looked me up and down. "Are those yer man's togs yer wearing?"

Even as he chuckled at my outfit, his eyes looked soft and full of sadness as he reached up and touched me lightly on the cheek.

I nodded. "I had a little swamp adventure tonight. It's not

important now. Please, you don't owe me an explanation, Ian," I said. "Precious was right; I had no business snooping around your library like that. I'm sorry. Really, I am. Won't you come inside?"

"No, thanks, if it's all the same to you, I'd just as soon stay here, outside. Can we just set here on the stoop for a bit?"

"Sure. I'd like that."

"I won't be staying long."

Ian sat on the big stone stoop to my cottage and stretched his long legs out in front of him. I sat down beside him, letting his heavenly woodsman scent envelop me. The night air was thick with the singing of crickets and frogs out in the yard. Ian looked up at the dark night sky.

Gosh, he's gorgeous.

"It was our wedding day when it happened, more than twenty years ago," he said slowly. "Fiona and I had met two years earlier in Scotland. Her father'd been a professor at the University in Edinburgh where I'd been a student. Her mother was a brilliant surgeon. Fiona was their only child. And from the moment we'd first laid eyes on each other, Fiona and I were desperately in love. Soul mates. We were crazy about all the same things, really—books, horses, long walks in the country-side. Cranachan and shortbread." He smiled. "Her shortbread was the best, that one."

He stopped for a moment, as if he was remembering the taste of Fiona's shortbread.

"She was smart as a whip, too. She had several scholar-ships in Celtic and Gaelic studies, and she spoke fluent Irish Gaelic and Scottish Gaelic . . . no easy task, either one. And she had the most lovely, soft, lilting, musical voice. I guess that'd be the Irish in her . . . not like the more gruff and gut-tural sound of so many of the Scots I'd grown up hearing."

"She sounds lovely."

Ian nodded. Without looking at me, he kept on . . .

"Although we'd met in Edinburgh, her mother's family was from a little village in County Antrim in Northern Ire-land. And that's where we'd gone to be married. All my fam-ily was there . . . my mother, father, and my two older brothers. And Fiona's family, her parents, grandparents, and some aunts, uncles, and cousins. Some were young children. Anyway, a few minutes after the ceremony, we were all standing outside the church, organizing ourselves before having our wedding photos taken, when Fiona realized that her little niece, Hannah, had left her flowers somewhere inside the church. So I raced back inside to find them. I had my hand on the bouquet when I heard the blast outside. A car bomb."

"Oh . . . my gosh. Ian . . ."

"Nineteen people were killed that day."

"I . . . I . . . I don't know what to say. How horrible. I'm so sorry . . ."

"Ye don't have to say anything. It was a long time ago, now. I'm only telling ye about it because when I saw ye standing next to the portrait, I was thunderstruck at how alike you and Fiona look. And that's even after knowing ye all this summer, and already recognizing how much you two look alike. It shocked the hell out of me the first time I saw ye a few months ago."

"I understand . . ."

"Also, I figure ye must think I'm some sort of nutcase, having feelings for ye because ye remind me of my wife. While it's true, ye look uncannily like her, and ye remind me of her, I want ye to know that I do see ye for who ye are, yerself, not as someone I want ye to be, or someone I remember. Yer much more athletic and outgoing than Fiona ever was. And I must tell ye, Eva, yer much more of a hammerhead."

He chuckled. I couldn't help but laugh.

"I used to sit and stare at Fiona's portrait and wish for a miracle. However, I don't look at it much anymore. It's just a fantasy. And lamenting for our lost life together distracts me from my purpose. Ye see, after that day at the church, I made a vow to spend the rest of my life working to stop people who make bombs that kill innocent people, like my family. And I'm still at it."

A vehicle pulled into the parking area up at the big house. Ian stood up.

"That'll be Mister Lurch, coming for me. I've kept ye long enough tonight, Eva."

"It's okay . . . really . . ."

Still processing everything he'd said, I couldn't find the words to respond as Ian started to head toward the big house. Then he stopped.

"Aw, I'm an *eejit*."

He walked back toward me, smiling softly.

"I meant to tell ye, Eva, that the photos ye brought to me today proved quite interesting. It looks like yer friends set up a company with a name similar to but not exactly the same as the Perennial Paper Company in Boston. Yer man, Buck, and I were talking about it earlier. He's thinking the Boston folks are using the legit Boston company's assets to research and lay the foundation to acquire land, and they're planning on tricking sellers into signing the actual deal with their phony company. Then the crooks will disappear before anyone figures it out."

"What? How can that possibly work?"

"It can't. Whatever they're up to, they won't be getting away with it. Their plan was sketchy at best. If they'd had a snowball's chance in hell of getting away with it, they would've had to have planned on hiding for the rest of their lives."

I remembered Dex's book about purchasing private islands. "I think they did. Or at least Dex did."

"It doesn't look like things went according to plan for him, now, does it? The FBI is on it now. Ye did good work, Eva."

"Thank you. I knew they were up to something . . . I just couldn't figure it out. Thank you."

Ian took my chin in his hand, tipping my face up to his.

"Just know that I care very deeply for ye, Eva. Like yer one of my own. And I'll always have yer back. And don't feel bad about uncovering the painting of Fiona. I should've told ye about her months ago. Actually, I'm enjoying looking at her now. So I thank ye for pushing my buttons, if ye know what I mean."

"No, I . . ."

Enveloped in a seductive swirl of earthy scents, Ian bent down and kissed me softly on the lips.

Then, without a word, he walked away.

I could barely take another breath.

CHAPTER 61

Lathered in coconut-scented sunscreen, I was lounging in my two-piece teal bathing suit on what seemed like the most luxurious, cushioned chaise in the world. Meanwhile, sheltered from the fierce summer sun, Dolly rested under the shade of a giant urn potted with an olive tree and cascading petunias. Snoring, she was taking a break from a ginormous T-bone that lay between her paws.

Precious handed me an obscenely huge virgin strawberry daiquiri sporting a straw and a giant skewer of tropical fruit before setting down her own obscenely huge tropical drink—most likely spiked with alcohol—on a little glass-topped patio table. Then, with a big, satisfied sigh, Precious plopped herself into the chaise next to me.

"This is grand, Precious. Thanks for the invite."

"Sure thing, Sunshine," said Precious. "I figured you could use a break. Besides, you and me, we never get to just hang out together. And Mister Collier says the pool here at Greatwoods doesn't get used hardly enough. Plus, we needed to make up, after yesterday and all."

I smiled.

"I'm happy to enjoy the Greatwoods hospitality, Precious. This is the first day of *nothing* I've had in years. I couldn't ask to spend it in a more peaceful, welcoming place."

"Well, you sure can use a spot of peace and quiet. After all, it's been a parade of drama and dead guys for you all summer long." She took a long sip of strawberry daiquiri from her straw. "I can't believe you almost got eaten by a gator last night! A gal can only take so much. Good thing Sheriff Sexy Pants got there in time to save you. You got some lucky stars, girl. Everyone in town is talkin' about it."

I sighed. "That's me. The talk of the town," I said, rolling my eyes.

Precious glanced at the little Cartier watch on her wrist.

"And I'm real sorry I barked at you yesterday," she added. "I get real protective of Mister Collier. You understand?"

"Sure. I shouldn't have been such a busybody. And after seeing the portrait in his library, I can appreciate how his seeing me standing next to it would be a shock."

"Honey, except for your pink hair and the freckles, you're a dead ringer for that portrait of Missus Collier."

"It's not pink."

"Okay, Sunshine . . . *strawberry-blonde*." Precious chuckled.

I nodded. "He must've loved her very much. Do you think he's somehow reliving his life with her through me?"

"I dunno, Sunshine. Could be."

"He said he wasn't."

"Then, I guess he isn't. He oughta know."

"Right."

"If it makes ya feel any better, I know Mister Collier cares about you . . . a lot. In fact, I ain't *never* seen him take to someone like he does to you. Never."

"Thanks. That means a lot."

I decided to change the subject.

"That's a fancy-pants watch there, Miss Precious."

"Goes with the shoes."

I laughed. Precious had coordinated her tiger-striped, one-shoulder maillot swimsuit with a pair of peep-toe, tiger-striped, gold-glitter slingback Louboutins. Added to that, she wore a giant pair of gold hoop earrings along with a bejew-eled, enameled leopard print and yellow gold Cartier sports watch. *Not only did Precious have the run of the Greatwoods estate*, I thought, *but it was clear that Ian Collier paid her handsomely.*

In fact, I'd seen a watch similar to hers once before. A woman at a Boston fund-raiser had worn one and bragged to everyone who'd listen that her husband had paid more than one hundred thousand dollars for it. I glanced over at Precious as she napped like a contented cat in the chaise next to me. There was still an awful lot about this woman that I didn't know.

Likewise, about her complicated boss, Ian Collier. He was sexy. Smart. Sharp-witted. And secretive as all get-out. And, even though he'd shared the story about Fiona with me, I was sure that he still had a ton of secrets.

The closer I get to Ian, the more I realize how little I know him.

A mockingbird chattered from an ancient live oak near the far side of the mansion. I took another sip of my tropical drink. *I'll figure it all out*, I thought. About Ian *and* Precious. *I just need a little time.* I popped a pineapple wedge into my mouth. *One day, I'll know all there is to know about each of them.*

I'd take it on as a personal challenge, I decided.

Next to me, Precious sighed on her lounge chair. Just a short distance past our feet, a warm breeze made little ripples in the bright blue pool water. I slid the Jackie O sunglasses over my eyes and watched sunshine dance over the water, like little twinkly lights. Around the patio, water from the rushing fountains caught the breeze, and spritzes of cooling mist fell from overhead, as carved marble cherubs danced and watched over us. Beyond the terrace, blue jays, robins, and mocking-birds chattered in the trees around the freshly manicured lawn. I stabbed my straw into my daiquiri and took a long, icy sip.

"If I'd died and gone to heaven, it couldn't be much better than this," I said.

"Yeah. Me, too, Sunshine. We should do this more often."

A bumblebee buzzed past my nose.

Precious checked her watch again.

"Listen, Sunshine, I gotta head inside and help Mister Collier for a while," she said, sitting up. "You just hang here and relax. We got all afternoon. I'll be back in an hour or so with some snacks. Meantime, why don't you take a dip in the pool."

"Okay, thanks. I might. Really, I can't think of anyplace I'd rather be. This is heaven."

"And it only gets better," laughed Precious.

"What?"

She seemed not to hear me as she clomped across the patio toward an opening between the Greatwoods mansion's tall French doors. She slipped between creamy, sheer drapes as they poofed and pillowed in the warm summer breeze.

I put my drink on the tiny glass-topped table next to me and settled into the cushy chaise, letting the warm sun wash over my skin. I closed my eyes and listened to water fountains gushing, to birds and frogs chirping, and to soft breezes moving the leaves in the great trees in the manicured yard. I took a deep, relaxing breath.

After a few minutes, I was almost asleep . . .

A shadow fell over me. Cold, wet hands pressed into my shoulders. I yelped and jumped up. The Jackie O's landed on the patio with a clatter.

"Hey!"

Dressed in pressed, perfectly fitted white twill slacks, a body-conscious black tee, and pricey leather moccasins, Buck stood behind the chaise lounge, watching me from behind his dark aviator glasses. He had that smart-ass grin of his. His hands were wet.

"Buck! What are you doing?"

"Sorry, I must've gotten my hands wet in the fountain." He held up his hands and grinned even wider. His flawless teeth looked bright white against his tanned skin. "Just playing with you, Babydoll. Sorry I startled you."

I couldn't help but notice how Buck's slacks draped beautifully as he bent down and picked up my sunglasses. Carefully, he set them on the little glass table between us.

I said, "I'd say that was exactly what you meant to do."

"Play with you? Or startle you?"

"Both! Why are you here, Buck?"

With the pool behind me, I stood facing him, shading my eyes from the glaring sun with a hand on my forehead. In his fitted shirt, brawny Buck's muscled form was impossible not to appreciate, even in the blinding glare of the sun. He looked slick . . . and he was full of his usual over-the-top confidence.

"I thought you'd want to know that we finally caught up with Pottie Moss and Skeets last night."

"Yes, Precious told me. Apparently, the local gossip-mongers are all over the story."

Buck laughed. "I should've known. I would've told you myself last night when I came to pick up my truck . . . but I saw you were sleeping."

"I was? You came into my cottage? I didn't hear Dolly bark or anything . . ."

"Dolly didn't bark. She never barks at me. Do you, Dolly?"

I turned to look at Dolly, gnawing on her big bone in the shade.

"Traitor," I said.

Dolly wagged her tail.

"Anyway, I figured you needed your beauty rest. So I didn't wake you."

"Gee, thanks."

"I know how cranky you get . . ."

I ignored the tease. "So, are Pottie Moss and Skeets going to jail?"

"They're both being held, at least for now. I doubt Pottie Moss will get bail; however, I don't know whether Skeets will actually remain locked up. For now, we're looking into him as an accessory. And of course, he assaulted you in the boat."

"What's going to happen with Pottie Moss?"

"I'm afraid she's put herself in some hot water, as they say. Detective Gibbit is still questioning her now, although she pretty much confirmed what we wanted to hear last night. It all matched what you'd told me, that she used a syringe to inject belladonna into an unopened Knox olive oil bottle then left it at the big house, ostensibly for Claudia Devereaux to ingest. When her plan went awry and Dex died instead, Pottie Moss thought she'd take another whack at killing Claudia during the planned picnic in the swamp. Only you and the twins were there to mix things up, and instead, you almost got the deadly dose."

"Right."

"I'm sorry, Babydoll."

"At least you showed up . . ."

"You have Daphne to thank for that."

"Never be late for Daphne or she'll call the law on you."

Buck laughed. "Gotta give the woman credit this time. She may have saved your life."

I nodded.

"So, I've typed up your statement from last night. I'd like you to go over it with me one more time to make it official. Tomorrow is fine."

"Okay. Sure. And what about the Bostoners and their land grab? What's happening with all that?"

"Ahh, that mess is going to take a bit more time to unravel. So far, what we know involves your friends—"

"Not my friends!"

"Okay then. So far what we know is that the group from Perennial Paper set up a shadow company based in the Caribbean with a name that was similar to but not the same as Perennial's so that legal paperwork from the two companies would be easily confused. Then the group went out and about, on Perennial Paper's dime, conducting themselves as Perennial Paper executives, acquiring land as you described to me the other day. Only at the same time, they scammed an equal number of sellers into believing that the legal documents they signed, selling property to Periennial Paper— spelled with an extra "i"—were for Perennial Paper Company in Boston."

"So, there were two paper companies."

"Exactly."

"I don't get it."

"Well, we're still sorting this out, but it appears that your old fiancé Dex, along with his other four cronies, used the real Perennial's resources to purchase land adjacent to land that the real paper company would purchase. They then planned to transfer their land, purchased under the fake company name, to another one or two of their Caribbean companies under different names, only to quickly sell it to an offshore investor at a huge profit. They'd make a killing. It's gonna take months, maybe years to sort it all out. Although, on the surface the plan looks like it would've been impossible to pull off. For some smart, educated people, it seems that in the end, they weren't smart enough . . ."

"Just greedy."

"Yes."

"So I was right about all the bird-watching being a crock. They were all pretending to be looking at nature, when they were really scouting land in preparation to scam people in order to make a giant profit."

"Yes. They used the bird-watching as a cover so they could check out land without drawing attention to themselves. And they came to Abundance because Dex Codman remembered this place, which used to be a relatively depressed region with cheap land and lumber, from his time all those years ago with you. According to the others, it was no accident they came here, Babydoll. The guy insisted this was the perfect place to pull off their scam, and he'd done the research to prove it. Of course, my personal opinion is that he still wanted you. I'm only sorry he died before I could get to him."

"Oh, Buck. Please don't say that."

"And I can't blame the dead bastard."

Buck stepped around the table and gave me an unabashed once-over. I felt myself blush.

"I don't mind saying that you're lookin' good, Babydoll."

Raising his sunglasses, he rested them atop his head. Then he smiled. His eyes had that mischievous sparkle that I knew only too well. I took a step backward.

"I wasn't expecting to see you here, Buck. If I'd known, I would've chosen another outfit."

"This one suits me just fine."

Buck stepped closer to me.

"I'm sure it does." I stretched my hand out, pressing it against Buck's chest to stop him from coming any closer. When he finally stopped and stood still, I dropped my hand. "Does Debi know you're here?"

I gave Buck a sideways glance as I turned to grab a tube of sunscreen off the small table next to the chaise. He tipped his head and gave me a silly, lustful little smile as I bent over, reaching for the sunscreen.

"Stop that," I scolded. I unscrewed the top from the tube of sunscreen and left it on the table.

"I'm just enjoying Mother Nature's beautiful bounty," he said.

"Hmm. Right." I rolled my eyes. "By the way, I'm still sure that Debi has a GPS device on your vehicle."

"Actually, you're right about that," he said matter-of-factly. "And I wouldn't have thought to look for it, if you hadn't teased me about it. So I owe you one."

"You're kidding, right? Debi actually put a device on your vehicle? *Your* vehicle? The sheriff's vehicle?"

"All my vehicles."

"*All* your vehicles? How many do you have? I mean, isn't that . . . illegal?"

"Yes, it's illegal. However, now that I know Debi thinks that she knows where I am at all times, it actually makes my job easier. Thinking she's outsmarted me with the GPS devices, it'll be easy for me to move the vehicles around to where I want her to believe I am at any given moment. Plus, I can always access other vehicles . . ."

"But I still don't get why you're pretending to be Debi's fiancé. You *are* pretending, right?"

"It's complicated. And I'm really not at liberty to say. However, since I *know* you, and I know that you won't let this go, and you have the potential to blow this operation for me, I'll tell you this much."

"Operation? I'm all ears."

"Debi's brother, Dickey, is about as slippery as they come.

He's been selling farm- and timberland to offshore investors for nearly a decade now."

"That's hardly illegal . . ."

"You're right about that. However, we have some evidence that he's also been involved with some extremely shady overseas operations that include money laundering, drugs, and trafficking."

"What? That's awful!"

Buck put his hand up. "I can't say any more. Just know that we're on it. So, back to answering your question—"

"My question?"

"Yes. You asked me a question. Don't you remember?"

I shrugged.

Buck continued. "To answer your question about whether or not Debi knows I'm here at Greatwoods this afternoon, yes, Debi knows that I'm over at my friend Ian's house. Later, I imagine that she'll even have the computer printout from her GPS device to prove it. And she'll share that information, no doubt, with her nosy brother. And he'll share that information with his criminal connections, and they'll all be relieved to know that the sheriff of backwater Abundance County is blind to their activities because he's just a playboy who likes to mooch off his rich ne'er-do-well friend at Greatwoods."

"The ne'er-do-well friend about whom they can discover nothing. At least on the Internet."

"I see you've been busy. Leave it alone, Eva. Don't dig anymore, about Ian, please."

I ignored Buck's warning about Ian.

"And just what, exactly, are you doing at ne'er-do-well friend Ian Collier's house right now?"

"My friend Ian, the rich eccentric who likes his privacy, and I are playing chess and smoking cigars."

"*Eeeew.* I hate cigars."

"So does Debi." Buck grinned. "I've learned that cigars make a very effective repellent."

"Please, too much information."

"If you say so."

"Still, you're really out here on the terrace with me, instead of inside, repelling the world, with Ian. Aren't you being kind of rude to your host?"

I stepped away from Buck to slather sunscreen on my arms. "No. Not really."

"Then why aren't you inside with Ian smoking cigars and playing chess right now?"

"Ian's busy."

Buck took the tube of sunscreen from my hand.

"Busy?"

"He likes spending time with his computer during the afternoon. Here, turn around."

Buck spun me around so I faced the pool. Standing behind me, his big, warm hands started spreading sunscreen over my shoulders. Slowly. He took his time, gently massaging the lotion into my skin.

"So much for chess and cigars," I said quietly.

Buck's strong hands felt marvelous as they massaged and moved tenderly across my back. They were both strong and sensitive as they caressed and kneaded my skin. I sucked in a deep breath and held it for as long as I could.

Step away, Eva. Step away!

Too late. Already I felt a flash of heat on my cheeks. My knees were weak. I exhaled my big breath.

"So, Buck, why are you *really* here?" My voice came out all low and hoarse. The back of my neck felt tingly.

Run!

I started to pull myself away, except Buck's firm hands held me in place. Then he leaned in close from behind me. His warm breath and soft lips brushed against my ear.

"What if I said that I came here just to see you?" Buck whispered.

"What if I said that I don't believe you?" I whispered back. I stood stock-still, trying to keep myself from shaking.

"What if I said that this whole afternoon-at-the-pool shin-dig between you and Precious is a setup, so I can spend a little uninterrupted time with my *ex-fiancée*?"

"Then I'd say that I'm not sure I believe anything you say,

and that you went to a lot of trouble to see your '*ex-fiancée*' for nothing."

"Really, Babydoll?"

"Really."

Still facing the pool, with Buck behind me—his powerful hands still holding my shoulders—quickly, I jerked free and spun around to face Buck.

"Don't you remember?" I said, with hands on my hips. "I have a man moratorium going on right now, since clearly, my man-meter is out of whack. Like, I keep falling for men for all the wrong reasons. Men who are unavailable. Men who are not who they pretend to be. Men who hurt me."

Buck didn't say a word.

I raised my voice. "And not only are *you* a man, Sheriff Buck Tanner, but you're a man who is, according to *everyone* in town, supposed to be marrying my archnemesis, the lovely Debi Dicer. The very same woman who would love to see me perish from this earth . . . accidentally, of course."

Buck raised his eyebrows.

"And according to *her*, your forthcoming nuptials could be *any day* now. So . . . that makes *you*, Buck Tanner, both unavailable *and* not the person whom you say you are, because you have managed to actually convince me that you're not at all *really* interested in marrying Debi. Or anyone else, as far as I can tell. Therefore, getting even *remotely* involved with you—a man who is both technically unavailable *and* not at all the man whom he pretends to be—would end up hurting me. Big-time. If Debi doesn't end up killing me first. So, that's three strikes. And I'm not going there. Not this time. Not again. Not ever."

"You don't say." Buck sounded completely skeptical.

"Yes. I *do* say. So you see, I'm not at all interested in pursuing a relationship with you, Buck, or even seeing you socially. I don't want to end up heartbroken. Or dead. And, of course, I have my reputation to consider."

I took a smug sniff. I was beginning to sound and act like Daphne.

Buck threw back his head and laughed.

"Stop that!"

He kept laughing. In fact, Buck laughed so hard, his eyes were tearing.

"Stop! I'm serious!" I cried.

With both hands, I shoved Buck away from me. He kept chuckling.

"Cut it out," I said. "I'm not kidding. *I don't want you.*"

Buck shook his head, still smiling. "Good to know that despite your lifetime of bad choices and heartbreak, you haven't lost one bit of your sass, Miss Eva Knox." He wiped the tears from his eyes with his hands. "Oh my goodness," he said, chuckling. "You're too funny, honeybun."

"Stop."

"Now, don't pout. It doesn't suit you."

"Good. Now, will you please go away? Go inside and smoke some cigars. Repel some people. Save the world. Just leave me out of it."

Buck smiled and took a big breath before releasing it slowly. Then, he stood quietly for a long moment, hands at his sides. He stared, taking me in. He seemed to be considering something as I stared defiantly back at him, arms crossed. It was like a game of chicken.

Who is going to turn away first?

Then all of a sudden Buck broke out into a big grin, tossing his aviators down on the table next to my sunglasses. With one giant step he closed the distance between us, drawing up against me. Wrapping his arms around me, squashing my folded arms between us, he pressed his head next to mine.

With his lips brushing against my ear, Buck whispered softly, "I think you know that I would *never* hurt you, Eva Knox. Never."

Gently, he kissed my ear, holding himself against me.

"Stop," I whispered.

Too late . . .

"And you know what else I think?"

He nibbled my ear.

"What do you think?" I whispered back hoarsely, half-heartedly wriggling to get free.

"I think . . ."

With one fell swoop, Buck leaned back, hoisting me up into his arms.

"Hey!"

"I think that you're *all wet*, Babydoll."

With that, Buck tossed me high up into the air and right into the deep end of the Greatwoods pool. And just as I'd swum back up to break the water's surface, Buck—stripped down to his fancy white slacks—cannonballed himself into the crystalline water next to me, making a huge splash.

He completely soaked the ritzy Greatwoods terrace.

And wouldn't you know it, little Dolly came flying across the terrace—ears flapping behind her. Then she leapt up and into the pool, right after us.

RECIPES

Bourbon and Ginger Barbecued Chicken

This marinated and barbecued chicken is sure to be a crowd pleaser. For the perfect complement, serve it atop or alongside a refreshing Limey Summer Pasta Salad.

- 1 cup bourbon
- 1 cup extra virgin olive oil
- ½ cup Worcestershire sauce
- ½ cup molasses
- 1 cup brown sugar
- ½ teaspoon fresh grated ginger
- ¼ teaspoon ground ginger
- ¼ teaspoon cayenne
- 1 garlic clove, crushed
- 8–12 chicken pieces, skin on or skin off
- Salt and pepper, to taste

1. Combine first nine ingredients in a medium bowl and mix well to make marinade.
2. Set chicken pieces in shallow pan and cover with salt and pepper, to taste.
3. Pour marinade over chicken. Cover and let rest for at least 4 hours.
4. Remove chicken from marinade and grill on barbecue over low, slow heat, turning at least once, until meat is thoroughly cooked.

Limey Summer Pasta Salad

This is a great, easy to make, bring-along dish, especially paired with Bourbon and Ginger Barbecued Chicken. The piquant lime flavor is a wonderful surprise, and the dish is most delicious served fresh, right after preparation. For a twist, try replacing the grapes with fresh cherry tomatoes or adding coarsely chopped fresh tangelos or nectarines.

- 16 ounces farfalle pasta
- 1 large Granny Smith apple, cubed, skins on
- 1 cup seedless grapes, halved
- 2 stalks celery, sliced
- ⅓ cup coarsely chopped fresh flat-leaf parsley
- ½ to 1 cup Roasted Sweet, Salty, 'n Spicy Pecans, chopped
- Fresh Lime Vinaigrette

1. Prepare pasta, al dente. Rinse with cold water to cool.
2. Add apple, grapes, celery, parsley, and pecans. Mix well.
3. Pour Fresh Lime Vinaigrette over pasta mix. Mix well. Serve immediately.

Fresh Lime Vinaigrette

Yum, yum, yum . . . this fresh and zesty vinaigrette will delight!

- Fresh zest from one lime (about 1–2 tablespoons)
- Fresh squeezed juice from one lime (about 1 ounce)
- 2 tablespoons sherry vinegar
- 1 tablespoon Dijon mustard
- 1 tablespoon honey
- 1 medium garlic clove, smashed
- ½ teaspoon salt
- ½ teaspoon ground white pepper
- ½ cup extra virgin olive oil

1. Whisk together first eight ingredients in a small bowl.
2. In a slow, steady stream, add olive oil while constantly whisking until vinaigrette is well mixed and smooth.
3. Remove smashed garlic.

Roasted Sweet, Salty, 'n Spicy Pecans

Delicious anytime, use in a salad, over ice cream, or eat as a snack.

- ½ to 1 cup pecans, shelled
- 1–2 tablespoons extra virgin olive oil
- Salt, to taste
- Sugar, to taste
- Fresh ground pepper, to taste

1. Spread pecans on roasting pan.
2. Drizzle olive oil over pecans, turning pecans to coat with oil.
3. Sprinkle salt over pecans.
4. Sprinkle sugar over pecans.
5. Grind fresh pepper over pecans.
6. Roast in oven 8 to 10 minutes or until fragrant and lightly toasted, turning several times.
7. Remove from oven and cool.

Heavenly Corn Pudding

A Southern staple, this is a family favorite. Delicious served hot or cold, summer or winter.

- 1–2 tablespoons extra virgin olive oil
- 1 large, sweet onion, chopped
- 8 ears of fresh corn, or 32 ounces canned or frozen (cooked until warm) corn kernels
- 1½ to 2 cups milk, or half-and-half
- 3 tablespoons flour
- 1 tablespoon cornstarch
- 2 tablespoons demerara or granulated sugar
- ¼ cup butter, melted
- Salt and white pepper, to taste
- 3 eggs, slightly beaten

1. Preheat oven to 350°F.
2. Heat oil in skillet. Add onions and cook until soft and translucent. Remove from heat. Drain onions on paper towels and let cool.

3. Add 32 ounces of corn kernels to medium bowl. Or cook fresh corn ears in boiling water, cool, and with small paring knife, cut kernels off husks and run back side of paring knife blade down each husk, collecting additional corn bits and juice, and add all to bowl.
4. Combine milk or half-and-half with flour, cornstarch, sugar, butter, salt, and pepper in saucepan. Whisk continuously and heat until mixture thickens.
5. Add eggs, onions, and corn. Mix well and pour into an 8-by-8-inch pan.
6. Bake for 40 to 45 minutes or until center is set.

Simply Scrumptious Chocolate Olive Oil Cake

A perfect, decadent ending to any meal. Still moist and scrumptious on Day Two.

- ½ cup hot water
- ½ cup cocoa powder
- 1½ cups cold water
- 3 cups all-purpose flour
- 1 cup white sugar
- 1 cup light brown sugar
- 2 teaspoons baking soda
- 1 teaspoon salt
- ¾ cup quality extra virgin olive oil
- 2 tablespoons white vinegar
- 2 tablespoons vanilla extract

1. Preheat oven to 350°F.
2. Oil and flour two 8-inch round cake pans.
3. In small bowl, add ½ cup hot water to cocoa. Stir to mix well. Add cold water to cocoa mix.
4. Place flour, sugar, baking soda, and salt into large bowl. Mix lightly before making a hole in the center.
5. Combine cocoa mix, oil, white vinegar, and vanilla. Pour into well in dry ingredients. Mix until smooth.
6. Pour batter into prepared pans and bake until done, about 30 minutes or until toothpick inserted into centers comes out clean.
7. Place on racks. Cool 20 minutes. Remove from pans. Coat with Yummy Mascarpone Frosting.

Yummy Mascarpone Frosting

- 16 ounces mascarpone cheese, room temperature
- 2 tablespoons heavy cream
- 3½ cups confectioners' sugar
- 1 tablespoon vanilla extract

Beat mascarpone, cream, and sugar until smooth. Add vanilla and continue mixing until soft peaks form.

Ready to find
your next great read?

Let us help.

Visit prh.com/nextread